Jane Linf

I write fun, flirty fiction with feisty heroines and edge. Writing romance is cool because I get to wear pretty shoes instead of wellies. I live in a mountain kingdom in Derbyshire, where my family and pets are kind enough to ignore the domestic chaos. Happily, we're within walking distance of a supermarket. I love hearts, flowers, happy endings, all things vintage, most things French. When I'm not on Facebook and can't find an excuse for shopping, I'll be walking or gardening. On days when I want to be really scared, I ride a tandem.

You can follow me on Twitter @janelinfoot.

PRAISE FOR JANE LINFOOT

'Jane Linfoot has got out the mixing bowl and whipped up
a truly gorgeous story... A deliciously scrumptious treat'
Rebecca Pugh, bestselling author of *Return to Bluebell Hill*

'Just like the perfect wedding cake, Cupcakes and Confetti
is beautifully crafted and wrapped in romance'
Heidi Swain, bestselling author of *The Cherry Tree Café*

'A pure delight... fabulous, fun and unforgettable'
Debbie Johnson, bestselling author of
Summer at the Comfort Food Café

'Simply stunning'
A Spoonful of Happy Endings

'Gorgeous book with characters full of heart,
and an impassioned story to make you smile'
Reviewed the Book

'This author packs a punch'
My Little Book Blog

'Loved this book. The main characters are
vividly drawn... the writing is fast and feisty'
Contemporary Romance Reviews

'With every book I read I fall more in love'
Booky Ramblings

Christmas at the Little Wedding Shop

Sequins & Snowflakes

JANE LINFOOT

Harper*Impulse* an imprint of
HarperCollins*Publishers*
1 London Bridge Street
London SE1 9GF

www.harpercollins.co.uk

A Paperback Original 2016

First published in Great Britain in ebook format by Harper*Impulse* 2016

2

ISBN: 9780008197100

Set in Minion by Palimpsest Book Production Ltd, Falkirk, Stirlingshire

Printed and bound in Great Britain by
Clays Ltd, St Ives plc

MIX
Paper from
responsible sources
FSC
www.fsc.org
FSC® C007454

For Anna and Jamie, Indi and Richard,
Max and Caroline, M and Phil xx

Women are like tea bags. You never know how strong they are until they get into hot water.

Eleanor Roosevelt

1

Friday, 16th December
Brides by the Sea: Crossed hearts and mermaid tails

'Leave the *Closed* sign up for now, Sera.'

Jess, my boss and mentor, is thinking ahead as usual, talking to me over her shoulder, as I wait for her to unlock the door to Brides by the Sea, the most popular wedding shop in all of Cornwall and where I'm lucky enough to work. Even though I pass them every day, the trails of frosted ivy and those cascades of tulle in the Christmas window displays still send shivers down my spine which are nothing to do with the icy blast of the December wind that's howling across St Aidan Bay. I know most brides choose to get married in summer, but when I see the whirl of hanging snowflakes and the sparkle of sequins against the snowy lace dresses, I completely understand why my sister, Alice, fell in love with the idea of getting married

1

at Christmas. In less than a week's time, a hundred and fifty guests will be descending on a Cornish country house for her four-day-long wedding celebration. Yes, it's as epic and ambitious as it sounds. Only a power house like Alice would ever try to pull it off. As for whether she'll succeed… Well, watch this space.

Coming back down to earth this morning, beyond the suspended silver baubles flashing with the reflections of a thousand fairy lights of the window displays, the remnants of last night's staff Christmas-drinks party are waiting for us inside the shop. As the warm air of the entrance hall wraps around us, I peer through into The White Room, where we were partying last night, then pull back sharply.

'Jeez, it looks as if a giant party popper exploded in there.' The low whistle I let out is to hide my horror at the mess. From the number of glasses, you'd have thought we'd invited the whole town, not just a few close friends from the business.

As I stoop to ease a cashew nut out of the gap in the floorboards and flick on the lights on the giant Christmas tree in the hall, my head throbs. There's a tinkle of dangling sleigh bells as I nudge the branches on my way back up, and set the white painted pine cones spinning on their ribbons.

I pick up a tumbler and shudder at the dying raspberries in the bottom. In the cold light of morning, I can't believe we got so carried away by Christmas that we flouted Jess's 'clear drinks only in the wedding shop' rule and went for red punch. Or worse, that we were rash enough to float exotic fruits in the Ruby Duchess cocktails next to so many precious and beautiful white dresses.

'We had a lot to celebrate, Sera, we've had a fantastic year.'

Jess is looking surprisingly upbeat for someone who was at the after-party until four, and has come in to find her main bridal room trashed. It's possible she might still be drunk. She's also building up to a purr, so even though she said it all last night ten times at least, it's obvious what's coming next. 'All thanks to you and your wonderful Seraphina East dresses.' Truly, someone needs to move her on from this loop to save me all the blushes. However hard I try, she doesn't take any notice.

In case you're wondering, I'm Sera, short for Seraphina, and I design a lot of the wedding dresses Jess sells in the shop. And if you don't already know, Brides by the Sea is four floors of bridal gorgeousness, in the seaside town of Saint Aidan. No prizes for guessing it's almost on the beach, which is where I wandered in from, with my scrap book of dress designs eight years ago. And I've been here ever since. Jess, the owner, began by doing wedding flowers in one tiny room, and built her way up to what is here today – a Bridal Emporium containing everything you could need for a wedding. And brides flock here from Devon, Cornwall, and the world beyond.

And what Jess is talking about here is me getting the chance to design a celebrity wedding dress earlier this year. Which obviously was great for the shop, and is why my designs now have a dedicated room of their own, and why my name is painted on every shop window. But given I hate the attention being on me, it's also meant I've spent the last few months trying to hide in corners.

'Weddings taking off at Daisy Hill Farm brought us a lot of business too,' I say. I'm trying to shift the glory off myself here, because last year Poppy, the wedding-cake maker who lived upstairs and worked at the shop, became a wedding organiser at a local farm. So if we've had a brilliant year, it's down to her too.

'It was so nice to see Poppy again,' I muse. However awesome the party, my high point last night was Poppy coming home after a couple of months in London, and looking so happy to be back. Come to think of it, I could murder a giant piece of Poppy's carrot cake right now.

'I'm so pleased Poppy's come to her senses and grabbed Rafe at last,' Jess says. 'We could all do with a farmer like him, he's completely yummy.'

Jess is talking about very own Brides by the Sea in-house romance, which was finally sealed yesterday evening. After a whole year, Poppy is finally going out with Rafe, her boss from the farm.

Jess begins to unwind her silk scarf. 'I haven't booked any brides in for this morning, because we've got so much work to do here.' She's not joking about that. And given most days she's meticulous enough to have us wiping away the rings on the coasters every time someone lifts a prosecco glass, we need to get cracking.

'Great, shall I collect glasses and you do surfaces?' I rub my hands together to show that despite my headache, I'm ready to get stuck in.

Jess sends me one of the despairing looks she saves for when I'm being dense. 'We aren't here to clear up, Sera.'

'We're not?' This is news to me.

There's more purring going on. 'Two tame and *very* sweet bar boys from Jaggers will be arriving any minute to look after that.' So that explains that purr. Jaggers Cocktail Bar is Jess's favourite hang out in town. Even though the clientele are half her age, when it comes to downing cocktails, Jess can drink most of them under the purple plastic designer tables, no problem. And given she spends so much time there, she's great friends with the staff.

'So what are *we* doing?' If Jess doesn't have cleaning plans for me, I'll head upstairs to my studio. Not that I've told her, but I'm very behind with my dress designs for next season's collection.

Jess sends me another despairing look. 'Sera, please tell me you haven't forgotten. We're sorting out your bridesmaid's dress. Obviously.'

'Oh shit.' My groan is long and heartfelt as I hitch up my shorts.

I *design* dresses, I don't wear them. Ever. And I know I have to make an exception for my sister's Christmas Eve wedding, but thus far I've been in denial. Although the bridesmaid's dress arrived weeks ago, despite Jess's best efforts, I've dodged trying it on. Although, as I think about Alice, I let out a shriek. 'Oh shit, Alice wants a Skype call, I need to set up my laptop. Like now…'

If someone said ditsy, I'd have to hold my hands up to that one. I'm the dreamy person, with the attention span of a gnat. The one who's so easily distracted that when I dunk a biscuit, it invariably falls in my tea. Let's face it, I'm creative. Coordination and organisation aren't in my mindset. Which is why Jess is so great for me to work with. She keeps me on track.

'Set up your Skype in your room, Sera, I'll get your dress from the store. That sister of yours can wait five minutes while you try it on.'

Jess deals in orders, not suggestions. She might be bossy, but I forgive her every time. In the last eight years, it's her hard business head and her drive that have taken me from a student with a sketch book to a designer with a studio and a dedicated room in her shop. Plus an annual collection, and more couture clients than I can handle. If it hadn't been for Jess, I would still be lazing on my beach towel, drawing and dreaming. And Jess has supported me all the way, financially too, which is unthinkably generous and why I don't mind her railroading me sometimes.

I mean who – except Jess – would have imagined that five minutes later, instead of washing up I'd be emerging from the fitting room in a dress…

'It's very pink.' As I gaze down at myself, a croak is the most I can manage. Imagine an explosion in a glitter factory colliding with an avalanche and you'll still only be halfway there. Although that might be the least of my problems, given the skirt is fluffing out to the size of a small tree. And right now I have to forget I'd ever hoped for cloud grey tulle, with tiny silver flecks.

'I'd say it's oyster rather than rose.' Jess's voice is breathy. 'And it's exquisite, just look at these seed pearls… did you ever see sequins so tiny?'

Don't worry about the hyperventilating. Jess can't help getting excited over anything with lace and sparkles. That's why she's got such a great wedding shop. At least she's temporarily suspended her disapproval of all things Alice, though.

Alice, importing her entire wedding from London to Rose Hill Manor, the Cornwall country house, where she's getting married, got the 'thumbs down' from Jess. Big time. Alice has somehow blagged *the* most spectacular wedding venue from a friend of Dan, her fiancé. But Alice not shopping at Brides by the Sea for her bridesmaids caused a tidal wave of discontent from Jess. As for Alice choosing a wedding dress from another designer when she could have chosen me, in Jess's eyes that's SO awful, we haven't even got onto talking about it yet.

'Forget about their size, did you ever see so many sequins in one place at one time?' I ask. No way can I be as enthusiastic as Jess when I'm the one wearing them all.

Don't worry, *I'm* completely cool with Alice shopping elsewhere. A bride has to find the perfect dress, and Alice and I have always been very different. Where I'm boho and scruffy, she's super-stylish and uber-smart. We live in entirely different worlds, our tastes don't coincide. So my dresses wouldn't be her thing at all. As for how we're going to get on when we're thrown together for the wedding… that's another instance of 'watch this space'.

I try a tentative swish with the skirt. 'Maybe maximalist bridesmaids will set off Alice's minimalist dress.' The sketch she showed me was so severe and pared back, it only had two lines. I'm guessing it's some kind of haute couture silk column. 'She's definitely embracing the "Snow Queen" theme.'

Alice's favourite book when we were kids was *The Lion, the Witch and the Wardrobe*. She starred in the Christmas production at school when she was ten and I was eight. Whereas I was a snowflake, and I fluffed my entrance, I'm not sure Alice ever forgot her triumph as Queen Susan. But Alice going for a full-blown Narnia wedding still came as a shock. Somehow I hadn't pegged my ambitious, order-obsessed, high-flying sister as nostalgic.

'If she's hoping for snow she'll be disappointed.' Jess is smoothing out my skirts now. 'This is Cornwall not Krakow. Someone should have told her – the climate's oceanic.' Jess drops onto her hands and knees, and begins to work her way around, giving the hem gentle tugs as she goes.

'Okay, stand still, I'll see how the length is. And while we're here, you can tell me how your collection designs are coming along.'

The question floats upwards through waves of tulle, but it still makes me stiffen so hard that my spine goes ramrod straight. Jess is talking about my ideas for my next collection of dresses.

'Alright… I s'pose…' I try to make the lie sound nonchalant and laid-back.

'Hadn't you hoped to be finished by this weekend?' Jess is slipping the questions between tweaks, but, believe me, there's nothing casual about them. This is the interrogation I've been dodging for more weeks than the dress.

We both know that I usually get all my design sketches consolidated easily, in two short weeks while I laze on some exotic beach in the cheap off-peak time before Christmas. And we both know, with Alice's wedding coming up, I'm here, not there. And somehow Cornwall in winter isn't doing it for me like Bali does. I'd promised myself and Jess I'd work my butt off, and whatever happened I'd have everything sorted by this weekend. But somehow it hasn't worked out like that. I'm a beachy girl, and that's where I do my best work. The designs flow much more easily when I'm flat out on the sand. Add in the crippling worry that I'm never going to be good enough again after designing for a celebrity, and I haven't been able to draw a thing. Between us, I feel about as creative as a turnip. I've got no designs finalised at all, but even worse, I haven't any ideas either. So where there should be a complete collection of worked-up designs, instead there's an empty sketch book. Sometime in the next week I've got a hell of a lot of work to do.

'Realistically, nothing gets going again until after Christmas.' I'm bluffing here. 'I decided it's way more sensible to give myself a New Year deadline.' I'm staring in the mirror over Jess's head, exchanging OMG glances with myself. Praying that the word 'sensible' will be the one Jess hones in on.

'I see…' Jess says, sounding like she really doesn't.

I'm dragging in a breath so huge it almost makes my eyes pop, waiting to see if I've got away with this when there's a loud squawk at floor level.

'Sera, what the hell have you got on your feet under here?'

Shit. I've been rumbled. Which is really bad luck, considering exactly how many layers of dress there are between Jess and my…

'Biker boots?' Jess's voice rises to a scream that makes my hangover head reverberate horribly. 'You have to be joking me. Where are the white bridesmaid's boots Alice sent you, Sera?'

My feet in those pointy toes? It's not happening. But I might as well come clean. 'The kitten heels are upstairs in the studio.' Buried under a week's worth of completely useless sketches. Along with the white fur jacket and the wedding manual she also sent. 'They *totally* kill my feet.' I can tell excuses are falling flat. 'The heels on these are pretty much the same height.'

Jess is staring up at me, her arm like a signpost, finger pointing at the door. 'Go.'

'Fine,' I say, with a sniff.

'And come back wearing the proper boots.' Her shouting softens. 'You'll have to break them in some time. You might as well start now.'

I look down at the skirt the width of the bay and know there's no way I'll make it up the narrow stairs to the studio in the dress. There's only one thing for it. I squirm, undo the zip, let the dress fall to the floor. As I leap across the bunched-up acres of skirt, being careful not to trample it with my biker boots, there's another howl from Jess.

'Sera, I don't believe it! You've got all your clothes on under there!'

'And?' I stare down at my leopard-print leggings, shorts and shirt. 'Good thing too, now I've had to strip off.' Honestly, it's December, there's no point being colder than I have to be. And if the dress is the size of a snowstorm, no one's going to notice a bit of underwear. Besides, Jess is the original inventor of the mantra, '*No one's looking at the bridesmaids*'. So I sense she's being a) a bit of a stickler and b) slightly hypocritical here.

Five minutes later, when we resume, I'm wearing the kitten heels – yes, they're agony, in case you're wondering – and I've compromised hugely by taking off my shorts. And Jess has gone in to attack the hem with her pins. My toes feeling like they're dropping off is a small price to pay when the heat's off my designs. Or the lack of them. Which Jess appears to have completely forgotten about now.

'You're lucky Alice hasn't got you in six-inch stilettos,' Jess says.

I don't bother to tell her that's really not Alice's look. Instead I lock my knees, settle down to listen to the gentle sound of guys washing up two rooms away, as I stare out of the window. Although, with the explosion of Christmas sparkle on the glass, it's hard to make out exactly what's going on in the world beyond, other than a solitary figure pausing to look at the displays.

'Jess…' One of the helpers has stopped clattering glasses and is calling through. 'There's someone at the shop door, wanting to come in.'

'Take a break, Sera, I won't be long.'

In a second Jess pushes herself up, shoves her feet back into her loafers and marches out into the hallway. Although the shop is technically closed, so long as Jess is in the building, there is the potential for trade. She's never one to let the opportunity of a sale slip by. Sure enough, next thing, I hear her opening the shop door.

'Come in… it's horribly cold outside… definitely no snow though… yes, we're closed, but we always make exceptions… do tell me, what can I do to help?'

Call me cynical, but from the welcome, I already know it's a guy. Thirty to forty, to judge by Jess's pitch. A smile spreads across my face, because the supercharge of charm tells me he's probably good looking too. And just because I'm nosey, and amused, and a little bit bored, I tilt my head to hear better.

'Yeah, I'm sorry to bother you…' Male, with a nudge of Scottish in the accent. And the kind of chocolate-fudge undertones that make you shiver. 'But there's something I spotted in the window…'

My back goes rigid. You know that thing when you instantly know a voice? Even though it's from years ago, this particular voice is indelibly logged, deep in my unconscious brain. Five tiny words, from twenty feet away, and my heart is hammering so hard that the sequins on my bodice are jolting.

Shit.

You spend years furtively looking round corners, in case a particular person might be there. Even though you know there isn't a snowball's chance in hell of them being around. And then you go so long without it happening that eventually you relax. Get lazy. You forget to look out. There are even days you forget they ever existed. And then...BANG! They're there.

The last person in the world I want to see.

I'll spare you the worst details. Enough to say, his name was Johnny, it was back in uni days, and my humiliation was complete. End of.

Shrinking back against the line of hanging dresses, I try to make myself invisible as I creep forwards to hear better. I'm literally turning my ears inside out, but as the voices move through into The White Room the volume fades. Which is extremely annoying, because they seem to be chatting for ages. And whatever I said about this being the last person in the world I want to see, part of me is aching to catch a glimpse. Just the teensiest peep to see if I'm right. And despite my sensible head screaming 'no, no, no' it's as if my bad-girl feet have a will of their own.

Before I know it, I'm through in the hallway. My bridesmaid's dress might be expansive, but desperate times and all that... A second later, I'm swirling the skirt, winding tulle around my legs, like I'm folding an umbrella. Hauling it into some kind of diagonal surrender. By the end my ankles are clamped so tight under the twists of fabric, I have to jump to move. But the good news is I'm slender enough to squeeze in beside the Christmas tree and duck behind the mannequin that's dressed in an Alexandra Pettigrew *Sophia* dress. And despite the occasional soft jingle from the sleigh bell Christmas deccies I disturbed, I'm enjoying an unrivalled, yet concealed, view of the shop door. What's more, I'm pretty certain so long as I don't move I won't be spotted.

'Cross my heart, promise I'll literally only look for a nano-second.' I whisper to myself, making ridiculous bargains with whatever fates hurled Johnny across my path. I mean St Aidan is on the edge of Cornwall. No one comes here by accident.

So long as I remember not to breathe, and not to let my heart bang too loudly, that's everything covered. Which is damn good timing, because the next thing I know, there's the clatter of loafers on floor boards and they're back.

'Well thanks for the bears.' That throaty lilt sailing over Jess's shoulder has to be Johnny's.

Even thinking his name makes me cringe. But bears? Everyone wants to buy the knitted bear wedding couple from the White Room window because they're unbelievably cute and dinky. But no one's allowed to because they're our Brides by the Sea shop mascots. They've been here as long as we've been open.

'My pleasure.' Jess's triple-volume croon says it all.

We all know Jess would sell her grandmother given half a chance, but surely not those particular six-inch-high, knitted bears?

Suddenly there's no need to move because Jess takes one step sideways and leaves me a clear view. There's that feeling where your whole stomach drops so fast you feel it's left your body. And then it's like there's water rushing through your ears, and a whole flock of seagulls just got loose in your chest.

It's him.

Except older. And thinner. And ten years more worn. But still the same hollow cheekbones, still flipping that same piece of hair back off his forehead. For a second I think I'm going to die. But then Jess begins to talk again.

She's got her hand on his arm as she reaches for the door handle. 'So enjoy the wedding… and Christmas… and good luck with your best-man's speech…'

Wedding? He's here for a *wedding?* I gulp so hard at that I almost inhale the veil that's dangling next to my cheek. As the shock of the word makes me lurch, there's the softest tinkle of a bell. And even though it's the tiniest sound, two heads whip round towards the tree. And just as my eyes lock with Johnny's dark brown ones, and I see his eyebrows shoot up in surprise, Jess lets out a squawk.

'Sera? What *are* you doing behind the *Christmas tree?*'

Just what I didn't need. But I can still bluff it. My brain's racing so fast it's already reached the excuses pile. Nuts between floor boards. Loose mice. Lost bears. I'm wavering, weighing up the long-term pitfalls of each answer. I've pretty much decided to go with the pistachio, and I'm *this* close to getting away with it when one kitten heel gets jammed in a knot hole in the floorboards. Had my feet been free to move, I might very well have got away with it. Working with the tourniquet of my twisted skirt, I don't stand a chance. Balance? I've completely lost it.

What begins as a tiny wobble, expands to a series of lurches. I'm aware I'm somehow in free fall, and from the hideously loud jangling beside me, I'm guessing I'm taking the Christmas tree with me. Before I know it, I'm in a nose dive, and the floor's rushing towards me.

'Waaaaaaaaaaaaaaaaahhhhhhhh…' My scream has to be huge, because I can't hear the sleigh bells any more.

In a last-minute effort to avoid a face plant, I hurl myself over onto my back. As the sequins on my dress splinter across the floorboards, and the tree comes crashing down, the face I'm looking up into is Johnny's. On the up side, the thump of the impact has apparently culled the entire seagull flock. And even though my breathing has turned to gasps, there still isn't enough force in my chest to make words.

Johnny's pushing the tree back to the vertical with one hand, still holding his bag of bears in the other. Which pretty much sums up my life. The guy catches the tree, while I end up on the floor. Sprawled horizontal is never the best look, even if my legs are wrapped up like a mermaid's tail. Especially when my beachy blonde hair and freckles look so bad with the colour of the dress. That's why I concentrate on my career, every time.

And for once, that cool sardonic smile of Johnny's is bursting into a laugh.

'Seraphina East. All in pink.' He rubs the back of his free hand across his forehead as he looks down at me. 'I knew there could only be one of you in the world. We must stop meeting like this.'

And then he's stooping, grasping my hand, and before I know it, a waft of delicious man scent whooshes past my nose, and he's whisked me back onto my feet. What's more, as I drag a stray pine cone out of my hair, my dress is unravelling as if it's alive. In the time it takes to blink, I'm back to the shape of one of those doll birthday cakes, with a Barbie body, and a sponge made in a pudding basin. Except in my case, it's without the boobs.

'You see… he said "pink" too.' I'm sticking my chin out at Jess. 'And what about the bloody bears? Who said you could sell them?'

It's not often that Jess is lost for words, but for some reason it must be catching, because she's opening her mouth and closing it again, and no sound's coming out. And we're all standing staring at each other when there's a warbling noise from The Seraphina East Room.

Johnny's the first to react. He raises his eyebrows. 'Anyone expecting a Skype call?'

Fate works in mysterious ways. Johnny disappearing at the speed of light? Or me? Either is good.

'That one's mine.' I hurl myself towards the sanctuary of The Seraphina East Room.

Johnny's voice echoes after me. 'Sorry to have disturbed your Friday. I'll let you get on, then.' So like him to want the last word. Although that's not exactly true. The last time I contacted him he didn't get back to me. At all.

A second later I'm in front of the laptop, staring at an empty chair on the screen, wondering where the heck my Bridezilla sister has got to.

2

'So is Alice online yet? I'm dying to see her.'

As Jess swoops in next to me on the chaise lounge, she almost knocks my laptop off my knee. With any luck, Alice will move her on from Johnny. Although I'm aching to find out if he mentioned where the wedding was he was going to. Not that he can possibly have any link to Alice's wedding. Can he?

'Alice will be along any second.' I'm whispering to Jess in case Alice comes back on screen. 'She's in Brussels, with an army of builders.' As planned, the 'b' words have Jess leaning in even more intently.

In case you're wondering, Alice works in international interiors. We're currently waiting for her to attend to urgent site

17

business, which probably means she's bringing her make-up up to speed before she comes on screen properly.

As Alice's figure sweeps past the webcam, Jess's voice shoots high with surprise. 'Oh, she's dark. And beautifully groomed. So you're not alike at all, then?'

Despite the insult, I can't help laughing, because it's true. Alice rocks the 'Audrey Hepburn, poised for the red carpet' look. Whereas I'm more 'Courtney Love, the morning after'.

'Great, I'm here now…' As Alice slides into view again, she's got her professional voice on, although it's less snippy than usual.

'And she's *so* glossy.' Given Jess is murmuring at my elbow, I take it she's set on joining in and making this a conference call.

As for the gloss, it's the expensive sort, not the flashy kind. The prefix high-end applies to every item in Alice's life. But despite ten minutes spent applying concealer, she's still got tired-shadows under her eyes.

'I've been trying to get you for *hours*, Sera…' She's exaggerating. Obviously. It's barely eleven and I've been next to my laptop for ages.

But whatever, the tension between us is already crackling. And I've no idea why exactly. When we were kids she was the kind of older sister who bossed me about without mercy, but she always stuck up for me when the going got tough. Since we left home, we respect each other's views and lifestyle choices. Although they're not the ones we'd choose for ourselves, we care about each other from a safe distance. And like so many other siblings, when we get together, we revert to type.

As for the Skype call, if I know Alice this is my reminder

to pick her up when she flies in tomorrow. So I'm getting in first.

'Don't worry Alice, I've set my alarm for six, I'll be in Exeter when you land… promise…'

There's a pause, as she rolls her eyes, not believing a word. 'That's why I've rung…' Her second hesitation is long enough for her forehead to pucker under her fringe. 'Actually I'm not going to be able to come tomorrow after all.'

'But why not?' My voice is shrill with shock. Alice never breaks appointments. And what about her wedding? There has to be shedloads of work left to do for that.

'I'm overseeing a polished-concrete installation, and the frigging mix hasn't set.'

It's a rarefied world she lives in. Only Alice would polish concrete. And she doesn't usually swear either.

'I see,' I say, even though I don't at all. 'Isn't it all a bit last minute?'

Her cheeks blow out. 'It's a rush job for a diplomat. I pulled it in to help pay for all the wedding extras.' The heartfelt groan she lets out is very unlike her. 'I *so* want all our guests to have a white Christmas they'll remember forever.'

There you go. I knew she was counting on snow. And with expectations like that, she's setting herself up for a fall. I try to let her down gently. 'I'm not completely sure it will be white.' In fact I'm a hundred percent sure it won't be.

'It simply has to snow, Sera.' She's wringing her hands, and her wail is so loud my laptop vibrates. 'What's the point in getting married at Christmas otherwise?'

Between us, a lot of people get married in December because it's cheaper. Not that I'm cynical, but Alice getting married in

Cornwall has more to do with the fabulous venue they've got their hands on, than the location itself.

'The sparkle will be seriously special with all your gorgeous touches,' I say, feeling weird that I'm suddenly trying to sell this to her. 'And the log fires.' I'm trying my hardest to reassure her here. 'And it'll be great getting everyone together.'

'Thanks for reminding me,' she says, calmer now. Although she can't be completely herself, because she doesn't usually go overboard with the gratitude. 'And I promise I'll be with you as soon as I can. But until I get there, *please* can you look after things for me? Be my stand-in project manager on the ground?'

I'm blinking, screwing up my face. 'What… me…?' She can't be serious.

It's no secret the rest of my family are all hugely brainy and successful. But where Alice surpassed all expectations, I'm the big let-down. From full-on public humiliation when I had to re-take GCSE maths, to going off to college to do fashion, I've been the family embarrassment my entire life. We both know I struggle to manage my own tiny life. Not to mention the designs I should be doing. Adding in more is asking for trouble.

'Don't worry, the earliest jobs are mainly humping stuff around,' she says, making me wonder why I'm needed at all. 'Dan's besties will be providing the muscle, but you'll oversee.' Her face lights up with a new thought. 'You can be navigator. You're the perfect person to guide them around. Go with them. Keep an eye on what they're doing.' Her nod is horribly decided.

'Navigator?' I mouth back at her, my voice a squeak. Alice really has no idea. I barely know my way round St Aidan, let alone anywhere else. I go from the shop, to the bakery, to the cottage, to the beach. And back again via the corner shop or café. I've barely done a thousand miles in gran's car in the three years since she died. The airport was going to be a *major* challenge. Then I have my own brainwave. 'There has to be someone better than me?'

We're family and we'll always have that tie. But the last few years you couldn't say we've been close. Although my parents appreciated me coming down to Cornwall to keep an eye on my gran when I gave up my gap-year travel, I'm not sure Alice approved. After that there was always a distance between us. And it was about more than the miles between here and London. Gran and I liked to think of ourselves as the Cornish free-spirit family outpost. And when Gran died two years ago, everyone in London was happy to let me stay on in her cottage by the harbour. But Alice has never been interested in my life down here.

'Actually I've thought about this very carefully.' She's tapping her pen on her front tooth. 'You're my sister, you're genetically programmed to stand up for me. I won't get better than that.'

'Really.' I can't hold back my ironic smile. It's so like Alice to analyse her problem so clinically.

She looks vaguely hurt. 'Truly, Sera, you're the only person I can truly trust for this. Deep down, you're the one who knows me best, you instinctively know the choices I'd make. Which makes you the perfect person to make them for me, until I arrive. And to back me up when I get there too. *Pleeeease* say you will. There's *so* much to do.'

If I'm blinking at her, it's because she sounds so desperate. She's strong, she never begs.

As she comes towards the screen her voice drops to a

whisper. 'I had no idea I'd find it this tough, it's all turning out to be a total nightmare. As for Dan and his friends, if I'm not there to control them, anything could happen. You're the only one who'll understand what I'd mind about. You're the one who'll care enough to fight my corner... head them off... sort them out... stamp on their wilder ideas. You know what guys can be like? Sometimes I get the feeling they don't give a damn at all...'

Actually I don't have the first idea about guys, given I'm singleton of the decade. But I am familiar with Alice's mindset. I know she's meticulous about every detail, and maddeningly uncompromising. And I can see how uptight she is. What's more, she's right. I completely understand where she's coming from, even if I don't always get it. The only problem is, I'm a complete wimp. I've never fought anyone in my life. I've never had to. Because Alice always did the fighting for me.

Looking back on our childhood we didn't have a bad time. It's just our parents were busy with other things. But Alice was the kind of big sister who looked out for me every step of the way. I can still hear her bawling at the kids who made fun of me because my corkscrew curls were almost white. And when my wedding Barbie's head dropped off, Alice toasted marsh mallows over a candle to make me smile again. Then my first week at senior school when I got to the top of the wall bars and froze, she ran out of her chemistry lesson to talk me down. I know I took her for granted back then, but looking back, she was the person who made every day okay for me. This is my first chance ever to pay her back. I owe it to her to step up here.

Alice smoothes her fingers across her cheekbones, then drags her bob behind her ears. 'If it's easier, think of yourself as head bridesmaid.'

'Oh my.' Worse and worse. When I signed up for bridesmaid duties it was to look awful in a dress for twelve hours, while carrying a posy. And smile for the photographer, so long as he wasn't arsey. Something tells me if I agree to this, I'm about to add in a whole lot more.

'Every detail's covered. It's just a matter of making it all happen. It's all in the *Wedding Handbook* – you've got that haven't you?'

'Of course.' Despite myself, I'm grinning. It's under the waste-paper mountain in the studio. I opened it at a random page, saw a sentence about the bridal party not sleeping together, and slammed it shut again. But given how fat it is, I suspect Alice has every item nailed. Apart from her late arrival, obviously. And the groom's friends who won't do as they're told.

'Stop worrying, you'll be awesome. You might even enjoy it.' She's suddenly sounding a whole lot better. 'Dan's best man's got your number, he'll pick you up in the morning. He said "ten at the Surf Shack". Does that mean anything to you?'

'Yes.' It's my local caf, but I'm hyperventilating too hard to say.

That's the thing about Alice. She isn't exactly a Bridezilla, because she never makes a fuss, she simply powers through. And if I've got to step in to keep her plans on track, even if it's only for a couple of days, it's a huge responsibility. What happens if I break the wedding?

'There you go. Knowing the Surf Shack, that's a great start.' Alice's air punch is so unlike her it leaves me blinking as her fist rushes towards the screen. 'We're Team Bride, Sera. We'll do this together.'

Which kind of sounds like a bit of a contradiction, given she's not going to be here.

'Any other queries, ring me, okay?'

Did I actually agree to do this? There's a thousand questions I should be asking, but my mind's gone blank. As for who the best man is, I want to weave that in too, but Alice has started again.

'Thanks so much, Sera, I'll catch you very soon, I promise. And good luck.' Then the screen goes blank. And she's gone.

***

'What a morning.' First Johnny, then this. I'm stomping around in my kitten heels, pink-sequined tulle flapping against my legs. Right now I'm thinking of heading for the beach, and running. And not stopping until I reach Scotland. Or maybe Wales?

'What am I going to do, Jess? I mean *you* know me, it'll be a disaster.'

Jess is still on the chaise longue, with wiggles in her forehead I haven't seen before. 'I know I "baby" you at times, Sera. But it's time you took more responsibility.' She narrows her eyes. 'Read Alice's *Wedding Book* carefully. Then go and smash it. And Dan's friends will be helping too.' That thought smoothes out the lines on her brow. 'Weddings are romantic times. Throw in Christmas, and who knows what will happen.'

Hang on. Whatever happened to our Brides by the Sea singles solidarity? Jess came to it because of a disgusting divorce, which makes it all the more surprising that she managed to rubbish our whole ethos in one tiny sentence there.

'Forget Christmas and cupid dust, Jess, I'm not on the market.' I grit my teeth. 'In any case, it clearly says in the manual "no hook-ups in the bridal party"'. Go Alice. Sometimes she really does think she can control the world.

'Really?' Jess looks gobsmacked.

If there's one teensy bit of silver lining in this very black wedding cloud, it's that I'm off the coupledom hook here.

As my pointy boots finally get the better of me, I sink down into one of the Louis Quatorze chairs that are meant for mums of our brides. The last time I collapsed into one of these chairs was when I found out Josie Redman wanted me to design her wedding dress. That pushed me a thousand miles out of my comfort zone, but it was *nothing* compared to this.

Jess beams. 'I've got a feeling this might be the making of you, Sera. Remember our mantra? "Feel the fear and do it anyway".'

I think she might have said that last time too. But last time, there was gin, which frankly I could do with now. And so long as I kept my nerve, last time I only had to do my job and design a fabulous dress. And if I'd messed up, there were a hundred people waiting to take my place. So that was easy in comparison.

This time failure is not an option, and I don't have the first clue what I'm doing. And this is Alice's wedding at stake. That's not just any wedding. This will have to be the most perfect wedding, in the world. Ever. Delivered *exactly* as Alice ordered it.

I scrunch up my face and try to find a thought to get me through. It's a few short days. It'll be over before I know it. And a few days never changed anyone, did they?

3

Friday, 16th December
In the studio at Brides by the Sea: After dark

A lot later that evening, hours after everyone else left, I'm up in the studio. Perching on a stool, in a pool of light, at the high cutting table. Sorting through swatches of lace, fingering pieces of silk. Staring out of the blackness of the windows, to see the distant lights of boats on the sea. Starting a drawing, then tossing it aside and beginning another. Even if I'm making no progress at all on the designs, at least I feel like I'm putting the time in.

I love my long workshop, three floors above the mews, with its stacks of magazines and the inspiration clippings pinned to a huge board. After the snowy neatness of the shop, the studio is a complete contrast, with its creative chaos of dressmakers' mannequins, ironing boards and giant scissors. Up here the tulle and silk are on rolls, and the rails are full of fragments of dresses. Bodices with ragged edges, half-finished petticoats.

Each of the beautiful dresses hanging in the shop downstairs began as a sketch. Those few first lines on paper capture the whole essence. You can't imagine the work that goes in to get from one to the other. But without those first sketches there's no guide to create the pattern. And without the pattern, the dress can't come to life.

I can't blame it all on Johnny. It wasn't as if the work was going well before he turned up. But since he did, somehow my brain can't get beyond those words.

'*Wedding... Christmas... best man...*'

I can't stop thinking how awful it'll be if he turns up at Alice's wedding. *And how gutted I'll be if he doesn't.*

But right now I have to forget that Johnny is in Cornwall. I have to block out that on a windy day we might almost be breathing the same air. And I've got to come up with some startling new sketch designs. Because if I don't, instead of bursting with an astonishing new collection, next Autumn the Seraphina East rails are going to be empty.

4

Saturday, 17th December
At The Surf Shack Café:
Dark chocolate chips and flashing decorations

Hi Sera, Alice's best man here, heading for the Surf Shack Cafe at 10. See you there :)

Texting? In St Aidan? I hope this best man – whoever he is – knows he's damned lucky that message arrived. Signal here is patchy. To be honest, in most parts smoke signals would be more reliable than a mobile.

Unless they're Cornwall devotees, most Londoners don't have a clue what it's like down here. When they arrive for the wedding, Alice's friends are going to have their eyes opened, big time. It's like the rest of the world used to be, in the days before technology. Locals scratch their heads over Wi-Fi, and give you blank looks if you mention broadband. Why would you want those when you can phone each other on the landline? Or – shock horror – talk, face to face. For me that's why I like it here. As for where Best Man has chosen to meet up, I couldn't have chosen better myself.

'So here we go.' I pull a face at Poppy, as we pick our way between the empty tables on the terrace deck of the Surf Shack Café. Poppy's the cake baker from the shop, who just came back from London, and one of my closest friends.

'You'll be fine, so long as you remember to breathe,' she says, making a good point.

Now I think about it, the last time I drew a breath was when we started walking along the sea front. When Poppy dropped in to pick up some baking trays from her attic kitchen, Jess muscled in, and sent her along with me, supposedly to make sure I don't chicken out and leg it down the beach. But this way Jess also gets a full report immediately Poppy gets back to the shop.

Unlike many of the beachside cafés which bear no resemblance to their names, the Surf Shack cabin is as rickety and weathered as it sounds, which is why everyone likes it. Add in excellent coffee, delectable cocoa and the fattest sandwiches on the bay, and you'll see why it's such a winner. What's more, it appears to have been knocked together from a thousand random bits of wood. Sometime most days, winter and summer, this is where I hang out. And while Poppy's been in London this is also where most of my calorie intake has come from.

On the dot of nine-thirty I shoot her a final grimace and brace myself. As we push through the swing door into the café, we're hit by a rush of warm air and the scent of fresh coffee. The owner, Brin, is grinning at me from behind a spikey electric-blue Christmas tree, perched on the counter.

'Mornin' Sera. Nice to see you back, Poppy,' he says, as he rubs his hands on his striped apron. 'Frothy hot chocolate, XXL, with dark chocolate sprinkles and a swirl of salted caramel?'

'Please.' I glance up at the glittery festive garlands that are criss-crossing the ceiling. That's my usual winter order. It takes at least twenty minutes to do justice to a Surf Shack hot chocolate, so the timing should be perfect. The mugs they come in are bucket-size, and the toppings aren't so much sprinkled on as added by the shovelful. 'What about you, Poppy?'

She wrinkles her nose as she studies the list on the chalk board.

'Hot chocolate… super-sized please… with whipped cream… and marshmallows… and white chocolate chips… and a double chocolate muffin please.' She gives a guilty grin. 'Rafe cooked me breakfast, but that was hours ago. And I've so missed the Surf Shack.'

'Have these on the house today, ladies, seeing as it's Christmas.'

I blow Brin an air kiss as we wander off to choose a table.

Poppy nods towards a table with its own mini Christmas tree, complete with flashing lights, then steers me towards a chair. 'This one's good, if you sit there it gives you a clear view of the door.' She tilts her head towards Brin. 'You still haven't been on that date he's always asking for?'

I laugh. 'You remember my gran always said it's better not

to have a guy at all, than to be with the wrong one.' I guess she repeated it so often it stuck fast in my head. 'Anyway, I'm too busy, guys aren't worth the trouble.' I say, as I slip my wool jacket over the back of a chair and unwind my scarf.

By the time Brin comes over with our order, Poppy's ready to dive straight in. As she begins to demolish her muffin, even though it's still long before ten, I have half an eye on my hot chocolate, half on the door, with its outline of multi-coloured chaser fairy lights. I'm more or less ignoring the boarding guys who walk in. Not pre-judging, but I'm guessing any friend of Dan's who's made it past Alice's eagle eye to be best man will stick out a mile as a smart London type. Especially given she's hanging out with diplomats these days.

And why did I think I'd be able to drink even a sip of hot chocolate, when there's a million-to-one chance Johnny might walk in the door any second? In a weird twist of fate, could he really be Dan's best man?

Poppy studies me as I sit, not touching my drink.

'I can see you with a surfer.' She scrapes a fingerful of cream from the top of her hot chocolate and sucks on it. 'I reckon a hunky, beachy, free-spirit type would suit you.'

'Just because you've finally given in to Rafe.' I laugh. 'For the record, I'm definitely not looking for a guy of *any* type.' And just to clear it up, I don't surf or swim either. My beach appreciation is definitely limited to the shore. 'But anyway, I'm hardly going to pull anyone in a suit, am I?' I gesture to my messy bun and general laid-back appearance.

'Who knows? Opposites attract.' Poppy teases. 'Some smart city barrister might have a thing for ripped denim shorts.' She leans in towards me. 'Actually, don't look now, but I think I just spotted your perfect soulmate. You know that thing where you're supposed to choose a partner who looks just like you. He's over by the coffee machines.'

'You don't say.' I'm not even going to bother to look. Sometimes Poppy is so unknowingly ridiculous she's hilarious.

'He's well fit. Pretty ripped under that baggy top of his, too.' She's not holding back on the details. 'All sun-bleached blonde hair, just like you. Stubble – not like you, but whatever, his denim's as threadbare as yours. You definitely look like you'd share an essence.'

If Poppy's talking about essences, it's time to stop her. 'Bollocks!' I say, meaning to hiss but it comes out a lot louder than it should. The momentary lull in the café's buzz gives me enough time to go crimson to my ear lobes.

Poppy leans in again. 'I'm right, he's totally checking you out now.'

This is why I avoid nights out in bars.

'Properly.' She takes another triumphant slurp of whipped cream.

I laugh at her. 'I just shouted "bollocks" at the top of my voice. *Everyone's* looking at me. Obviously.' But I might as well prove her wrong. Out of all the thousands of surfers who've wandered through St Aidan in the last ten years, I have clicked with zero this far. Enough said. I might as well do the job properly and make my point. I give it a second, pray this won't be the moment that Best Man chooses to walk through the door, and sneak the fastest-possible glance over my shoulder.

I only mean it to be a nano-second. But when I flick around and take in the ragged blonde hair and the sloppy sweater, something holds my gaze. And I can't turn away. I'm smiling at scuffed suede boots that could almost belong to me. One minute I'm running my gaze up over that stubble, the next there's a flash of blue green and our eyes have locked. When his delightfully lived-in face breaks into a grin and the skin at the corners of his eyes crinkles, my tummy flips. Nothing so huge that it officially leaves the building. But enough to throw me right off.

Shit. I force myself to wrestle my gaze away. As soon as Best Man shows up I'll be out of here, and I'll never have to look at this 'soulmate' guy again.

'See what I mean?' Poppy's laughing. 'So what's the verdict?'

I make sure my shrug is spectacularly diffident and make a big thing of trying to stir my hot chocolate. Then I clear my throat and swallow madly, because somehow all my saliva has disappeared. 'Nothing special,' I croak, desperately playing for time. 'Although you've got a point about his jeans. They could make great summer cut-offs.'

'Oh my God...'

At first I assume Poppy's perfect 'O'-shaped mouth is because she's so shocked and disgusted I've rejected my perfect match.

'Oh my God...oh my God...' The third time she says it and her voice is mounting to a shriek, it has to be something else. 'Oh my God, you might be in here...'

'What...?'

'Don't look now,' she says, completely unnecessarily, 'but he's... COMING OVER.' She mouths those last two words silently. Which frankly is a bit stupid seeing as the whole café's been scrutinising us since she screamed OMG.

I can tell he's arriving way before I see him. First there's

Poppy's completely uncool flapping of her fingers in front of her face. Although strictly, with my puce chops, I'm the one who should be doing the hand-fanning. And second, there's the way she's puffed out her cheeks so far she looks like a football about to pop. And bear in mind surf hunk is getting the full benefit of this as he comes towards us. Which I assume he has, because there's suddenly the most fabulous scent of hunky male. Definitely not salty skin and seaweed, with an undertow of testosterone, which, let's face it, is what most guys smell of here when they drag themselves up the beach. More, expensive cologne, crashing into a motorcycle engine, in a cedar forest.

I draw in a long breath as he circles the table and swaggers to a halt. After waiting a couple of seconds – I'm guessing to maximise the swoon effect – he seeks out my gaze with a disarming grin. As his broad hand extends towards me, I grit my teeth, and will my heart to stop galloping.

'Hi, it's Sera isn't it? I'm Quinn,' he says, his low voice resonating as he hesitates. 'Quinn Penryn…?' The questioning tone of his introduction makes him sound even more super-confident than he obviously is. It's as if he's so famous he thinks I should know him, and believe me I don't.

Random guys hurling themselves at me is the last thing I want. And I'm not about to bend my rules now. Not for anyone, no matter how much I covet their jeans. The faster I stop this, the better for everyone. What's more, I'm horribly aware that the whole café is watching us like we're some kind of floor show. There's no time to lose, so I launch.

'Sorry,' I say, throwing in the most distant, yet benign and unsexy, smile I can muster. 'I'm going to cut you short here, Quinn. Because I'm *really not interested.*' I'm actually feeling bloody empowered here. Not to mention proud of myself, for the small detail of slipping in his name too. 'It'll save us both a lot of time and trouble if I'm honest here,' I add, by way of explanation. Because although I want to sound decided, I don't want to come across as a complete bitch. Especially as we've got an audience.

The way his eyebrows shoot up, I'm guessing he's not used to getting the knock back. Which is very probably the case, because close up, he's even more delectable than he was from across The Shack. But something about his surprise super-charges my new-found confidence. I'm on a roll here.

'Pickups by strangers really aren't my thing.' I say, and fix my smile, determined to hold it until he's backed off. 'So, thanks, but no thanks.'

I look back at my hot chocolate, give it another stir. And wait for him to go. How much more of a dismissal does Quinn Pen-whatever he's called expect? He's still here, because when I look down I can see those distressed boots of his. Which is the exact point I remember that eternal question we were obsessed with at school. That thing about the relationship between a guy's shoe size and something else significant. Which, embarrassingly, is exactly what I'm staring at, at table level beyond my hot chocolate. If schoolgirl legend is true, and there is a link between the two, his feet are going to be size twelves. At least.

Screwing up my eyes to block out the view, I will Quinn to leave. To make it clear that I've moved on with my life, and I expect him to do the same, I take a massive gulp of hot chocolate. As my cup clatters back down, Poppy begins to flap again. From the way her eyes are popping like saucers, I'm guessing she's trying to tell me something hugely important. But I'm not getting it. As she draws her forefinger under her nose, my frown deepens. If this dammed Quinn wasn't still hanging around, Poppy and I would probably have collapsed in a heap of giggles by now.

Finally I give in. 'What?' I hiss at Poppy across the table.

There's a low growl, which seems to be coming from Quinn. As I turn my face towards his, I see he's biting his lip and holding in his laughter.

'Don't worry, Sera.' Quinn says, completely misreading my feelings. 'We've all been there. Chocolate moustache alert!'

He swoops, napkin in hand. Before I know it, he's right in my personal space, dabbing at my upper lip. By the time I've formed my squawk of protest, he's backed away again.

'All done.' He's scrunching up the serviette and rubbing his hands on his thighs. 'Drink up, then, and I guess we're good to go.'

I tilt my head and my voice rises in disbelief. 'Go where exactly?' Surely I couldn't have been clearer?

'I know you were sounding reluctant before, but we *do* have a date.' He slides out his phone, with a twitch of those lips of his. 'Ten at the Surf Shack? Alice and Dan's wedding? Ring any bells?' He wrinkles his forehead.

Triple shit. There are times when you want a tidal wave to rush in from the sea and whoosh you away. And this has to be one of them. I'm frantically clutching my cardigan sleeves, winding my foot around my leg under the chair, as I try to hang in here. Surely this can't be? Or can it? 'Right, so you're…' This is so embarrassing, and what's more, if I try to apologise that will only make it worse.

'I'm Quinn Penryn, Dan's right-hand guy.' He butts in, but the words come out slowly, one syllable at a time, as if he's explaining to a child. He's still smiling, but this time there's less sparkle and more relief. 'Great to have cleared that up. Good to meet you… at last… Sera.' There's the smallest ironic twinkle in his eye as he holds out his hand. 'I must say, you're very different from your sister.'

I'm not going to show how happy I am he's noticed. I shrug. 'What is there to say, she's in Brussels, I'm here.'

'And cutting too. This kitten has claws.' There's a glint in his eyes as he lets out a laugh.

Whatever. That wasn't what I meant. But I can't help being pleased I've surprised him.

He leans towards me. 'This is going be a lot more fun than I'd thought.'

As his palm finally hits mine I throw myself into the hand-shake. But even as I'm grasping and shaking Quinn's hand for all I'm worth, my brain's jumped somewhere else entirely. *So what the hell happened to Johnny, then?* That thousand-to-one outside chance. The one that had me awake all night, rigid, in case it should happen. The reason I've had butterflies dancing in my stomach since the moment Jess closed the shop door after him yesterday. I completely refuse to believe that my stomach feeling like a wrinkled pancake now is down to disappointment that I'm not going to get to see him. That he was on his way to another wedding entirely.

Quinn's voice pulls me back to reality. 'These wedding plans are epic. We're going to have such a blast…'

'Sure,' I say. Not that I've ever thought of Alice's marriage quite like that before.

As I get to my feet and drag on my coat, out of the corner of my eye I catch Poppy's manic double thumbs-up signs beyond the flashing fairy lights of the table decoration. And it's not just because she's going to snaffle the hot chocolate I'm leaving behind. If I'm doing mental eye rolls it's because I can just imagine how this is going to get reported back to Jess. Essence and all.

As for me, I've no idea what's coming. But that one enthusiastic burst from Quinn just put the next week in a whole new light.

5

Saturday, 17th December
The sea front in St Aidan: Pretenders and parking tickets

'So my wheels are right outside…'

At a guess, if Quinn's chilled-out surfie style transfers to his transport, we'll be trundling around in a clapped-out camper. Not that I'm a car snob – I can't be, when I drive my gran's cast-off mini, as rarely as I do. But whereas those characterful vans are fabulous fun in summer, their heaters are non-existent. Given it's December, I'm preparing to freeze my butt off.

'We're over there, where the sand ends.' As we cross the deck Quinn's arm casually flops round my shoulder, steering me left. He's come in so close behind me now, he's bumping on my satchel.

'It's all double yellows, there's a strict "no parking" policy, the wardens are like Rottweilers.' I say, shivering as a gust of wind blows my coat open. He's obviously got confused somewhere. But I might as well give him the benefit of my inside information, seeing as that's what I'm here for. 'Driving isn't my strongest point, but people definitely aren't allowed to park along here.'

'I'm not "people", Sera.' He sounds indignant, as we clatter down the steps from the terrace to the seafront. 'My policy is "park where I please". I live dangerously, risk the wardens every time.' As he pulls his keys from his pocket, he tosses them high and snatches them out of the air.

I blink as I hear a beeping and scan the empty seafront for a van. It's only when the headlights flip up and flash, I notice a sleek, low car tucked in around the side of the Surf Shack. I try to make my eyes less wide and attempt to keep the surfie vibe going. 'Your wheels?' This serious bit of metallic London bling looks lost and out of place, up to its hubs in a sand dune.

'Yep.' He flings open both the doors and rips a plastic bag off the windscreen with a snort. 'Complete with complementary parking ticket.'

'What did I tell you?' As I poke my head into the car, I'm met by the scent of leather with a heavy overtone of seaweed.

He dips into the car and grabs a damp wetsuit and towel from the front seat. 'I'll just put these in the back.'

I can't hide my surprise. 'You've been swimming?' And there was I, writing him off as a pretender the minute I clapped eyes on the car.

'I had a quick dip before we met up.' He slams the boot and rubs his hand through his hair. 'One life, live it and all that. It was damned cold, but it woke me up.' Another of those understated shrugs, and the next minute he leaps into the driving seat.

When I attempt to do the same on my side of the car, I discover squeezing into the low, narrow seat isn't as easy as he makes it look. Getting my legs into the foot well is about as easy as fitting a baby giraffe into a crisp packet. On the plus side, I'm guessing there'll be a heater.

Quinn leans across me, flips open the glove box, and stuffs the crumpled-up parking ticket on top of a heap of others. 'Into the filing cabinet. They'll keep my PA busy in the lull after Christmas.' He lets out a long sigh. 'As for parking wardens, whatever happened to hanging loose in Cornwall?' But the grin he sends me as he slams the glove box shut is entirely unrepentant.

I open my mouth, intending to expand on the perennial problem of narrow streets, tourist crowds and selfish parkers. But the engine roars, and the next thing, the wheels are spinning up a sandstorm. As we scream along the seafront at what feels like a hundred miles an hour, but may only be ninety-nine, I'm gripping the arm rests so hard my fingers hurt.

'Mark Ronson okay for you?' Quinn says, as he leans forward and flicks on the stereo. 'We hang out sometimes, these are some of his unreleased tracks.'

Oh my. Is this guy is for real?

'Great.' I force out a smile and decide it's not cool to ask if he means 'the' Mark Ronson. I've a feeling I should be reacting more to what sounds like plain old bass guitar with a drum backing. 'Anything's good for me.' So long as it's not "go faster" music. We're going fast enough as it is.

By the time we hit the road out of St Aidan, I'm a) thanking my lucky stars the windows are tinted so no one will have recognised me in the car that broke the sound barrier going up the high street, and b) fully understanding the term white-knuckle ride.

As we zoom into open country, the winter landscape is passing so fast it's little more than a grey blur, so I decide to look inside the car instead. Now I'm close enough to examine the stitches, Quinn's sweater seems less surfer, more designer. As he rests his forearms on the steering wheel, he eases up a sleeve, and I let out a gasp. Tattoos? On Alice's best man? Surely not?

I shuffle in my seat and end up resting my chin on my propped-up satchel. 'So where exactly do you work into this wedding picture then? How do you know the happy couple?' From where I'm sitting he seems an unlikely fit for one of Alice's friends, for every possible reason.

'Dan and I have an app-development company we started at uni.' As he eases up his other sleeve the colours on his skin are dazzling. 'Dan does the geeky code stuff, I'm the creative one with the street cred and persuasive powers.' His sideways glance twinkles with a dash of self-mockery. And a bucketful of self-assurance. 'I'm a no-brainer choice for best man.'

'I see.' It's amazing how strangers can give you an immediate insight into what your soon-to-be family gets up to.

'And I'm the one with the contacts too,' he goes on, as he drags the car round a left-hand bend on two wheels. 'Like, I arranged to borrow the wedding venue from my uncle.' He's definitely not bragging about it either. From his dismissive shrug he might be talking about blagging a box of chocolates for a raffle prize. 'We all used to holiday down here at Rose Hill Manor as kids, so we know people in Rose Hill village. It's the most magical place. My uncle mostly lives in London, and goes to Klosters for Christmas, so we had the perfect "in".'

Due to Quinn sorting the venue, I've already forgiven him for the last corner. What's more I'm beginning to see why Alice might be overlooking his shortcomings too.

I start breathing again now we're back on four wheels. 'So you know the area then?' Which kind of rubbishes the argument that I'm here for my local expertise.

He grins and taps his fingers on the steering wheel. 'Enough to know where to swim and not get caught out by the tides.'

How cool a reply is that?

'And you thought that was why you were needed?' He raises an eyebrow and stares at me for so long I think we might crash.

I take a while to find the best way of answering. 'That's what Alice… kind of implied.'

His voice drops. 'Well she would… wouldn't she?' He rubs his forehead and shakes his head. 'Actually, way better than that, tell me about you. So far all I know is you live here and you're a painter.'

So that about sums it up. Mostly I'd have let the misinformation go and left it at that. But something about his ragged left cuff makes me comfortable enough to put him right.

'My *gran* was the painter. She used the same colour pallet as the tats on your wrist.'

That has him nodding. 'So what about you?'

I say it quickly, hoping we can move on. 'I design wedding dresses.'

His eyes open wider and he's bouncing with enthusiasm. 'Great, so you designed Alice's then?'

I don't hold back putting him right on that. 'Definitely not.'

'Ouch...'

That one word tells me he completely understands.

'As you said before, Alice and I are very different people. My dresses wouldn't suit her at all. I'm a bit dreamy, whereas she's...' I hesitate, wanting to be fair.

'Uptight and dictatorial? Controlling and completely un-chilled?'

I wince. Quinn filling in the gap sounds a lot harsher than me thinking it.

He laughs. 'Don't worry, we don't have to pretend, we both know her. And mostly we forgive her.' He leans across and taps my bag. 'I'm guessing that's where you're hiding Alice's *Book of Wedding Law*?' He gives a conspiratorial nod towards the back of the car. 'Mine's in the boot.'

'You got one too?' I ask, fumbling with the buckles on my bag.

'I did,' he says, amusement lilting around his lips

Somehow I've been so blown away by Quinn, I completely forgot to check the small print for today. I look at my watch. 'So did you read what we're supposed to be doing now? Ten-thirty, Saturday, what job did the itinerary say?'

His face cracks into a smile. 'Much as I love Alice, there's more than one way to skin a cat.'

'Sorry?' I have no idea what he's driving at.

'You have two hundred pages of detailed instructions in your bag. But given the person who wrote them isn't here we

45

don't have to follow them to the letter.' He slaps the steering wheel triumphantly.

'Isn't that all the more reason we should stick to them?' I'm starting to see why I'm here.

A low laugh comes from Quinn's throat. 'You're more like your sister than you like to think, Sera. From where I stand, what you're clinging onto in that bag of yours is a whole load of suggestions. And it's our job, as creative directors, to implement these to the best of our ability. But we'll do that so much better if we do it in our own way.'

Actually I think he might have lost me a mile out of St Aidan. 'There's a difference?'

'Of course there's a difference.' He's almost shouting now. 'I'm a free spirit, I'm categorically incapable of obeying orders. But I'm damned amazing at making things happen. What you're holding is a blueprint, but we're not going to be enslaved. We're going to wing it.'

'Oh shit.' I sigh. All Alice's hard work and I can see it imploding in front of my eyes. What's more, I'm kicking myself for not reading every single page of the wedding manual. Three times. At least. By only skimming the first two pages, I've really let Alice down. Because without the facts, I have no idea how far off course Quinn is taking us.

'Let's face it, we'd have no fun at all doing it Alice's way,' he says. 'These days she sucks the joy out of everything.'

I hate hearing him talk about Alice like this. But he might have a point. She used to like to steer, but lately she's become horribly rigid. But only because her wedding's so important. 'But at least we could *try* it Alice's way?' I reason. 'And go *off-piste* if it doesn't work?'

Quinn gives a loud sigh. 'So currently, in the world according to Alice, we should be picking up snow machines in Truro. Whereas as I see it, it's way more important to let you see the venue first. That way you'll get a real handle on the event.'

I wince at the jargon. 'Snow machines? What are they for?'

'Sera, please tell me you didn't just ask that.'

I know Alice wants a white wedding in every way. I screw up my face and my courage, and hazard a guess. 'You mean they are *literally* what it says on the tin?' Don't blame me. I spend a lot of time in my own little design world, either on the beach or in the studio. Sometimes I miss out on crucial cultural developments. Somehow I've missed out that snow machines even exist.

'You put water in, fire them up and end up with a snow storm. Of sorts. They can be a bit hit and miss. You only have to read the reviews on Trip Advisor to know they disappoint more often than they thrill. Which is why I suspect she's ordered so many.'

I think I get what he means. 'So if it really starts to snow, we get to skip a whole trip to Truro.' I'm hoping to show I've got the idea and I'm willing to give it a go, at least in part.

'It won't,' he says, making no sense at all.

'Won't what?'

'It's not going to snow.' He sounds definite on that, as he jumps on the brakes and makes a sharp left-hand turn off the lane we're racing along. 'So we will need those machines, but they're not top of our list.'

As we accelerate out of the turn, the cluster of buildings coming into view on the hill ahead is comfortingly familiar. 'But this is Daisy Hill Farm. Where the wedding guests are staying.'

'Got it in one.' He gives a low laugh. 'See, you know your way around better than you think.'

I'm trying to keep up and failing. 'But I thought we were going to the venue?'

'I'm staying in the cosiest little holiday cottage at the farm, and there's a fridge full of food.' There's that unrepentant grin again. 'So unless you want to spend all day sitting next to someone who smells like the beach, I reckon our first priority is a shower and breakfast.'

'Brill.' I say, because I'm really regretting not finishing my hot chocolate earlier. What's more my tummy is growling at the mention of breakfast. But all the same, my alarm bells are ringing.

Something tells me I'm going to have to up my game here. And fast. I'm going to have to pull out all the stops to keep Quinn in hand. Or Alice's wedding will be careering off the rails quicker than I can say 'fried eggs'.

6

Saturday, 17th December
In Quinn's cottage at Daisy Hill Farm:
Scrambled eggs and second glances

'Come on in…' The warmth hits us the moment Quinn pushes
open the pale grey door of the cottage. He leads the way into
a wide open-plan living room with exposed beams and white-
washed stone walls. 'This is home… at least it is until we move
up to the manor house for the wedding.'

Quinn wasn't joking when he said the cottage is cosy. Daisy
Hill Farm is the most amazing summer wedding venue, owned
by Rafe Barker, who is the guy Poppy has finally got together
with. I came up to the farm a couple of times last year with
Jess and Poppy, but I haven't been in the holiday cottages
before. The converted outbuildings, clustered around a court-
yard could literally have come off a picture postcard. And

they're the ideal accommodation for the guests who won't fit into the manor.

When he kicks off his boots by the door, Quinn's feet are bare, with traces of sand between his toes. 'Help yourself to a hot drink,' he says, nodding towards the kitchen area. After pushing on some flip flops, he strides across to a wood burner in a huge rustic fireplace, throws on a couple of logs, and rattles the fire back to life. 'I'll grab a quick shower and then I'll cook. Farm eggs, scrambled, with local sausages and cherry tomatoes okay?'

By the time I swallow my drool enough to reply, he's already disappeared to the bathroom.

Sipping hot chocolate, toasting my toes in front of a roaring fire, when we should be out collecting snow machines? As I look at it, I'm re-grouping. And making up for my previous slacking. And this time, curled up on a velvet sofa with lots of squishy cushions, and Alice's *Wedding Book* resting heavy on my knees, I'm reading with a new urgency. And what's more, I'm making sure every word of it is logged in my brain. So much for fast showers. I've actually got as far as page ten, when there's a knock on the outside door. As there's still no sign of Quinn, I go to answer it, and find Immie, the holiday-cottage manager, on the doorstep. Immie has known Poppy since they were toddlers. I've met her at the shop over the years and seen a lot more of her lately, with Alice's wedding coming up. After a flying visit to see the venue, Alice has organised most things remotely, occasionally using me as go-between. So no one at the farm has actually met her in person yet.

'I saw you and Quinn arrive, so I thought I'd pop over,'

Immie says, as I step back to let her in from the cold. 'Alice rang to tell me you're in charge for now, Sera. I've brought you a key for the office, so you can help yourself to all the cottage keys when you need them.' She runs her fingers through the short spikes of her hair, dropping her voice as she comes in closer. 'Between us, I'd rather not trust Quinn with it. I've known him a long time and I know he drives a flash car and he's meant to be a squillionaire, but he's also a bit "hello clouds, hello sky" when it comes to other people's stuff. Always has been.'

Once I've got over the shock of my 'in charge' label, I can't help smiling. Usually I'm the one who loses things. If they're trusting me over Quinn, he *must* be a disaster.

As for access to the holiday lets, in the last twenty minutes I've discovered that Alice, bless her perfectionist heart, has a welcome pack waiting for every holiday cottage, with enough Christmas decorations to fit out Oxford Street. Which all need collecting and installing. No pressure there, then. I can see I'm not going to get to bed between now and the wedding.

As Immie's Barbour gapes open, I notice she's clutching a familiar fat file to mine. 'You got one too?' I ask.

'Yes, Alice made this booking years ago, she's covered every aspect. In spades.' Immie gives the file a doubtful tap. 'Although Alice has to realise, the best-laid plans can go tits up.' From the snort she gives, Immie's viewing the file as fiction rather than fact. 'The good thing with weddings is it's all between friends. Everyone pitches in and no one minds.'

The phrase 'tits up' makes my eyes go wide. As for 'not minding', that doesn't sound like Alice. The slightest deviation from the plan, we'll all be for the high jump. I hug my shoulders as a shudder ripples through me.

Immie laughs. 'There's no need to look that scared.' Which obviously goes to show she knows zilch about Alice. 'I know it's a lot different from making those beautiful dresses, but we've all got your back until Alice takes over.'

Which is nice to know, but might not be enough. Some things it's best not to think about, so I change the subject. 'You sound like you know Quinn well?'

'Hell yes.' Immie's dramatic eye roll says it all. 'He used to turn up at the big house – Rose Hill Manor – every summer.' She pulls a face. 'When we were teenagers, we did a lot of underage drinking together at the Fox and Goose. Back then he was as bad as they make them, but charming with it.' She gives a gruff laugh. 'And I don't think he's changed any.'

Immie's famed for telling it like it is. And the more she says about Quinn, the more it sounds like she's got him to a 'T'.

There's a click as the bathroom door opens and the next moment we hear Quinn. 'Who hasn't changed?'

Shit. I wince as he saunters across the wooden floor, naked except for a hand towel knotted around his waist. Okay, on second glance – yes, I'll admit I looked again – it's a long way below waist level.

'Bloody hell, sight for sore eyes or what?' Immie shakes her head and groans. 'Still just as much of an exhibitionist, I see.'

Right now I'm thanking my lucky stars Immie's here to slap Quinn down. Although maybe this was all to wind her up. Whatever, I'm glad I'm not alone with this un-clothed version of the man, even if he does look completely relaxed in his own skin. There are so many ripped torsos on the beach, I barely notice them. Whereas this almost-naked guy rocking up on the tufted rug has me entirely horrified, with a tiny undercurrent of thrill I'd rather not admit to. And I'm hoping the others will assume my burning cheeks are down to the fire, not the hormonal flush. I'm definitely going to need a few pointers from Immie on how to handle him.

Quinn seems impervious to Immie's accusations. 'Not guilty, I promise.'

As he turns to me and holds up his hands, I'm praying the knot in his towel is well tied. Otherwise we're all in trouble.

'I thought I'd get the sausages underway before I got dressed, that's all.' As he rubs his arm, the biceps he's flexing are pretty damned honed, so maybe Immie's spot on with what she says. 'And these days I'm fully tamed, house-trained too.' He's upping the protest now. 'Jeez, I'm cooking breakfast, aren't I?' The next thing, he's wandered over and he's giving me the smallest and cheekiest naked elbow nudge on his way to the fridge. 'You couldn't ask for anything more domesticated than that, could you, Sera?'

Immie shakes her head at me and lets out a long sigh. 'You've got your hands full with that one.'

'It's fine,' I say, meaning anything but. I need to start as I mean to go on, even if I'm dying inside. 'We've got so much work to get through it's unreal,' I say, completely truthfully. My recent reading's revealed a 'To Do' list of mind-boggling proportions. 'We're keeping it fun, so we're definitely saying "stuff the snow machines" for now. We'll be starting with Christmas deccies in the holiday cottages, if that's okay with you, Immie?' Let Quinn have what he wants, but at the same time make sure we do something useful. If I don't stand up to him from the start, I'll be dead meat. 'All good, Quinn?' I make sure I'm smiling, then turn to check out his reaction.

There's a string of sausages dangling from his hand, and he's opening and closing his mouth like a guppy. Given he's pretty much lost for words, I'm guessing surprise is a good tactic.

'We'll take that as a "yes" then.' Immie winks at me. 'Let yourselves into the cottages, the keys are all in the office.'

While I've got Immie here for back up, I go again. 'Be careful in the kitchen, Quinn, if you're playing the naked chef. We can't have the best man burning himself.'

Immie's straight in after me. 'Make sure you cook the right sausages too.' She gives a guffaw and holds out the key to me. 'I'll let you get on. I got you a Santa keyring that flashes,' she says. 'So you can keep track of it.'

Seeing as the light-up Santa in question is at least eight inches high, I'm guessing someone tipped her off about me losing stuff.

'A flashing Santa from Immie? Why does that not surprise me?' Quinn quips, as he emerges from behind the kitchen units.

Immie rounds on him. 'You… Stop cheeking people and damn well go and get some clothes on.'

Surprisingly, he saunters across the room like a lamb.

I wait until he's almost at the bedroom door. 'Nice tats, by the way.' I note the way he jerks to a halt, then laugh at Immie. 'But now I've seen them once, I won't need to see them again. Understood?'

'Okay,' he says grudgingly, and gives us a crestfallen-puppy shrug. 'Your loss, though.'

Immie heads for the other door, but when she reaches it, she drops her voice. 'I can tell he likes you. Joke around, but stay firm. You'll have him eating out of your hand.'

I really hope she's right.

7

Anyone who cooks a breakfast as delicious as the one we just ate deserves to get a little bit of their own way, even if they did do it with too few clothes on. So when we finally get to work on the list of stuff to collect for the cottages, Quinn gets to decide the order of the pickups. By the time we turn into the drive to Rose Hill Manor to pick up a consignment of boxes, the hire van Alice had thoughtfully had delivered to the farm is already groaning under the weight of fifty Christmas trees in pots for inside and out at the cottages.

He gives a satisfied nod as we make our way between the avenue of huge trees flanking the approach road. As we round the final corner, and the house comes into view, the steep roofs and mellow stone facade are glowing gold in the pale-pink afternoon light.

He pulls the van to a halt. 'There you go, Rose Hill at its rosy winter best.'

'Wow... beautiful.' Squinting at it through the wide windscreen of the van, I'm almost lost for words. The house is larger than I'd imagined, but its higgledy piggledy mix of windows make it wonderfully welcoming. 'Alice is *so* lucky to be getting married here.'

Of everyone I know, Alice and Dan are one of the most perfect and solid couples, and they truly deserve this. And I don't mean to imply they're boring. It's just I couldn't actually imagine settling down together as early as they did myself. They met on their first day at uni and have been going out ever since. As soon as they got their degrees, Dan set up the business and Alice zoomed up her career ladder. Next came the most gorgeous Hampstead flat, and fast-forward to a textbook romantic proposal on a private launch on the Thames. Now three years later, this fabulous wedding is the icing on their perfect cake.

'I thought you'd like it.' Quinn's smile is full of warmth. 'There's a formal garden and more parkland round the back.' From the way Quinn's talking, he could be describing a pocket handkerchief lawn with a barbecue on a patio. 'Oh, and a bit of a lake too.' Just as an afterthought, then.

I pause for a moment, trying to take it all in. 'It's so wintery, with the bare trees silhouetted against the land.' I can imagine how it looks, dusted with the rime of a hoar frost. If Alice gets one of those for the day of her wedding, even though I know they don't happen very often, it'll be worth freezing our butts off for the pictures.

He nods at my satchel, clamped between my feet. 'Not sure if you've got that far in the *Wedding Story*, but they've got a hot-shot photographer coming down. One of the best in London. Friend of a friend. I blagged them a four-figure discount.'

The more I hear, the bigger Quinn's involvement seems to be. 'Alice must be very grateful,' I say.

He gives a sigh. 'Alice and I have our moments. She doesn't always approve of me, or my methods.'

'She's always been conventional,' I admit. After a few hours with Quinn, I can see his individual brand of anarchy probably drives Alice up the wall. 'You should be in her good books after this, anyway.'

'I'm not sure I'll ever make it that far.' He gives a laugh. 'Thank Christmas you're more Team Dan than Team Alice.'

Whoa. 'I wasn't aware we were taking sides here. Isn't this a joint effort all round?'

'My point entirely,' he says.

I'm not certain, but I think he just contradicted himself hugely there. Not that I'm going to point it out.

He goes on. 'Which is exactly why you should come and join me and stay at the cottage.'

'What?' For some reason I haven't kept up with the logic here. Worse, I seem to be squeaking like a strangled mouse.

He drums his fingers on the steering wheel. 'It makes perfect sense, given we get on so well. At least until the others arrive. Bunking in together would save you running back and forwards into town.'

When I turn to examine his expression, there's not an ounce of flirt in his eyes. Just a very direct, honest, blue green gaze.

Which is actually way more unnerving. Because now I don't know what the hell to think. Other than knowing this would be completely banned by Alice. And remembering there's no way he'd be attracted to me with my non-existent figure and scruffy clothes.

As I open my mouth I'm unsure how to reply, but it doesn't matter as he cuts me off short.

'Obviously we don't have to decide now.' He gives me another elbow nudge, but this time there's the thickness of an extra sweater between us, so it's way less jolty than this morning's naked one. 'For the record…' There's a bit of a dramatic pause. 'I do think hanging out with me twenty-four seven would do you a lot of good.' He tops that off with one of those unapologetic grins of his.

'Thanks for the offer,' I say. *For the record*. Was that completely arrogant of him? Or just plain cheeky? Or an extremely kind thought to save me travelling time? As for exactly what he thinks I'm going to be hanging out… After this morning the mind boggles. 'I'll stay at home. At least for now.'

For a moment, thinking back to the shop and the best man that could have been, I consider a parallel universe where Johnny and I had just loaded fifty potted pines into the back of a van. Where he asks me to stay over. But before I decide how to answer, my sensible self takes over and stamps on that thought. Hard.

'Okay, next job,' Quinn says, rubbing his hands together. 'Decorations for the cottages, from the Coach House.' He's suddenly sounding like Mr Efficiency. 'And there should be a handyman guy in there doing repairs to the pony and trap Alice is hoping to arrive in.'

'Cool.' My reading hasn't got as far as the bridal carriage yet. Hopefully I'll get onto that tonight. On my own sofa.

As he pushes the gear stick forwards, his forehead creases into a frown. 'You do realise, people don't often turn me down, Sera.'

He seems particularly perplexed that I have. Although it's really not exactly clear what I've said 'no' to here.

'I don't imagine they do.' My lips twitch into a smile, but I can't resist the next bit, because he said the same thing to me only half an hour ago. 'But then I'm not "people", Quinn.'

Me? I'm wary enough to put that easy charm and those aching good looks on hold every time. At least until I get to know him better.

In the meantime, we need to push on.

8

Saturday, 17th December
In the kitchen at Daisy Hill Farm:
Mistletoe sprigs and hearts on strings

As I reach the farmhouse, later that evening, I walk straight into Rafe giving Poppy what looks like the good-bye snog of her life on the doorstep.

'Don't mind him, he's acting like he's disappearing for a year,' Poppy laughs, as she peels herself away. 'He's only going out to check the cows.'

It's taken these two a year to make this work, but it's been worth the wait. Believe me, if there was a guy who looked at you the way he looks at her, you'd reconsider your single status. Every time.

'Are you still here working?' As Poppy steps back to let me past, the scent of warm spice whooshes up my nose. 'Come on in and warm up, I'm trying out Rafe's Aga.' She's got her hair in a twist and icing sugar on her nose.

'Thanks, it's so cold out here, my fingers are like ice pops,' I say. It's dark and after stringing lights on trees, by every cottage door around the farm, despite my woolly gloves my hands feel like they belong to someone else.

Poppy peers down at the light-up Santa poking out of my pocket as she leads the way into the kitchen. 'I see Santa's doing his job, if you still have the office key.'

Between us, keeping track of all the cottage keys has been a nightmare. Quinn might be enthusiastic and strong, and know some hilarious jokes, but he's a total ditz when it comes to losing things. For the first time in my life I completely understand why I've sent people round the bend with my vagueness in the past.

'Look at your hessian hearts on strings, there's so many of them,' I say, as I take in the garlands criss-crossing the room. I thought we'd got a lot of deccies for the cottages, but seeing the number of hearts and bows in here, I'm not so sure we've got enough.

Poppy laughs. 'This is Rafe's welcome-back effort. Not a tractor part in sight either, though I'm not sure how long that'll last.'

'Are you baking?' My mouth's already watering, as I see the bowls and drifts of flour on the long kitchen table. It's been three long months since I last wolfed down Poppy's cakes, and I've missed them almost as much as I've missed her. Seeing as I was often in the studio at Brides by the Sea when she lived and baked her cakes in the top-floor flat, I was officially her chief taster.

'You've timed it well. Fancy testing my gingerbread men?' She nods at a pile of biscuits on a cooling tray. 'They haven't got any eyes yet. My icing pipes are still at the shop.' She slides the kettle onto the Aga. 'You've got roses in your cheeks from the cold. Like a drink to warm up?'

I'm suddenly so hungry I'm practically swooning at the thought of gingerbread. 'Tea would be fab, please.'

'I'll make one for Quinn too.' She pulls some mugs from the shelf. 'You two looked like you were having fun when I saw you earlier.'

'He's a long way from the stuffed shirt I was expecting,' I laugh. 'He'll be along soon. Great with fairy lights, too.' Since he put his clothes on and covered up that disgustingly deep tan of his, we've got on better.

Poppy frowns. 'Immie said she'd have been happy to put up the usual cottage decorations, but Alice wouldn't hear of it.'

I pull a face. 'I'm sorry Alice is a bit fussy. She wants every cottage themed, to match the wedding and the occupants.' This won't be the last time I apologise for her. 'Actually I came to check if it's okay to take the pig pictures down?' Another of Alice's specific instructions.

Poppy's face breaks into a grin. 'We're all with Alice on that one. Those pigs are hideous. Leave them in the office, with any luck they won't go back up again.' She puts three mugs on the chunky wood table and piles a plate high with gingerbread men. 'Is there much left for you to do in the cottages?'

Sliding onto a chair, I slip off my jacket, then grab a tea and dunk my biscuit. 'Loads.' I sink my teeth into a delicious gingerbread leg to stem my panic. Because 'loads' is a huge understatement. Each cottage has an individual tree with hand-made decorations. Then there are bespoke toiletries, wicker wreaths, pillow chocolates, rose petals, scented candles, boxes of Turkish delight, hampers, fruit bowls and a mistletoe sprig. And tasteful pictures to replace the pigs. And Christmas garlands. 'The job's so massive, if I hadn't had a gingerbread intake at exactly this minute, I might actually have given up.' I'm not joking either.

Poppy stares at me over the top of her mug. 'Maybe Immie and I could help?'

'No, I couldn't possibly expect you to do that. You haven't even met Alice yet.'

'Really, it's fine, Sera. We're all here for each other. Look how you stepped in with my bestie last summer. The dress you lent Cate gave her the wedding of her dreams.'

'But Cate let us use her photos for publicity…' I'm hesitating, knowing the difference more hands would make.

Poppy comes over and squeezes my shoulder. 'Think of this as payback for you making Cate's day wonderful. That wedding might not even have happened without your dress.' She's being very persuasive.

'You really have time to help?' If I didn't have my mouth full of gingerbread man, I'd kiss her.

She smiles. 'I'm just back from London, with no cake orders, and no weddings to sort out. And who doesn't love Christmas decorations?'

'You might not be saying that when you get to the end,' I groan. 'But if you're sure, I'd be *so* grateful.'

'Call in first thing, show us exactly how you want things. Then leave it with us.' Poppy's still patting my hand when the door opens.

'Can I smell gingerbread?' Quinn's rugged face appears as he dips under a heart garland. 'I let myself in, I hope that's okay?'

This is the measure of the guy. He's laid back and confident enough to walk right in like he owns the place. And he gets away with it every time. Unless there's a parking warden involved.

Poppy's pushing crumbs into her mouth. 'Sit down, grab some tea and tell us how the biscuits are.'

'The good news is Poppy and Immie are going to help with the cottages.' I say, knowing he'll be ecstatic.

'Amazing,' he says. 'Thank Christmas for that.' He folds himself into a chair, helps himself to a biscuit and takes a bite. Then takes a few seconds to deliberate. 'Delicious,' he says eventually, turning to Poppy, waving his biscuit. 'But look, you've bitten off the head of yours, which is pretty cruel.' He sends me a wink. 'Whereas Sera and I are both eating ours feet first.' He leans over and gives me another significant nudge. Which makes four today. If you count the one where we had hysterics because I dropped the Christmas tree on his foot.

I pick up what's left of my gingerbread man – just the head – and pop it into my mouth. Not that I'm trying to eat the evidence, but I'm not sure it's *that* significant. I help myself to another and try to start at the top, but I can't. So I begin to nibble the toes, except this time I'm eating more slowly, because I feel like I'm being watched.

'It's the same with chocolate teddy bears,' Quinn goes on, chomping his way up to chest level on his biscuit. 'The world is split into two groups – people who start with the head. And people who start with the feet. There's no switching sides. You are how you are.'

'When did eating gingerbread men get this complicated?' I twist my sleeve around my fingers, take another bite and try to work out what he's getting at here. Or if he's just bullshitting. Which he might be.

Quinn carries on eating until only the head's left, then he holds it up. 'Twelve out of ten for taste.' He nods at Poppy. 'I'd score even higher if he had a grin.'

'Waiting for icing pipes,' she explains, even though Quinn probably has no idea what she's talking about. 'I think what Quinn's trying to point out, Sera… very subtly…' Poppy's nipping back her smile. '… Is that you two have quite a lot of common ground.'

'Excuse me?' I say. I'm not sure this is what I need to hear. Because it's patently not true.

Quinn's waggling his next biscuit at Poppy. 'Twelve out of ten for observation there, Pops.'

Listening to this, I'd say they're the ones with the common ground. She didn't even flinch when he called her Pops and she usually hates it.

'It's not just the gingerbread. Look at you both.' Poppy's laughing now. 'The same ripped denim, the same sun-streaked hair, your sweaters are practically identical…'

Pretty appalled, I look down to remind myself what jumper I pulled off the bedside chair this morning. Yes, it's one of my favourites. Burnt orange, sloppy. I chose it as my comfort blanket because I was stressed about this random best man I was going to meet. With good cause, as it happens. *Was that really only this morning?* The end of my sweater sleeves are fraying where I've been tugging them over my hands, which is what I'm doing now. As I turn my gaze onto Quinn, my tummy sinks.

Shit. 'So, we're both wearing orange sweaters.' I'm praying Poppy won't pick up on his ragged cuffs. 'And your point is?' As I push back my sweater sleeve, because actually I'm getting a bit hot here under all the scrutiny, Poppy lets out a yelp.

'Omigod, you've got the same leather wristbands too.' She gives a guilty shrug. 'I'm sorry, Sera, but it's much more than what you're wearing. Your expression is so similar, it's unreal.' She chews her thumbnail as she studies us. 'You're like a couple of beachy twins.'

I pull in a long breath. Twins I may be persuaded to go for. Non-identical ones, obviously. Where the siblings disagree over most things. It's the 'couple' bit that has me lifting off the chair.

'Actually we have really different views on practically every subject.' Even as I blurt it out I can see Quinn smirking behind his hand.

'Really...' Poppy sounds unconvinced.

'Yes,' I'm determined to fight my case here. Quinn and I have been together for less than a day and we've been at odds right left and centre. 'Like I really disagree with inconsiderate parking... which Quinn does all over the place.' I stick out my chin. One to me. 'And I completely disagree with guys walking around the cottage nine-tenths naked...' It's out before I think. This is how crap I am under pressure. And it's way more embarrassing for me than anyone else, which is why those roses in my cheeks have now spread to the tips of my ears. Dammit.

Poppy's elbow is on the table and she's propping her chin on her hand, widening her eyes at Quinn in mock horror. 'Don't tell me you've been walking around without clothes, Quinn?'

He grins, but looks entirely unashamed. 'I have. But only to put the sausages on.'

Poppy blinks at that. At least the sausage part slowed her down a bit. But then she turns to me. 'Not wanting to put you on the spot, Sera, but what about that string bikini you walk round in the entire summer? The one that covers a whole lot less than a tenth of you. The one you wear all the time. In the studio, down the mini market, in the Cats' Protection shop. Basically everywhere, except if there are customers around?'

Quinn laughs. 'So we park in different places. But it sounds like we definitely both like to chill...' He pauses, and the skin at the ends of his eyes crinkles as he smiles. '...Nine-tenths naked, that is.'

I'm kicking myself for coining that phrase. And although I'm hungry enough to eat for an army, if I have one more crumb of gingerbread man I might just choke.

'Talking of chilling...' Quinn's suddenly much more serious. 'If I see another fairy light, I might just explode, so it's probably time for some down time.' He claps his hands. 'I've got wine and supper waiting across at the cottage for anyone who's interested.' He switches his gaze to Poppy. 'We were thinking it might be easier if Sera stays over at mine tonight.' Smooth as anything. Just like that.

My eyes practically pop out of their sockets in shock. What part of 'no' does this guy not understand?

I take a deep breath and count to nine... 'Actually, I was hoping to get back to St Aidan, if anyone's going that way?' The look I send Poppy is pure desperation. What's more, she did create the opening for Quinn here, although I've a feeling he'd have made it regardless. 'I've got too much reading and designing to catch up on to spend time… chilling.' Naked or otherwise.

'Maybe another night, then.' Poppy smiles at Quinn, then turns to me. 'No problem, I'll pop you back home, Sera. Let's face it, I can hardly ice a Christmas cake without my piping bags. And I might grab some cupcake cases too.'

Now she's talking. Right now I could kill for one of Poppy's cupcakes. Plain sponge. With lashings of vanilla buttercream. All white, like the wedding dresses. Just in case the crumbs get in the wrong place in the shop.

As for tomorrow, I'm going to need all the calories I can get, to keep the Naked Chef in hand. There I go again. Definitely not in hand. Anything but that.

9

Sunday, 18th December
At Brides by the Sea: Blaring horns and short circuits

Sera, Pls can you bring me some pieces of lace – working on Christmas cupcake designs – cd always make a few Chrissy cupcakes for Alice's cake table? Poppy xx

I'm in the studio the next morning and as Poppy's text pings into my phone, I can hear Jess's loafers clattering up the stairs. Although, if Poppy imagines there will be a place for unscheduled cupcakes at Alice's wedding, it's because she doesn't know Alice.

'How long have you been here?' Jess pops her head around the doorframe, frowning, her voice high with surprise. 'Aren't you supposed to be on wedding duties today?'

Poppy's text gives me the perfect excuse. 'I just called in to get some lace scraps for Poppy.' I'd rather Jess didn't know I've been here since five, bent over the sewing machine. Having hit a brick wall with my as-yet non-existent designs, I've gone back to basics. I've been messing around with silks and satins and scissors, trying to free myself up by skipping the drawings and working very fast, straight onto the mannequin. If I stop worrying and work entirely instinctively with the raw materials, like I used to do when I was a student, maybe, just maybe, I'll short-circuit my creative block. Come up with some entirely new ideas and shapes for wedding dresses. Although thus far, all I've got are a line of limp shifts, dangling from hangers. Like ghosts waiting for a Halloween party.

'Are you okay? You've got very dark circles.' Jess motions to her eyes, although if she thinks I'm looking sleep-deprived, she should find a mirror.

'I was up late, reading up on the wedding strategy,' I say. It was well after midnight when I crawled into bed, my head throbbing with wedding facts. I definitely don't need to admit the pre-dawn start to work on my collection. 'What's your excuse?'

She rolls her eyes. 'Jaggers until four.

'Again?'

'It was the "Grab a Granny and a Cocktail" Christmas do. Believe me, some of these forty year-olds really know how to whoop it up. Jules was there, with his mum.'

'That was nice.' Jules is Jess's tame and very talented photographer, who hasn't actually untied the apron strings and left home yet. As for age, Jess's is a closely guarded secret. Between us, forty is a long way short of the real figure, but she talks a good job. And she swears by what she calls her 'hope in a jar' products – anti-gravity potions and wrinkle repair creams. She keeps them in the prosecco fridge and slaps them on by the gallon.

'Actually Jules' ma was drinking like a bloody fish, I couldn't keep up with her at all.' Jess gives a grimace. When it comes to alcohol, Jess is the original hollow-legged woman, so who knows what Jules' mum is like. 'So many Christmas parties, I'll be damned relieved when it's January. What are you doing today?'

And now she has me. Alice rang last night to say she's finally got a flight into Devon later on. Which is brilliant news, because that'll take the heat off me. Right now I'm actually putting off the awful moment when I have to leave the building and drive to the airport to pick her up. Exeter's a bloody long way when the furthest you usually drive is to the launderette, once every two years, when the washer breaks down.

'As I said, I'm taking Poppy some pieces of lace.' I recap, for both our benefits. 'Then she and Immie are helping with the cottages.'

If Jess gets a sniff of the truth about where I'm heading she'll go into overdrive. If she starts reeling off road numbers and asking if I've got life insurance, I'll get so hot under the collar, I'll melt into a pool of grease. Driving round St Aidan I'm fine. But dual carriageways and turning-right arrows in the road give me the willies. And somehow I have to get all the way to Exeter. And it's no good saying 'use your sat nav', because that just confuses me even more. And half the time there's no connection anyway.

A car horn beeps down below in the mews and makes me jump. Omigod, this is how nervous and wound up I am. That'll be me in half an hour. Getting lost. Causing hold-ups because I don't like driving over forty. Everyone beeping me because I'm in the wrong lane.

When I peer past my fabric samples and magazine piles to see out of the window at the car roofs three floors below, I seem to be looking down on a log jam. Except these are cars not logs. There are three or four horns blaring now, their discordant notes clashing. At first I think I'm having some weird fast-forward see-into-the-future vision of me, having a mid-road crisis, en route to Exeter. When I blink myself back to the present and force myself to calm down, even from above I can tell the car at the front is sleek and low. Even though it's one of those cold, murky, December mornings, when the daylight never really takes a hold, the highly polished, metallic granite paintwork of that car sticks out a mile. Given that by rights Quinn should be miles away, I'm bracing myself for something. I'm just not quite sure what.

'Sera...' It's the Sunday girl calling up. 'There's a guy waiting for you downstairs. I put him in the White Room.'

If this is Quinn, it's an entirely unscheduled visit. Right now he should be at Rose Hill Manor, taking delivery of the starry ceilings for the ballroom. Thank goodness he didn't do his usual trick of walking right on in like he owns the place, and make it all the way up to the studio. I hurl myself down the stairs, and thirty seconds later I'm skidding to a halt on the bleached floor of the White Room, gasping.

'What the hell are you doing here? What about the heavenly ceilings?'

From the way Quinn's holding back his smile, he looks like he's trying not to laugh 'Nice to see you too.' His hands are deep in the pockets of a well-worn duffel coat. 'Poppy told me I might find you here.' He's really rocking the laid-back thing this morning. Which is really damned annoying, when I'm in such a razz.

I pull out my phone and check the time. 'Well I'm in a hurry, even if you're not,' I snap, and give him the most threatening stare I can drum up at short notice. 'Some of us have to get to the airport.' Between us, this is the kind of move I usually practise in front of a mirror for a few weeks before I let it loose on the outside world. But we all know there's no time for that here. 'If you miss the Celestial Ceilings people...' Alice will go apoplectic/through the roof/ape – or maybe even all three.

But before I can get that far, he interrupts. 'Okay, take a chill pill, Sera...'

If he knew how patronising he sounded, he really wouldn't say that.

He carries on. 'The flight's not in until this afternoon, there's no need to set off yet.'

I've done the calculations and I know better. 'At forty miles an hour it takes...'

He cuts me off mid-sentence. 'That's what I came to say. Given you said yesterday how much you hate driving, maybe we should swap jobs. You stay at Rose Hill and I'll do the airport run.'

'Right...' I'm not sure how he picked up on that, but I'm relieved enough to go momentarily floppy. 'That would be so brill,' I say weakly, propping myself up on the tilting mirror as my knees collapse with gratitude.

'But then I got side-tracked by your flamingos.'

'Flamingos?' I really have no idea what he's talking about here.

He lets his smile go. 'On those very smart pyjamas you're wearing…'

For a second I think he's joking, then I look down. As I catch sight of my favourite Topshop shorts sleep set on top of my woolly winter-night tights, my tummy takes a nose dive. How the hell did I forget to get dressed before I came out?

As I squirm in embarrassment, my mouth is gaping, but no words are coming out.

Jess, who's arrived without me noticing, swoops to my rescue. 'Sera often wears leisure wear in the studio. Basically talented designers *have* to feel relaxed or they can't come up with the goods.' She's beaming at Quinn, extending her hand. 'We haven't been introduced yet, lovely to meet you, I'm Jess.'

I wince at how horribly close Jess is to the truth there. She'd have a complete hissy fit if she knew about the state of my current non-collection of wedding dresses.

'So this is your shop? What a fabulous place.' Quinn's turned all his attention onto Jess now. 'I'm Quinn, by the way, Alice's best man.'

'Lovely.' From the way Jess's purr has switched on, she's warming to Quinn. 'Do come through and have a peep at Sera's room, while you're here.' As Jess steers him through, the heat's right off me, because, true to form, she's pretty much taken him over.

In a last-minute move, she grabs my wrist and yanks me with them. Before you can say petticoat, there's a flurry of tulle and lace and whispering voile and she's whipping dresses off the rails right left and centre. In thirty seconds flat she's whisked Quinn through the key pieces in the Seraphina East collection, and she's onto the celebrity pictures.

'And this is the couture dress designed by Sera, which Josie Redman wore for her celebrity wedding.' She sounds like a cat that got double cream.

'*The* Josie Redman?' Just this once Quinn is gobsmacked enough to look shocked. 'Impressive…When you said you made wedding dresses, Sera, I had no idea you meant real ones.'

Even though I hate being around when people see my dresses, I'm indignant enough to chime in here. 'What other kind are there, Quinn?'

For a moment he's chastened. 'Okay, what I mean is, I had no idea they'd be this beautiful… or high end.'

'Well thanks a bunch for that.' Talk about wrapping a compliment up in an insult.

He frowns. 'I can see I'm digging a hole for myself here. But even when you're not in your jim jams, there's a big gulf between Sera's holey denims and Seraphina's exquisite dresses.'

Even though I think he just said 'exquisite', he's still coming over as pretty insulting, overall.

'You'll see.' I stick out my chin in protest. 'I scrub up.' It's complete bull. The furthest I go is black silk shorts rather than ripped denim. But I can't let him talk down to me like this.

He laughs. 'I'm not saying it's a bad thing. It's a surprise, that's all. In a good way.'

As a particularly long and loud blast on a horn in the street resonates around the room Jess hangs up the dress she's holding and covers her ears. 'Whatever's going on out there, it's playing havoc with my head.' She pushes back a swathe of tulle and fairy lights and peers down the mews. 'Looks like some kind of traffic jam...'

Quinn puts his hand to his mouth. 'Ooops... I think that might be me...'

Jess is at the window in a flash. 'No, it won't be, it's actually a sports car causing the trouble. Dark grey. There's a traffic warden too.'

Dark grey? I groan. It's the traffic warden that's the real giveaway. 'Quinn, what did I tell you yesterday?'

'Sounds like my free parking's over.' He pulls a face. 'Sorry to rush you, but we'd better run. Sera, I'll take you home to get some clothes and drop you at Rose Hill...'

'But why didn't you tell me Quinn drove a Ferrari?'

Actually I told her as little as I could. Not that she needed my info, after she'd pumped Poppy dry. As if I noticed the car make. 'Maybe I was too busy counting the parking tickets.' As a reply it's completely true. One blingy car is very much like another, after all. Let's face it, they're all totally impractical on the roads round here.

'Sera's not the only one full of surprises.' Quinn's laughing over his shoulder at Jess, as he heads towards the door.

As I hurtle off towards the stairs to grab my coat and satchel I can't help hoping there won't be any more surprises today

10

Sunday, 18th December
At Rose Hill Manor: A cottage by the sea

It's no surprise that Quinn drives at the speed of light, all the way to Daisy Hill Farm, where we show Poppy how Alice would like her cottages. Then we head over to Rose Hill Manor, which is quarter of a mile down the lane. Yesterday, in the van, we went around the back to the coach house, but today we roar all the way up to the front door.

'The great thing about this house is it's relaxed rather than starchy and grand.' Quinn leaps out of the car and digs deep in his duffel coat pocket for a key. Seconds later he's pushed open the wide oak door and his arm's sliding around me, as he shows me into the hall.

It's a shame he wasn't this efficient with the cottage keys yesterday, but whatever.

Blinking as I spin away from Quinn's grasp, I take in a tall white hallway, washed with pale light from high leaded windows. A staircase that's wide, but definitely more 'Sleeping Beauty in the country' than 'Cinderella at the ball'. Given he smells of something manly and expensive rather than salt, I'm guessing he hasn't been for a dip in the sea today yet.

'See what I mean?' He leans a shoulder on the stair post as he gazes around. 'Small, yet perfectly formed.'

I'm not sure where Quinn hangs out if that's how he sums it up. There's nothing small about the rooms I'm glimpsing behind the half-open doors. But despite the lofty ceiling and the expanses of white walls, the warm pine-drenched scent of the house immediately wraps itself around me. I feel welcomed rather than intimidated.

'And what a whopper of a Christmas tree.' I get a crick in my neck as I look up at the branches, tapering up the stair well. It has to be the largest I've seen outside Oxford Street. For a moment it spins me back to the last Christmas at uni when one of the guys from the upstairs flat hauled in a tree from someone's garden that was so big and spiky we couldn't get down the hallway.

'And like the rest of the house, it's still waiting for its decorations.' Quinn raises one eyebrow. 'How are you on step ladders?'

I don't reply, because right now I'm remembering that somewhere upstairs there are bedrooms for the entire bridal party, and more, plus all the ground-floor rooms, where the wedding celebrations will take place on Christmas Eve and roll straight on into Christmas next day. With everything still to do, I can't believe we're hanging around in the hall. 'Maybe we'd better hurry up.' My voice rises as my chest tightens with the stress. That's possibly the understatement of the year. 'We haven't got time to stand around chatting.'

'Chill, Sera, you've done the most important thing for the morning. At least you're dressed now.' That same old smile is lilting around his lips. And no surprise he's making a dig about the pyjama blunder. 'As for the wedding, it's all in the manual…' He leans over and taps the file I'm clutching, then glances at his watch. 'There's time to whizz you round the rest of the ground floor before I leave for the airport.'

'About that…' I say, as we push through a door and I take in a series of simply furnished interconnecting rooms, which might have come straight out of an *Elle Deco* magazine. 'How did you know I hated driving?'

'The ceremony will be in what we call the winter garden, by the way.' He pauses and points to a room with doors looking out onto the garden, then carries on where he left off. What begins as an elbow nudge, somehow ends up with his arm closing around my rib cage. 'As for the driving, you're neurotic about parking and a terrified passenger. I joined up the dots.' The squeeze he gives me forces every bit of oxygen out of my lungs. 'At a guess you'd rather fly to the moon than drive to Exeter? Which is why I'm going instead.'

Given I haven't any air to form words, I nod and offer up a silent 'thank you' for what he's saved me from.

'You could always come too?' he says, with a wistful look I can't quite judge.

For a second the idea of racing across into the next county, even with Quinn driving like a crazy person, is quite appealing. Then reality hits. 'Someone's got to stay to let the ceiling guys in.' How can he have forgotten that? Then another thought. 'Plus, you're driving a two-seater, and picking up Alice.' Not to mention all the work there is to do.

'Shit, so I am.' He smacks himself on the forehead. 'Maybe another time then.'

'Great,' I smile. Suddenly I don't feel so bad about going out in my pjs.

He moves on through the house, talking as he goes. 'My uncle calls this his "cottage by the sea". He had it redone to look like a beach house a few years back.' Quinn's propelling me through the winter garden into an enormous room with sloping ceilings. 'This was originally built as a ballroom. It's perfect for the wedding breakfast and the party afterwards. This is where you'll bring the guys to install the ceiling, okay?'

I screw up my face as I take in more white criss-crossing beams in the roof space.

Again Quinn reads my mind. 'I don't understand why Alice would want to hide this either.' He gives a bemused shrug. 'But she insists she wants a ceiling with stars that twinkle. They're the current must-have. Can't get married without one. It's the same with the disco floor.'

'What?'

'Tut, tut, you really are behind on your wedding reading.' His lips twitch into that grin again. 'It's a kind of electronic light-show dance floor that changes colour with the music. They're very cool. It's coming later in the week, once the sky is up.'

'I suppose she's only getting married once...' I muse, wondering why the perfect uncluttered backdrops aren't enough.

'We are definitely doing this for one time only,' Quinn echoes my thoughts as he whisks me through more rooms. As the white painted walls and floors give way to the polished stone and stainless steel of several interlinked kitchens, we come face to face with a wall of cardboard boxes.

The packaging is familiar. 'Bedroom supplies, for here?' I'm pointedly ignoring the tray of mistletoe.

'I brought them in earlier. I thought you could put them out while you were waiting for the ceiling to arrive?'

'Sure.'

Quinn must have had a very early start, then.

'And not being sexist…'

I frown at him, because I've spotted an ironing board across the room, already erected. 'But…?'

He nods at the boxes. 'Somewhere in that lot there are a few hundred seat covers and bows that all need pressing. Don't worry, the hire chairs have arrived, and they're in the coach house.'

As it happened, I wasn't worrying about chairs, because I don't even know about them yet. I can't believe he's a) got so far ahead of me in the instructions, and b) is dishing out the jobs. Which actually is what *I* intended to do, but whatever.

'Before you shoot me down, I *can* iron…' he says. 'I would iron… but I'm off to get Alice.'

Even though this arrangement couldn't suit me better, I can't resist staring at the creases on his shirt. 'Yeah, I can *really* see how much you like ironing.'

'Designer wrinkles.' He laughs as he smoothes his hand over the cotton. 'I prefer my clothes this way. Just like you obviously do with yours.'

Damn. Just my luck that the flowery silk cami I grabbed from the bedroom floor looks like the original crumple zone. Sometimes it's best to back down gracefully.

'Don't worry, you get off, I'll look after the ironing.' I'm not going to tell him that I iron anything I can get my hands on. Apart from the clothes on my bedroom floor, obviously.

'Okay.' He sticks his hands in his pockets. 'Help yourself to lunch, help yourself to the bedrooms, and remember...' He flashes me the 'hang loose' hand sign. 'Stay chilled. Alice is on her way and it's all going to work out fine.'

With Alice here I'm not sure how much chilling there will be. But I'm giving silent cheers, because I've avoided an upstairs tour, complete with all the nudging and squeezing opportunities that offered. 'And Quinn...' I know he's already had at least one parking ticket today. And possibly a whole load more I don't know about. So I may as well give him the benefit of my local knowledge anyway. 'If you park on the runway, they'll tow you away. Every time.'

As he backs out of the kitchen, he drops the 'hang loose' sign and flashes the 'birdie' at me instead.

11

When I finally screw up my courage and dare to tiptoe upstairs, I find a dozen lovely bedrooms, all decorated in the same chic yet uncluttered style as down below. There are a couple of gorgeous master suites, with understated four-posters and French-style wardrobes practically the size of my cottage. Between us, if I had one of those at home, I'd put more effort in and the pile of clothes by my bed might be less chaotic. The rest of the bedrooms are still luxurious, in diminishing sizes, all with en suites. And then there are attic rooms too. Lingering by the window, I'm looking out over what could almost be a hidden kingdom nestling in the surrounding hills. Beyond the gardens, there's parkland and fields, then the lake beyond, which is huge.

It's much easier putting out goodies in the guest bedrooms here than in the holiday cottages. I zoom from room to room, being careful to keep an ear out for the delivery van, or vans.

By the time Quinn should have reached the airport, each bedroom has its own table-top tree, complete with burnished gold baubles and matching pine cones, and swags across the fireplaces. I've put out candles with the scent of angel's wings, – yes, really – warming bath essences, hessian bows, cashmere throws, cinnamon-spiced pot pourri in hammered metal bowls, spring water in glass bottles with snowflakes on. Oh, and champagne truffles, Turkish delight and crystallised ginger. Everything's there, except for the mistletoe. Let's face it, when there's a hunk like Quinn rampaging around the place, mistletoe is better left until the last possible moment.

By the time I step outside to take the empty boxes out to the old stable block, it's way past lunchtime and a biting wind cuts through my cardi. Although there's no sign of the elusive ceiling, there's a white van parked by the coach house. I'm guessing, from the distant noise of grinding metal, that the handyman Quinn mentioned yesterday is working on Alice's horse-drawn carriage. As I pass and peer in through the half-open door, I can see some kind of cart, which isn't quite the Cinderella coach I'd imagined. In the yellow light beyond, there's a figure in a welding mask leaning over a work bench.

If I were more like Poppy, I'd bounce over and say hello. If I were Jess I'd probably go and try to sell him a wedding suit, or at the very least, I'd invite him to Jaggers. As it is, I'm dithering, wondering if I should go and offer him a sandwich, or some tea. But then I spot a kettle and mugs, and if he's busy he won't want me to disturb him. So instead I pull my cardi more tightly around me and hurry back to the house. As I dive for the back door and the warmth of the kitchen, if I didn't know better I'd have sworn there were specks of snow blowing. Which reminds me, we still haven't collected the snow machines yet.

I know some people hate ironing, but pressing the fabric is so much a part of making dresses that I love it. When I unpack the chair covers, they are dreamy cotton voile and when they're pressed they come up a treat. With the steam iron hissing, the repetition is so soothing that the afternoon whizzes by.

I was hoping that hours of ironing would provide the space for some design ideas to pop into my head. But it hasn't happened. As the afternoon light fades and I finally stop for a coffee, I get the latest copy of *Vogue* out of my satchel to flick through as I drink.

When you're a designer it's a bit like being a sponge. You devour magazines, absorb the trends. Find out everything you can about styles and fabrics and celebrity fashions. When you've soaked it all up, you let your brain work on it, to give it your own individual spin. Then the designs come out pretty much on their own.

At least that's what's always happened in the past. But this time, something's gone wrong. Because nothing's coming out. And the more I'm worrying about it, the worse it's getting.

I've moved onto *Hello!* when I finally hear the throb of an engine outside. This time I pull on my coat, shoot out of the kitchen door and rush around the front of the house, expecting to see a lorry. But instead it's Quinn, climbing out of his car. Alone.

'What have you done with Alice?' I know for sure she won't have missed her flight.

Quinn rolls his eyes and tugs at his hair. 'Long story.' For someone so chilled, he looks remarkably stressed. 'Alice's cases were too big for the boot of my car.'

'Ouch.' I can imagine how that went down.

'First she hit the roof,' he confirms. 'Then she hired a car of her own. She said to tell you she's going straight to the farm.' He shakes his head. 'Talking of roofs, give me some good news. How's the ceiling coming on?'

'It's not,' I say flatly. 'It hasn't arrived yet.'

'Shit.' He looks at his watch. 'I seriously doubt it'll be coming now. Probably best not tell Alice, unless she specifically asks.' As he stares over my shoulder, his frown lines deepen and he mutters. 'What the hell is he doing here still…?'

As I turn to discover exactly what Quinn is so pissed off about, I see the guy from the coach house coming towards us in the dusk, welding mask in hand.

'Hey, I thought I heard voices…'

Those six words are enough to send a seismic shiver down my spine. I try to ignore the fact that my heart is pounding so hard that all three of us will be able to hear it. If my feet weren't rooted to the spot, I might just run. As for what Johnny's doing here…

Quinn cuts in. 'Actually, we're just leaving.'

If I hold my breath Quinn might just pull off his second fairy godmother trick of the day and magic me out of here.

'We?' There's a mocking antagonism in Johnny's voice. 'Anyone I should be introduced to before you rush off?'

Right now I can't dwell on why the guy who was doing his

PhD on car engines in Bristol back in the day, should have popped up here of all places, doing something as ridiculous as welding Alice's Cinderella coach. As if coming face to face with Johnny all over again isn't bad enough, doing it all in front of Quinn makes it ten times more embarrassing.

Between us, I'm the last person in the world to think on my feet. Whatever I've done, for the last eight years, fast-thinking Jess has always been there to leap in and save me. But suddenly it's all down to me. And just this once I astonish myself so much, I'm surprised my mouth doesn't lock into a wide-open 'O'.

Before I know what's happening, I'm smiling a very broad, very rigid smile. Next thing, I've whipped around to face Johnny, head on. And even though my voice is hoarse and I sound as breathy as Marilyn Monroe, at least the words are coming out.

'Hi Johnny… again. Alice is my sister, by the way… and I'm her bridesmaid.' And then his words from two days ago pop into my head and straight out of my mouth. 'We must stop meeting like this…' I hurl out my hand towards Johnny, daring him to grasp it.

'Sera…?' He's blinking at me in the half light.

At least this way I have the unexpected advantage of seeing smooth-talking Johnny being the one who's struggling to find words.

Quinn's staggering backwards. 'You two know each other?'

I make it as airy and throw-away as I can. 'Our paths crossed at uni. Briefly.' That should make it even less significant. 'And the other day in the shop.'

I'm so busy basking in my own glorious moment, I entirely

miss Johnny getting his act together. When his hand comes towards mine, I jump.

'Great to meet you again too, Sera – or is it Seraphina now?' His narrowed eyes are glittering with irony. 'And vertical not horizontal this time. It must be my lucky day.'

There's a second when my hand is lurching wildly in space and then he grasps it, and anchors me. And then he lets go again.

It only seems right to turn back to Quinn and involve him in the conversation. 'And Johnny is here because…?' Somehow Johnny's not acting like the lowly handyman he's been billed as.

Before Quinn can reply, Johnny's in there. 'I'm Dan's best man.'

'Sorry? Is there something I'm missing here?' I look at Quinn. 'But aren't you…?'

Johnny's back in there, looking like he's laughing at some private joke. 'He's best man's assistant.'

Quinn quashes that in an instant. 'We're *both* best men. Best man one – me – and he's best man two.'

'There are *two* of you?' Excuse me for being incredulous, but…

Johnny gives a shrug. 'Actually it's the other way around. Dan and I go way back. I sat next to him on my first day at junior school in Suffolk, when my parents flew south from Edinburgh. Whereas Quinn's known Dan since uni. And J comes before Q in the alphabet. Just saying.'

So that explains it. Strange we never made the connection before. But Alice and Dan never visited me at uni and Johnny rarely spoke about home. So how could we?

And there's another question I have to ask. 'Does Alice know she's doubled up on her best man?' Because somehow I can't see her being happy about an arrangement this unorthodox.

Johnny's doing all the talking here. 'She got her head around it eventually. In the end she put us down in her book as our generic title, without names.' Ahh, the book. He's got one too, of course.

At least it explains why I couldn't find who the best man was when I looked. And funny how Quinn didn't admit to this earlier, because it was sure to come out eventually. But maybe that might explain why he's looking particularly pissed off as he turns to me.

'Come on, Sera we really should go and get those snow machines. They should have been picked up yesterday.'

I might have avoided gawping before, but I'm making up for it now. When did snow machines suddenly go back on the agenda?

'Probably not that urgent.' Johnny's low laugh sounds as if he's mocking again. 'Given there's snow coming in on the forecast.' All these years and he still hasn't lost that Ewan McGregor lilt. It killed me then and it's killing me now. But this time I really *don't* want to hear it.

'It won't snow,' I say quickly. Not that I'm taking sides, but I've hung out with Quinn for the last thirty hours. And I'm eternally grateful he did my airport run. What's more, this is the perfect excuse to be air-lifted away from Johnny. I wrack my brains to remember why it isn't going to snow. 'It doesn't snow here because the climate is… err… Pacific.'

There's a second of silence while the guys momentarily suspend hostilities and stare at each other with puzzled frowns.

Then Quinn jumps to the rescue. 'I think "oceanic" is the word you're looking for,' he says, helpfully.

'Thank you, Quinn, that's the one.' I knew it had something to do with the sea. In fact I was pretty damned close for someone who doesn't have the first clue. 'So we'll be off then,' I say, as I dive towards Quinn's car. 'Catch you later, Johnny.'

This is where we make our quick getaway. A squeal of tyres on the gravel and we'll be away. I fling open the car door. And that's where the fast part ends. By the time I've managed to contort myself enough to squeeze into the seat, Johnny is standing right next to me. Staring down at the tangle of my legs like I'm some comedy show.

'Catch you later then, Fi.' The interior light illuminates his sardonic smile. And that last word makes my chest implode. He's the only person I ever knew who shortened Seraphina to Fi.

We're half a mile down the road by the time I remember I've left my bag in the kitchen and the house unlocked.

12

Monday, 19th December
In Alice's cottage at Daisy Hill Farm: Fingers and toes

'When you've got your coffee, come and talk to me in the bathroom.'

As I push down the plunger in the cafetière, I'm literally gagging for a caffeine hit. And Alice is calling me through for a chat, like it isn't ten in the morning, with a thousand things we should be getting on with. I already seem to have been dashing around for hours and yet here she is, luxuriating in the bath.

Welcome to Alice's world. Where everything is perfect. The bride has finally arrived, a couple of days late, but hey ho. And even though she just flew in from abroad, her pre-planned outfit for the day is hanging, clean, pressed and waiting on the bathroom door. I know without asking that she hasn't had to scrabble through the clothes pile to find a clean thong, and dig under the bed to find some shorts that aren't covered in hot-chocolate slurps. The upside of being super-scheduled is that Alice can factor in time for home spa treatments. Whereas with a super-chaotic life like mine, when I add in a whole heap of extra bridesmaid duties, there's barely time to brush my teeth.

'It's lovely to see you,' I say, as I wander across the huge bathroom to the Lloyd Loom chair, being very careful not to wreck the chances of a good start by spilling my coffee on the floor. As bride, Alice has claimed the star holiday cottage for both of us to stay in, at least until we move up to Rose Hill for the night before the wedding. Which is why I'm here with my car and a beach bag stuffed with any clean clothes I could lay my hands on. Meanwhile, she's enjoying the 'whistles and bells' gargantuan bath tub as we speak. Actually, there's barely six inches of Alice showing above the bubbles. And that glossy dark-brown hair of hers I wish was mine is safely stowed inside her shower cap. But we all know what I mean, because I *am* pleased to see her. If I sound as if I'm gushing, it's because I'm having that immediate rush of sisterly love that happens every time we meet. Super-sized with wedding emotion.

'You too,' she smiles. 'And you've been *so* busy already – I'm *so* sorry I'm so late, but I *knew* you'd be fine without me – thank you *so* much, Sera, you're *such* a star.'

Given she's not the world's biggest praiser, and she hardly ever apologises, I suspect she's feeling the wedding warmth too.

'Any time,' I beam. I'm riding the wave, because with Alice

the love fest doesn't usually last long, simply because her standards are so much higher than mine. 'And what about the snow? Isn't it beautiful?'

Seeing the view from the window, with the hills dusted powder-white makes me momentarily forget that I came the whole length of the lane from the village in a sideways skid. And it also rubbishes the fact that Quinn and I were running around until eleven last night, collecting and delivering snow machines, with only a drive-thru Big Mac for dinner. But whatever.

'If only it had come later. I was hoping for snow on the day.' The sigh that seeps over the bath edge is straight from the heart. 'Can it *possibly* last until Saturday?'

Oh my. So she *has* set her heart on a white wedding. That's just crazy. I mean, how often is there a white Christmas? And I can see that snow coming a few days early and disappearing again is more disappointing than it never coming at all. What's worse, she's looking at me as if I'm personally responsible for the weather.

Of course it won't last. It's a miracle it's here at all. It'll probably be gone by lunchtime. All of which I ignore. 'Fingers crossed it'll stay,' I say. Hoping that's positive enough to give her temporary hope, but non-committal enough to avoid a shitload of recriminations when it melts in two hours' time.

'Yes.' There's a few seconds of reflective silence, when she closes her eyes, and she might actually be praying. But when she opens her eyes again and goes on, her voice is sterner. 'About the cottages…'

Here we go. I take a deep breath and make my smile bright.

'You might need a pen... or your tablet?' The sad thing is, she isn't joking.

When I come back I'm armed with sketch book and pencil. The next ten minutes are filled with listening to a never-ending list from Alice. Hampers in the kitchens not the living rooms. Scented candles on the fireplaces, not in the bedrooms. Turkish delight on the coffee tables, not in the kitchen. Times twenty. How could we have got this so wrong?

At the same time, Poppy, Immie, Quinn and I have busted a gut on those cottages. And Alice is being a total bitch queen, with her nit-picking. Even if she does wrap it up in fancy packing by calling it 'attention to detail' she's still being a grade-one arse. She seems to be forgetting – she's not 'woman in charge on a building site' here. There isn't a client waiting to come down on her like a ton of bricks. We're doing this for her friends and approximate should be completely good enough.

But everyone knows the first rule for a bridesmaid is to avoid challenging the bride. Even when they're bang out of order. It's a bridesmaid's job to take every outrageous wish the bride has and turn it into reality. And unfortunately, weddings can bring out the worst in the mildest brides. But sometimes when Quinn is making snide comments about Alice, however treacherous it makes me feel, I find myself silently agreeing.

Although her reaction is no surprise, given how Alice was even before the wedding came along. She can't help that she's naturally one of life's bossy people, who has no margin for error. When we were kids, she was the one who ran the show. And I was the one who did as I was told. All made worse by our mother, who thought she was a stay-at-home mum. Whereas, in fact, she worked all hours, doing translation work in the summer house in the garden, while we were in the house being looked after by a string of dodgy au pairs.

And whereas my childhood memories are of hunkering down under the kitchen table, being told stories about far-flung places by a series of teenage girls who smelled of Gauloises and had exotic foreign accents, Alice had a very different time. She was older. Old enough to step in and try to bring order to a home where our mum had all but given up. Alice was the one who made sure I had clean clothes to put on every morning and socks that matched. And when those socks went to sleep in my shoes on the walk to school – my all-time childhood hate – Alice was the one who was kneeling down on the pavement, making things alright. While I was having fun hanging with the au pairs, honing my fashion sense, dreaming of travelling and learning to blow smoke rings, Alice was running around emptying the ashtrays.

'So what about the rest of the year's most perfect wedding?' I say, when she runs out of steam on the criticism four pages later. As I'm learning fast, perfect doesn't happen all on its own.

'All coming along brilliantly.' She brings her hands out of the bath so she can count off the points on her fingers.

'Hetty's in charge of the food.' Finger one. 'She's flying her entire team in from New York, arriving Thursday. The food's coming in refrigerated lorries.'

And this is how Alice has pulled off this mega-wedding. Because her friends love her enough to pull the biggest favours for her. Bridesmaid Hetty's day job is catering for rock stars on world tours and she's bringing almost as many hand-picked helpers as there are guests.

'Flowers were a nightmare so close to Christmas.' Finger two. 'But I'm using a London florist and making it affordable by getting them couriered down myself.'

This is Alice for you. She ducks and dives and gets what she wants every time.

'Jo's sorted the cake and Dan's bringing it down from London.' Finger three.

Bridesmaid three happens to own a patisserie. Yum to that one. Which also reminds me I haven't had breakfast yet.

Finger four. 'We're having the most awesome ceiling, because without it the ballroom would be horribly austere, but Dan's guys have got that covered.'

Well, what would you do? In the face of so much optimism on Alice's part, I keep my mouth tightly shut about yesterday's no-show.

Finger five. 'Oh, and the disco floor and the disco. That's the guys' department too. Along with the drinks and the furniture.'

At least there's some good news there. 'The chairs are here, and the covers are mostly pressed.' It's sounding as if we're getting ahead of the jobs.

'That's brill.' She pushes her shoulders out of the suds. 'Because there's something extra I've got to fit in today...' There's an uncertain note in her voice I don't recognise.

'Really?' I refuse to believe there's anything she's not covered on her multiple spread sheets and in her manual.

'I told you I ran into Iris a few weeks ago?'

Actually she didn't, because if she had I'd have remembered. We used to see Iris every summer when we came to stay with my gran in St Aidan. But way more important than Iris was Iris's brother, George. I'm guessing he was Alice's first real love. They hung around every holiday for years, before he smashed her heart into a thousand tiny pieces. And I suspect Alice knows she forgot to mention Iris. Because whenever we've spoken, it's been wedding details all the way.

'She's meeting a few friends for drinks; I thought I might pop over.' Alice's expression is blank and she's making it sound completely throw-away. 'Seeing as I'm here.'

So throw away, I can't imagine why she'd even be bothering. 'Just Iris?'

I watch her throat bulge as she swallows. 'Actually George might be there too…' Her voice is so low it's almost a croak. 'He just got divorced and he's been asking after me… apparently.'

'Alice…' My alarm bells aren't just ringing, they're clanging. Which is my excuse for sloshing my coffee all over the tiles and shrieking. 'You're about to marry the love of your life, at the wedding of the century. And you're running across Cornwall to see the guy who broke your heart? Are you sure you know what you're doing here?'

At least one of us is calm and collected. 'I'm simply ticking a box, now the opportunity has come up. It's not as if Dan's arrived yet. If he had, and we were doing things together, that would be different.' She hands me a flannel for the coffee spill.

'Right.' I mop up, without thinking. Dan turning up is something else I haven't had time to focus on. I know he's not here yet, but I assume that, as with Alice, his work deadlines have slipped.

'George never gave me closure. Whereas I'm on course for my perfect wedding and I'd like him to see that.'

It's years ago, but that summer is still as fresh as yesterday. Hearing Alice crying herself to sleep. Seventeen and waiting all holiday for George to arrive, as he always did. And he didn't have the guts to tell her he wasn't coming. That he was going out with someone else. And he never came to St Aidan again.

'He's a GP now, near Truro.'

If we're talking parallel lives, I'm not sure sophisticated, metropolitan Alice would ever have fitted in as a GP's wife, in Cornwall of all places. She'd have hated every minute.

'Some dragons are best left to sleep,' I say. Cliché alert, but it's true. If this were me, I'd be slipping this particular dragon a tranquiliser dart, not surprising it awake by drenching it in cold water, then dangling a hot human bride under its nose. 'Leave the past alone.' It comes out as a shout, because I know. I came face to face with Johnny. No good comes of it.

'This is why we're so different.' She juts her chin out. 'We disagree every time on the most important things. I've already decided I'm going. You can come too if you want.'

'Me?' Worse and worse. 'I've got important wedding jobs to do...' I say, knowing I shouldn't be looking forward to a day with Quinn quite as much as I am. I'm squirming, hoping I'm not completely letting her down here. Is it really my job as a bridesmaid to stop her making kamikaze moves like this one? I'm supposed to be helping Quinn pick up a consignment of extra-special glasses Alice has ordered. Not baby-sit Alice while she goes to do whatever it is you do with old flames. Stamp on them? Re-ignite them? *Please don't let it be that.* I'm doing mental equations. No glasses means no fizz. But then if I don't keep Alice in check, we might not need either.

13

Monday, 19th December
At Rose Hill Manor: Blowing cold and hot

When I arrive at Rose Hill Manor to meet Quinn an hour later, I cautiously drive around the bend at the end of the drive and go headlong into a blizzard. As for Alice, in the end I decide that at thirty-three she's old enough to make her own mistakes. Yes, there's a twang of guilt that I'm here and not with her. But she's got to do what she's got to do. And picking up bespoke cocktail glasses is what I've got to do.

As I climb out of the car, a flurry of snowflakes hits my face, blasting from all directions. I put my arm up to shield my eyes and hear a burst of throaty laughter, which has to be Quinn.

'So what do you think? Great snowstorm, or what?' He ambles into view around the side of the house. As the sound of the snow machines dies, the flakes waft in the air. 'That was five machines, full on. Impressive or what?'

'Pretty cool.' In fact, the drifting flakes look totally magical against the snow-covered ground. I'm suddenly seven again, remembering one idyllic Christmas when we were kids, when the whole family went to a cottage in the Lake District and we were snowed in. When, just for once, our dad wasn't on another continent doing a visiting lecture tour. And he looked up from his papers for long enough to take us out sledging. Maybe that little bubble of childhood happiness is what Alice is trying to recreate here. And if Alice has to settle for fake snow, it's not the end of the world, apart from the way it's clinging to my jacket like polystyrene. But I don't want the success to go to Quinn's head. I have to ask, 'How long have you been playing?'

'All morning.' His shamefaced grimace turns to an indignant grin. 'And? Someone has to do the testing. I'm happy to report they're all working.'

'And I'm pleased to hear it.' I get out my phone to glance at the time. 'No pressure, but aren't we going glass-collecting?'

'The van's round the side. Jump in, I'll run the snow machines back into the stables and be with you in five.'

We've got to head a couple of hours' north for the glasses. I know lots of people drink out of plastic flutes at receptions, not hand-blown crystal, but that's not Alice. And for once she bucked the London trend and ordered locally. As I clamber into the van, there's a vague fluttering in my tummy, and not just because Quinn's going to be driving at the speed of light. There's something tingly about the thought of a five-hour road trip with a guy who doesn't give a damn. Let's face it, anything could happen here.

As he swings into the driver's seat my tummy gives a growl. He rubs his chin. 'Have you had breakfast?'

I wrinkle my nose and try to decide if I'd describe his jaw as bearded or stubbly. 'Can we pull in for lunch along the way?' Not that I'm a flashy kind of girl, but somewhere more upmarket than a drive-thru would be nice. Maybe even a cosy pub.

'There's a place I know not far away, where the chips are double-fried and the sea food is…' He stops mid-sentence. 'What the hell…?'

I'm busy sucking in my drool, but when I see the reflection in the wing mirror, my stomach deflates faster than a whoopee cushion under a sixteen-stone bottom. Johnny? Again? Except this time he's lost the overalls and found a disgustingly hunky parka.

Quinn exhales as he winds down the window. Not that he went into details, but from what he said last night, Quinn's as anxious as I am to avoid Johnny. Which is why I had no worries at all about bumping into him, at least for today.

'We're just leaving for Torrington…' Quinn revs the engine, as if to emphasise he means this instant.

Johnny's smile is laid-back. 'Move over, I'll come along too. We can call in the wine merchants on the way back.'

Quinn's squawk of protest is desperate. 'Don't you have a carriage to mend, mate? Or horses to harness?'

'All done.' Johnny's response is as cool as they come. No change there, then. 'So it might be best if I drive…'

'What?' Quinn's blinking in disbelief.

'Given the icy roads…' Johnny's pause is pointed. '…and my experience on the skid pan.'

Welding *and* skid pans? I know it's been years, but whatever happened to the Johnny who spent every waking hour in the lab or in the library?

Quinn gives a snort of disgust and makes speech-mark signs in the air. 'Err, excuse me but…"My other car's a Ferrari." I think I can handle a van in an inch of snow, thanks all the same.'

'Up to you.' A second later Johnny's yanked open the passenger door and it's me he's smiling up at. 'In that case, I'll come in next to you.'

As re-introductions go, this one is sudden and horribly up-close. In an ideal world this three-seater bench seat would be twice as wide. When Johnny slams the door shut his thigh is practically welded to mine and I'm staring down at sharp designer jeans that couldn't be more different from Quinn's lived-in version.

To take my mind off Johnny's thigh, I'm watching Quinn's broad fingers heading for the gear lever. At the last moment, they veer off course. As his palm lands flat on my knee my gasp leaves my eyes popping. Somehow the shock freezes my vocal chords, because although I feel like shrieking, I don't even squeak. Johnny and I watch, mesmerised, as Quinn's hand clamps into a tight squeeze. If I'm gob-smacked, Johnny's worse. And Quinn's grinning like he's a kid who's found the key to Santa's grotto. If I'd known my leg was going to get this much scrutiny, I'd have made sure I picked some tights without a hole in.

Out of the corner of my eye, I catch Johnny frowning like a storm. The best I manage is a 'what the fuck?' glare in Quinn's direction.

He responds with one last pat and a low laugh. 'Ready to go, Sera?' Then he's pushing the van into gear and we're pulling away.

Once Quinn's let go of me, Johnny settles back into his seat. At a guess, he's trying to act like nothing happened. 'Leopard legs, Sera? Aren't they very 2006?'

Another snide reference to the past there. And who'd have thought animal print would have run and run the way it has? Not that anyone can take any fashion comments seriously from a guy who's dressed head to toe in John Lewis' casual menswear.

'My tights came from the H&M summer sale. *This year.*' I say, pointedly.

When I mentioned cosy lunches, I was *not* thinking me squished in the middle of a best-man sandwich. Apart from the leg-grabbing – and who knows what that was about? – there are two clues that Quinn isn't exactly thrilled that best man two – or should that be best man one? – has come along for the ride: a) the furious bull snorts coming out of Quinn's nostrils, and b) the deep furrows on his forehead. He flips on the radio, turns up the volume, and the next minute Pirate FM is perforating our eardrums.

With *Frosty the Snowman* reverberating around the van cab, Johnny digs in his pocket and pulls out a set of battery operated fairy lights. I watch as he unwinds them along the dash. As we head between the avenue of trees along the drive and he clicks the tiny lights on, Quinn's brow descends into a full-blown scowl.

Somehow I seem to have inadvertently landed in the middle of a territory war. The lights have lovely copper wire and flat, white illuminated stars, and I'm desperate to say 'Sooo pretty'. Instead I take a deep breath and stare down at my knees. Big mistake.

The one and only time my legs were this close to Johnny's was years ago and back then they were naked. If that sounds bad, the rest is way worse than anything you're imagining. He invited me to be his 'plus one' for the department formal, the Christmas after I left uni. More fool me for going. I've re-lived that weekend in my head a thousand times and every time it makes me feel like I want to crawl into a hole and never come out. You don't want the gory details. Not with Johnny sitting right next to me. The upside is that it's whooshed every bit of this morning's hunger away. If we stopped at a gourmet restaurant, I couldn't even manage an amuse-bouche. Locking my eyes on the snowy hills we're whizzing past, I hope for Alice's sake that her 'blast from the past' is giving her more space than mine is.

The A30 passes in a blur. If the atmosphere hadn't been so awkward, I'd have been singing along. Let's face it, it's impossible to listen to 'I Wish It Could Be Christmas Every Day' and not join in. We sit through Chris De Burgh, the X-factor finalists and numerous adverts for garden centres and chipped windscreens. 'Let It Snow' is just beginning when I have a thought that makes me lean forward and turn down the volume. Because there's something I need to ask.

'So when's Dan arriving?'

These are the guys who should know, but there's a stiffening either side of me.

'He'll be along any day now.' Quinn twitches his nose and fiddles with the fog-light knob.

'Still tying up loose ends...' Johnny adds raking his fingers through his hair.

'Celestial skies don't come cheap.' If Quinn's thrown that in as a distraction, it's worked.

The ceiling! I was so preoccupied with Alice and her after-bubble-bath plans, I forgot to ask. 'So when's the ceiling coming?'

Quinn shakes his head. 'Not today.'

I screw up my face. 'But don't they need two days to fit it?'

'This is why we're all here in advance.' Quinn's drumming his fingers on the steering wheel. 'To give us tolerance when things go wrong.'

That's a word I seize on. 'It's gone *wrong*?'

Johnny cuts in, 'No one said that.'

If I didn't know better, I'd swear these two guys, who aren't exactly the best of buddies, were closing ranks.

I go back to my original question. 'So where did you say Dan is?'

'Still working...' That's Johnny.

'We've got things covered here...' That's Quinn again. And they've actually said diddly squat.

Johnny joins in... 'I mean, Alice only just got here herself.'

Oh shit. Alice is the last person I want to talk about. Even as we speed along at a hundred miles an hour – well, that's what it says on the speedo – she's probably meeting George. Air kissing, at the Shark and Shrimp, moving straight through to recriminations over canapes. By the time they've got hot and bothered over mulled wine and mince pies, anything could have happened. Suddenly, adverts for garden centres and

Christmas shopping seem so much less dangerous than talking about Alice.

'And we were managing fine before she turned up.' I say breezily, as I reach for the volume knob. 'It's only a wedding, after all. Who needs a bride and groom?'

14

Monday, 19th December
In the hire van: Salt and frosted glass

So you know those times when things are so dreadful you can't imagine they could possibly be any worse? It's bad enough that I have to listen to 'All I Want For Christmas Is You', and hold back my werewolf howl on the '*Youuuuuuuuuuu*' part. But when we get to the glass factory, there are way more boxes than we'd anticipated. We're expecting cocktail glasses, but it turns out we're collecting glasses for every eventuality. Martini, flutes, tumblers, wine. As for how many ways are there to pack a van, I'm guessing that depends on how many best men you have. And how hard-headed they are.

'It's obvious, we stack them high.' Quinn's indicating hand is way above his head. 'Like a tidal wave.'

Which sounds logical enough to me. But total bollocks to Johnny.

'Or...' If Johnny's being cool and persuasive, it's probably because by rights he shouldn't even be here. 'We put them one box deep across the floor... like the sea.' Despite that empathising watery afterthought, Quinn isn't going for it.

'No, so long as we keep them upright we're good to go high.'

At this rate we'll still be here when it's dark. What's more, if they don't hurry up, my numb toes may have turned to ice blocks. I'm turning to hear Johnny's counter-argument, but as Quinn stands back and folds his arms, he accidentally moves into a phone-signal area. The pocket of his duffel coat is suddenly jumping and beeping. And the minute Quinn answers his phone, he's out of the game.

Johnny grabs me by the shoulder. 'Quick, jump to it, load as many in as you can while he's talking.'

By the time Quinn comes back, it's too late. The boxes are safely stowed and the back doors are slammed shut.

'Everything okay?' I send him a pacifying smile, which is way more than he deserves, considering the knee-grabbing incident, earlier.

His dismissive head-shake suggests exactly how pissed off he is that he hasn't got his way. Which is weird, because thus far I hadn't got him down as a bad loser. Although somehow I doubt he loses often.

Johnny holds out his hand. 'Have you got the keys? Precious cargo and all that. I'll drive back.'

Quinn shakes away his frown and a grin spreads across his face. 'Like hell you will.' He's in the driving seat faster than you can say 'High Ball'.

They say people don't change, and it's true Johnny was always the cleverest person out. But I don't remember him being this domineering with other guys back in the day. Yes, he had girls queuing round the block to go out with him. I mean, no guy should have it handed on a plate every time. It can't be good for them. But maybe he's met his match with Quinn. Quinn's easy confidence and rugged good looks are a dynamite combination for any woman looking for a guy. Which – just saying – definitely isn't me. But the threat of male competition might be why drop-dead gorgeous Johnny feels he has to prove himself here.

'We'll take the scenic route, there's too many speed cameras on the main drag,' Quinn says, as he veers off onto a side road half an hour later.

I brace myself. Last time out, Quinn did St Aidan to Rose Hill in seven minutes, so I know what's coming. That's half the time most people take, and a quarter of what it takes me in Gran's mini. I try to find a handhold that doesn't involve Johnny's thigh.

'They won't have salted these back roads,' Johnny says, flatly.

Quinn gives a sneer. 'Okay, Johnny, we all know you've driven on every racing track in the world, but Sera and I are the Cornish experts.'

By the time we round the next bend, I'm practically on Johnny's knee. *Every racing track in the world.* This is Johnny, who was so busy getting on with his career he had no time to travel. Okay, he was heading for some high-flying engineering job, but it was in the Midlands. He went for the mortgage route too. Not being rude to people who live there, but Coventry was hardly the most exotic place to tie himself down in. I was the one who was free as a bird and hooked on gap-year exploring. But as Quinn just pointed out, with all the subtlety of a sledgehammer, I'm tied to Cornwall now.

Johnny shoulders me back into my seat, but leaves his arm across my body, pinning me into place. 'Isn't this the bit where you tell us you're a dot-com billionaire, Quinn?' The laugh he gives is mocking and bitter, rather than amused. 'And that everything Dan has is down to you?'

Ouch. When did this turn into best man wars? Not that I'm one to tell people what to do, but they need to stop this. I take a deep breath, hold up my hand and go for it.

'That's enough, guys. Chill!' I don't sound like me at all. It's half way between Jess on a bad morning and Alice in a razz. But it's worth it if it stops them. As for Johnny, how did I once spend a two whole years hanging on his every word, aching to be the one he draped his arm around at the back-yard barbies? Back in the day, I must have been blind as well as stupid.

Quinn sends me one of his unrepentant smirks and floors the accelerator.

Johnny sniffs. 'Watch out for ice, that's all I'm saying.'

Not that ice will be a problem, given the wheels are barely touching the road. By the time we go over the next bump, we're going so fast I swear we take off. Before I know it, I've grabbed a fistful of Johnny's jeans to steady myself. And to hell with the consequences. The next hour literally scares the Brazilian briefs off me so much, I get my organ donor card out of my purse and slip it into the pocket of my shorts. Just in case.

But at the same time it's exhilarating, in an omigod, silent screaming kind of way. I reckon my heart has been pounding at a steady two hundred beats a minute for the entire time. I'm not sure I've taken a breath the whole way back to Rose Hill Manor. So when Quinn does a handbrake turn at the top of the drive and we set off down the snow-covered avenue, I'm starting to exhale with relief.

Quinn lets out a triumphant shout. 'See, what did I say? We're back home and no problem with ice at all.'

I've let go of Johnny's leg and I'm flapping my fingers in front of my face like an angsty adolescent from an Australian soap. As Elton John drifts out of the speakers telling us to 'Step into Christmas' I'm thanking every god I can think of that I'm still alive. Then on the last corner, Quinn jumps on the brakes. The back end of the van slips and the next thing, despite Quinn's yanking the steering wheel every which way, we're spinning backwards off the drive. Even though the scenery's moving really fast in the wrong direction, it feels as though time's standing still. We veer sideways across the grass, then plough an arc through the shrubbery, and as we finally bump to a halt at an angle, the noise from the back of the van sounds like a bottle bank's being emptied.

For a moment we just stare and listen to Elton John, who hasn't missed a beat. When Quinn speaks his voice is a hoarse whisper. 'I think we maybe hit the ha-ha.'

It sounds like a joke, but none of us laugh. Instead, one by one, we ease ourselves out of the fug of the cab and into the raw afternoon air and begin to assess the damage.

Johnny's breath billows as he prods at the scuffs on the bumper and the dents on the wing of the van. 'It'll take your billionaire bank account to pay the excess on this, Quinn.'

He shakes his head. 'I damn well knew you couldn't handle this van.'

'Shit.' Quinn's hands are deep in his pockets as he kicks the splinters of the flattened azalea bushes and stares at the gouges of fresh earth sticking up through the snow. 'My uncle will possibly throttle me for this. On the up side, we made a whole trip without getting a parking ticket.' He catches my eye, then thinks better of it.

I'm still not laughing. Padding round to the back of the van, I pull on the handle and prop the door open against my back. When I peer inside, I'm hopeful, because the boxes are all pretty much as they were when we put them in, just not so neat. I pick one up, hold my breath. Then I give it a tentative shake. There's a jingling, like a distant wind chime in the breeze and my stomach plummets. Shards of crystal clinking. 'We are so screwed.' I'm talking to myself, but Johnny and Quinn have closed in too. And if either of them start to criticise the other, I'm going to throw the damn box at their heads.

'How am I going to break this to Alice?' I grimace at the hideous accidental pun, but the others don't even notice.

'Maybe you could tell her later?' Thank Christmas Johnny's switched to being reasonable. 'But only if you need to.'

'I'll sort this.' Quinn's cheeks are ghost-pale under his tan. 'Tomorrow. I'll go back tomorrow. I'll take more care…'

Johnny's glaring. 'You damn well better had.'

With any luck they'll both go. And leave me to have a quiet day on my own.

15

Monday, 19th December
In the farmhouse kitchen: Lost and found

'So do things often go wrong at weddings, then?' I ask, as I'm sitting opposite Poppy and Rafe, a lot later that evening, in the farmhouse kitchen.

We're all tucking into a delicious Aga-cooked hot pot, made by Rafe. I probably said it before, but that guy's a keeper if ever I saw one. And so damned in love with Poppy. And yes, I did check that I wasn't going to be playing gooseberry before I crashed their dinner. Apparently Rafe's on his way out to take a wrench to his mate down the road – no idea what that means, but whatever – so when Poppy spotted me skulking round the yard searching for Alice's car, she came out and dragged me in. Given they've had a full summer of weddings here at Daisy Hill Farm, they should be able to answer my wedding question. As a designer, I see the dresses, and some-times the brides, but only if it's a bespoke order. Occasionally I get to see the pictures afterwards. But my experience of the weddings themselves is limited. Sometimes I pick up snippets of gossip in the shop, but, let's face it, although I'm usually up to my elbows in satin and tulle and beads and bows, the mechanics of weddings have passed me by. When Poppy and Rafe hear my question they exchange glances and then practi-cally fall off their chairs laughing.

'Things go wrong all the time.' Rafe pulls a face.

I'm not sure this is what I want to hear.

'Put it this way…' Poppy's chewing her last forkful, as she takes in my shocked expression. 'There aren't many weddings where everything goes right. But on the day it's rarely a problem.'

'Really?' I'd completely forgotten how hungry I was until I started tucking in to the crusty potato slices and the tender meat and veggies in thick gravy. I'm already on my third helping. But this news is restoring me as much as the delicious food.

'You name it, we've had it.' Rafe says. He's sounding strangely enthusiastic considering he's talking about disasters. 'Everything from guests stuck in a sea of mud, to a baby who arrived on the wedding night. We even had a bride who didn't come to her wedding at all.'

'Fuck…' I say, thinking of Alice, who's still not back. 'I mean… wow.'

Poppy puts down her fork, props her chin on her fist, and leans towards me. 'So how are things working out with Alice and Dan's big day?'

'Fine,' I lie, making my voice as light and unbothered as I can. A glimpse of Poppy's one raised eyebrow tells me she's not buying it, but I barely know where to begin. 'The venue's beautiful.' That's one place to start.

'So that's good,' she says. Her smile is encouraging me to go on.

'And the Cinderella carriage is on track,' I say. 'But it goes downhill from there.' That's a serious understatement. 'The electronic sky's gone missing and I suspect the groom has too. The best men are pistols at dawn and the snow's not going to last. Today we accidentally smashed an entire van-load of crystal into tiny pieces. Even the Turkish Delight is in the kitchens when it should be next to the sofas.'

Rafe rubs his chin. 'Sounds about right. Anything we can do to help, just shout.'

Poppy frowns. 'Sometimes when brides are stressed, they can get very exacting. And that's very hard for everyone who's trying to help.'

'Yes.' I say. 'Thank you.' It's such a relief that someone understands.

'People get caught up with the small things,' Poppy says gently. Probably thinking of all that Turkish delight she put out, six feet too far to the left. 'But so long as the bride and groom are strong as a couple, whatever else goes wrong won't matter. Especially if you have a lovely venue.'

'Alice and Dan are rock-solid,' I say. 'They've been together forever.' Everyone knows couples don't come any stronger than them. But suddenly, in my head I'm replaying a YouTube clip of a Cornish cliff collapse, up near Dead Man's Cove. Thousands of tons of rock tumbling into the sea. Not so solid that day, then. It comes out of nowhere and I blink it away fast.

'It's all going to be brill.' Poppy reaches across and pats my hand.

If I'm picking up negative vibes, it's probably just the fall-out after spinning off the drive in the van earlier.

Rafe stands up and takes the plates over to the dishwasher. 'Remember, we've got burly guys, generators, lanterns, four-by-fours, tractors and trailers. And an office full of tame chickens. You're welcome to any of them.' He drops a kiss on Poppy's head on his way to the door.

Poppy gives his hand a squeeze as he goes. 'So are you up for icing some Christmas cupcakes, Sera?'

My ears prick up at the word 'icing'. I know I'd planned to spend this evening working on dress designs but let's get real: it's a choice between a warm kitchen and cupcake decorating with a friend I haven't seen for weeks, or drawing, when my ideas are about as exciting as an unsugared doughnut. Well, which would you choose?

'I made the icing earlier.' She dips into the huge fridge and brings a bowl to the table. Then she puts down a tray of deep cakes, next to it. 'Snow-white vanilla buttercream.'

I'm licking my lips as she fills two piping bags, then pushes one in my direction. 'You're expecting me to do *icing*?' Surely not.

She laughs at my squeak. 'Squeeze and swirl, like I'm doing. You'll soon get the knack. Then we'll do the decorations together.'

When a bare cupcake lands in front of me I screw up my courage. Pick up my bag. And go for it. Buttercream has to be the stickiest thing in the world. My fist squirt misses the cake and hits the table. So I scoot that into my mouth before Poppy sees. The next squeeze is gentler and gives a pathetic squiggle that ends in a smudge. So I scrape that off and eat it too.

'It's only a trial run, but more on the cake, less in your mouth.' Poppy sends me a grin.

By the time I'm on my fourth cake, I'm getting better, but Poppy has done at least twenty and she's already bringing the decorations over.

'I've got pale-pink edible glitter.' As she shakes some out, it glistens like sunrise on the buttercream peaks. 'And tiny gold-and-silver stars and balls. You can make some ties, to go with these miniature holly leaves and Christmas labels.' She hands me some scissors and the bag of lace I brought her.

'When do we get to taste?' I ask, twisting a lace strip through a miniature luggage label and tweaking it into a bow.

'That's so pretty.' Her face lights up as she sticks the label into the icing. 'Let's taste as we decorate and wash it down with some fizz.' She's back with glasses and a bottle and she's popped the cork before I've sprinkled the stars on my next cake.

'Great idea.' I peel back the gold paper case, take a monster bite of cupcake. Then I lean back and let the cake and sugary vanilla melt on my tongue. Wherever heaven is, I've arrived.

Poppy scrapes a crumb from the corner of her mouth, licks her finger and takes a slurp of fizz. 'So did you say there are *two* best men?'

I let out a sigh and nod. 'Scrapping like little boys.' Since we started with the icing I've been concentrating so hard, I'd almost forgotten the gruesome twosome and how awful today was. Which is probably why people ice cupcakes at hen parties when they want to relax. Although Alice didn't go in for anything quite that enjoyable. She opted for a Japanese afternoon tea – bite-size cucumber squares on rectangles of bamboo. If you're looking for something yummy and comforting, I don't recommend it. Followed by a trip to the opera, which was cancelled six months in advance, due to work commitments.

Poppy's lips twitch. 'And is the second-best man as dreamy as Quinn, then?'

'I'd hardly describe Quinn as…' I haul on the brakes, determined not to rise. If my cheeks are warm, it's down to the cold weather and the wine. Nothing else. 'They're *very* different. Johnny's efficient, serious, and a little bit Scottish.' That just about covers it. I leave out the bit about knowing him.

She's grinning now. 'So there's McSteamy, who walks round in his towel, and McFlurry, who gets things done. And I bet you ten cupcakes they're fighting over *you*?'

'Loving those names.' But she's *so* wrong about the rest. 'Their conflict's nothing to do with bridesmaids, it's pure power struggle. All the way.' I know, I've spent five hours squeezed between them. I bury my teeth in my cupcake, hoping to blur them out again.

'So do you have a strategy to handle them?' She's scooping icing up on her finger now.

Good question. As if I'd have a plan for anything. But now she mentions it, strategic point one is to keep my hands off. Both of them. At all costs. 'I think they're easier apart than together.' I'm thinking aloud. Although it's the opposite of

safety in numbers. And given I'd prefer to avoid Johnny alto-
gether, that leaves me with Quinn.

'You need to up your game. Make sure you're the one who
calls the shots.' Poppy's sounding a lot like Jess since she's been
in London.

It's all very well her talking about calling the shots. 'Up my
game?' It's almost a wail. 'I'm not even *in* the game.'

That eyebrow's shooting up again. 'Maybe it's time to play.
Find your inner sass and start telling them what to do.'

'As if.' When they were giving out balls to girls, Immie, Jess
and Poppy got my share. I back off every time.

I'm about to say as much when I'm saved by the landline
ringing. Poppy crosses the kitchen and finds the handset under
a pile of Christmas wrapping paper. As she answers she catches
my eye and mouths, 'Alice…'

Oh my. Calling the farm to leave a message, no doubt.
Poppy's pointing to the phone, asking if I want to talk, but I
shake my head. If Alice isn't coming back, I'm not sure I know
what to say.

'There's snow coming in, so she's staying over.' A moment
later, Poppy's back at the table, looking puzzled. 'Although the
forecast I saw earlier said rain.'

I sniff, and poke at the holly leaf on a cupcake. 'Probably
an excuse because she's off her face.' It's a better thought than
what I suspect is happening. And, between us, it's unlikely
she's drunk. Alice is great at getting drinks down everyone
else, but less good at drinking them herself. Somehow I have
to carry on the excuses on her behalf. 'If she's been knocking
back the Christmas cocktails like we were the other night at
the shop party, she won't be able to drive.' My face cracks into

a grin at the idea of Alice ever getting as legless as we were.

Poppy's leaning into me, suddenly delighted. 'There, that's your sassy smile.'

She slaps me on the back so hard I almost drop my fourth cupcake.

'Flash that at the guys,' she goes on, 'and wrinkle that deliciously freckly nose of yours – they won't be able to refuse you anything.'

Except the one time I tried this smile on Johnny, that's exactly what he did. Turned me down flat. Maybe now's the time to come clean.

'Actually Johnny was in Bristol when I was there.' I leave it at that, but then toss in a last-minute confidentiality clause. 'Not that I'm broadcasting it.'

'Better and better.' She's bypassed surprise and she's sticking both her thumbs up. Waving them around looking way too pleased. 'Quinn's got a lot of ground to make up to win the girl here. Guys love it when they've got to put in the effort.' On balance, shock would have been way easier to cope with than a gallop to this conclusion.

'Stop.' I put up my hand, because I need to make it completely clear. 'Seriously, the girl is not available. Not for Quinn or anyone else. Really I'm not.' And just to get in a bit of practice, I broaden my smile and twitch my nose. It feels very odd, but some part of it worked, because Poppy gives a whoop.

'There you are, you did it again.' She punches the air and grabs her glass. 'Seraphina East, you just found your bossy. Jess will not believe this when I tell her. Let's drink to that!'

16

Tuesday, 20th December
At Rose Hill Manor: Breezes and good calls.

So Poppy was right about the weather and Alice was wrong. By the time I get to the Manor next morning, it's drizzling, and every bit of snow has gone. And there's no sign of Quinn this morning, up at the farm, or here. Given that Alice hasn't appeared yet, with half a mind on what Poppy said yesterday about me calling the shots, I flip through my wedding manual to check on the outstanding jobs. I've been dying to see the tree in the hallway with all its decorations, so seeing as I'm on my own today I'm going to please myself and start that.

I'm rooting around the stables looking for step ladders when the door pushes open.

'Fi, is that you?'

If my gran's red mini parked outside was my big giveaway,

calling me Fi was Johnny's. Along with the low burr of his accent.

'I'm collecting decorations for the big tree.' I stifle my sigh of disappointment at being disturbed. 'Weren't you going for new glasses?'

'No, I'm working on the carriage.'

I frown. 'Isn't that done?' I'm certain he said it was.

It's Johnny's turn to sigh. 'When I saw you heading off with Quinn yesterday, knowing what he's like, I thought I'd better come. Spur-of-the-moment decision.'

'Sorry?' I can't believe I'm hearing this.

'A good call, given how it ended.'

I'm not sure I need a protector. Especially one I didn't ask for. What's more, Quinn might have been calmer if Johnny hadn't forced his way into the cab and wrecked our day.

'And what exactly *is* Quinn like?' If I'm pushing Johnny here, it's because he's sounding so derogatory.

He snorts. 'You don't need me to spell it out. Surely you saw for yourself?'

Johnny being judgemental is not a good look. We all know Quinn's a bit bonkers behind the wheel, but in every other way he's a breeze.

'Quinn had an accident and he's making it right.' Even if he has totalled Alice's crystal-ware, I have to defend him. 'At least he knows how to have fun.' Which counts for a lot, given Johnny's apparent sense of humour by-pass. I'm sure he never used to be this serious.

'You really don't see it do you?' Johnny sighs again. 'Hang around long enough, you'll find out how much fun Quinn really is.'

'Actually, I'd better get on.' Not that I've got the first clue where to find the boxes I'm looking for, but there's no point listening to Johnny bad-mouthing Quinn. 'So unless you can point me to the step ladders and decorations…' It's meant as the end of the conversation, not a question, but he comes straight back with a reply.

'They're all next door, next to the broken glasses. I'll help you into the house with them.'

Given the tree is the size you see in shopping centres, we have to make several trips, working in silence. As Johnny puts down the final box, he turns.

'There's a lot to do here. Shall I help?'

'Absolutely no. Definitely not.' It comes out in a rush before I can stop it. Like a knee-jerk reaction. Because I really don't want to spend any more time than I have to with Johnny. Yesterday was more than enough. Although seeing the height of the ladders I've got to climb up, I must be mad. Then I see the hurt on his face. 'Sorry, I didn't mean to be ungrateful, but…' I grind to a halt.

His voice is low. 'When I found out about this, I knew I'd be the last person you wanted to see, Fi.'

Something about his sudden frankness makes my breathing go shallow and I shrink back against the stair post. 'When did you find I was going to be here, then?'

'When Alice said Sera, at first I thought it was her Hampstead take on Sarah. But then I saw the name Seraphina East on the windows at that wedding shop. And as I said when I saw you in there, I guessed there couldn't be too many of those around.' His lips curve into a smile that's gone before it arrives. 'Let's face it, your name's indelibly printed on my brain after seeing it on the post in the hall most mornings for two years at uni.'

'Right.'

He goes on. 'But let's not make this any harder than it needs to be. From now on I'll keep out of your way as much as I can. You're right, it'll be easier for both of us like that.'

'Great. Thanks. Another good call.' I say, trying to keep my voice steady, because it's wavering all over the place. 'I'd appreciate that.'

He couldn't be more obvious. He's telling me to back off, to save both of us the embarrassment of me throwing myself at him again. Save him the trouble of turning me down a third time. Thanks for the heads-up.

'Good to clear that up.' He's almost through the door when he stops. 'Just be careful with…'

I already know the next word is going to be Quinn, and my neck is prickling, because it's really none of his business what I do. Or who with. 'I can do without the free advice, thanks.'

Johnny isn't quite done. 'If you're happy to be the latest beach bunny Quinn spits out, go ahead. Be my guest.'

And there's something so hypocritical about Johnny saying that, I don't even bother to reply.

17

Tuesday, 20th December
In the hallway at Rose Hill Manor:
Mood boards and white-outs

Anyone else think decorating a Christmas tree is one of the most magical parts of Christmas? As soon as I begin to open the boxes of decorations, my excitement takes over and the stress of the last few days melts away. Alice's theme for the hall tree – surprise surprise – is white and silver. As the baubles, hearts, angels and stars tumble out of the boxes in their hundreds, I try not to get over-awed by the task ahead.

'Keep calm and decorate,' I'm whispering to myself, as I circle the lower branches. But where do I start? After dithering for at least five minutes, I grab a white-painted wooden heart and loop its shimmery white ribbon over a branch. There. One down, five thousand to go. I'm all good here. Beginning at the bottom, I grab a handful of ribbons and ornaments and begin to work my way upwards and around the tree.

Even though it's a completely different scale, I'm whisked back to Christmas when we were kids. Back to the times in Gran's cottage when the dusty boxes would come down from the attic and Alice and I would stand on the table and take it in turns to hang the decorations on the table-top tree. Of course, she was the oldest so she always thought she should get first go. And she always demanded first choice of the miniature trumpet that blew, because that was our favourite. Gran was the one person who used to be firm with Alice. She'd make Alice let me have first go, then send me a wink and give Alice a chocolate instead. It was the only time it ever happened.

Back then there were moulded-glass ornaments in the bright colours Gran loved so much. Tiny foil-covered parcels, pine cones we'd painted and whelk shells we'd collected from the beach. It took all afternoon to decorate the tree and apart from the day itself, for me it was the best part of Christmas.

After working solidly for two hours in the hall, I'm at the top of the step ladder. I've got a crick in my neck from concentrating so hard and despite the festive soundtrack on my phone being on repeat, the Christmas magic is wearing thin. As I stand back to get an overview of progress, I'm thinking how whelk shells would look really pretty on this tree too, but I know better than to mess with Alice's design scheme. Even though the effect is already awesome, there are still a scary number of decorations left in the boxes waiting to be hung.

I've loved the peace and quiet of today after yesterday's best men arguing in stereo either side of me, but I'm beginning to wish I wasn't doing this on my own. This is the exact thought in my head when I hear the scrunch of tyres on the gravel outside. By leaning over, I can get a view of the drive, and Alice climbing out of her hire car. *About bloody time too.* I stamp on that thought. I'm just so relieved to have some help here, I'm really not going to ask about what took her so damned long.

As the front door opens, I wave down at her from my perch at the top of the steps. Despite being knackered and having a chronic case of decoration overkill, I make my voice light and merry. 'Hey, you're back.'

Her trench coat is open and there isn't a crease in her cream polo neck. As she runs her fingers through her hair, every gleaming dark-brown lock falls back into a slightly better place than before. I guess what she learned from our French au pairs was how to dress like their mothers. Although somewhere along the line she also picked up how to look totally disapproving without even trying, which is what she's doing now. What's more she barely seems to have noticed the tree.

'Ta-da!' I fling out my arms in an expansive gesture she can't possibly miss, given I'm also halfway up a ladder. 'So what do you think, Alice?'

It's a moment before she replies. 'It's December, Sera. Why are you wearing shorts?' Her tone is so incredulous; my shorts have eclipsed everything else in her head.

In the face of a twenty-foot Christmas tree, I fail to see why we're talking about this particular item of clothing, even if the decoration is only two-thirds finished.

'I always wear shorts.' How it's taken Alice thirty years to notice I have no idea.

'But that's ridiculous.'

In her world maybe, less so in mine. 'No, shorts are what I'm comfy in. They also make me think of summer and the beach. Is there a problem?'

She closes her eyes. 'No, but I hope you've got something more suitable to wear for the wedding.'

Now who's being ridiculous? 'My bridesmaid's dress, obviously.'

She's firing straight back at me. 'What about the other days? It's my special day, not a hippy festival.'

I'm completely mentally unprepared for this attack from a style dictator. 'You're getting married, not launching a lifestyle brand.' And who's going to notice me anyway?

'But surely you got the dress code mood board in with the invitation? The "smart country-house party" one? A4 envelope, with embossed initials? Recorded delivery. You definitely signed for it.'

'Mood board?' I wrack my brains. I'm not sure I even remember an invitation. Let's face it, it probably came light years ago. When I was really stressed designing the wedding dress for Josie Redman I didn't open my post for weeks.

She sticks out her chin and glares at me. 'If you're going to turn up looking like a beach bunny who lost the wave, I'm going to have to un-invite you.'

'For fuck's sake, Alice.' What's the obsession with beach bunnies? That's the second time in as many hours.

'Back at you, Sera. Really, I'm not going to argue. I've got enough to do without planning your outfits too. Just get yourself something decent to turn up in that's not what you're wearing now.'

Back at you? When did Alice say that? She sounds like she's been spending too much time with Quinn.

'Okay…' I say weakly, even though it obviously isn't. When am I going to have time to go outfit shopping? Or find the cash? Despite my wedding dresses selling, I plough the profits back in. I already owe Jess loads. I'm basically a single-person family, with every penny spoken for.

'So what were you saying about the tree?' She rubs her hand across her forehead and it's as if she's focusing on the tree for the first time. 'No, something's definitely not right with it.'

No surprise there, then. But frankly it's a relief to get the spotlight off me.

She narrows her eyes and looks doubtful. Then she gives a sharp nod. 'Got it. No wonder it looks so bad. It should be white.'

I ignore that she's even uttered the word 'bad' and stare at the dazzling decorations, in every shade of white there is. 'That's right, every *single* decoration is white.'

'No, the branches should be white too, silly. Someone's screwed up here, big time.' She gives an exasperated snort and marches over to where my wedding manual is lying next to my bag.

My tummy is squelching, because it's blindingly obvious that 'someone' isn't just any old 'someone'. The 'someone' she's gunning for is me.

A second later her pale-oyster frosted nail has located the exact point on the relevant page. 'It's perfectly clear. It's here in black and whatever. That tree should have been painted white *before* it was decorated.'

Sometimes there are no words. 'Oh fuck…'

'How the hell did you miss the paint?' She's firing the words like she's wielding a machine gun. 'It should have been with the boxes of decorations.'

A minute later, I'm down the ladder, being frog-marched round the side of the house towards to the Coach House, to track down the crucial missing element.

'Quinn's back.' It comes out as a half whisper as I glimpse the van we bashed around yesterday outside the stables. Its scuffed back door is propped open.

'Sera…' Quinn's face appears around the door, lights up for an instant, then fades. 'Shit… and Alice too.' He reassembles his grin. 'Alice, at last. Long time no see.' In one seamless move, he swoops over, drops a kiss on Alice's cheek and swoops out again to a safe distance.

Although I'm not sure anywhere in the county would qualify as safe, given Alice's mood. Somehow we've been so busy discussing inappropriate dressing and inappropriate tree painting, we haven't got to the bit about how things went with George.

'Where's the paint for the entrance-hall tree? One of you should know, surely?'

As Sera barks at us, Quinn and I roll our eyes at each other and shuffle our feet.

'Paint?' If Johnny knew what he was walking into, he wouldn't be looking this unbothered as he wanders into the yard. 'I think I saw some in here.'

So much for promising I'd keep my distance. We all troop after him into the stable.

'Here it is.'

How we missed the two huge drums he's pointing at, I don't

know. Although, to be fair, paint wasn't what I was looking for. 'Sometimes things are so big, you don't see them.' Ridiculous, I know, but it's the only excuse I can come up with under pressure.

I'm staring at Alice, expecting her to shout me down, but she's left the paint behind and her eyes are gleaming as she heads straight for the pile of boxes marked "Fragile".

'Why didn't you tell me you'd got the glasses?' She lets out a squeal of excitement and her face illuminates in a delighted smile.

Behind her, the three of us let out a collective gasp. Horror doesn't begin to cover what I'm feeling as she heads, with outstretched arms, towards the stack of ruined glassware we brought in here to hide. There's enough adrenalin coursing through my veins to make my heart beat at a hundred miles an hour, yet my feet won't move. The soles of my Converse might as well be bonded to the ground with Superglue. It's like one of those moments when a bomb is falling and you're watching it. Just waiting for the impact and the explosion. On the plus side, it looks like I might be off the hook for forgetting the paint.

It's as if our intake of breath has sucked away all the air and left a vacuum of silence. And then Alice's hands make contact with the cardboard. As she lifts the first box there's the teensiest tinkle and she freezes.

One more tiny shake, then she sets the box gently on the floor. When she turns around, her face is putty colour. 'Do any of you have a knife?'

Johnny dips in the pocket of his overalls, and a moment later he's slicing through the red-and-white parcel tape, and pulling out the polystyrene packing. 'Careful, don't cut yourself.' He is one brave guy for doing this. We already know about the shattered shards he'll be looking down at here, because we did exactly the same yesterday afternoon.

Alice is crouching over the box. Her voice is a croak as she pulls out the base of a cocktail glass. 'Broken?' But she doesn't wait to see more, she's already on her feet at the next box. As she shakes it and the next one, and the one after that, they jingle like a percussion section. 'ALL of them?' She lets out a howl of rage.

Johnny's voice is low and controlled. 'You weren't actually meant to see this. There was an accident on the ice, we've been for replacements.' And good on Johnny for not actually dobbing in Quinn.

'Err...' Quinn is staring at me, eyes popping, shaking his head.

'What do you mean replacements?' If Alice is shrieking like a banshee, we all forgive her. 'I ordered these two years ago, you can't just go and buy more.'

Quinn's finally found his voice. 'My point exactly. But I have actually pulled off the impossible and got a few more boxes of the same glasses. Then I improvised for the rest.' He inclines his head. 'We'll take them into the house and see what you think.'

Five minutes later the new boxes are lined up along the stainless steel worktops in the kitchen. Quinn may have been careless yesterday, but not many people could have deferred Alice's explosion so deftly just now.

The glasses he's bringing out look spot on. 'Champagne flutes. I took all they had.' He sends Alice a tentative smile.

'And…' Even if the boy's done well, she hasn't been won over yet.

'I had to go elsewhere for the rest, to get the quantity.' He dips into the next box. 'These are very now. I already know you'll love them.' As he slams the glass down, his beam suggests he's particularly pleased with himself.

Alice's impassive expression crumples as she looks at the glass and when her voice arrives, it's a ferocious growl. 'You are joking? I'm not drinking out of fucking jam jars.'

'Bang on trend.' He's grinning at her and there's a teasing shine in his eyes. 'Toughened. Very Cornwall. And much less likely to break.'

'We'll see about that.' Before I can stop her, Alice picks up the jam jar by the handle and hurls it down onto the polished granite tiles.

I'm waiting for it to shatter, but there's a thud and it spins and bounces across the floor, and comes to a halt against the kick board of the quadruple cooking range. Which is a bit of an anti-climax and probably much less satisfying for Alice than if it had splintered into a thousand pieces. But on balance I'd say, overall it's a good thing.

Quinn looks as gobsmacked as the rest of us as he picks up the jar. 'Guaranteed party proof. What did I tell you?'

'I know we wouldn't be here without you, Quinn.' Alice hisses. 'But right now you are *so* full of shit.' Alice, that would be Alice who has trained herself never to swear, is speaking through gritted teeth now. 'Why are you *all* so damned incapable? My glasses are in pieces, the snow's been and gone, and my bloody husband-to-be hasn't even shown up yet. Where the hell is *he*?'

She's holding us all equally responsible for stuffing up here, but thus far she hasn't mentioned my tree blunder. And obviously Quinn has pulled so many strings to make this wedding happen, he's pretty much beyond reproach, whatever he does.

'Actually there's more. More not-so-good news… if that's what we're doing here.' Quinn's got a strange go-for-broke look about him. If this is his way of taking the heat out of the 'where the hell is Dan' question, I'm not sure it's the best idea. Or the best time.

'Well go on…?'

'Celestial Skies are going bust as we speak. I'm sorry, but you can wave goodbye to your starry ceiling.' And finally, Quinn comes in with an apology. For something he's completely not responsible for. 'And probably the disco floor too.'

18

Wednesday, 21st December
In Poppy's kitchen at Brides by the Sea:
Hanging lanterns and chocolate input

'Nothing picks me up like maple syrup pancakes for breakfast.'
I'm eating my fourth, and smiling gratefully at Poppy as I lick
my fingers. 'I was feeling *so* guilty for bailing on Alice.

My big admission is that last night I left Alice in a full bath,
loaded with as many relaxing bath oils as I could lay my hands
on. I poured her a very large glass of wine I knew she wouldn't
drink. Topped up her crystallised ginger supply. Then ran.
Back to my own bed. And now I'm sitting in Poppy's kitchen,
in the top-floor flat at Brides by the Sea, pouring out my
troubles and comfort eating.

Poppy puts down the pancake pan. 'You talked Alice down

137

before you left. And it made sense to sleep at home if you wanted to do some work in the studio this morning.'

She's doing a great job of making me feel better, on every level. Alice was calmer by the time she got into the bath, although for obvious reasons we skirted around controversial subjects. So I'm no wiser about what happened at the lunchtime drinks party it took her twenty-four hours to come back from. But I did squeeze in a long session in the studio earlier, experimenting with satin slips. And tulle and ribbon. And chiffon twists. Although I'm not really any wiser about that either.

'It's so great to have you back again, Pops.' My voice is thick with syrup. It makes the whole shop feel more homely again, with Poppy running up and down the stairs, and clanking her baking tins. Just being back in Poppy's tiny kitchen, with its bird's-eye view of the sea, is making me feel better. With its blue-painted cupboards and the shelves crammed with mixing bowls and brightly coloured crockery, it could have come out of one of my gran's pictures.

She laughs. 'I'm making marzipan stars and chocolate truffles for Christmas pressies. I'm doing it here so Rafe doesn't wolf them all.'

'Yum. Definitely the right morning for me to drop in to the shop, then.'

'I might be able to help with your other stuff too,' she says, patting my shoulder as she passes. 'If Alice insists you wear something other than your shorts, you're welcome to raid the hanging rail in the bedroom here.' Poppy whisks out of the kitchen and comes back in with some pretty print dresses on hangers. 'I'm bigger than you, but there's a silk shift you might like and a couple of culottes mini dresses. Take them to try.' She slides them into a carrier, then gets a bowl of chocolate-truffle mix out of the fridge and puts it on the table.

'Alice's friends will hate her if she's this dictatorial about the wedding with them.' I take the foil cases Poppy hands me and start to arrange them on the waiting tray. 'I forgive her, but she's my sister.' That's the unwritten rule. Your relations will put up with stuff no one else would.

'Inside every bride, there's always a Bridezilla hammering to be let out. And sometimes she escapes.' Poppy takes a scoop of truffle mix, rolls it between her palms, then drops it into a cup of cocoa powder to coat it. 'So hopefully that's your dress problem solved. What else did you say?' She delivers the first perfect truffle into its case and begins the next.

I sigh, because it's so hopeless. 'Any ideas how we can recreate a twelve-thousand-pound starry sky? Alice thinks the exposed roof timbers in the ballroom make it feel too cold.' This from a woman who, in the next breath, is demanding snow.

Poppy scrunches up her mouth as she rolls the next truffle in a tray of crushed nuts. 'People created amazing effects in the marquees at the weddings at Daisy Hill Farm last summer. I'm sure there are photos on the website.' She wipes her hands on her apron and flips out her phone.

A moment later I'm staring at the most amazing pictures. Twigs and branches, suspended and dotted with thousands of tiny fairy lights, lines of dangling lanterns, long tables with clusters of lighted candles along their centres. And all of them beautiful.

'Wow.'

Poppy smiles. 'There's no reason you couldn't do something like this at the Manor.'

There's a flutter in my chest. 'It might just work.' My voice is high with excitement and relief, and I'm babbling as I think out loud. 'We could use the beams to hang things from. We'd need shitloads of fairy lights and twigs. Omigod, what kind of trees are they from?' Maybe Alice doesn't have to be stuck with her stark roof after all.

'Hang on.' Poppy puts down her phone and dashes off down the stairs to the shop. A few minutes later there's a clattering of footsteps and she's back with Jess.

'If you'd told me you were making truffles, I'd have been up hours ago.' Jess is gasping after running up four flights of stairs.

'Here.' Poppy shoves a truffle into Jess's hand.

'Best man anywhere around, then?' Jess takes a bite of her chocolate.

'Not today.' I haven't actually broken it to her that there are two of them yet.

She's rubbing cocoa off her lips. 'If I were you and he was my date, I swear, I would *not* let him out of my sight.'

Who'd have thought she'd be so impressed by a flash car? But I have to smile at her direct approach. 'Well a) you're not me, and b) he's not even close to being my date. So we're all good.'

Poppy's holding a second truffle at the ready. 'Actually we got you up here because we need your floristry expertise…' She flashes her phone at Jess. 'For twig identification. Are these any particular sort of twig or branch?'

Jess takes a moment to unglue her eyes from the waiting

truffle and focus on the screen. 'I'd say they're birch. Most birch varieties have delicate branches and lots of twiggy growth. They're fairly common. Where do you want them for?'

'Thanks, Jess, we need some for the ballroom at Rose Hill Manor.' I say, slightly underplaying how many. That's the thing about problems, they keep on coming. You solve one, then there's another. Next up: where to find a birch forest.

'Look in the grounds, there'll probably be birches there you can take them from. If there aren't any there, shout and I'll help you find some.' Claiming her nut-truffle prize from Poppy, she strides past me to look out of the tiny window as she eats it.

Poppy might be here so Rafe doesn't snaffle her chocolates, but so far she's made two truffles and they've both been eaten. And I haven't even had any yet. If my next job's locating a forest, with the size of chocolate input I'll need for that, Poppy's going to have to make another batch.

'The sea's not very sparkly today. It's so cold, can you believe there are actually people swimming out there?'

'People?' Why have my ears pricked up at the word swimming?

'Actually only one.'

Before I can stop myself I'm at her elbow,

She points. 'See, wading out of the sea.'

I zoom in on a figure in a wetsuit down by the shoreline. 'It looks like Quinn.' Something about the laid-back way he's strolling, swiping the water off his face, as he strides up the beach, tells me there's probably a parking warden not far away.

'You can recognise him from up here?' Poppy's grinning. 'I knew you two were close, but…'

'Well, what are you waiting for?' Jess rounds on me. 'Get on down there, see if he knows if there are birch trees at Rose Hill.'

There's a nanosecond of deliberation, when I weigh up whether I should wait for truffles or nail the birch twigs. But sadly for my sweet tooth, with the wedding so close, there isn't a contest.

The next thing I know, I've got my carrier bag of Poppy's dresses in my hand and I'm hurtling down the stairs.

19

Wednesday, 21st December
On the island at Rose Hill Manor:
Highwaymen and toasted tea cakes

'When I asked you for birch trees, I wasn't counting on spending the rest of the morning in a rowing boat.'

Quinn laughs as he pulls on the oars, battling into a head wind as he rows. 'Pretty twigs don't grow on any old trees you know. They have to be the right trees and the only place birches grow is on the island.'

In case you haven't got that yet, that's the island in the middle of the lake. Although the wind is whipping up so hard today, the lake actually has waves on, like the sea. We've been chopping down branches from the wood on the island, and ferrying them back to the house. After working all morning, the pile in front of the ballroom doors is pretty huge.

And, yes, I have run a twiggy ceiling past Alice, in a hurried conversation. I rang her from the shop and she checked out the Weddings at Daisy Hill Farm website. Either that website has fairy dust sprinkled on it or maybe Alice sensed she was stuck between a rock and a hard place. But whatever the reason, she's said 'yes' – in principle – to the idea of twigs and lights.

'It's taking a lot more branches than I realised,' I say. We're on our fifth trip. On reflection it was rash to say twigs across the whole ceiling, without actually realising how humungous the ballroom is.

Quinn laughs. 'When I told you you'd get to great places if you hung out with me, I wasn't joking.' He nudges the boat up alongside the jetty, throws a rope around a short post and pulls us into the side. 'We used to love hanging out here when we were kids. It's why I'm a natural sailor now.'

'I bet the summer house is lovely when it's warmer.' The building is like something out of *Swallows and Amazons*. It's an idyllic hideaway, with a lovely wooden-plank building and a veranda overlooking the water. 'I've always loved verandas ever since I saw one in the "Alfie" books when I was little.'

'This'll be the last load.' Quinn leaps onto the jetty then gets hold of my hand and yanks me after him.

'Ooops…' As my foot hits the boards, I stumble, crashing against his padded gilet as he breaks my fall.

Immediately his arm closes around me. 'Whoa… watch it, we don't want you in the water.'

I'm with him on that one. The smell of sea salt and waxed cotton wafts straight up my nose, as his warmth spreads through me. For a moment I'm wedged under his armpit. As

I close my eyes and lean into his body, suddenly in my head we're running along the shoreline, hand in hand. Jeez. I can't quite believe I'm thinking this. But the more I try to blank it, the worse it gets. We're muffled against the cold, in matching scarfs, dodging the frothing breakers as they roll up the beach. Really? Then we're in the Surf Shack Café, our foreheads touching, as we wait for our double order of large mochas and toasted teacakes, dripping with butter. And thankfully that's where the dream breaks, because I always have hot chocolate not mocha, and the currants in teacakes are like dead insects. Bleughh. I give a shudder. Even if they're hot and butter-drenched I couldn't be tempted.

'Cold?' He's grinning down at me and for some reason he's still hanging on to me as if I'm about to dive into the water at any moment.

If my heart is skittering, it's only because I almost fell in. And nothing whatsoever to do with a certain pair of gorgeous blue eyes looking at me.

Pulling away, I head towards the safe end of the jetty. 'No worries, carrying twigs will soon make me warm.'

I'm not wrong. We tramp backwards and forwards through the undergrowth, dragging branches behind us, piling them into the boat. I'm starting to wonder if Quinn ever heard of the Plimsoll line and the dangers of overloading vessels, when he finally says, 'Okay, one more lot should do it.'

'Great,' I say. 'Because those maple-syrup pancakes I had for breakfast are a distant memory.' My stomach is literally growling with hunger. As the branches tucked under my arm swish along behind me, I'm already planning my raid on the fridge in the Manor kitchen. Then as we round the bend on the path and come to face the jetty, I realise there's something significant missing. 'Quinn, where's the boat?'

He blinks and scratches his head. 'Did you see me tie it up?'

Not exactly the line I'm expecting from the guy who twenty minutes ago was claiming to be a natural sailor. I give a shrug.

'I'd swear I tied it in a highwayman's hitch, so one tug on the rope would cast us off. As used by highwaymen back in the day when they wanted to undo their horses quickly. The wind must have tugged it free.'

I'm not sure what horses have to do with anything when our damned boat is nowhere in sight. And I'm also surprised Quinn looks so unbothered. 'So what do we do now?' I ask. 'Swim? I'm so damned hungry I might have to.' That's a joke, obviously. While I love the beach, I hate going out of my depth. Not that I broadcast this in a town where everyone except yours truly swims like a dolphin.

There's a strange lilt around Quinn's lips. 'I was going to suggest we stopped for a picnic anyway.' He picks up his tool bag from the jetty. 'We can build a fire and hunker down in the summer house for as long as it takes.'

'What?' I'm appalled on so many levels. Lack of lunch is only one.

'If no one's found us by morning, I promise I'll swim for help.' He's got his bloody 'hang loose and chill' voice on.

'Morning?' I echo, weakly. Surely not? Everyone seems to have forgotten there's a wedding rushing towards us at a million miles an hour. And we're a million miles from being ready for it. Just when things seemed to be looking up too. As for getting marooned in a cabin alone with Quinn…

'How about I cook you an island all-day breakfast of hot dogs?' He's grinning. 'For starters.'

My mouth is watering. I swallow loudly. 'You've got food?' The promise of lunch momentarily eclipses my doubts. Sad to say, at this exact moment the hole in my stomach is so huge, this is what I care about most.

'Obviously. How does lunch by a log fire sound? And we can wash the hot dogs down with buck's fizz.'

'Sounds like a plan.' That seriously qualifies as a contender for understatement of the decade. I frown as he pulls a bottle of champagne out of the bag. 'I thought you had your saws in there?'

'Saws and a few of life's other essentials.' As he gives a low laugh, his eyes are locked on my face, as if he's watching for a reaction. 'So let's take it from here, shall we?'

If he's talking about hot dogs, I'm in. As for the rest, I'll worry about that later.

20

Here's another instance of Quinn being good with keys, even if he does have a tendency to lose boats. Along with the well-stocked bag and matches, he also has the key for the summer house in his pocket. There's a stack of dry wood and kindling on the veranda and it turns out his fire-building and lamp-lighting skills are as impressive as his cooking. Okay, thus far I've only seen him cook sausages. Twice. There may be a bit of a theme going on there. And both times I was hungry enough to have eaten a proverbial horse.

'More Bolly?' Quinn holds up the bottle. He found a shelf of beautiful champagne flutes in the cabin kitchen, which seems ironic after all the smashed glass of the last couple of days. 'There are some candles in the bag, if you'd like to light them. And I'll get some more wood in.' For a picnic, thrown in at the last minute, he's pretty much thought of everything. As I hold out my glass, I'm sitting on the thick floor rug, toasting my toes in front of the roaring fire. With my back propped against the comfortably faded sofa, I can't remember when I last felt this lazy and relaxed. The fistful of jam jars that he drops beside me for the candles makes me smile.

'Thanks.' As he pours, I can't resist the tease. 'Although I can't think why you gave us flutes to drink out of when you had on-trend jam jars to hand.'

He drops a box of matches next to me and I drag his bag towards me as he heads out to the veranda for logs. I pull out a pair of pruning shears and a couple of saws, so I can dig in better. As my hand closes around the box of candles, my heart misses a beat. Surely he hasn't brought...? I squint closer, praying to the god of winter breaks in summer houses, that I'm mistaken. But, damn me, I'm not. Nestling between the spare matches and a sleek stainless steel cork screw, I can't miss the dayglow pink-and-orange box. *Of condoms.* I peer in closer to read the label.

'*Surprise and Delight*? Quinn, are these yours?'

'Shit, you found them.' By the time he's back in the room and stacking the wood on the fireplace, his initial dismay has been displaced by a familiar unrepentant grin. 'And?'

'What the hell did you bring these for?' And why the hell have I challenged him on it? If I hadn't been so shocked I'd have been sensible and pretended not to see them.

He gives a smirk. 'I'd have thought that was obvious, even to a sheltered Cornwall girl like you.'

'It's a box of twelve.' I'm almost wailing.

'Un-started,' he says. 'That should count for something.'

Somehow, it makes it worse rather than better that he's even thinking along those lines.

'But we hardly know each other…'

'As if that matters.' His sniff suggests I'm stupid. What's more, he's entirely unembarrassed. 'I'm laid back about many things, but in my book it's very bad manners to leave a woman hanging for want of a condom. You may well be thanking me for my vigilance at some point down the line.'

Now I've heard it all. 'Sometimes you are so full of shit, Quinn.' Even as I'm spitting it out, I'm aware I'm stealing Alice's line here. And I'm also aware that something about the combination of his straight-up delivery and his enthusiasm makes him damned hard to stay annoyed with for long.

'Not at all.' Now it's his turn to protest. 'Sex just happens to be what I'm good at. Along with making deals and being persuasive. I promise, you would – you could – have the time of your life with me.'

'Per-lease… that's enough.' I'm noting that persuasion seems to be a common factor here. This time when I clamp my eyes closed and shake my head, I don't get any couple pictures at the beach. There is a tiny thought about once, a very long time ago, when I did have the time of my life. I push that to the back of my mind. I haven't found it since, and between us, it's a search I gave up on years ago. And I'm not about to re-start now.

'No, really, think Michael Hutchence, or Prince.' Quinn's eyes are wide with truth. What's even more unbelievable, he's being serious. 'Both renowned for being phenomenal in bed – and out. That's the standard you'll be looking at with me.

When you get to know me better, if that's how you're comfortable.'

He's making it sound more like he's delivering a service. I mean, who bigs themselves up like this, in the cold light of day? What's more, he seems to have missed that the guys he's comparing himself to are dead. Which is hardly sexy, is it?

He's still being as matter of fact as if he were talking about an app. 'Let's hope there's a time when you decide I'm irresistible.' He's laughing now and when he laughs it's very tempting to believe the publicity.

'Sure,' I say, ironically, meaning exactly the opposite. Somehow I think I'll fight and resist, however husky his laugh is. 'So what do you do when you aren't using up your condom supplies?' This seems like a good way to move the conversation on.

He flops down next to me on the floor and props his chin on his hand, being careful not to take the heat from the fire. 'Work, play. Lots of play.' He laughs again. 'I take the company team to Escape Rooms.'

'Keep going…' I have absolutely no idea what he's talking about.

'They're video-game adventures, recreated in real life. You get locked in a room and you have to solve puzzles to get out. We've done them worldwide.'

'Wild,' I say, meaning anything but. It sounds like a typical geek-guy thing.

'Talking about escaping…' The way he pauses adds to the dramatic effect. 'With your talent, you really shouldn't be stuck in this backwater.'

'No?' Only Quinn could have got from games to this veiled insult in one over-exuberant leap.

'You should come to stay with me in London for a while. You're wasted here – on every level. With my contacts, your career could be stratospheric.'

Only Quinn would use that word. When Johnny warned me about him, I assumed he was talking about him playing the field, not rolling through my life with the force of a seismic wave.

'Thanks, but I'm happy here.'

He shakes his head. 'Don't get me wrong, it's a great place for holidays. But unless you're a surfer or a seal, it's a dead loss full time. The only reason you're living here is because you gave up on yourself. So how long ago did you get hurt?'

I drive the surprise out of my eyes and flatten my voice. 'W-why would you think that?' How on earth can he work out what no one else has, in all the time I've been here? Not even my gran knew I was running away. That selfishly, me staying to look after her was as much for my benefit as for hers.

'Easy.' Shifting his legs, he pulls down the corners of his mouth. 'It's the only possible reason a woman like you would be living here, behaving like a monk.'

'Monks are men,' I point out. If he makes a mistake that basic, he can be wrong about the rest too. 'How would you have the first clue, anyway?'

His eyes narrow. 'Instinct. I can sense it a mile off. You haven't had decent sex in years.'

So sure of himself and he's back to *that* again? 'You're *so* wrong.' It's my word against his. And luckily there isn't a lie detector in the room.

'I'd bet my life on it, but I'm not going to argue. The important part is, you need to move on. And I can help you do that.'

'A fling with Mr Shag-around? That's going to be really helpful. Not.'

He sighs and his foot moves very slowly, and comes to rest on my ankle. 'I've been wild, pretty much forever, for a lot of reasons. But there comes a time when even the crazy guys get to settling down – we're hard-wired that way.'

Deep down I know I should readjust my legs to push him off. But I don't. Simply because it feels comfy. And because somehow he sounds so sincere.

'Have you got any Christmas songs on your phone?' I ask. Getting stuck on the island was bad enough, without throwing in the analysis too. At least a sing-along might stop him dissecting my life. Given there's zero signal, it's not as if his phone's useful for anything else.

I laugh at his very guilty nod. Between us I doubt he'd admit this to his bestie music producer mate. But a second later 'The Power of Love' is echoing off the walls so loud it's making the glass on the oil lamp vibrate.

After a few glasses of Buck's Fizz, I do a pretty good job on the chorus to this one, but on balance, given the loaded lyrics, I decide to leave singing along until the next track.

'Shall we light those candles?' Quinn's eyes are shining.

All I have to do is watch his broad thumbs as he lights the candles and drips the hot wax to stand them up. And every time there's a match to blow out, he offers it to me. As he lines up the jars of flaming candles in front of the wood burner, the first notes of 'A Winter's Tale' tinkle around the room.

Where are all the up-tempo tracks? This one is way too dreamy to be listening to in a wood cabin that could have come off a poster from the Lapland Tourist Board. It's the kind of emotionally loaded track they play on Pirate FM, when couples phone in to say what was playing the night they got together. I must have drunk way too much champagne, because the melody is almost making me tear up. The fire light is flickering on Quinn's face, illuminating the shadows on his light brown stubble. I've heard of beer goggles, maybe I'm suffering from champagne shades here.

'I'm truly sorry about the "Surprise and Delight", Sera.' He rubs his chin. 'Bad call on my part.'

'No problem.' I give a sigh. Apologies aren't what I'd expect from Quinn. '"Surprise and Delight" sounds more like the name of a pudding.' The box is still on the floor at my feet. If it's anything like my toes, it'll be getting scorched by the heat of the fire. I'm silently daring him to make a tacky quip about using the contents for dessert, but it doesn't come.

'Hey, our rips match.' He hooks his finger through the ragged hem of my shorts.

'So they do.' However inviting the ripped denim on his thigh looks, I'm not going to reciprocate.

Then next thing I know, he's sliding his finger through my belt loop and giving a gentle tug. And you know what? I haven't even protested. If I lean in, I know what's going to happen next. The rub of his stubble on my face, the tingle, the taste. Exactly what Alice banned. It's not that I often agree with her. But even through my wine haze, I can spot a bad idea when it's this wrong. If my legs didn't feel so damned relaxed, I'd get up and walk away. Pretend to do the washing up. Instead

I clamp my eyes closed and try for a mindfulness view of the beach to calm me down. But the image that flashes into my head is an open glovebox full of parking tickets. *Parking tickets?* I'm trying to work that one out when a sharp rap on the summer-house door makes me jump so hard I kick the champagne bottle over.

'What the eff…?' Quinn jerks his hand back, makes a dive to save the last inch of fizz, then squints over his shoulder. 'Johnny? How the hell did he get here?'

One more knock and the door swings open. The gust of wind that bursts in with Johnny is so strong it blows out all the candles.

'Sorry to break up the party…but I found your boat.'

21

Wednesday, 21st December
By the coach house at Rose Hill Manor: Not quite perfect

'You were stranded? On the island? But how? Why? When?'

If I'd forgotten how thorough Alice could be when she turns her mind to interrogation, I'm remembering now. It's embarrassing enough already, being careless enough to not only lose a boat, but also get found half sozzled with Quinn. Having a welcoming committee waiting when we get back to The Manor makes it ten times worse. While I'm thanking my lucky stars Johnny came across the drifting boat while he was test-driving Cinderella's carriage, it's a shame that Alice didn't arrive for her personal carriage inspection a teensy bit later. That way she need never have known. She's also brought Poppy and Immie along with her too, as a 'thank you' for decorating the holiday cottages, so there's no chance I'll ever live this down.

'It wasn't a big deal, it was over before it began...' I say, ignoring three puzzled frowns. Quinn definitely had the right idea. He disappeared into the house faster than you could say 'desert island', muttering something about wine deliveries. 'And anyway it's *great* we're all here to see the carriage.' I'm putting a positive spin on this. Given how picky Alice is, it might have been better if she had her first view of the carriage without Poppy and Immie as an audience. If she dishes out her usual criticism she'll look like an even bigger bitch queen than she does already. As we stand in our huddle in front of the coach house waiting for Johnny and the coach to arrive, Alice is already tapping her toe impatiently and looking at her watch. Poppy snuggles further inside her parka hood and sends me a sympathetic grin.

As we hear the rumble of cart wheels on gravel coming closer, we turn. I'm not sure what I was expecting. But the sight of the sturdy white horse tossing its head and slowing to a walk in front of the small open carriage is so beautiful, it takes my breath away.

'Wow,' Poppy and Immie chorus.

And then there's Johnny, sitting up in front, holding the reins, grinning down at us.

'Isn't the horse lovely?' I say, trying to hide that I'm doing a total double-take at this particular incarnation of Johnny. I'm also trying to make sure I head off Alice's criticisms. Whereas Immie, Poppy and I are so impressed we're almost speechless; if I know Alice-the-Bride, any minute now she'll break her silence with a crushing comment. I'm so used to her barbs, I shake them off. Part of me suspects she doesn't actually realise she's doing them. I know Johnny is nothing more than someone I once knew and he's also a hundred per cent able to stand up for himself. But knowing how hard he's worked to make the carriage run makes me want to leap in and save him from Alice.

'This is Snowball.' Johnny secures the reins, jumps down and pats the horse's neck as he passes.

'Aren't white horses supposed to be lucky?' I ask.

'You can make a wish when you see one,' he laughs. 'Although the catch is there's no such thing as a white horse, they're called greys. If you look closely, this guy's got some dappling on his bum too.' Johnny gives him an affectionate rub on the rump. Anyone coming for a ride?' Opening the side door of the carriage, he pulls down a step and holds out his hand to Alice.

I'm praying to the god of pumpkins that she's not building up to some withering dismissal. When Alice doesn't step forward we all turn to look at her. She's standing, her face all bunched up, scraping her nail under her eye.

'Alice?' As I step towards her she gives a loud sniff. 'Are you okay?'

'Fine.' She pulls a hanky out of the pocket of her trench coat and blows her nose. 'When we talked about the carriage, I had no idea it would be so perfect, that's all.' Her voice has gone small and croaky, and she sniffs again.

'Babe,' I say, because I'm not sure I've ever seen her cry before. She's tough as nails. Tougher even. Crying isn't her bag at all. It's amazing how the emotional charge of weddings can crack the hardest people. As I put my arm around her, and squeeze, my own eyes are bleary with tears. I'm so happy that something has finally met her expectations. This is obviously important to her.

Johnny swallows. 'It's buffed up well.' Serious understatement alert there, considering the dusty wreck he had in a hundred pieces only a couple of days ago.

'You've done so much work, I can't begin to thank you.' Alice reaches up to give Johnny a peck on the cheek. 'Really, arriving in this is going to make my wedding day. I mean, imagine the pictures.' Her voice is high and dreamy. It's a minor detail, but we're staying at the Manor the night before the wedding, then Johnny's going to draw up outside in the carriage, so it looks as if she's just arrived.

'It's open, so it's pretty cold when you're moving,' Johnny says, as he helps her in. 'We'll go up the drive and back now, that's far enough to give you a feel for it.'

Immie and Poppy get in after her and I'm about to follow, when Johnny puts his hand out and stops me.

'Probably more room if you sit up on front with me, Fi.' Johnny jumps up front and pulls me up after him. Being ever so slightly alcohol impaired and reacting slowly, I wobble horribly when he shakes the reins and we set off with a lurch.

When he said more room, he must have been joking. It's like the front of the hire van re-visited. Except this time I'm on a slippery wooden seat with nothing to hold on to. Think of riding a roller coaster without a safety bar and you'll be close. The only way to anchor myself is by putting my arm around Johnny's back and clinging onto him. I hesitate at first, but it's either that or end up being pitched into the road. As we lurch around the first corner I steel myself, and grasp a handful of his North Face jacket. Then I turn and grin at the girls huddled together in the open carriage behind me, as we speed towards the drive.

'Fucking freezing, but bloody brilliant,' Immie yells. 'Even better than arriving at a wedding in a fire engine.' Immie's been going out with a fireman called Chas since last summer, in case you missed that. Although she's not technically engaged yet, that's obviously not stopped her planning ahead.

'Are you having a jacket?' I yell back to Alice, remembering my bridesmaid's one.

She shouts back at me. 'A floor-length fur cape.'

'Of course.' It would be. Thinking of the Queen of Narnia. Why hasn't she gone for broke and done this in a sleigh, in Norway?

'So how come you got stuck on the island?'

Bugger. That's Alice, back on my case, and I'm wishing she'd stayed teary for longer. I know Johnny is hanging on every word. And judging. It was not the best moment of my life when he accidentally kicked the *Surprise and Delight* box. Awkward.

'The boat blew away because the quick-release knot came undone in the wind,' I yell, hoping if I blind her with technicalities, she'll back off. 'We made a fire to keep warm, then Johnny rowed out to pick us up. That's it.'

'That bloody Quinn doesn't change.' Immie lets out a chuckle. 'He used to pull that "lost boat" stunt once a week back in the day. Caught out more hapless holiday-making females than I've had hot potatoes. Quinn and his damned highwayman's knot.' From the loud guffaws and kicking, it sounds like she's rolling around the carriage floor. 'Good on you for not falling for it, Sera.'

Even if Immie's having a ROFL moment, I want to curl up and die. She may have nailed the highwayman bit, but maybe she's wrong about Quinn this time. The wind was really strong. Although I'm looking forwards, I can feel Alice's appalled stare boring into my back. Johnny, to his credit, doesn't look at me, and he doesn't add anything to blow my cover any more than it has been. I think Immie did that job, single-handed.

'Good thing you were here, then, Johnny,' Alice shouts.

Judging by the ironic twang in her voice, she knows that's not the whole story. And Johnny is definitely her new favourite person. What she's totally overlooking is that Quinn and I were getting twigs for her damned ceiling when the excursion went belly-up.

'Lucky coincidence I was around.' The pointed sideways glance Johnny shoots me makes me suddenly less certain that it was pure chance on his part. 'Although rescuing bridesmaids is only what a best man *should* do.'

When the other best man has screwed up. Thanks a bunch for highlighting this, Johnny. He couldn't have done a better job if he'd gone up to that little top-floor bedroom here, where I've found out he's staying, and shouted it from the attic window. I know it's what they're *all* thinking. Which is probably why there's a hole in the conversation the size of Greater London, all the way back up the drive.

'Bells…'

When Alice breaks the silence with her cry, at first I think it's a substitute swear word, given she's trained herself not to curse in front of clients. But then she says it again.

'Bells… We're supposed to be having bells on Snowball's harness… so they'll jingle all the way down the drive and the guests will hear me coming.' She's being more specific now. And wagging her finger at the coachman. 'I knew there was something we'd forgotten. It's definitely in the manual. We need to sort this, Johnny.'

Perfect is a momentary state for Alice. I knew it was too good to last.

'Bells? Of course, thanks for reminding me, Alice.' Johnny appears to be forcing his smile. 'Sera and I will pick some up when we're out later.'

My ears prick up at my name. 'Out?' This is news to me. 'Doing what, exactly?'

'Shopping.' He says that word more enthusiastically than any straight guy I've heard. 'Given the size of the ballroom, I reckon we need to buy every fairy-light string in Cornwall. Candles might be good too. But we need to get a move on or we won't be ready for the wedding.' At last someone else seems to have woken up to the fact that the wedding is only days away.

But just for a moment I'm wishing I'd stayed on that desert island.

22

Let's face it, I brought it on myself. If I hadn't got rat-arsed on the island, I'd have been able to drive myself around the DIY stores in search of every last fairy light. They've mostly got huge car parks and one tends to run into the next, after all. If it had been a choice between going on my own, or being run around by Johnny, believe me, however much I hate bay parking, I'd have managed.

'So you think we need candles as well as lights?' I ask, shivering and turning my collar up against the biting cold. It's almost dark. As we hurry towards the entrance of the first shop and make our way past a huge pile of Christmas trees out on the tarmac, the brightness of the shop is warm and inviting.

163

'The extra glow of candlelight will help make up for lost sparkle.' Johnny sounds decided. What's more he's showing a shedload of decorative insight, for a guy. It's less surprising that he's done that man thing and taken charge of the trolley. He looks up at the lights dangling over the entrance canopy, being whipped around by the wind. 'Would Alice go for multi-coloured icicle chasers like those, then?'

Maybe take back what I said about the decorative insight. 'Absolutely not. She wants single white bulbs, as tiny as possible.' And as many as we can lay our hands on.

While the upside of shopping this close to Christmas is that most places have home-grown Santas handing out complementary sweets, the downside is that stocks are low. And while there are aisles of display lights, flashing like bad migraines, the shelves are far from full. By the time we hit the sixth shop, I've already devoured five free chocolate tree decorations and a candy cane, but we still haven't found enough lights. We're met at the door by a pensioner in a dayglow elf costume, whose huge stick-on ears are so impressive I can't say 'no' to the lolly he's giving away. As I twist off the wrapper Johnny stops pushing the trolley and stares at me for a second.

'What were those lollies you used to eat at uni?' He scratches his head as if that's somehow going to help him remember.

Thus far we've both kept strictly to the 'here and now', and I'm taken aback by the abrupt departure. I carry on walking, in the hope he'll follow. 'Chupa chups?' I used to buy them in industrial quantities because I always had one in my mouth to suck on when I sewed at my machine. Which was pretty much twenty hours a day.

His legs must have started working again, because he draws level with me. 'Yes, you'd fight anyone to get a cola flavour.'

Bloody hell. I'd almost forgotten. 'They were the blue ones.' Although I'm laughing, I'm wary. Somehow even if we are only discussing confectionary, the past is a dangerous place to go. But now he's crossed that invisible barrier into forbidden territory, I might as well ask what I've been aching to find out. 'So how come you're so good with horses?' One tiny question, and then I promise we'll go back to discussing road layouts and local trivia.

'Horses?' His tone suggests he can't quite work out how we got here. 'I worked with a blacksmith in the village where Dan and I lived when I was at school. I wanted to work with metal, but I learned how to handle ponies too. I moved on to cars later.' So that explains why he was mending the carriage.

'You just never said.' I stick the lolly in my mouth, to make sure that comes over as a passing comment rather than the start of an interrogation. Two years of drinking and student parties and crossing in the hall. Not to mention cups of tea in our kitchen if I could ever tempt him in. Although maybe those teatimes were mostly filled with *me* talking about *my* dreams. My obsession to travel the world. Lists of must-visit beaches.

Once I found out he had a soft spot for apple cake, he came round quite a lot. All those late afternoons putting the world to rights over the kitchen table, and yet he never mentioned working with a blacksmith. Although, come to think of it, he was probably way too hung up on the future too. Of everyone I knew, he was the most focused and obsessed with where he was heading next. Although maybe it was because he was older and already on his second degree. Plus he was the only one around who was sponsored and getting paid to be there.

He rests his elbows on the trolley. 'It's strange at uni. Everyone's so busy with the study and the social life. You live with people for two or three years and end up knowing nothing more about them than what degree they did and what their favourite shots were.'

He makes it sound like a lifetime ago. Which it almost is. And we didn't even share the same flat. We only used the same front door and hallway. Which is probably his way of gently pointing out that I didn't know him. Don't know him. At all.

A half-smile passes across his face. 'Do you still drink Sambuca then?'

Bleughhh. Even the word makes me feel queasy. 'Hell no. One really bad drunken night and I've never touched it since.' Which just goes to show how we all change. And we all move on. Although I'm pretty embarrassed to admit that back in the day I'd volunteer to go on the party booze-buying trips, just to see how it felt to push a trolley around the cash and carry with him. To try out how it felt to sit in the passenger seat of his car. Another bleughhh to that thought. That's the kind of cute-yet-silly thing you do when you're twenty-one. Looking back, those trips were the closest I ever came to coupledom. Thank heavens I came to my senses.

Right now I'm making damn sure I stand far enough away from the trolley and make my body language stiff and hostile. I want to make it perfectly clear to the rest of the store that we're definitely not a joined-at-the-hip pair, this time around. Although, to be honest, my trashed shorts and snagged tights hardly look like they come from the same washing basket as his sharp navy chinos. And my baby-pink wool jacket with the bald patches is so far away from his North Face jacket, I probably look more like a bag lady he's taken pity on than anyone more significant.

He turns the trolley into the Christmas lights area. 'I was forgetting, you're more of a champagne woman now, aren't you?' he quips, referring to my boozy picnic earlier.

Ouch! How cheap is that? Especially since my lunchtime hangover headache is starting to kick in. I scrunch up my face in disgust, but at least it's brought us neatly back to the present. I'm saved having to look for a suitably barbed reply, because suddenly I come to a rack, fully stacked with boxes of lights.

'Yay. I think we've struck gold.' I bend down to read from the shelf label. 'Here we go, "Indoor outdoor. LED string. Warm white. Five hundred. Christmas party." And a shedload too.' So there is a god of twinkly ceilings after all.

23

Wednesday, 21st December
At Rose Hill Manor: Amnesia and baking trays

'Looks like Robinson Crusoe got lost again.'

We're back from St Aidan, carrying candles and fairy lights into the ballroom. It doesn't take a genius to work out Johnny's referring to Quinn here, who, between us, has made no progress at all while we've been away in town. When Johnny flicks on the lights and illuminates the outside terrace, we can see the branches are still in a pile in front of the French windows, where we left them this morning.

I glance at my watch. 'It feels later than seven. Maybe I can fit in another job.' Especially given the alternative is going back to the cottage, to be told off by Alice, no doubt. Not that I've done anything wrong since getting stuck on the island. But she's so stressed, there's not much she doesn't find fault with.

We called in for a pizza on our way back from St Aidan, so it's not as if I'm rushing back for dinner.

Johnny puts his hands in his pockets. 'We could carry on decorating the big tree in the hall?'

I was planning on working on my own, so the word 'we' comes as a jolt. Although 'we' are currently firmly back in real time again, the conversation tends to make unnerving quantum leaps. One second we'll be chatting about something completely innocuous, the next it's toxic. Sentences begin by being cosy and safe and then move somewhere excruciatingly uncomfortable. And all without warning. To be honest, it's easier without the stress.

'Alice wants that tree white.' Waiting for Alice's decision on what to do with the tree is the perfect get-out. It's still as it was when she came in and stopped me – was that really only yesterday? 'She needs to decide whether to strip off everything it took me hours to put on, paint the tree white, let it dry. Then re-decorate from scratch. Or to leave it as it is and end up with – horror of horrors – a tree with green branches under the thousands of white decorations. But only Alice can say.' And I'm sure if I locate my wedding manual – which should be with me at all times, so how do I not know where it is? – I'll be able to find another, equally pressing, job to do instead.

Johnny sighs. 'I'm going to make an executive decision on this one. Realistically, it's too late to have the tree white. We'll finish decorating it now and I'll take the consequences with Alice.'

That's one brave man. And put like that, I'm not going to get out of this. I hope he realises that just because he's been

Alice's favourite person today, there's no guarantee for tomorrow.

'Okay then, rebel, are you going up the steps or on the floor?' I ask.

A moment later I'm looking up at him.

'Pass me some deccies, then,' he says. 'This reminds me of the Christmas the guys brought that tree into the hallway at uni. We couldn't get it up the stairs, remember?'

Here we go. Why does Christmas make everyone so bloody nostalgic? As I pass him a handful of sparkly cones hanging on white-and-cream gingham ribbon, my heart is sinking to new lows.

In a bid to keep control, I throw in my own bit. 'And someone sawed the branches off so we could get past. We were still walking the shavings and the pine needles around the flats when we moved out the summer after.'

'I did the sawing.' He says it proudly, reaching down for more decorations. 'And we had that massive Christmas dinner that went on all night. Someone served up Paxo stuffing raw. Remember that?'

Shit. He's nailing every detail.

'As if anyone could forget.' I hurriedly grab some hearts and shove them up at him.

He takes them from me, but instead of stopping and concentrating on what he's doing, dammit, he carries on. 'You made the rum sauce, and the guy with pink hair fell into it – was it Graham?'

'Grant,' I say, only because I've got a good memory for names. 'Curvy Sally from the top floor brought him. Remember her? Film-star face, beautiful figure; all the guys adored her.'

She's imprinted on my brain too, if only because she had the kind of pneumatic boobs I'd have loved at the time. Still would. Although these days I'm more resigned to how I am. Boob-free and hip-free, that is.

'Those red lips didn't do it for me.' Johnny pulls a face. 'I was a 'less is more' guy back then. Still am really.' He hooks on another heart. 'Anyway, didn't Grant overdose on aperitifs, pass out in his rum sauce, then nearly suffocate when he inhaled?'

And there I was, I remember, flushed and trying to make a roux for twenty-four, when there weren't any pans left, and nothing like enough milk. All so I could impress damn Johnny. Which was an epic fail, because he ended up leaving with Sally. Which was the same epic fail that happened every evening out with Johnny. He always went home with someone else. The only difference was the girls changed. I pass up a handful of baubles.

'Sally could barely walk, I had to haul her all the way up to the attic,' he says, sorting out the silver balls from the white ones. 'I was fifty minutes late for the nine o' clock tutorial I was giving.' He's looping a silver bauble over a branch when he stops and curses. 'Damn, we forgot bells. For Snowball's harness. Alice will eat us for breakfast.'

Strange how we both forgot something from an hour earlier and yet we can remember things down to the last minute from years ago. But if Johnny can remember this particular Christmas in so much detail, what about the Christmas after? When I'd left uni, but for some unknown reason he asked me back to the department ball. After that whole weekend went tits up so spectacularly, I comforted myself by erasing it from my mind. And then I went off travelling. And afterwards, when it was obvious we weren't ever going to meet up again, somehow I assumed he'd erase the whole thing too. But if he can remember raw stuffing, I suspect he'd be able to recount the whole ball weekend back to me word for word too. Minute by cringey minute. And, believe me, that thought is pretty appalling. If there's a good-luck charm that saves you from having your significantly embarrassing moments and mistakes shoved in your face, mine's gone badly AWOL.

'And there was that time we went brambling down the waste ground and when we ate the crumble all our teeth went purple.' He's on a roll with the baubles now. 'And what about that apple cake you used to make?'

I shake my head and push a whole load more decorations his way, to try to shut him up. 'It was all a *very* long time ago, Johnny.' I throw up a fistful of stars, then follow with a handful of angels.

'But surely…?' He's refusing to believe I've forgotten.

'Sorry, I gave up baking when I was twenty-two.' True, in a way. After that my gran was the one who cooked. I rattle through the boxes and piles, scooping up the last few toys. 'Here, this is for the top.' Something pretty to take his mind off cake. 'A fairy bride and groom, how cool is that?' All the more so if it brings us back to what we're doing. Rather than what we once did.

'Brilliant, if a little kitsch.' He gives a sniff. This from the guy who paid to steal away our knitted bears when they weren't even for sale? He takes the fairy couple and stretches to hook them into place. 'That's the finishing touch. Is it all looking white enough?'

As I stand back to admire it, I have to say the effect is awesome. 'Pretty damned white. We can always blast it with some fake snow spray from a can tomorrow if not.' Why didn't Snow Queen Alice think of that?

He's down on the floor again and folding up the steps. 'It's taken no time. Some jobs are way faster with two.'

Whatever he's hoping, I'm not joining in the congratulatory couple-fest. 'Thanks for your help, anyway.' And just because we're so close to going, there's one more thing I want to slip in. 'Skid pans? Where do they fit in, exactly?' I know I've surprised him, because he blinks. And takes a step backwards.

'Remember that PhD in automotive design?'

As if I wouldn't. 'But all over the world?' I'm repeating Quinn here. 'Weren't you in Coventry?' Back in 2008 he sounded like he would be there forever.

'I moved on, to motor-racing teams.' He gives a shrug. 'Travel goes with the territory.'

Not that I'm jealous, obviously. But back then he was only interested in engines. Seeing the world didn't even figure.

He picks up the steps, then hesitates. 'Fancy a Winter Warmer now we're done?'

'I'd better be getting off.' I'm stuffing the empty boxes into bags like a dervish, so I can make a run for it.

'Pimms No 3 and hot apple juice?' He's staring at me, leaning on the door frame, a smile playing on his lips. 'A great way to warm up and wind down at the same time. It might help your amnesia... about the cake?'

I manage to ignore that last teasing comment. 'As you said, I shouldn't drink and drive – and as you also pointed out, I'm more of a champagne girl now, anyway.'

It's a relief when the door slams behind him. I sink onto the bottom step of the staircase and bury my head in my hands. I'm only halfway through letting out a long sigh, when the door bursts open again. I look up to see Johnny. Back. And obviously on the war path.

'You know what...' He's staring at me, a tiny bit bemused, but mostly just annoyed. 'For the last few years, I've been walking through airports, everywhere from Milan to Mexico. And that whole time I've been looking, somehow expecting to bump into you. And now I find out you've been in damned Cornwall all along. So what the hell happened, Fi? What went wrong?'

Where has that come from? It's hardly fair, when my question was only the tiniest query about skid pans. And why is everyone so opposed to living in Cornwall?

The end of a long, long day is the last time you want to deal with a tirade like that from someone as up himself as Johnny. Especially when it rubbishes your whole life. Mostly I'd back down. Or step back and let Jess come in and fight for me. But maybe, because of my antsy champagne hangover, or maybe because this guy stuck his size-ten feet through my plans for the second time in as many days, I'm going to let him have it.

'Wherever that came from, it's pretty insulting.' I stick my chin out, to make sure he knows how cross I am. And furious. And hurt, although maybe I'd rather he didn't see that. 'Just because you once knew me – though as you said before, you probably didn't – and it certainly doesn't mean you know me now. So back the hell off and stop judging what's none of your business.' I mean to hiss, but by the time I finish it's pretty much a yell.

On balance, I should have picked up my bags before I let rip. That way I could have flounced out and let the door bang shut behind me. As it is, I take a few minutes to gather what feels like a hundred carrier bags. Then Johnny ends up opening the door for me and holding it as I squish through with all my bags. Having to say 'Thank you', then 'Sorry' as I accidentally brush my bum on his leg is diminishing.

When it comes to being assertive, I'm a no-hope amateur. Next time I'll definitely do better.

24

Wednesday, 21st December
In the yard at Daisy Hill Farm: Cold nights and gold spots

Some days just go on and on. Today felt like it should have been over when we came back from the island, but that was almost ten hours ago. And it's still not finished yet. As I pull up by the farmhouse, Poppy and Rafe are coming out into the yard.

'Hi, Sera, how's it going?' Rafe asks, as he zips up his Barbour jacket and slips his hand onto Poppy's shoulder. 'Found your groom yet?'

Shit. Somehow I thought he was going to say 'boat'. With everything that's been going on, I never even thought about Dan. I suppose I should be grateful he isn't cheeking me for getting stuck on the island.

'Have you got a minute?' Poppy's trying not to smile, but it's bursting out. 'I promise it's something nice.'

'Nice?' At this very moment my dream would be to sink my teeth into one of her coffee cupcakes, with mocha butter-cream swirls and a topping of toasted almonds. But there's no hope of that, because she's heading away from the house.

'You'll have to come with us.' Jet the dog is rubbing on her legs and wagging his tail as they wait for me.

A moment later, instead of heading towards Alice in the holiday cottage, we're hurrying in the opposite direction, down the yard.

'It's going to be really cold tonight.' Rafe's breath is steaming in the night air as he rubs his hands and looks up at the sky. Between us, it's starrier than anything Alice could have ordered.

'Here we go.' As Poppy pushes through a stable door her voice is squeaking with excitement. 'You're *so* going to love this.'

Unless it's high-fat, high-sugar, with a mega-calorie count, and a caffeine burst thrown in too, I can't imagine being that ecstatic about anything on a farm. But the stable I follow them into is warm and dim.

'Over here.' Poppy gently closes the door and leads the way to where there's a light shining in the gloom.

As we peer over the wooden panel I can't help smiling too. 'Baby pigs?'

In the light pool there's a huge black-and-pink-spotted sow, lying on her side in the straw. Along her stomach, under a stronger light, there's a line of piglets, all suckling.

'This is Pandora. Her piglets were born yesterday.' Poppy whispers. 'Aren't they *so* cute?'

The babies are clean and golden, with black spots, and they're totally huggable.

'I didn't know this was a pig farm.' I'm wondering where the rest of the pigs are.

'It's not.' Poppy laughs. 'Rafe's started a pig family. So far he's got two mums both with babies. We're building up a variety of animals for the weddings. Guests love to see them and they're great for the photos too.'

Rafe scoops up a piglet, which is barely longer than his hand. 'Here.' He holds it so I can see its face. 'They grow really fast. When they're a few weeks old they'll be running around completely independently.'

'Whoa.' I step back as a speckled hen flutters out of nowhere, lands on the rail, and begins to peck at Rafe's hand. As farms go, this is a fast-forward introduction.

'Don't worry, this is one of Henrietta's children.' Poppy scratches the hen on the head. 'Henrietta's the office chicken and her children hang out anywhere they can around the farm buildings. The only place they refuse to roost is in the hen house.'

I lean my chin on the rail and count eight babies. 'I could watch them all night. You're going to need lots of names.' It's so calm in the half light of the stable, but hanging out with the pigs rather than with my sister maybe isn't the best plan. 'I better go and see how Alice is.'

'I popped some coffee cupcakes into the cottage earlier.' Poppy puts the hen down on the straw. 'After this morning I thought you might need them.' She pulls a face. 'I hope Immie didn't put her foot in it too much about Quinn and the runaway boat. She's world-famous for talking first and thinking later.'

'No worries.' Whatever Immie said about Quinn in the past, I'm sure today was an accident. 'And thanks for the cupcakes, they might just save me.' As I tiptoe out of the stable and back to the cottage, I'm wondering what Alice is going to say about it all.

25

'Hi Alice, I'm back.'

After everything that happened earlier today, I'm bracing myself as I open the door to Alice's cottage. As I throw down my jacket and my bag and make a beeline for the tin on the kitchen counter, I notice an open bottle of Pimms. 'What are you drinking?'

Her reply comes from the open bathroom door. 'Winter Warmer. Johnny gave me this lovely cordial. You put a big slurp in a glass, top it up with hot apple juice, then wind down and warm up. All at the same time.'

Where have I heard that before? Although Alice doesn't usually do alcohol.

She emerges, flops on the sofa, drops her full glass onto a

180

coaster on the table and tucks her feet up under her bathrobe. 'I think I almost prefer it to my Bottle Green lemon grass and ginger. It's even nicer than their festive spiced-berry cordial too.'

Alice is the only person I know who can keep fluffy snow-white bathrobes looking pristine for whole days, rather than five minutes. Especially when drinking coloured squash. Although if she's comparing those to Pimms she's hardly comparing like with like.

'You do know what Pimms is?' From where I'm standing, the word 'brandy' figures high up on the list of ingredients.

'Obviously.' Only Alice can say one word and wholeheartedly imply that I'm an idiot. But then she has had thirty years' practice. 'It's that lovely long summery drink with mint leaves you get at Henley and the Chelsea Flower Show. This is the Christmas version and it's not only delicious, it's very relaxing too.' She holds her glass up to the light. 'It must be the special herbs they put in.'

Just for now I'm not going to enlighten her, but I grab an orange. 'Like a slice of citrus in there?' All those fruit bowls are coming in useful after all.

'Thanks,' she holds out her glass for the orange. 'I borrowed your robe, by the way. Given you don't seem that keen on baths or lounging.'

So maybe the secret to looking like a washing powder ad is simple. Take someone else's dressing gown. And ask about it later. Note to self: Watch and learn.

Alice picks up a pencil and a book, which catches my attention because it's the first time I've seen her looking at anything other than a wedding list for ages.

When I realise what she's doing, I do a double-take. 'Are you colouring, Alice?'

She pauses and looks up. 'Actually colouring's not as relaxing as you'd think. The pressure to finish is immense.'

'I can imagine.' Only Alice could make colouring a high-stress activity. The way she's tapping her crayon on her teeth could get quite annoying if she's going to do this a lot. 'What's the theme, then?'

The look she sends me is another of the ones where she despairs of my intelligence, or rather my lack of it. 'Our wedding. Obviously.' That thought softens her expression. 'I had the books specially created to send out with the invitations. I'm surprised you haven't brought yours with you.'

Oh my. Something else I'm missing from that damned A4 embossed envelope. My excuse is the first thing I can pluck from the air. 'I had no idea we'd have time for colouring…' Catching Alice's horrified frown I try again. 'We're very behind here with social trends. Colouring therapy hasn't hit St Aidan yet.' I'm onto a winner this time, judging by her eye roll.

'That figures.' She's surveying her page with a critical eye. 'It's such a backwater. And so dull. Seriously, I have no idea how you survive here full time.'

And we're back on track again. Finally, I brace myself to ask. 'So how's things?'

As she selects her next pencil, she lets out a sigh. 'Not good.'

'Any sign of…?'

She fills in her own blank and cuts me off. 'No.' There's a snap and her pencil point skims across the floorboards. Without comment, she pulls out another crayon.

Given she wrecked her crayon, I presume we *are* both talking about Dan here. 'Don't worry,' I say, determined to do my job as bridesmaid, and offer positive support. Regardless of my own panic, or doubts. 'I'm sure he'll be along as soon as he can be.' Let's face it, if he doesn't damn well hurry up, he's going to damn well miss his own damn wedding.

She lets out a bitter laugh, then bites her lip. 'Apart from that, Quinn says the disco floor's a write-off. And Hetty plus her entire catering team are stuck on the tarmac at JFK. Grounded by a blizzard in New York.'

'Shit... fuck... bollocks...' I'm working through for a suitable Alice-friendly expletive. 'I mean "bells". Hells bells, even.' At least someone's got snow.

'I know.' She runs her fingers through her bob. 'It's only thanks to this Pimms stuff I'm not losing it completely. It's a total godsend. Like bloody rescue remedy. Only stronger. And longer.' She holds out her glass. 'Be a sweetie and pour us both some more before you sit down.'

Given Alice is being nice enough to call me that, I assume she's well on her way to alcoholic oblivion. So I deliver her a stiff drink to make sure she reaches her destination a.s.a.p., and get a plain apple juice for myself. As I flop down in front of the log burner, I'm half worrying we're going to struggle to find things to talk about, but she gets in first.

'I told him exactly what I thought, you know.'

Oh dear. This isn't sounding good. I summon my inner confident bridesmaid again. 'Really?' Maybe this is why Dan's still AWOL.

As she goes on there's a note of triumph in her voice. 'Finally, after half my life, I have closure on my first relationship.'

And the penny drops. How slow am I? She's not talking

about Dan here at all, she's talking about George. And what went down along with the spicy crab canapes at The Shark and Shrimp. Or was it The Shrimp and Shark?

'You have no idea how good it made me feel, Sera.'

I'm pleased one of us did. I was worried sick all day. But it seems too long ago to bring that up now. 'You stayed over?'

'I blamed the weather, but that wasn't the whole story. There was so much to say, we stayed up all night.'

Those few Pimmsy alcohol units are acting like a truth drug.

My happy inner bridesmaid is withering by the second. 'You stayed up all night? With your ex?' If my voice is going high, it's because I'm shocked. Appalled even. I suppose it's marginally better than going to bed with him. But all the same, right now I'm feeling like one of those judgemental, narrow-minded people who write to the papers and sign themselves 'Indignant, of St Aidan'.

'We had so much to talk about.' She isn't even apologetic.

From what she's said so far, we're lucky she's come back at all. Sorry, it might be nothing to do with me, but I have to ask. 'So what was the outcome?'

'It was wonderful.' The more she's gushing, the more my heart sinks. 'He was so easy to talk to. It was as if fifteen years never happened. Although, obviously it did. He has kids now, and an ex. The woman he went on to after me.'

More and more dangerous. And, not wanting to take the spotlight off Alice, but so different from me and Johnny, and our awkward half lines.

'You didn't want to…?' I can't bear to say the words.

Alice fills in. 'Get back with him? Not at all. That was why it was so awesome from my point of view. All these years I've wondered about this parallel life I might have been living, with the guy a tiny part of me never gave up loving. And yesterday made me see that it wasn't something I'd ever have wanted at all.'

I'm open-mouthed at what I'm hearing.

'What's more, I saw why we'd never have worked. George was lovely, and clever, but he was so ordinary. So lacking in style. And so happy with his country town lot. Believe me, I wouldn't have lasted two minutes as a GP's wife in deepest Cornwall.'

My thoughts exactly, but I can't say that. So I just say, 'So was he hoping to get back with you?'

She thinks long and hard about that. 'Maybe. At first. But by the end he realised it was the fantasy of first love he was hooked on rather than me. Me in the flesh, years older, wasn't the person he thought he loved at all.'

'Don't you think it was a risky game?'

She purses her lips. 'I believe if we'd worked as a couple, we'd still be together. We had our time when we were teenagers. It ended when we grew into different people. I was pretty confident of that before I went to meet up. But it's still nice to have set myself free, after all this time. Him too.'

Note to self: *If we'd worked as a couple, we'd be together.* I mentally underline that. Twice. And stick it in my pending box. Where I can see it clearly, with every blink of my mind's eye.

'Clever old Alice.' I give her a thumbs-up, and waggle my glass at her. This is why she's so successful. Because she's so damned smart and has so much self-knowledge. 'And what a great way to go forward to marry Dan. With that one tiny doubt wiped out.'

That's what's so funny with sisters. How one can be so damned perceptive – Alice. And the other hasn't a clue – moi. Although that reminds me, I'm better at pidgin French than she is, but that's the only area I beat her in. And it's only because of our au pairs. It's the same with the drive. Alice has enough for both of us and it passed me by entirely.

'I'm not exactly sure about the going-forward part.' The way she's rubbing her nose is a sure sign she's not a hundred per cent happy.

'So where's the problem?' She spent the night with her ex, found out she's marrying the right guy. How could it possibly be any better? People say every cloud has a silver lining. But I'm not sure which is the cloud here and which is the lining.

'When George and I talked, it was easy. We couldn't stop. But it reminded me how it used to be with Dan.'

'And it isn't like that now?'

The pencil is rattling on her teeth again. 'Dan and I haven't talked like that for years. These days we barely see each other, let alone talk.'

'You've been busy planning a wedding.' For three years that I know of. 'And working to afford it.' I miss out the bit about it being gratuitously enormous, and the strain that must bring. I'm sure she doesn't need me to rub that in.

'Seeing George might have been good to lay the ghosts to rest. But if I come back seeing there's a bloody great chasm between Dan and I, that wasn't so damned clever after all, was it?'

Oh my. It's like she's been taking swearing lessons from Immie.

'Some days I feel like the wedding is bigger than the relationship. As the wedding grew, it strangled the love. Like I'm marrying a stranger.'

Fuck, fuck, fuck. Any one of those statements would be a bombshell. But three in the same breath? What is the insightful supportive bridesmaid's reply to that lot? Is this the Pimms talking? Or the bride who's shitting herself with pre-wedding nerves? Or the smart, insightful woman who's had a moment of clarity? And do I agree and talk her out of the whole thing? Or try to change her mind and talk her into a loveless marriage? Talk about being out of my depth here – more like I'm drifting in the Pacific. Or maybe the Atlantic? I'm still no nearer deciding how to answer when Alice saves me by going on.

'I'm not sure about the bridesmaids' dresses either.' Her voice is small and shaky. And it's such a relief she's moved on to this more tangible problem.

'Really?' Great. Empathy. I know exactly where she's coming from on that one. Although I wouldn't advise her to change anything as radical as dresses at this point.

'I haven't seen the dresses against mine. I'm not sure they'll go together. I'm not sure I even like my dress.' She's getting pretty whiney now, as the negativity snowballs.

'First thing in the morning, we'll try them.' It's the best this sub-standard bridesmaid can offer, for now. And then I spy it. The cake tin on the side. How could I have got side-tracked enough to forget Poppy's cupcakes? I thunder across to them and grab some plates. And a fork. I can't see Alice proceeding without, can you?

A second later I'm wafting nuts and mocha buttercream right under Alice's nose. 'I guarantee this cupcake is going to make *everything* feel better.' Which may be asking a lot of a cupcake – but it's my only hope.

As I bite into mine and the bitter-sweet flavours of coffee and dark chocolate fuse on my tongue I know this will hit the spot for me. I'm just not so sure Alice's problems are the kind that can be wiped away with a sugar rush.

26

Thursday, 22nd December
At Brides by the Sea: Zip codes and parental boxes

Bringing Alice's London designer wedding dress into Brides by the Sea was pretty much top of my 'not to do' list. Frankly, as bad ideas go, it's scoring top marks. When Alice woke up this morning, luckily for me she wasn't talking about loving – or not loving – Dan. But she was still wanting to see the bridesmaid's dress next to hers. Alice's dress is so minimalist it travels in the kind of slender cover that is barely there. Whereas my bridesmaid's dress is so huge and humungous now it's fully fluffed out, it pretty much requires its own removal van for transportation. So, despite my better judgement, by nine on the dot we're creeping into the shop. I've warned Jess we're coming and flagged up that we're wobbling. So if Jess isn't happy, just this once she's going to have to suck it up.

'Here we go…' I'm holding Alice's dress in the air with one hand, struggling to hang onto it in the force-ten wind, and fumbling to unlock the door with the other, when Alice's hangover fog suddenly clears.

'Sera, Sera, why's your name painted on the shop window?'

How a few white letters can bring her back into the room, when a kale and kiwi smoothie completely failed, I have no idea. Between us, I had to hide the Pimms earlier too, because she was hell-bent on having a high ball of 'that delicious cordial' again. Sometime soon I may have to tell her the awful truth about the alcohol content, but maybe I'll wait until after the wedding. Let's face it, every bridesmaid needs her Bridezilla-taming weapon and Winter Warmer could be mine. Johnny might be sticking his oar in right left and centre with Quinn, but at least he came through on that one.

'Paint on the window?' Pushing through into the entrance, I flick on the tree lights and fling out an excuse. 'Graffiti… happens all the time… we just haven't cleaned it off yet.' In my rush to sort out Alice's problems I've momentarily over-looked how family scrutiny makes me wither. They can't help being critical. At home they make me feel about as important as a worm. They were so dismissive of my fashion choice, I didn't bother to send them invitations to my degree show. And thus far I've managed to keep them out of my professional life. If Alice wasn't having a bride crisis of epic proportions, we wouldn't be within ten miles of the shop.

'Enjoy the Jimmy Choos, I'll be back in a minute' I hang her dress on a hook in The White Room and point her to a Louis Quatorze chair. With any luck the shoe display will keep her occupied while I grab my bridesmaid's dress from the store.

I swear it's only a few seconds before I'm haring back, hurrying so much I'm stumbling over the bursting dress bag. But when I reach The White Room it's empty.

'Bugger.' I'm cursing under my breath. 'Alice… where are you?' When I call it's in the kind of sweet voice you'd use to tempt a naughty kitten to come back. I'm rustling back across the entrance hall with my bundle, when I catch a glimpse of her flicking through the dresses on the rails beyond the Christmas tree. And holy shit, somehow she's wandered into the Seraphina East room. I accelerate and arrive breathless at her elbow.

When she turns to me, her brows are knotted into a puzzled frown. 'Graffiti, my foot. Why didn't you tell us what you were doing, Sera?' She's using that accusing stare she does. On a scale of one to ten, where one is low and ten is off the scale, the intensity is twelve.

I ram my dress onto a hook in the fitting room and hurtle back into The White Room to get hers. Then I hang that up too and find the patch of wall to lean my back against. 'There was nothing to tell.' My chin's jutting now. 'Who in our family would have cared I was a designer?' No one was ever interested in what I was doing. Apart from going ape when I failed.

Alice gently fingers a lace strap. 'But these are beautiful.' Her voice is almost a whisper now. As she runs her fingers through her hair and shakes her head her frown softens. 'I can't believe we didn't know, that's all.'

'Fashion didn't exactly tick the parental boxes.' When I hook my foot around my leg I feel less stressed. *A worthless waste of time.* Not that I'd throw it back at Alice now, but that's what my entire high-flying family said about my degree. Including her.

Alice has worked her way around to the celebrity photos. As she picks one up she's literally gawping. 'And you even did a dress for Josie Redman? *The* Josie Redman?'

I blow upwards to clear the sweat from my forehead. Sometimes it feels like that celebrity dress is going to haunt me forever. And how come starchy old Alice has even heard of Josie? She wouldn't be seen dead near anything as down-market as a copy of *Hello!* magazine.

'It was no big…' I'm about to say 'deal', when I'm cut off in mid-sentence.

'It certainly was *the* Josie Redman.'

Oh my. It's Jess. Still exploding with pride about Josie. And from the way she's stamping, she's come to give Alice a piece of her mind. If I wasn't leaning on the wall, I'd have to collapse on the sofa because the thought of this confrontation has turned my legs to jelly. Disapproving Jess, bumping into London-centric Alice, in the sodding Seraphina East room. Add in the treacherous dress and worst-case scenarios don't get any more awful. My best hope is to make a run for the kitchen and leave them to fight it out.

But just this once I don't. Much to my surprise, I'm moving my mouth. What's more, words are coming out. 'This is Jess, the force behind Brides by the Sea. She's my mentor and butt-kicker.'

'And you must be Alice?' As Jess jumps forward to shake hands, the force almost snaps Alice's wrist off. 'If you don't mind me saying, it's time you woke up to how wonderfully talented your sister is and how much she's done for this shop.'

As Alice takes back her hand, she's rubbing her arm. 'If you don't mind me saying, it's lovely to be let into the secret of what Sera's actually doing with her life,' she says icily.

Jess is peering at Alice like a hawk. 'You didn't know?' As Alice shakes her head, Jess's eyebrows go skywards and she lets out a snort. 'Well, that explains a lot.'

I'm bracing myself for the fallout. But Jess isn't looking at me. Instead her gaze falls to the floor, and she's honing in on the cream-leather toes sticking out from under Alice's pale grey cigarette pants.

'Excuse me, but are those Gucci Horsebits?' Jess is drooling the way I do when I come face to face with a coffee cupcake.

'Yes.' Alice's mouth softens. 'I'm afraid I have some in every colour.' She sounds as if she's confessing a deep vice here, but I assume they're talking shoes.

'Me too.' Jess lifts up the hem of her wide-leg trousers to show a navy version. 'Have you tried the driving moccasins?'

Oh my. Who would have thought they'd be bonding over loafers.

Alice clasps her hands. 'Yes. They're so comfy, aren't they? Did you find any of the backless flowery summer ones?'

Staring down at my beaten-up ankle boots, I'm suddenly feeling marginalised.

Jess rolls her eyes. 'The Princetown grey ones were like rocking-horse shit. I had to have mine couriered from Paris. Did you get your hands on any?'

As Alice nods I cough. 'Not wanting to get in the way of the Gucci love, but are you going to try your dress on, Alice?'

'Of course.' Jess is straight in there. 'But how about some

prosecco first? Or better still, while Sera helps you into your dress, I'll make you one of my bride's specials… guaranteed to relax you.' We all know Jess's drinks veer towards coma-inducing rather than relaxing, but given I'm driving it probably doesn't matter what Alice has.

As she hears the word 'relax', Alice perks up. 'Thanks, that sounds fab.' And hooray that for once she isn't insisting on boring old mineral water.

Jess whisks back the fitting-room curtain and comes to a strategic halt, her hand hovering over Alice's dress cover. 'May I?' Sometimes she's such a pro. Well, every time, really.

'Please do.' Alice is perching on the sofa edge, her arms tightly crossed.

Jess smiles her 'cat in the cream factory' smile, as she eases down the zip. 'I've never un-wrapped a Givenchy before. This one's so light, it's barely there.' As she steps back and pulls the cover off the slimmest satin column, she lets out a low purr of appreciation. 'Wonderful.' She looks at Alice. 'Come on then… we'll help you into it, then I'll sort the drinks.'

As Jess and I stand outside staring at the white-on-white stripes of the fitting-room curtain, and waiting for Alice to strip and wriggle into her dress, I can't help thinking how different that dress is from anything here. When I come back to earth, Jess is scrutinising my nose.

'I couldn't see it on Skype, but you two are very alike, you know.'

I pull a face 'I don't think so'. I'm twirling a lock of wavy blonde hair around my fingers, because in thirty years, no one has said that before.

She frowns. 'Obviously your hair isn't the same.' At least

Jess is conceding that. 'But if you look beyond that, you're like two peas. Especially your expressions.'

What? Surely I don't look that uptight and constipated. I'm about to take her up on this when the curtain moves and Alice's face pops out. 'Please can you do me up?'

That's the cue for us both to fight our way through into the fitting room, which thankfully is wide enough for the worst-case capacity of a bride with a massive entourage in tow.

As I catch a view of the front of the dress, I can't help gasping. 'Oh, Alice, it's amazing.' The high collar is slashed at the throat, and the bodice somehow skims and clings at the same time. It's simple, yet so sophisticated. 'And it's so fab with your bob.' What's more it's pure, unadulterated silk. There's not a single sequin, or bead, or bow.

Unsurprisingly, Jess has got into pole-fastening position around the back, so I don't fight her. But from where I'm standing I can see Alice grimacing.

'It's feeling a bit tight.' She's smoothing the fabric over her ribs.

'That's probably just the cut,' I say, because it's very unforgiving. There's nothing to spare. Straight up and down doesn't begin to cover it, but Alice has the figure to carry it off. 'It'll be better when the fabric warms up and gives.' I'm thinking how a millimetre or two will make all the difference, when I'm awestruck for a second time. 'Alice, for the first time in your entire life you look like you have boobs.'

Alice stares at me blankly. 'No, I definitely don't.'

We all know I won't be arguing. It's probably the clever cut of this super-high-end dress. Or the fact that the cashmere jumpers she wears every day fit so loosely, I haven't noticed her filling out. Maybe there's hope for my flat chest after all.

'Sera, can you come and help me here.' It's Jess, with her tetchy voice on. And although she's frowning, she can't possibly have got the zip stuck. She knows better than to do that on a Givenchy. 'When did you say you had the fittings for this, Alice?'

'About a month ago.' Alice runs a hand through her bob. 'The dress was perfect. All they had to do was the hem. I tried it on again when I picked it up a week later.'

As I join Jess around the back of the dress I take in the finest of zips, with loops and buttons that fasten across once the zip's done up. But most of all I take in Jess, frantically trying to squeeze the zipper edges together. And a wide strip of bare flesh right either side of Alice's spine.

'And you tried the dress and saw them pack it up?' Jess is asking. She's skilfully twisted Alice around, so Alice can't catch a view of her back in the mirror opposite.

As we exchange wild-eyed glances, I can't believe Jess is managing to sound so calm.

'Yes, I zipped up the dress cover in the fitting room myself. They make you do that.' Alice is as definite about that as she is that her boobs haven't grown. 'Why, is there a problem?'

I'm so pleased Jess is with me to handle this. I've no idea what the hell has gone wrong, but how do you break it to your sister that she's chosen a dress with nothing to let out in the seams, which is currently looking like it's at least four inches too small.

Jess purses her lips. 'It's actually a very good thing you've tried your dress on today, Alice, this far ahead of the wedding…' Her voice is incredibly level and controlled, given the bombshell she's about to drop. 'You suspected there might be a problem, and I'm going to level with you here…' She's doing as much preparation as she can, but eventually she's going to have to come out with it. 'I'm not sure we're going to be able to get the zip up.' She holds my gaze behind Alice's head.

As we wait for her to blow, my eyes feel like they're going to explode from the pressure in my head. One, two, three, four…

'Wh-a-a-a-t?' When it comes it's a howl.

Jess waits for the werewolf noise to end. 'You were so right when you said the dress was feeling a bit tight.' Carefully Jess guides Alice's hands onto her back so she can feel the width of the problem for herself. 'Here.' She spins her around by a few degrees so she can get a complete back view.

'Oh my fucking…' Alice wails. 'What the hell happened?'

Jess moves around to face Alice and as she takes her hand she's talking quietly. 'You aren't the first bride to have a dress that doesn't fit. And you won't be the last. It's a dreadful shock and completely devastating. But there are two things working in your favour. First, you have time to spare, and second…' She scans the rails of white dresses. 'You couldn't be in a better place. So stay calm and trust us. We're going to sort this out.'

When people talk about wringing their hands, until this moment I thought it was a move that only existed in the heads of soap-opera directors. But here I am, one hand clenched inside the other in front of my chest, living out my own dramatic cliché. And even though Jess has pointed out we have wedding dresses coming out of our ears, I know there's nothing remotely like Alice's dress on the rails at Brides by the Sea. As for what went wrong, Jess leap-frogged that question very neatly. She's right that we need solutions not explanations. But how the hell did we end up here?

'Why don't I get those drinks?' I say. For one time only, it's not an excuse for me to hide in the kitchen. It's just because Alice and Jess couldn't look paler if they'd been sprayed with fake snow. They need something to bring them round.

Jess suggests instead, 'You stay here and look after Alice. I'll go to the kitchen.'

Unlike me, Jess hates doing the fridge run. There's only one time Jess takes charge of drinks – when she knows they have to be super-strong. I hope Alice likes gin.

27

Thursday, 22nd December
At Brides by the Sea:
Medicine bottles and Christmas macaroons

'English Garden meets Christmas Crash,' Jess says, as she drops dashes of elderflower cordial and ginger ale into tumblers, then adds gin. 'With some *Anges de Sucre* macaroons.'

As I top them up with prosecco and toss in a mint sprig, I can't help thinking a strong cup of tea and half a ton of short bread might have been better. After helping Alice out of the dress, I left her on a sofa, doing a pretty good impression of a mute ghost, and came to hurry Jess along.

'Is it okay if I grab a bottle of Bride's Mum's Fentimans?' I ask, hoping the sugar rush and gentle fizz of the lemonade might revive me.

Jess passes me a glass. 'Help yourself. You might want to

pick up a couple of pregnancy tests later too.' She says it as airily as if she's telling me to buy a packet of rich tea biscuits.

'Sorry?' I feel like I've accidentally landed in the wrong conversation somewhere along the line here. Which is weird. It's not as if anyone's even started drinking yet.

'You'll need at least two,' she says, which wasn't the bit I was querying. 'Probably more. People rarely believe the first one.'

I shake my head. 'Why would I need *any*?' When, as Quinn so deftly pointed out, I live like a monk. I assumed Jess knew that too.

Jess does her 'no hope' eye roll. 'Not you, Sera, obviously. I'm talking about Alice.'

Oh my. 'But why would you think that?'

'Brides always lose weight before the wedding, even if they stuff themselves. It's physically impossible to keep weight on with all that adrenalin surging around their systems.' She's whispering at me now. 'The only way to grow four inches too big for your wedding dress in a month is if you're... well, you know...' She makes her eyes wide. But thankfully this time she's stopped short of saying the word.

'In which case, maybe gin's not the best idea?'

The way Jess scoops up the tray, I know she's going to override me on that. 'The gin's entirely medicinal. But slip her a test, just to be on the safe side.' She sends me a significant look as she clatters through to The White Room.

'Sure.' I'm being ironic here, muttering as I follow her. 'Bridesmaids get all the best jobs.' And let's face it, they don't come much worse than telling your sister you think she's pregnant, when she obviously hasn't got the first clue herself.

Like I'm going to be able to bring up the subject at all let alone persuade her to pee on a sodding stick.

It's a long time since I've seen Alice this silent. She takes a few sips of her cocktail when Jess gives it to her. 'Thank you...' she says eventually. 'That's nice. Is there elderflower cordial in here?' She sounds like she's swapped voices with someone else while we were in the kitchen. The one she's ended up with is too weedy and shaky for a no-nonsense power house like her.

Jess nods. 'Bottle Green.' She says it as if it couldn't be anything else.

Alice nods appreciatively. After a few more sips, she begins to look slightly less like a corpse bride. 'The grapefruit and honeysuckle they do is good too.' At least now there's more colour in her cheeks. Before they were as washed out as her cream cashmere polo neck.

As soon as Jess finishes her next slurp she replies. 'Have you tried the apple and plum one?'

Oh my. What are these two like? First Gucci loafers and now Bottle Green cordials. As a reformed Red Bull addict, whose soft drink of choice would be Lime Pepsi, I have nothing to add here. The best I can hope for is that they'll do a quantum leap and end up discussing hot chocolate. I can enthuse over that all day. I'm wondering if it would be really rude to leave them to it and nip up to the studio, when I hear the door opening. A moment later Poppy and Immie breeze in, bringing a large gust of the Siberian gale that's howling outside.

Poppy's taking down the hood of her parka. 'Great we've found you, Sera. We went across to Rose Hill first, but we missed you.'

Jess beams. 'Macaroon anyone?' She hands the box to Poppy. 'And how are things going at The Manor?'

I try to catch Jess's eye by doing a frantic eyebrow wiggle to flag up to her she's on very dangerous ground here. I know she's trying to steer the conversation as far away from the dress 'situation' as she can. But she'd have been better sticking to juices and cordials, because when we called into The Manor on our way over, nothing was moving forward. And Alice was not a happy bunny.

Poppy offers the macaroons to Immie, who takes a handful, then crashes onto a Louis Quatorze chair.

'It's that bloody Quinn,' Immie says, as she hoovers up her first macaroon and swallows it whole. If she carries on like that she's never going to work out if all the different colours have their own tastes. 'He couldn't organise a piss-up in a pig farm.'

'He couldn't?' I watch as the next three macaroons disappear from Immie's palm. Pink. Peacock blue. Orange. They're gone in as many seconds.

'For someone who supposedly makes things happen, he's made shit-all progress.' She gives a snort of disgust. 'If he thinks he'll be ready for a wedding in two days' time, he's deluding himself.' Reaching over she scoops up another fistful of macaroons.

Not that I'm biased at all, but I think she's being a bit unfair on Quinn. It's down to more of us than just him. And it's all very well dishing out the criticism. But what we need are solutions. And people who will concentrate on a job and finish it. Rather than start it and waft away ten seconds later. When I dare to steal a look at Alice, instead of looking horror-struck,

I'm shocked to see that behind the ginger macaroon she's nibbling on, her lips are twitching.

'Quinn always leaned on his PA more than his publicist.' Alice sighs and shakes her head. Immie's 'tell it how it is' attitude might be blunt, but it's resonating with Alice.

Poppy gently lifts the macaroon box out of Immie's reach.

Immie clears her throat. 'Actually I've come to offer Chas and his fireman mates… to help. Honestly, Blue Watch will sort you out in no time.'

Poppy chimes in with her support. 'They're ace on ladders, and they did a great job with the twigs and lights in the tipi last summer – when Chas *didn't* get married.'

Long story. He and Immie met when his Daisy Hill wedding went off the rails at the eleventh hour, but the party carried on. Not that we want to dwell on weddings getting called off.

'The guys are on their Christmas pub crawl tonight, so tomorrow will be a write-off.' Immie's eye roll ends up as a broad grin. 'But they're free today. Say the word and they're all yours.'

It sounds too good to be true. We've got the branches, but only because it was the kind of adventuring Quinn enjoyed, I was starting to doubt they'd ever get off the ground. As I send Alice a querying glance, she's nodding so vigorously, for once her hair is a total disaster.

'Brilliant. Couldn't be better. Thanks so much for that, Immie.' I'm mentally punching the air.

'I'll get them along right away.'

'We've got a tiny bit more to do here,' Jess adds. She can be so diplomatic.

'Go for it.' Immie's up, ransacking the macaroons again.

'We'll get straight off and see you at Rose Hill later.' She's in such a rush to round up her firemen she careers out into the hallway and crashes headlong into the Christmas tree. 'Fuck… shit… festering snowmen…'

But along with the string of expletives as colourful as the macaroons, there's another sound.

'Bells?' Alice leaps to her feet. 'Sleigh bells? Exactly what we need for Snowball's harness.' She's been reunited with her own voice and as she dashes across The White Room she's sending Jess an imploring smile. 'I don't suppose we could borrow a couple?'

A second later we're in the hall, stripping the Brides by the Sea Christmas tree.

But even though Alice is having a momentary distraction from her bigger problem, as we unhook the bells from the branches, I'm wondering where the hell we're going to find her a couture column wedding dress two days before Christmas.

28

Thursday, 22nd December
On the way to Rose Hill Manor:
Strategies, jitters and surprises.

'Phone signal? That's almost as much of a novelty in Cornwall as having your husband-to-be turn up for his wedding.'

It's Alice, we're zooming along the road towards Rose Hill, and if she's said that once since we left St Aidan, she's said it... Well, put it this way, who would have thought it was possible to express two random thoughts a) Cornwall's a bit quiet and b) you could be happier with your fiancé, in so many different sentences that all mean the same thing.

Okay. I know we should be at Brides by the Sea, focusing on the 'where the hell do we go next?' wedding dress question. But just as we got the last bell off the tree, there was a beep from Alice's phone, announcing – ta-da – there will be a bridegroom after all. What's more, he's heading for The Manor as we speak.

As we drive through Rose Hill village, past the pretty stone cottages that line the high street, Alice finally stops running her fingers through her hair. A second later, her hand lands on my arm. 'Slow down, Sera. Or maybe, stop. I need to decide if I want to get there before Dan. Or after him.' It's rare for Alice to be this indecisive. Although going in with a firm strategy is her all over.

I pull over by the green, next to the village Christmas tree. 'So, what are you thinking?' It's a tentative question and I've deliberately left out any emotive words. Like 'feeling', 'problem', or 'wobble'. As I listen to her breathing, I count the lights on the tree. Seventy-six red. 84 blue. I'm up to ninety-nine yellow when she finally breaks my concentration.

'I'm a bit jittery.' Her voice has done that disappearing trick again. She dips into the pack of jelly babies I bought her earlier, then offers me one.

'And?' I ask, taking a red one. Maybe I'll get to count the green lights while she thinks about this. But no.

'That's all.' She sighs, then lapses into silent chewing. When we were kids we used to fight over the red jelly babies. Alice always won, obviously. But she's not that fighty today. Let's face it, if she's let me get a red one, she's really off her game.

When Quinn drummed his fingers on the steering wheel I thought he was being a bit of a poser. But suddenly I'm doing it. What's more surprising is, it's helping me see we shouldn't be dithering. So I go for it. And if we're talking new voices, the one I've found belongs to someone pretty damned bossy and uncompromising.

'Well, we can sit here all day counting lights on Christmas trees…' Understandably I get a blank look from Alice for that but I haul out that sassy smile I learned with Poppy. 'Or… how about we roll with the punches, get up to The Manor, and take it as it comes? I'm sure you'll be fine as soon as you see Dan. You can always hide behind the crowd of firemen.' Given they're fast responders, I'm assuming Blue Watch are already there, transforming the ballroom. And what is the collective name for more firemen than you can count on one hand? A hose? A splash? An engine-full?

'Okay. You could be right,' she agrees, kicking the bags at her feet as she recrosses her legs. When she dips down into own her bag her squawk is loud enough to startle a passing dog-walker. 'Sera, what the hell's this?' Even the dog stops in its tracks and stares at the car, as Alice scoops up my crumpled carrier from the mat well.

'Oh.' As the Tesco Metro bag splays open, I watch, helpless, as a Clearblue pregnancy test falls out into her lap. Talk about screwing this up. It seemed such a great idea to hit the shop for sweets and the tests, so I was fully equipped and ready, should the moment arise. I just wasn't expecting it to be quite this soon.

Before I can say any more she's jumped in. 'Sera, you're not…? Really…? Are you…?'

Talk about a happy accident. The ideal opening to bring up the subject. Or maybe not. The appalled expression on Alice's face makes me chicken out completely. 'A teensy false alarm.'

I say, knowing I have to take this on myself. 'I'm pretty sure it's nothing. But I just wanted to check, anyway.'

As she peers into the bag she laughs. 'What three boxes? That's six tests. Buying them for all your friends too? I've heard of fertility festivals but this is ridiculous. Are pregnancy tests a group activity down in Cornwall?'

I pull a face. 'It's always good to have a backup. Just to be certain.' It's the perfect opening to suggest a mass pee on sticks behind the hedge for the two of us, then we could get this over with here and now. But I'm not that brave. And although I grabbed the tests on impulse along with the jelly babies, in reality the pregnancy question is probably be the last thing we want to throw into the wedding mix right now.

'Sorry, I didn't mean to joke about something this serious.' An anxious frown has chased off her smile, as her hand lands on my arm again. 'If it isn't good news and you need to talk, I'm always here. You know that, don't you?' She gives me a squeeze, firmly back into big-sister mode. Strong. Concerned. Responsible. And between us, that's a thousand times easier to handle than wobbly bride.

'Back at you,' I say, with a lot more irony than she suspects. Although the jolly thump I give her on her shoulder is only to hide how bad I'm feeling for not coming out with the truth – as I suspect it. 'Great, well if you've got all those boxes safely back in the bag, shall we go then?'

As I slam the car into gear and roar off up the lane, I probably deserve the disgusted looks the dog-walker and the dog are dishing out to me. Yes, from the spinning wheels and the shower of gravel I'm leaving behind, I'm driving like Quinn.

But it's only so I can get Alice to Rose Hill before she has a chance to go weak again.

As for what will happen when we get there, as we race up the drive and catch sight of Snowball out in the field, I'm definitely grabbing a white horse wish.

29

Thursday, 22nd December
At Rose Hill Manor: Rare beasts and sharp edges

In the race to get to Rose Hill Manor first, Alice wins. When we pull up outside the house in my gran's mini, Dan's Range Rover is spectacularly absent. But on the upside, from the mini bus and handful of cars, it looks like Blue Watch are already here. So to take Alice's mind off Dan, rather than freezing our butts off waiting out in the car park, which is what she wants to do, I bundle her through the house to the ballroom.

I'm not being sexist here. And I definitely don't want to get caught up in the male objectification trap. I mean, some people disapprove of stopping for too long to admire muscly men up step ladders. But, on the other hand, the sight of a great team of guys working well together is heart-warming in a peculiarly satisfying way. And even though Blue Watch – plus Rafe, who's tagged along too – can't have been here for more than half an hour, by the time Alice and I get to the ballroom, there is plenty to smile about. And before you jump to conclusions, this has nothing to do with me and my one-woman-strong 'Quinn Appreciation Society' either. Because Quinn is nowhere to be seen.

'The branches are flying up,' Poppy says happily. She and Immie are directing from the ground, as Chas and his friends work like lightning, running up and down ladders, hanging branches off the ceiling trusses, and threading fairy lights through the twigs. Poppy steps back and nods up at the ceiling. 'The first truss is finished and lit. What do you think? Is it working?'

As Alice and I stand, gazing up at the cloud of twigs hanging across the room, studded with a galaxy of tiny light spots, there's a long, long silence. Eventually I dare to sneak a sideways peek, to judge her expression, but her fist is over her mouth so I can't tell. At least she's not running her fingers through her hair.

'So?' I prompt, holding my breath. Somehow I daren't say how dreamy it looks, in case she's about to shout it down.

Alice purses her lips. 'It definitely isn't anything like the celestial sky I was wanting…' Up their ladders, the guys stop their hooking and winding and tying, and are suddenly still. In the ominous pause that follows, every eyeball in the room is glued to Alice, and every stomach in the room is hanging, ready to plummet.

'But…' She takes a breath. 'It's just like the pictures you showed me, Sera… And from what I can see this far…' She scrunches up her face as she deliberates. 'It's looking promising.'

'Phew.' I say, beaming around the room, trying to compensate for my sister being queen of the understatement. 'Woohoo, we'll take that as a "yes" then.' I punch the air and do a little circle and high-five everyone in reach with a free hand. Although right now, I might be a bitch, but I *wish* Alice could be just a little less matter of fact and a bit more enthusiastic.

She looks up at Chas. 'Thanks so much, guys, you're doing a great job. I really appreciate you stepping in to help with my wedding like this.'

Which is better than nothing, so that wish just came true. Although if we're talking white-horse wishes, I saved that for something a lot more crucial than the ceiling. There's a minor rumble of gratitude for the appreciation among the guys as they go back to work.

Immie's beside us now, muttering. 'Quinn buggers off, things get done. Anyone noticed the reverse correlation?'

Alice hones straight in on Immie's criticism. 'So where's our dandy highwayman gone today, then?'

'Does chasing a disco floor mean anything to you?' Immie rolls her eyes at Alice. 'Exactly the kind of wild-goose chase our Quinn specialises in.'

Alice shakes her head. 'The sky was my dream, the disco floor was for the guys'. Guess which one they're running around the country after?'

'Who's talking about wild-goose chases?'

Alice stiffens as a low voice resonates from the next room.

A second later Dan appears in the doorway, pulling his woolly hat off his dishevelled dark hair, rubbing his stubble behind his huge scarf. 'Hey Sera… lovely to see you.' Given he practically falls over me as he walks in, I'm the first to get one of his trademark bear-hugs. 'I can see you're all busy here.'

'Great to see you too.' I go in for a squeeze that's so hard it whooshes every bit of air out of my lungs. If I'm laughing like a mad thing, that's more to cover up my relief that he's here. 'How's my future brother-in-law? Still as handsome as ever, I see.'

Between us, he's going to scrub up into a fabulous groom. Now he's arrived, that is. Dan's one of the rarest of beasts – a geek in hunk's clothing. Six-four and built, but behind those boy-next-door good looks, he's hiding a super-brain. What's more, he's kind and easy-going, and best of all, he adores Alice. Has done since they were teenagers. There's something about his relaxed warmth that smoothes down her sharper edges.

'To be honest, I'm effing freezing.' Dan shrugs further into his duvet jacket and rubs his hands. 'Whatever happened to the warm wet west?'

Rafe who's wandering by with a branch, stops. 'Too cold for snow, too,' he says with a laugh. 'Unless it warms up some we won't be having a white Christmas.'

Or a white wedding either. But has Alice taken this on board? Right now she's standing apart from the crowd, hanging onto her wedding manual like it's a life buoy in a stormy sea. With the belt of her Burberry trench coat pulled tight and the branches strewn across the floor, she's doing a great impression of a frozen scarecrow in a winter field. As she offers her cheek to Dan for the briefest of pecks, the muscle in the side of her jaw is flickering. When he gives her arm a passing squeeze, she whirls out of his grasp and ends up out of reach. Glaring.

'So you decided to turn up then…' Alice says. '… finally.' If Dan was cold before, after that sub-zero stare from Alice he'll have hyperthermia.

From the way he barely shrugs, it looks like he's expecting the frost-bite treatment. 'You knew I had like a thousand apps to wrap up before I came.'

'Please.' Alice gives a snort. 'Spare me the bloody app excuse. There's so much to do here I've actually had to get the fire brigade in to help. The fire brigade… How embarrassing is that, when it should have been you?'

Dan closes his eyes, drags in a deep breath and tries again. 'But the guys have been here to cover for me.'

'Quinn? All Quinn's done is cause havoc.' Her voice soars. 'As if smashing the bloody crystal wasn't enough, he then goes on to kidnap poor Sera. My bloody sister, of all people…'

I can't believe that me getting stuck on the island is up there with the smashed glasses at the top of Alice's catalogue of wedding disasters. I can't decide if I should be honoured or horrified. What's more, even if she's repeating herself an incredible amount – I mean who says bloody *that* many times? – it's a major breakthrough that uptight Mrs Clean Mouth Alice is swearing at all. She's always been crap at cursing. Not that I can afford to be a competitive sibling when she's better than me at everything, but expletives are *the* one area where I can beat her hands down. Although it's maybe not the best sign, given her knuckles are shining white where her fists are clenched across her chest.

If Dan's eyes are wide with horror at the kidnap allegation, it doesn't come through in his voice. 'Calm down… breathe… it's fine, I'm here now…' His words couldn't be more soothing.

Alice's eyelids flutter. 'Okay…' She takes a breath and when she speaks all the yell has gone from her voice. She's back to Mrs Organise. 'Great. So have you brought the post box?'

Dan smiles and blinks. 'The post box…' He takes care to make it a statement, not a question, but it's obvious he's not quite with her. 'Remind me again…?'

'The Mr and Mrs Bradwell post box.' From her twitch of a smile she thinks he's teasing her, although he'd have to be a crazy adrenalin junkie to dare to do that at this point. Although these gaming guys do sometimes lose the link between real life and fantasy in danger terms. 'Full-size, cast-iron, custom-made. With our names on… You were picking it up…'

She couldn't spell it out for him in any more detail. I'm a wedding slacker, and even I know what she's talking about. It's in the section on sundries. The replica post box. For safe receipt of guests cards, cheques and cash gifts. Maybe someone else is behind with his manual reading too. I'm gritting my teeth, desperately trying thought transfer, but it doesn't look like it's working.

He's screwing up his face. 'Hmmmmm…' And playing for time.

As Alice's half-smile slips, her voice slides upwards. 'Dan, please tell me you're joking.'

'No, seriously. I'm really sorry…' He gives a momentary grimace, but his voice is steady as he levels with her. 'Confession time… I have absolutely no idea what you're talking about.'

In five seconds Alice has gone from pale to puce. 'You had one bloody thing to bring. One bloody thing to remember.

And you bloody screw it up.' As her yell bounces off the white walls of the ballroom there's a sudden lull in the chatter.

Then a shout from Chas cuts through the silence. 'Guys, outside. Now.'

You can tell they're trained to drop everything in an emergency and run. Next thing, Blue Watch are sliding down their ladders and there's the thunder of feet as they stampede through the house. A second later the front door slams and we're on our own.

Immie drops the curly mass of wires she's untangling. 'Great, we'll give you guys some space then too.'

As Rafe grasps Poppy's hand and yanks her after Immie, I catch their 'please never let this be us' grimaces. As for me, I'd love to run, but my feet are stuck to the floor. Alice is so close to losing it, I have to hover in case I can help.

Dan's opening and closing his mouth, probably in shock, but nothing's coming out.

'And now look what you've done.' Alice spits the words at him.

'What?' At least he's found his voice, even if he sounds incredulous, 'Hold on here. You're the one who frightened the firemen away. By yelling like a banshee.' He's shaking his head.

Alice narrows her eyes and comes two steps closer so she can hiss in his ear. 'Do you know, Dan, I'm starting to think you don't give a damn about this wedding at all.' Somehow the words sound way more chilling now her voice is quiet.

Dan puts his hands on his hips and his jaw is jutting. 'If we're talking home truths, how about you try this one, Alice. I've worked for this wedding day and night for the last three years.' His expression is strangely detached and his grey blue eyes have lost every bit of their sparkle. 'But if you're going ape over a post box I'd say *you're* the one who's stopped caring.' His low laugh is bitter. 'Seeing as you've got everything so well in hand here, I might as well go. Mostly we forgive you for being bossy, because we love you, and it's part of who you are. And your drive is a wonderful quality, and often we need those rockets up our backsides. But this is something else. Right now you've crossed a line. When you decide to stop acting like a power-crazed Bridezilla cliché, give me a call.'

He's walking away, but even I can see he's doing it slowly. When you compare him to the firemen, who left the room at the speed of light, Dan doesn't look as if he's trying at all. Like those excruciating toe-to-heel walks you do when you had those back-to-front slow-walking competitions at school to see who can keep moving, but get across the room last. He's aching for Alice to call him back. He hangs in the doorway for ages, waiting. But she doesn't say a word. She lets him go. And then the front door slams again. And as we hear his Range Rover roaring into the distance, Alice and I still haven't started breathing.

30

Thursday, 22nd December
In Poppy's kitchen at Brides by the Sea:
The recovery position

Ever heard the phrase 'When life serves you lemons, eat chocolate brownies'? Me neither, but it doesn't matter, because an hour later, in Poppy's kitchen, we're hell bent on doing it anyway. This was Poppy's life-saving suggestion when I brought her up to speed on the double disasters of the dress that doesn't fit, and the groom that came and went again in five minutes flat. Even if Alice was partly to blame for putting in the metaphorical lemon order in the first place, the brownies seem like a great way forward. For me, if not for her. Watching Poppy whip up the mixture was exactly the stress-buster that Alice and I needed after the shock of watching Dan leave the room.

'Six eggs in one cake.' There's a rush of steam as Poppy opens the oven door. 'Good thing I'm staying on a farm, then.' As she carries the tin over to where we're sitting at the table, and peels back the baking parchment from the edge, we're engulfed by the scent of warm chocolate.

And we all know hot is the only way to devour brownies. 'Spoon anyone?' As I pass out the dishes, Poppy eases a sticky slice onto each. Then she dips into the fridge for the cream carton. As I dribble on the cream, it sinks into the dark crevasses of the cake.

Then Poppy heads into the fridge again, but this time she comes back peeling the lid off a plastic box. 'Anyone up for testing my Christmas pudding ice cream? It's laced with rum, so it should go nicely with the brownie.' Before we can say 'yum' she's dished out two scoops all round.

I take a corner of brownie and a slice of ice cream and slide them into my mouth. The hot, dark cocoa hits the rum, freezes on my tongue and explodes in an amazing taste sensation.

'This is lush, Poppy. Orgasmic even.' My voice is thick with chocolate and alcohol as I grin at her. 'I hope Rafe didn't mind us stealing you. Again.'

Poppy laughs. 'Not at all. He was happy to spend the afternoon working on his old tractor with Immie's son. Rafe and I get on so well and his kitchen is awesome, but I can't ever imagine giving up this little kitchen in the sky.'

I laugh. 'That's definitely good news for me.'

Alice waggles her spoon at her cake and nods at Poppy. 'Delectable.' It's the first word she's said since we left Rose Hill Manor.

While I sympathise with her frustration with Dan, I'm hoping her outburst was partly down to hunger. So I wait until she's finishing her third piece of brownie before I launch into today's 'wedding speech'.

'So, I know you and Dan just had a bit of a...' Disagreement? Tiff? Nuclear blast? In the end I decide the dot dot dot version is the one to go with. But before I can get onto the next bit Alice finds her voice and cuts in.

'He's a bloody arsehole. What kind of a bloody wanker walks out like that?'

Oh my. She's obviously found enough signal to Google 'swear words' then. What I'd like to reply is: 'Maybe the kind of wanker whose girlfriend has pushed him to the edge and doesn't call him back'.

But instead, because I'm a scaredy-cat sister and a brides-maid who doesn't contradict the bride, even if she's momentarily resigned from that position, I bite my tongue and send her a smile. And carry on as if I haven't heard. 'So how about we make a fall-back plan for the dress? Just in case...' I hope that last part is a cover-all euphemism.

She sticks her chin in the air and stares at me like I'm the one losing the plot. '*In case* you've failed to notice, given my wedding has dematerialised, why would I even need a dress?'

I let out a long sigh. What does Alice think we've come here for if not that? We aren't sitting upstairs above a wedding-dress shop so we can get sugar highs from the brownies and Christmas ice cream and enjoy views of the sea. Which is fittingly dismal and grey, in case you wondered. Although admittedly the pudding was sensational. In fact I'm gritting my teeth at the idea of showing her my dresses. I do anything to get out of showing them to normal customers. Family members are a thousand times worse, especially when it's certain she won't want any of them.

I'm kicking myself for trying to get this show back on the road too early when there's a clattering on the stairs and Jess appears in the doorway.

'How's it going?' We brought her up to speed on the bad news as we passed through the shop earlier. Her beam is lighting the entire room, but it's mainly directed at Alice. 'Seeing as you have a free afternoon, I was hoping I could borrow you and your fabulous cheekbones, Alice? There are a few things Jules and I want to play around with... in the studio.' Free afternoon? Nicely put.

If my brow furrows into a deep frown, it's because I have no idea what she's talking about. 'There are?' Along with my squeal of surprise, I send her what I hope is a searching stare.

Jess goes on without meeting my eye. 'Jules is our photographer – you'll love him. We're wanting to grab a few shots of a fledgling collection we're pulling together.'

Any collection at all is news to me, given the only one I can think of is my non-existent one. As for how she's summoned Jules so fast – when Jess gets going she's like a one-woman tornado.

'Sure...' Alice says, even though she can't have any more idea than I do of what she's letting herself in for. But it's not as if she has any other pressing plans.

'Lovely.' Jess is starting that purr she does when everything is going her way. That is, when people let her steam roller them into submission. 'So if you're ready, let's all go down to the studio…' She's holding out her arm.

And before we know it, we're all following her down the stairs.

31

Thursday, 22nd December
In the studio at Brides by the Sea:
Sea views and Jimmy Choos

'If I'd known you were all coming to visit, I'd have tidied up.'
I'm squawking like a teenager who's about to have their bedroom
invaded, but as we spill into the studio, no one's listening.

Poppy and Alice march past the chaos on the cutting table
and head straight down the long room to the seaward windows.
Then they start gasping about the view. When you know how
startling the azure sparkle of that view can be, it's hard to
understand why they're this ecstatic about today's slate-grey
sea, meeting a sky that's the colour of a battleship and just as
threatening. It's not even as if the breakers are doing anything
spectacular. They're arriving on the shore like limp frills on a
petticoat.

At the other end of the studio from Alice, I'm frowning past my magazine piles and fabric rolls at Jess. It's obvious she's been up here already, because all lights are on, including the Christmas-tree ones. Hurrying, I whisk my scattered sketches into piles, pick up pencils, straighten the ironing board and gather up a hundred bits of fabric. I bang my phone into the doc and flick on my Christmas tunes, so whatever stunt Jess is going to pull, at least there's something jolly playing in the background. And finally, scooping up a couple of half-finished tops from the armchair so Alice has somewhere comfy to flop, I shove my high stool in Poppy's direction.

Jess, meanwhile, is on some mission of her own. She heads straight for one of the rails, where the silk shifts and slips I made recently are hanging. Sticking out a loafer, she deliberates for a second, then plucks a hanger.

'Right, Alice.' From somewhere she's found a pair of Jimmy Choo diamanté sandals and they're dangling seductively from the fingers of her other hand as she shakes the slip. 'Strip off and pop these on, please.' It's not the kind of order you'd stop to question. For one time only, in-charge Alice has met her match and is being bossed around.

Alice grabs the shoes and slip, follows Jess's nod and scurries behind the folding screen. I'm about to corner Jess for a 'what the hell?' moment, but she waltzes past me to the top of the stairs.

'Jules, almost ready up here.'

He must have been waiting on the landing, because a second later he springs into the room.

'Hey, Sera, Poppy, great to see you.' As his camera bag lands on the end of the cutting table there are enthusiastic air kisses for all of us, plus a double waft of that pricey aftershave he wears so much of.

The way he's running his fingers through his wavy brown hair, he and Alice could almost be related. And dammit that every hair of his hair falls back into perfect place. Just like hers, only better.

'And this is Alice…' As Jess says her name we all turn to look. From the synchronised way our jaws drop open, we could be in a choir. Alice scrapes her fingers through her hair and picks her way across the uneven painted floorboards in her heels. The slip she's wearing is so minimal it's almost translucent. Yet something about the way it flows over her angular body takes our breath away.

Jules jumps towards his bag. 'Wow, spectacular. Hello and hold that right there, Alice, I'll grab my camera.' A moment later, he's snapping her from all angles. When he stops and flicks back through the results, his face breaks into a secret beam of satisfaction. Then his eyes flash at Jess. 'You were completely right, sweets. These are *awesome*.'

Jess comes, and as she looks over his elbow for herself, her face lights up in triumph. 'Great work, Jules and Alice. Now let's play.' Snatching up a length of ribbon, she twists it round Alice's waist and twitches the silk dress into place. 'Okay, take a few shots standing, then try that sitting on the windowsill.'

As Alice sits and shrugs, and looks effortlessly sultry, Jules bounces around her. There are times when her neck is so slender beneath her dark bob, it looks as if it could almost snap. Meanwhile Jess is flicking through the tulle and ribbon skirts I've been making, tapping her foot as she mulls. Eventually she chooses one and takes it across to Alice. Another twist later, Alice's slinky silhouette has been transformed by the gauzy tulle gathers of her skirt, caught at the waist by the simple ribbon tie. As she leans a shoulder against the white-painted fireplace, there's the smallest glint of Jimmy Choo sandal peeping out below her hem.

'Simple, yet completely exquisite.' Jess is beaming at me. 'Let's add one of those tiny tulle jackets.' Next minute, she's slipping a tulle top onto Alice and doing it up. And tah-dah, Alice has changed again, and now the cropped top is hanging off and accentuating the nip of her waist.

Jules is shaking his head. 'No embellishment at all and yet they look stunning.'

Jess laughs. 'Not a bead in sight. A minimalist bride's dream. The perfect starting point to dress up, or down. You really have hit on the most brilliant capsule collection concept here, Sera. And all without a sketch in the book. You are such a unique talent.'

I'm screwing up my face at Jess. 'You see this as a collection?' And how does she know my sketch book is empty?

A narrow diamond-covered ribbon is trailing from her hand, and she's moved on to one of the simple lace tops I made. 'It's completely innovative and inspired. By taking the different combinations of slips and skirts and tops and belts and sashes, it means every bride can have a dress completely unique to them. Which is what so many brides want now. And yet your simple cuts are so sophisticated that they look completely amazing.'

'You think?' I have to come clean here. 'I didn't actually plan this…'

Jess smiles. 'That's what makes you all the more amazing,

Sera. You did it by pure instinct. All I had to do was show you it's perfect.'

Poppy is perched on the high stool. 'They're beautiful, Sera. And with a few simple changes you end up with a dress for day and a completely different look for the evening, too.'

Alice is standing, her arms stretched along the top of a huge vintage storage chest, her narrow diamond belt blinking as it catches the light, as Jules moves around her, still taking pictures.

Jess calls down the studio. 'Okay, that's enough for today, Alice. Thanks so much, now we know for sure we've got our collection, you can get dressed again.'

As Alice turns and catches sight of the Christmas tree standing on the top of the chest she lets out a cry. 'Sera, are these the decorations from Gran's tree?' As she fingers a shimmery blue hanging fish, then a battered felt Santa, her voice glows with warmth. 'I remember these. We used to stand on the table to hang them on the tree, didn't we?'

I laugh, if only because it's so far away from what Alice would choose for herself. 'I bring the toys down from the loft in the cottage every year. Nothing matches, but somehow Christmas wouldn't be the same without it.' It's in the studio, because that's where I spend most of my time. I send her a mischievous grin. 'Christmas trees don't have to be all one colour to be magical.' Although sadly in Alice's world, they might.

'It's lovely.' As she says it she almost sounds teary. 'And your dresses are wonderful too.' All these compliments, she really can't be feeling herself. As she makes her way back to the folding screen to get changed, she lingers by the cutting table. 'What's this?' She points to one of the half-finished tops I bundled off the chair.

'Something else I was playing with.' I give a shrug. Chiffon with the tiniest sparkle, so light it's barely there. 'It's still only pinned together.' And for possibly the first time ever, I don't feel like running away when someone's looking at my clothes. Maybe it's easier when they aren't finished.

'It's beautiful.' Her voice fades to nothing as she swallows. 'Like sequins and snowflakes.'

If she was in the shop downstairs, and was anyone other than Alice, we might have thought she was having her fall-in-love moment. With the dress, obviously, not the groom. The bit with the groom will have to wait until later and, believe me, I'm putting my faith in fairy dust for that one. We'll be needing it by the lorry load.

As she picks up the sleeve that's almost sheer, she smiles as the minute sequins catch the light. 'And long sleeves too. Perfect for a Christmas wedding.' She gives a wistful sigh. 'For anyone getting married, that is.'

Dammit. Obviously not her, then. Which reminds me that white-horse wishes really aren't reliable. If they were, right now Alice and Dan would probably be drinking Winter Warmers in the Goose and Duck and laughing together about the missing disco floor. Instead of which, they're both miserable and contemplating life as single people. Stubborn single people. In my book that doesn't go down as a desirable outcome. Which also reminds me how much work there is to do, if we're going to make this damned wedding of the year happen at all.

32

Thursday, 22nd December
In St Aidan: Pompoms and great excuses

As I drive back into St Aidan after dropping Alice back at
Daisy Hill Farm there are already a few groups of people
spilling out of their offices onto the pavements after work,
hitting town for Christmas drinks. Although I'd rather have
stayed at the cottage with Alice, I can't help remembering how
she lingered over the 'sequins and snowflakes' top in the studio.
Not that I'm getting my hopes up that she's going to need it,
but in case there's the slightest possibility, I want to finish it.

I leave my car down by the harbour and head back up
towards the mews and the shop. As I pass The Hungry Shark
it's already buzzing. Beyond the tinsel-clad windows, the inside
looks warm and inviting. I'm willing myself to walk past
without popping in, when the door opens.

'Hello, stranger…' It's Quinn, glass in hand, his crumpled checked shirt half in, half out of his jeans, hanging down below his floppy sweater.

And if I take a moment to recognise him under the yellow glare of the street lights, it's because he's wearing a red-and-green-striped elf hat. I can't help grinning. 'Nice ears you've got there.'

His face creases into a smile as he pats the pointy bits of latex stuck to the side of his head. 'Being a pixie's a great excuse to be naughty. Check out the pompoms and the bell.' He waggles the end of his hat that's dangling over his shoulder.

I take my cue and lean in to admire them and get a waft of whisky too.

'Coming in for a drink, then?' When he smiles the dimples behind the stubble are pretty impossible to resist.

It takes a nanosecond and one more glimpse of that laconic smile to decide. 'Just one… then I have to sew.'

As he walks behind me to the bar, his hand's already dropped onto my shoulder. 'I'm warming up with a toddy, but the mulled cider's looking good if you'd like one?'

Even as the fug of the bar hits me, in my head I'm already picturing wonky stitching on the chiffon. 'I'll stick to the spiced apple, thanks. I'm on my way to work.' From the way his face falls as he orders, I'm guessing he was hoping for a drinking mate for longer. 'So what have you done with Dan?' Between us, I'd pinned my hopes on them being together. At least that way we'd know where Dan was.

Quinn carries my steaming jam jar to a space along the bar and pulls out two high stools. As I unwrap my scarf, slip off my jacket and clamber up beside him, he squeezes my knee, then gives a shrug.

'Dan came and went before we touched base. I don't blame the guy for being pissed off. Or for pissing off, either. He didn't exactly get a warm welcome from "Ice Queen" Alice.' Quinn's lip curls as he says Alice's name.

Before I know what I'm doing, I'm leaping in there to defend my sister. 'It wasn't just Alice's fault.' I know Alice was pretty unreasonable, but I can't let that sneer go, even if it is softened by those baby blue eyes of his. 'Dan gave as good as he got. They're both stressed and overwrought. It's up to us to help them through.'

Quinn seems to find that funny. So funny, he almost falls off his stool laughing. 'Couples counselling might be in your job description, but it's certainly not in mine.' His elbows are on the bar now and he's rolling his whisky around in its glass.

'So you're not even going to attempt to find Dan? Or smooth things over?'

The corners of Quinn's mouth drag downwards and he seems to be searching for something in the bottom of his drink. 'Nope. Dan's a big boy. If he wants to tie himself down for life to the bitch queen from hell, that's entirely up to him. But, similarly, if he decides to save himself the bother, that's his decision too.'

'Holy frigging crap, Quinn, that's a bit harsh.' I'm so shocked by what he's come out with, my juice sloshes all over the wood-block bar, and I almost lose a cinnamon stick.

'Not at all. I'm simply telling it like it is. Take your sickeningly rose-tinted wedding specs off, forget the party hype – and you're left with two people who are going to have to wake up and look at each other every morning for the rest of their lives. It sounds brutal, but it would take a brave guy to commit to your sister the way she's been these last few months.' His pointed stare tells me he's not joking.

As I sip my lukewarm drink and pick a clove out of my teeth, I've gone all shaky. My tummy's dissolving on Alice's behalf. She may have been hard work, but she doesn't deserve this.

I screw up my face, because however much I run away from conflict, for once I have to fight this one. 'If you knew *half* the effort Alice has put into making this wedding *completely* amazing for *everyone*, including Dan, you'd cut her some slack.' Even as I'm saying it, I'm suddenly furious Quinn's being so cutting. 'Not that you'd know about work, given you seem to cause a lot more than you actually do.' It might sound mean, but he hasn't exactly been knocking himself out to help. What's more, my whole childhood, Alice stuck up for me, but this is probably the first time in my life I've been able to return the favour. When you're fighting for something you really believe in, especially for someone else, it's a lot less hard than you'd think.

Quinn's face breaks into a beam. 'Whoa, go Sera.' As he laughs and his cheeks slide into the kind of creases that should be to-die-for sexy. 'None of this needs to bother us. It's really not our business. Forget about the wedding, we'll have some downtime of our own. Drinks, laughs, hanging loose – how about a night for *us*?' He's holding my gaze with his. If he wasn't so damned cool, I suspect he'd be smouldering. One delish beach-ready, Ferrari-driving guy. Delivering himself on a plate. Should be a no-brainer. As the barman walks by, Quinn's stare slides off me and he waggles his empty glass.

'How many have you had?' Not that I ever count, but I'm sensing he's a long way ahead.

'What, are you the drinks police now?' There's another throaty laugh. 'You are *so* like your sister.' And despite the tease in his voice, I suspect he doesn't mean in a good way.

I can't let that go without protest. 'Actually, I'm really nothing like her.' Apart from being stone-cold sober. And indignant. And being less than enthusiastic about the Quinn I'm seeing right at this moment. And fighting someone else's corner. Okay, so maybe he is a teensy bit right.

He leans in towards me, so close his temple is almost touching mine. 'Just because you're related to Alice, you don't have to sign a fun disclaimer.' His hand slides over my knee and he grasps my fingers. 'If you'd rather have a night in, we could grab some champagne. Curl up in front of the fire?'

Talk about déjà vu. This is highwayman island re-visited, and now I'm the one seeing the funny side. 'You mean pick up where we left off the other day?' My lips are bursting to smile, but I hold it in.

His grin is playful. 'Think of it as a pre-emptive Christmas present – to us both.' However decorative he looks, it's not happening. 'Or even a late one.' His low chortle tells me he's alluding to the other day.

'I'd hate to spoil the surprise this far ahead.' Clunking my jam jar of juice down on the bar, I finally let my grin go as I slide down from my stool. As for the present I already missed – there are no words.

His chin shoots upwards. 'Where the hell are you going?'

'There's a wedding dress waiting. I have to go.' On a need-to-know basis, that covers it.

He frowns. 'If you think Alice will be needing one of those, you're deluding yourself. Running out on me for that is bollocks.'

'Whatever.' So much for home truths.

'Seriously, Sera, you're wasting your time. Jeez, just for once, let go, enjoy the ride.' Cool and ripped. His denims *and* his body. All blonde stubble and cheekbones. He's even got the frayed sweater to match mine.

And I'm still walking away. 'Thanks for the drink.' I grab my coat. 'Sorry to miss the fun, I'll catch you later.'

33

Thursday, 22nd December
In the studio at Brides by the Sea: Better in daylight

Whenever I sew, the outside world always fades. Tonight, as I sit up in the studio, in the pool of light next to the twinkling Christmas tree, the whirring of my sewing machine is the perfect way to block out reality. All I'm thinking about are the pieces of chiffon. As I ease them under the flying machine needle, the wedding manual seems a long way away. Dan and Alice's argument begins to blur. And the way Quinn shook it off as if he really didn't give a damn isn't important any more. As I hand-stitch the tiniest pearl buttons into place down the back, and ease them through loops made from the narrowest satin ribbon, all that matters is the whisper of the fabric in my hands. Once the little cropped jacket is done, I carefully drape it onto a hanger. As I hold it up, the colours of the

Christmas tree shine through the sheer fabric and the miniscule sequins glint. It weighs so little, it moves as a draught of air blows up from the stairs.

'Sera… are you up there?'

I jump, and kick myself for being careless enough to leave the door unlocked. If this is Quinn… I brace myself and rush to hang the top on the rail as I hear the thump of feet on the stairs. Quinn, four hours more drunk than when I left him, is the last thing I want to deal with.

'I hope you don't mind me coming up…'

As I catch the lilt of the words, my ribcage relaxes and I sigh with relief. 'Johnny?'

'I saw your shadow in the window from the street.' His hands are deep in the pockets of his North Face jacket as he appears in the doorway. Below his uncharacteristically messy hair his face is lined and pale. 'Sorry, I know it's late, but I was hoping to tap your local knowledge.' He sounds like a line from the wedding manual. On the upside, he's not slurring or waxing lyrical in an over-emotional way. What's more, he's made it up the steep winding studio stairs without falling over. So that can only be good.

'Sure, how can I help?' Given the awkward way we parted last time, as I flick off the power to the machine and the iron, I don't meet his gaze.

His deep sigh heightens the shadows under his cheekbones. 'I've been all over the county, trying to locate Dan, and I finally found his car down by the harbour. At a guess, he's out in town.'

I've already picked up my coat to leave. 'And you want me to…?'

'Come round the pubs and bars with me to look for him. It's a long shot, but I reckon it's worth a try.'

'Okay.' Even if I'd rather not be doing it with Johnny, after Quinn's attitude earlier, it's a relief to have some positive action from Team Groom.

Johnny hesitates as he turns for the stairs. 'Believe me, this *is* all about Dan. I'm not trying to change history here. For us, I mean.'

I hope someone knows what he's going on about here, because I don't. I stare at him blankly. As I flick out the lights and join him on the landing he's trying again.

'Whatever I said the other day, and however bemused I am at how your life has turned out, I promise I'll back off.'

'Okay. Thanks for that,' I say, throwing in a bright smile, even though I still haven't got the foggiest what he's getting at. 'Shall we make a start, then?'

As we head out onto the street, we run straight into a guy with a monster Christmas pudding for a body, surrounded by a cluster of people dressed as crackers.

Johnny pulls up his collar and leans down to me. 'It's party time out here. At least we'll stand a better chance with two of us.'

I dodge an inflatable snowman, then a guy who appears to be riding a stuffed camel. 'Trust Dan to go AWOL the one night everyone's out on their festive pub crawls.' If Dan's dressed up to blend in we won't stand a chance. 'Shall we start in The Hungry Shark?'

As we shoulder our way through the crowds spilling out onto the pavement, I'm aching for Quinn to have moved on. I brace myself, dive into the melee, and begin to scan the faces. There's a snowman on the stool where Quinn was.

'When did plain old Santa suits and fairy dresses go out of fashion?' Johnny's shaking his head, as we meet up again back at the door. 'I've checked the Gents, but on balance I'd say it's a "no" in here. So where next?'

'We'll start with The Jolly Sailor, The Ship, The Balcony Bar, Hot Jacks, The Hub and The Smugglers' Inn.' I count them off on my fingers. 'Then we'll try The Yellow Canary and The Rum and Crab, then pull in The Harbour Hotel. And work our way down to The Beach Hut and The Surf Shack.' Even as I reel them off, it seems like an impossible task.

'The quicker we go, the more chance we have of catching him rather than missing him,' Johnny points out.

We're shooting in and out of bars so fast, there isn't even time to unwind my scarf, let alone enjoy the decorations or join in the Christmas songs playing in the background.

'Should we be checking them all, or should we be targeting the places Dan would choose?' I'm panting and half running, as I try to keep up with Johnny's long strides as he steps off the pavement to overtake a dawdling turkey. On the upside, there's no breath left for conversation in between bars.

'Best do them all.' As he hops back onto the pavement, he pulls me up beside him. 'You never know where he'll wander in to.'

We're about to dodge a group of guys in angel dresses, arm in arm and singing, or rather shouting, 'We three kings…' I'm scanning, just in case Dan's hiding in amongst the group when I come across a familiar face under a very crooked halo.

'Chas?'

He narrows his eyes at me for a second, then it clicks. 'Sera, hi, how're you doing?' The enthusiastic punch on the arm he gives me is pretty forceful for an angel. As the line slews to a halt, the angel carol subsides. 'Are you partying too?'

I'm shouting over the noise from the nearby Rum and Crab. 'Looking for Dan, the groom. We've temporarily misplaced him.' At least that's halfway to the truth.

Chas gives a grimace. 'We've just come from The Harbour Hotel; he wasn't there. Wasn't in The Beach Hut earlier either from what we could see.'

'Thanks.' I can't imagine how they ever got into the up-market Harbour Hotel in their angel dresses. Maybe there are special dispensations for festive firemen. 'If you see him, tell him we're on our way down to The Surf Shack,' I yell as an afterthought as I nudge Johnny across the road.

'Will do.' Chas shouts over his shoulder as the angel line sets off again.

Probably because Chas just saved us a half-hour round trip or more, as we make our way down the hill and along the sea front to The Surf Shack, our pace slows.

'Must be cool to wake up this close to the beach every day.' Johnny's hair is flattened against his head as he yells at me. As we hit the sea front he's struggling into a head wind so strong, it whips his words away.

I shove my hands deep into my pockets and pull my jacket closer to my body. 'It isn't always blowing a gale like this.' I yell back and jump to dodge the spray as the high tide smacks against the sea wall and splatters foam over the railings. By the time I skip up the steps to the decking at the front of the café heading for the chaser lights around the door, I decide some context might help. 'This is pretty much my local.' It's easier to explain away the welcome in advance.

As we push our way into the sudden calm of the café and sidle up to the bar, sure enough Brin bobs up from behind the electric blue Christmas tree, beaming. 'Hey, Sera, you're out late tonight. What can I get you? Beer, hot punch, hot chocolate…?'

I grin at him. 'Actually I'm not here to order, I'm searching for a lost bridegroom.' When you put it like that, it comes over as a bit dramatic. As I catch sight of the muffin plate on the bar, my mouth begins to water, so I yank my gaze away from the cakes. 'Although we're running out of places to look.' When I look over my shoulder and check the tables, it's obvious Dan's not here either.

'No, let's have a drink.' Johnny's come to a halt beside me. 'We can warm up and regroup. What would you like?'

I hesitate, but only for a moment. 'Double chocolate muffin, please, and my usual please.'

'Which is?' Johnny's head is tilted.

'Frothy hot chocolate, XXL, with a swirl of salted caramel and dark-chocolate sprinkles. It's to die for.'

There's a smile lilting around his lips. 'Two of those, then, and a muffin for me too, please.'

Five minutes later I've sunk onto a chair and I'm dipping my spoon into the froth on my drink. 'After all that rushing around it's nice to sit down. As for lunch, it's so long ago I can't remember it.' I peel back the paper on my muffin and slide a knife through the cake, and take a delicious, sticky bite. 'Best, most gigantic muffins in town.' I mumble, pushing the crumbs into my mouth, then taking a deep drink of hot chocolate.

'It's a pain we've lost Dan. But it's nice to see you where you live, at last.'

This is the downside of stopping. Though why he makes it sound like something he's been waiting for all his life, I have no idea. 'It's better in daylight in summer, to be honest.' I rub the corners of my mouth. 'Have I got a chocolate 'tache?'

He laughs. 'How could you not? Don't worry, I won't let you go back into St Aidan with a dirty face.' His eyes narrow. 'So remind me how you ended up here?' For someone with a mighty muffin and a delectable hot chocolate in front of them, he's paying way too much attention to other things.

'I came to help out my gran and never left.' That should cover it. 'It was cosy. Like getting back the childhood I missed out on first time around.' I'm not sure he knows about our too-busy parents, but whatever.

He still hasn't attacked his muffin and his brow has wrinkled into a frown. 'But what about the travelling? And working abroad? When we were at uni that was all you talked about.'

This is why you should never come face to face with people from the past, who can remind you what your dreams were at twenty-one, when they turned out to be bollocks.

'I was the world's worst traveller.' I might as well come clean. 'It was knackering, I was lonely, I got ill. Then my gran had a stroke, I was the only one not working, so I came back to help. Jess was starting the wedding shop and she took my designs, and that was that.' If I say it fast enough I might skip the bit about my world tour only lasting a couple of months, rather than the year, or even the lifetime that I'd planned. And I'm definitely not going to pinpoint that the one and only time I came back was when I got in touch with him. The time he didn't reply.

'So where did you get to?'

Locations are better than dates. 'Malaysia, Thailand, Indonesia. Those kind of places.' When you say it in a list you can fudge that it was barely a couple of weeks in each country.

'Australia? China? South America?' He's prompting from my bullshit list of destinations that I reeled off to him so often over tea.

I shake my head, get the better of my embarrassment at failing so spectacularly, and make my smile bright. 'As it turned out, I'm a package tour kind of girl. An occasional all-inclusive burst on a beach is enough for me. If it wasn't for the wedding, I'd be baking in Bali as we speak.'

'Oh.' He's put down his knife and he's staring at me in the weirdest kind of way. 'Back then I was tied down, committed in every direction, and you were so free. I used to imagine you doing all the things I wanted to do, but couldn't. And now I find you weren't doing them at all.'

He was the one who got paid for his degree by signing on the dotted line for his job in advance. He was the one who came out debt free, when the rest of us are still paying it off, so there were compensations. As for the living-vicariously part, I had no idea. But he doesn't need to sound this badly done to.

I let out a snort. 'Well, I'm sorry for screwing up *your* fantasy of *my* life.' Even as I'm apologising, I'm indignant for having to. 'You're the Mr Stay-home, who ended up all over the place, and I had the big plans that came to nothing. It's like we got each other's lives. But you got what you wanted in the end, so it's all okay.'

He stirs his chocolate slowly. 'Or maybe I didn't.'

Something about that faraway look in his dark grey eyes

makes my stomach clench. I can't believe I've dropped my guard. I promised myself I'd never let that happen. Ever again. Unrequited love is a hell hole you only go down once. Been there. Done that. Got the 'learned my lesson' T-shirt. That's why I'd rather have done this with Quinn. Even if he is a handful, and offers unwanted presents at every turn, I can just about handle him.

I shake my head. It's too late at night to be enigmatic. 'Shut up and eat your muffin, Johnny. We're supposed to be looking for Dan.' *Not raking over the past.*

34

Thursday, 22nd December
At Jaggers in St Aidan: Job descriptions
and ice-cream cones

'So this is Jaggers, the place where Happy Hour never stops.'
As we battle our way past a crowd of very young people, most
of them holding at least two jam jars of cocktails, some more,
it's only fair that I give Johnny a taste of what's in store. Even
if it means I have to yell very loudly in his ear for him to hear.
'It is also an advantage if you're barely eighteen, like Strawberry
Daiquiris, and have hollow legs.'

'Okay for you, then. I meant to ask, how come you haven't
changed a bit, even after all this time?'

I take it he's talking about my apparent age, not my empty
legs. Although I'm not sure that's actually a compliment.
'Probably I stayed the same because I live in a seaside time

244

warp and refuse to grow up. My gran used to joke she'd be eighteen 'til she died too.'

That makes him smile. He's looking at the chalk board, rubbing his hands enthusiastically. 'Great timing, anyway, we've hit White Christmas Special Offer Night.'

I'm not going to break it to him that every night is special-offer night at Jaggers. What's more, I'm sending silent thanks to my fairy godmother that we haven't hit that other Jaggers favourite, three for two *Sex on the Beach* night. Although I'm hoping he doesn't think if we stopped for a drink at the Surf Shack that we're getting stuck in here.

'And there's not so much full-blown costume love here either,' I say. Most punters have made do with sparkly wings or variations of Santa hats. I can't see Dan being here. Any sensible thirty four year old would have run a mile at the door. 'Saving their cash for cocktails, no doubt.' Pulling in our stomachs, we wiggle our way through the crush by the door. I'm staring down the length of the bar, trying to work out a search strategy when a tap on my shoulder makes me whirl around.

'Jess. What a surprise.' Although, if I stopped to think about it, lately it would be more of a surprise for her to be anywhere else at midnight on a Thursday.

'Ditto,' she says, beaming as if she can't believe her luck. I make my excuses and stay in the studio working every time rather than coming out to play. She leans closer, in a vain attempt to keep her yelling confidential. 'You'll never guess who I'm with?'

'Jules? Immie? The ex-soldier turned sheep farmer who came to Grab Granny night?' Although, by all accounts, Jess scared the corduroys off her guy by drinking him under the trendy purple tables last visit. I'm just remembering it might be Jules' mum she's with, when Jess cuts in again.

'No, we did see all of them earlier, but I'm actually with…' She pauses for dramatic effect and does a little ta-da hand waggle. 'Your future brother-in-law…'

It takes a second to sink in. 'Dan? What the hell are you doing with Dan?' I want to scream 'Holy effing crap, we've been all over effing town looking for him' at the top of my voice, but somehow I hold it in. If my knees are sagging, I'm not sure if it's with relief we've found him at last, or shock that he's been abducted by aliens. 'Since when?' I mean, it's not as though Jess exactly knows him is it?

'I'm on my way to the bar, but *do* come and join us.' She's smiling like a cat who caught a pigeon. 'He came into the shop looking for a post box when you took Alice home. We've been here ever since – having a quiet chat in the corner. '

Between us, it's hard to imagine anyone describing anything at Jaggers as quiet. As for her spiriting away my future bro-in-law… there are no words.

Johnny smiles at Jess. 'Hi again, I'm Johnny, one of Dan's best men.' His one very ironic eyebrow raised at me says it all. 'Let me go to the bar. What are you drinking?'

'Lovely.' Jess has already pushed the empty jug she's carrying into Johnny's hands. 'Dan and I are moving on to the Ice Queen cocktails. But Wonderful White Christmas is good for starters, and the Snowballs and White Russians are fun too.' No surprise they've worked their way down the whole damned board. She grabs my arm. 'Come on, Sera, I'll take you over to Dan.'

If you ever need to power your way through a crowd, Jess

is your woman. She'd cut a swathe through a Sleeping Beauty forest faster than a Disney prince. By the time Johnny arrives to join us a few minutes later, complete with cocktails and bottles of Diet Pepsi – and how did he remember that? – I'm fully flopped in Jess's VIP alcove. While everyone else in the bar is standing or wedged onto high stools, Jess has somehow blagged her own leather benches and a dedicated chill-out zone.

'Guys…' Dan's eyes pull into focus as Johnny sits down and slides a cocktail pitcher the size of a bulk tanker onto the low table. '… You brought cocktails too…' He beams, tilts forward, gropes for the jug and wobbles it towards the glasses.

If Dan hadn't already failed his sobriety test with his slurred speech, the splashing overflow of Ice Queen flooding across the table top and dribbling onto Johnny's leg is enough to tell us he's hammered.

Johnny slides a coke to me and takes one himself. Overlooking the sticky mix of vodka and peppermint seeping onto his chinos, he flops an arm around Dan's shoulder. 'So, mate, how're you doing?'

'Pretty damned fine… considering…' Dan takes a slurp from his glass and crashes it down again. 'Photographer's FUBAR… cake's FUBAR…but o-on the u-upside, I f-found a post box.'

'FUBAR?' I squint at Johnny.

'It's an acronym,' he says helpfully, shaking his head. 'Fucked Up Beyond All Repair.'

'Really?' My heart just did a nose dive. I turn to Jess, hoping she knows enough to fill us in.

The fact she raises both her eyebrows at once says it all.

'Apparently the wedding cake came out of the car with seismic cracks in it. And as if that wasn't enough, the photographer's been run over by a Range Rover while lying in a car park.'

Dan sits up. 'Photographer's got a femured fracture...' He's mumbling, but it's close enough for us to get the idea.

Jess goes all dreamy. 'The price of the perfect shot.'

'You couldn't make it up.' I take a sip of Pepsi, in a desperate bid to pump up my caffeine levels. But all I can think of as I sigh is poor Alice.

'When Alice went postal about the post box, obviously Dan couldn't begin to tell her the rest.' From the way Jess is closing her eyes, she's thriving on the drama.

'What a good thing Poppy's back.' I say, knowing we'll be able to count on her for some kind of cake, even if it isn't the same kind Alice planned. 'I'll see her at the farm first thing. How about Jules? Will he step in for the pictures?'

Jess nods. 'I called him from the Ladies', he's on stand by for Saturday. But that might be the least of our problems.' She gives me one of her extra-significant stares and lowers her voice. 'A groom who can't face the bride needs very careful handling. I was planning to take him back to mine when we finish here. It's taken hours to talk him down from the edge.'

'I can imagine,' I say. Hours. And a few gallons of White Russian, no doubt. Then I suppose Jess planned on tucking him up like a stray puppy.

Johnny smiles at Jess. 'We really appreciate you catching Dan, but we can't impose any more. Sera and I will take it from here.' He looks at his watch, as if to warn Jess her time's up.

'One groom not a million miles away looks like he's in need of his beauty sleep. We really should be getting him home.'

Now it's my turn to have my eyebrows on the ceiling. 'We should?'

'Come on, Dan…' Johnny stands up.

Dan shakes his head and settles back against the cushions with a squawk of protest. 'Can't go before the ice cream.'

Johnny's face crumples. 'Who said anything about ice cream?'

The look Dan sends Johnny is pretty withering, considering. 'You were the one who bought it…'

My lips twitch into a smile. 'You mean the Ice Queen cocktail, Dan?'

'My point… exactly.' A beatific beam spreads across Dan's features as he stabs the air with his forefinger.

Inebriated grooms are like horses – easier to coax than to force. Grabbing a jam jar, I pour in a huge slurp of Ice Queen and dangle it in front of Dan. 'This one's a carry-out. We'll drink as we go.'

Dan staggers to his feet too. 'Okay then… whadda we waiting for ' For a second, he bobs back down to scrabble on the seat. When he wobbles into view again there's an antler head, band clamped to his temples. 'Ready when I am…'

'Come on, Rudolf, come on Prancer.' I send a bemused grin behind me as Johnny hauls Dan's arm over his shoulder and yanks him after me. 'Ice cream as soon as we're outside.'

Was someone talking about job descriptions earlier? Because whatever else was in Alice's wedding manual, I'm damned sure leading a reindeer with wonky antlers along the sea front wasn't in mine.

35

'You'd think the cold would wake him up.'

I'm shouting at Johnny over the roar of the wind, across the front of Dan's sagging body, as we stagger across the cobbles of the harbourside. I say stagger, but actually our shuffle is so slow we're almost stationary. As for Dan, if you overlook the antlers, he's doing an excellent impression of a guy who's been out drinking with Jess. After eight hours most of them go out like the fairy-light strings around the town are doing now.

'Dan wasn't anything like this bad on his stag weekend.' Johnny's panting with the exertion of keeping Dan upright.

'He actually had a stag do?' Even though I'm peering out from under the arm of Dan's parka, talking as we lurch along

250

is making this easier. Somehow I didn't think Alice's fiancé elastic would stretch further than sandwiches and a snooker game for the guys.

'Three Eastern Bloc escape rooms... that was Quinn's part.' Johnny's voice comes in bursts. 'Then we flew to Iceland... saw the Northern Lights on the way home.'

I free my hand and scrape my hair away from my eyes. 'That was your bit?'

Johnny pauses. 'How did you guess?' He laughs as he readjusts Dan, who lets out a snort. 'Iceland's big on vodka. They have this stuff called Black Death that makes your legs de-materialise. Made from potatoes and caraway seeds. Alice sent us last winter, so Dan had plenty of time to sober up.'

'And still not as lethal as an evening with Jess.' So much for Alice's forward planning. I can't help rolling my eyes at the irony. 'Are you parked at the top?' The road up to town is steep at the best of times. Dragging a six-foot-four dead weight all the way up there, it's going to take forever. My leg muscles are already burning with the effort of holding him up.

'Yep.' Johnny heaves Dan up again. 'At the rate we're walking, I reckon the wedding will be happening round about when we get back to the car. In thirty-six hours' time.'

'Or...' I can't believe what I'm about to offer, given how determined I am to keep Johnny at a distance. 'We could go to mine – it's that cottage at the end of the row over there, with the blue front door and leaded windows. It's less than a hundred metres.' Blame the sheer desperation, but I'm pointing towards the harbour end. My sanctuary, which is how I wanted to keep it. But suddenly all I care about is getting us all into the warm. I'm hoping Johnny won't get all judgemental.

'Best news yet.' Johnny drags in a breath. 'Let's go. One big last push and we'll be there.'

So many times when we were at uni, my über-secret fantasy was to bring Johnny to my gran's place by the sea. I mean, everyone has fantasies about walking on the beach, don't they? Although what difference I thought that was going to make to anything, I've no idea. And now, ten years on, when we're finally here, after all, and it's the last thing I want. Whoever said 'be careful what you wish for' wasn't wrong. But with our destination in sight, we speed up. There's no going back, and next thing I know, I'm shouldering the cottage door open and flicking on the lights, and we're bumping off the painted board walls, knocking Gran's tiny pictures every which way, as we head down the hall. We pretty much fall into the living room. Then with a final heave, we roll Dan onto the sofa.

His stubbled cheek is pale against the blue-linen cushions. As he mumbles and scratches at his hair, I reach in and untangle the antlers.

'Bridesmaid to the rescue – again.' Johnny blows as he stares down at Dan. 'Thanks for this, Fi. I owe you. He's sleeping like a proverbial baby now.'

'Excuse the mess, I'll grab him a duvet.' Plucking a pair of abandoned lacy tights off the sofa arm, I set off to race upstairs, and stop halfway to the door. 'What about you? There's a spare room?' Damn that sleeping arrangements always have to be so loaded. To be honest, though, unexpected guests landing rat-arsed at two in the morning can't expect to be sniffy about a few empty mugs and a scattering of random shoes. Or underwear.

Johnny grins at the tights I'm bundling into my fist, but

brushes the offer away. 'I'm best here, to keep an eye on Dan. Make sure he doesn't go AWOL a third time.' His eye roll pretty much acknowledges what we've been through to get to this point.

When I get back down from raiding the spare room for covers, Johnny's sitting on the floor, his long legs stretched in front of him.

'Tea, coffee, beer, Wotsits, fish fingers, cornflakes?' As a hostess I'm not only out of practice, I'm also bluffing wildly about my fridge contents. Since I've been dashing up and down to the farm and the manor, I can't remember the last time I even bought milk.

'Actually I'm fine, Fi.' As he takes the duvet from me, he's re-arranging magazines and shopping receipts to make a space on the rug. 'Maybe I'll get some water later.'

Right answer. 'Help yourself, the kitchen's at the back, bath-room's at the top of the stairs.' As I rattle off directions, I make a mental note to keep my bedroom door firmly shut so he doesn't glimpse the devastation in there. Then, probably thanks to that last bottle of cola, my mind whirls ahead to morning. And making my escape. 'I'll be creeping out early to see Poppy about the cake.' Great excuse there. 'Dan can sleep for as long as he wants. Let yourselves out whenever you're ready, and leave the key under the Christmas-tree pot by the door.' That pretty much covers it.

'Great.' Johnny gives me a nod and then suddenly looks a little bit sad. 'You know I always wanted to come and see where your gran lived.' He gives a shrug. 'And now I have.'

'What?' Where did that come from?

'Your summers at uni always sounded idyllic. You can't

blame me for wanting a piece of them.' He's eyeing me levelly and moving on fast. 'You know, whatever Quinn says, and however much Dan tried not to arrive, Alice is brilliant for Dan. They make a great couple. When they're *not* getting married, that is.'

'Dan put off coming?' Now I'm blowing my fringe up. Stupid o'clock in the morning is hardly the ideal time to find out Dan's app excuse was fake. What's worse, the fact that Dan's cold feet are real sends a chill down my spine, even though I'm backed up against the radiator. 'How am I ever going to sleep now?' I'm starting to understand why Alice needs her colouring books. What's more, if I'd been in her place when Dan finally showed up, I'd probably have gone through the celestial ceiling too.

'Don't worry. If we're both on their case, fingers crossed, we can help them see what's important. Get this show on the road.'

Johnny is so right. Truly, I have not lived through the last week to end up with my sister still single. As I head up the stairs, I'm just hoping he's right.

36

Friday, 23rd December
At Rose Hill Manor: With bells on

Alice is the list queen. If I had a list, which I never do, it would say one thing: design dresses. Come to think of it, when I do have any more than that to do, like bespoke appointments, Jess is on my case, like some kind of super personal assistant. Although after what she did to Dan last night, I'm not sure Jess deserves to be mentioned in the same sentence as super-anything. Jess's excuse this morning, 'The poor boy needed a blow-out to face his demons' isn't cutting it. I mean, really? This is my sister's future husband we're talking about here. Getting him wasted to the point he was so legless he couldn't run away is a lame excuse.

As for the list thing, for one time only, due to the extreme extenuating circumstances, I broke with tradition. Earlier, while I was waiting for Alice to come out of the bath, I made one for myself. I'm guessing cute stationery is an upside of lists I'd overlooked. In case you're wondering, I blagged a heart-print Paul Smith notebook of Alice's and prettied it up using Pritt Stick and glitter borrowed from Poppy. And if I'm sounding super-lively (super being my mot-du-jour for today) for someone who barely had four hours sleep, it's because I've said yes to every extra-strong coffee I've been offered. Which so far totals five.

Sera's pre-wedding day to-do list A (status: public)

Photographer – break bad news to Alice, ring Jules
Cake – break bad news to Alice, see Poppy
Flowers – e.t.a. of hire van – 10 a.m. at
Rose Hill Manor – be there
Put on chair covers and tablecloths
Catering lorries – arrival to be confirmed
Catering team – currently 48 hours late – have they even
left New York yet? – arrival to be confirmed, everything
crossed for this
Move Alice and I over to Rose Hill Manor
First guests – arriving from 8pm onwards – OMG!!!

This is my general 'anyone can look at over my shoulder' list. It's for huge things only, not the small stuff I don't give a damn about e.g. the post box. I can barely say the words without rolling my eyes, after all the trouble that damn thing has caused. Jess is in charge of bringing it, on the condition she keeps her hands off the groom.

Between us, there's also a second super-confidential list... which is strictly more of a wish list:

Sera's highest priority, to-do list B (status: top secret)

1. Make Alice and Dan fall in love again
2. (In case of success with item 1) Wedding dress
   for Alice?????

So there you go. By the time Alice and I are heading over to Rose Hill to meet the flower van, we've already knocked off the first two items from list A. What's more, Alice just heard the catering team are airborne, so we may not be cooking on gas after all.

'It's great that Jules has agreed to stand in, even though you might not need him.' I say, as we zoom along the lanes between Daisy Hill Farm and The Manor. I'm careful to add in the end disclaimer, because as far as Alice is concerned, the wedding is still very much on hold.

It helped that Alice had met Jules and already fallen under his floppy-haired, azure-eyed spell.

'As for the cake, it was useful of Poppy to point out the damaged cake will still be fine to cut up and eat,' Alice says. 'And it's so good of her to do a nude cake too. Even if we don't... you know...' The way Alice tails off is the way it's been all morning. We're in a kind of half-way limbo-land, where we have to go ahead and do things. But no one's heart is in it.

So Poppy's going ahead with a four-tier nude sponge, with vanilla buttercream, for the – fingers crossed – wedding cake. And she's baking as we speak.

'The cupcake towers will be a nice addition too,' I say. Trying to keep Alice up-beat this morning is, understandably, hard work. 'I mean, who doesn't love a cupcake?' Piped with vanilla and orange and peppermint-flavoured buttercream, with colour-coded 'I do' labels to show the flavours. It'll only take a minute to whip the cute 'I do' stickers off if Alice and Dan decide to say 'I don't.' Because, let's face it, like it or not, the guests will be stuck here for Christmas. Even if the 'I do's' don't happen they still need to eat.

Even though I've told Alice about the photographer and the cake, there's a news blackout on Dan. Although it's too early to count my chickens – can you tell I've been hanging around a farm? – with Alice agreeing to so many fall-back solutions this morning, it feels like we might just be on a roll here. All we need now is for Dan to waltz in for a quick kiss-and-make-up, and we'll be back on track, job done. Although given the hangover he'll be dealing with, it's going to be a while before he waltzes anywhere.

Alice is beside me in the front of my gran's mini. Even though it doesn't feel as cold this morning, she's still hugging her trench coat around her knees, like some kind of comfort blanket. As we pull up in front of the Manor, her hand lands on my arm.

'Thanks, Sera, you're amazing. And your friends are wonderful too. I so…' Halfway through, I feel her touch go heavy on my arm. As she sits up, her eyes widen. Wedding or no wedding, the shriek of excitement is loud enough to make my ears buzz. 'Oooooo, I think the flowers have come early.' In two seconds flat, she's thrown open the car door and she's hurtling towards a white van.

By the time I catch her up, she's flinging open the back door and poking at the contents.

'This doesn't look like flowers… there should be boxes.' She deflates along with her voice as she pokes at some wires and a pile of plastic slabs.

A low laugh comes from the front of the van. 'Of course it doesn't look like flowers, Alice, because that's not what we're unloading here.'

'Quinn, hi. In a pixie hat too.' Alice's tone is more sarcastic than playful. If she doesn't go on to say "lovely to see you" at least she's being true to herself.

'You'll be smiling when I tell you what *is* in here.' As Quinn pops into full view around the end of the van his grin stretches from one plastic Elf ear to the other.

Alice has regained enough of her composure to be sticking her nose in the air and feigning complete disinterest. 'I can't begin to guess what you've got to look so self-satisfied about, so you might as well tell us.'

Quinn's so bouncy, he's either impervious to Alice's put-down. Or maybe he's used to ignoring her. 'This is the one and only disco floor. I've chased the length of the country to get this baby.' As he pats the side of the van with his palm, his beam is ecstatic. 'I promised Dan I'd come through on this, and I damned well have. It's going to blow you away, believe me.'

If Alice could raise one eyebrow, I think she would have done. As it is, she has to make do with a head tilt and a hard stare. 'Not that you have the best record of being believable, Quinn.' She rearranges her hair and gives a sniff. 'Thanks anyway, I'm sure our guests will be very appreciative.'

Whatever Alice misses out with the eyebrows, she makes up for, times ten, with her snippy remarks. If I had a quarter of her tongue-lashing genes, I wouldn't be the wimp I am.

Quinn smirks. 'You're very welcome, Mrs Bradwell – or will it still be Ms East? I hear the odds on a wedding happening are about the same as the odds for a white Christmas. But at least we'll have great dancing.' He practically cuts himself off laughing at that, before he goes on. 'Anyway, did you mention flowers?'

'Why?' If Alice sounds suspicious, I reckon it's only because she knows Quinn so well.

As Quinn nods the bells on his hat jingle. 'Flowers are in the next van along. You're very welcome. My pleasure to be on hand to help Team Bride. Covering for absent grooms is all in a day's work.' His mischievous grin warms slightly as he turns to me. 'Even if the prettiest bridesmaid did leave me drinking on my own last night. You won't slip away from me that easily if there's a wedding party, Sera.'

I'm opening and closing my mouth like a guppy trying to think of a suitable snappy come-back. It's not that I mind for me, but I hate the way he's taunting Alice. 'Actually Quinn… do us all a favour and shut up.' There's something so satisfying about the shock on Quinn's face.

Quinn's face soon splits into a grin again. As he leans towards me, he scrapes his nail across the corner of my eye, then examines what he's found. 'No panic, it's just a bit of glitter. Sorry to steal your sparkle, princess.'

As I pull away from him poking me in the face, I'm a million miles away from a nifty reply to that one. I'm standing wracking my brain when a howl slices through the air.

'Waaaaaaaaaaaaaaaaahhhhhhhh…'

I've heard that scream before. As I follow the yell, I see Alice, at the next van along, wedged between the open doors, and dipping into a box.

I tiptoe towards her, even though every atom of my survival instinct is telling me to hang back. 'Anything I can help with?'

Her eyes are flashing as she turns and when she replies, she's literally growling. 'Not unless you're a bloody flower wholesaler… or a bloody florist. These roses aren't cream and white, they're bloody pink. Someone must be bloody colour blind.'

'Oh my.' I can see that's going to be an 'end of the world' situation for Alice. But as I peer in over her elbow, it's not the dusky-pink colour that hits me first. I screw up my courage. 'Do you think some of them are looking a bit… well… droopy?' I'm no expert, but I know frost-bitten roses when I see them.

'Droopy… where?' Alice pokes deeper into the box

'They're just like a bunch I had from the mini market last year. I got a refund, because they'd been…' I hesitate to say the words '… frozen in transit.' As I say them she lets out a tiny whimper.

But given it was polar last night when we were walking around St Aidan, it's completely possible that's what happened to these flowers. And as Alice organised the transportation, that's down to her.

'Let's see how the next box is.' I'm desperate to be positive, but it's like the broken crystal all over again. Just without the chinking noise.

As Alice pulls the cardboard open her anger fades to despair.

'This one's the same – the roses are weird and wilting. It has to be the frost.' Her face crumples and for a moment she looks as if she's going to cry. But then she tugs at her hair instead, and talks through gritted teeth. 'This is my fault and no one else's.'

'There's no point beating yourself up.' I can't help sending a quick thank you to my fairy godmother, because bad as this is, we're not dealing with actual wedding bouquets and wedding flowers. As things stand, strictly they're only decorations. I look more closely and a fresh scent tickles my nose. 'Actually, maybe they're not *all* ruined. Qui - i - nn…' No one could ignore a yell that loud. Sure enough, seconds later he comes trotting up.

'You called, princess?' He waggles his bell in my face.

For now I'll overlook the princess. And the bell waggling. And give him a light smack on his beard. 'Be a sweet elf and take the flower boxes into the house. We're nipping into town.'

'We are?' Alice is staring absently.

'For reinforcements.' On a need-to-know basis, that's enough. I'm just hoping Jess is around to pitch in with this one.

'Great. Consider it done.' Quinn leans across to Alice, flicking a shiny fleck of glitter off her cheek with his finger. 'Someone else losing their sparkle?'

I just know there's only one place this is going. One more dig about lost fiancés from Quinn, and I will personally throttle him. 'Quinn, just back off.' As I send him the scowl of my life he jumps at my shout. 'You're an elf, so stop acting like an arse. And for one time only, get some bloody work done.'

He grabs a box and shoots off towards the kitchen door. I'm still laughing about the look on his face as Alice and I reach the car.

Not only have we got to salvage the flower situation. We also have to persuade Dan that he wants to have a first dance with Alice.

37

Friday, 23rd December
In the Butler's Pantry at Rose Hill Manor:
Sour apples and blood-shot eyes.

'So how's it going with that delectable best man out there?'

We're in the utility room, aka the butler's pantry, at Rose Hill Manor, and before she so much as sniffs at the pile of flower boxes and the disaster of what's inside them, Jess is preparing for business like a surgeon putting on scrubs. I was so relieved she could drop everything and come running, I completely overlooked avoiding Quinn on the way in. Bumping into him flexing his muscles, humping a massive disco speaker into the house was obviously a bad mistake.

'Hey, aren't the fairy lights pretty?' I'm looking up, desperate to move Jess on from eligible groomsmen. 'What a lovely idea of Alice's to hang them on the Sheila Maid.'

Jess frowns. 'Back on task, Sera, we're talking Mr Muscle here, not clothes airers.'

'Remember the bridal party celibacy agreement,' I laugh. 'Not that we need it. Those plastic pixie ears are killing the passion all on their own.'

'When he swaps that hat for a wedding suit, it'll be a lot harder to stay hands off.' She's massaging her hand cream into every individual finger. 'So you're telling me after a week of rubbing shoulders on wedding work with a Ferrari owner, you still haven't…?'

'What, wiggled my eyebrows at him?' I say, because that's what she's doing. 'This far I've said "no" to moving to London, a night in a log cabin and sex by the fire. We'll have to see what Christmas brings.'

Her eyes grow wider as the list grows longer. 'My God, I hope you put your foot down hard about London.' She pops a khaki apron over her head, winds the strings around her middle and knots them into a bow.

'We both know happiness isn't man-shaped, Jess. My life is completely great, I'm entirely fulfilled as I am, thanks.' No change necessary. Between us, I'm shocked at Jess. Who'd have thought she'd be so swayed by one flash car.

'On the other hand,' she says, eyeing me coolly, 'so long as you don't do a disappearing act, filling that man-sized gap in your life may be no bad thing. The upgrade you didn't know you wanted, but would be wild about if it happened. Like getting bumped up from business class to first?'

That is *so* not going to happen. 'I'm not sure Quinn's worth the effort.' The funny thing is, the more I get to know Quinn, the more he makes me wary rather than comfortable.

Her eyebrows are off again. 'You wouldn't buy a car without a test drive.' She breaks into a smile. 'Once a woman got her hands on those abs she wouldn't let go in a hurry.'

I take it she's still talking about me here. 'The whole point is, I'm a metaphorical nervous driver, who isn't looking for a car.' Before Quinn, Jess and I have always seen eye to eye on guys. We didn't want one, full stop.

'Okay. We're good to go.' She lifts the lid off the first box and begins to tweak out the flowers. 'I'll take the arrangements apart, save anything I can. Then we'll work our magic.' The 'good' pile is already encouraging. 'Did I see a jam jar as we came through the kitchen?'

I dash off and retrieve the famous jar Alice bounced across the kitchen floor. 'This one?'

'Great.' Jess's hands are flying as she works. 'Got any more of those?'

My lips twist into a grin. 'Only a few hundred.' Seems like Quinn's bulk buy is coming in handy after all.

'Brilliant. Next I'll need twigs to make the flowers go further. Something straighter than the ones on the ceiling.'

Here we go. Why does the mention of more twigs make me lose the will to live? Then I have an idea. 'How about the kindling sticks they use for lighting the fires?' A minute later I'm back from the boot room with a basketful. 'There's a stack of these in the coach house.'

She shoves a handful of sticks into the jar, pops in some roses, adds a twist of eucalyptus, then stands back to assess. 'Run these down the table centres. Job done.'

That's the fab thing about Jess. I knew she'd make it look easy.

'Awesome, you've saved the day again! I'll bring more jars and sticks.'

I'm careering across to the coach house when I bang into Johnny. His hair is spiked up in all directions and there are creases in everything including his face; he's looking exactly like he spent the night on someone's floor and had no sleep at all. Although I'm not going to tell him that.

'What have you done with Dan?' If I blurted that out, it's only because I'm panicking Johnny's lost him again. And technically I don't need to say 'good morning' anyway, because it was morning when I last saw him and I'm not sure there's anything good about it.

'Don't worry, Dan's upstairs having a shower, negotiating to re-join the human race.' Johnny gives a grimace.

I might as well ask. 'Did you get any clue as to how he's feeling… about Alice?'

Johnny blows out his cheeks. 'A little. He knows how much Alice has put in and that he shouldn't have let the wedding get so big. But I think he got a shock how hardline Alice has been. And right now he feels very disconnected.' Johnny's being suitably tactful here.

The sigh I let out is only because I get where he's coming from. 'Disconnected isn't the best way to feel when you're about to make a lifetime commitment.' But in a way I think that's exactly how Alice feels too. 'I'll have a word with Alice. Maybe we can get them together later.' Let's face it, if we don't, we're all in for a very un-merry Christmas.

'Thanks for catching us last night.' Johnny reaches out and gives my arm a squeeze. 'Maybe I can come to stay again sometime – when I haven't got a comatose best mate in tow?'

If we're all talking bollocks this morning, it's probably because we're knackered. One of those mornings after, when you say whatever sounds great and instantly forget about it. I'm cool with that.

'Sure.' I'm not going to hold him to it. Or ever think about it again.

As he rubs his hair he sends it in even more wrong directions. 'I'm checking on Snowball before I freshen up, how about you?'

Where do I start? On balance I decide not to bother explaining that things are so bad Alice has gone back to the cottage for a Winter Warmer and a colouring session. 'Probably best not to ask.' Pulling down the corners of my mouth should give him a clue of how it's going this far. 'If I can find Quinn's jars and a bulk supply of kindling sticks we should be back on track.'

'I'll give you a hand. Just a minute…' Johnny's squinting at me.

He's moved in so close I can see how bloodshot his eyes are. The individual pricks of stubble on his upper lip. Even after a night on the tiles his scent is still achingly familiar. 'What?'

He traces an arc across my cheekbone with his finger tip. 'Been playing with glitter again?'

The shiver that skips down my neck is like the taste of sour apple sweets. Disgusting, yet weirdly thrilling, both at the same time. And compellingly more-ish.

He pulls his hand back and blinks. 'Okay, where were we?'

For a second I've almost forgotten. 'Quinn's jars… we're on our way for those.'

'Great.' He marches into the coach house and goes straight to the stack.

He's another one like Jess. No fuss, he gets on and does the job. Ten minutes later, Johnny's heading off to see Snowball and I'm back with Jess, unwrapping jars.

'You kept that quiet.' Jess eyes me over the top of her twig pile. 'Talk about smokin' hot.'

'Let's not start…' More fool me for letting Johnny shuttle a few boxes around.

As she puts down her scissors, there's a strange glint in her gaze. 'He looked at you like he wanted to eat you. Whole.' She tweaks the petals of a rose. 'Actually I got that wrong. Quinn's the one who looks at you like you're prey. That was a far more tender look.'

Now I've heard it all. 'No, he really didn't…' Even though my protest is so high it's a squeak, I do know I'm right here.

She's looking pointedly at me. 'He literally couldn't take his eyes off you. And you were looking at him *exactly* the same way.' She's talking slowly, as if she's working it out as she goes along. Then suddenly she gets it. 'Omigod, he's the best man you slept with.'

How the hell does she know that? I'm opening and closing my mouth in shock.

She's down on me like a ton of bricks. 'Don't say anything – I already know from your face you have.'

My mouth is so dry I can't swallow. 'You're right.' My voice is a hoarse whisper. 'But it wasn't this week. It was a very long time ago. And a big mistake for both of us.'

'For goodness sake, Sera.' Her lips are curling into a smile. 'I take back everything I said about Elf Ears. It's about opposites attracting. This one's yours.'

'Soul mates come once in a lifetime. You've paired me off

with two in half an hour.' I'm crashing jars onto the work table in increasing frustration.

'I can't believe I got this so wrong first time round.' Jess's tweaking her head scarf. 'This second one is definitely "the one". No doubt about it.'

No doubt in her mind, maybe. Some of us know better.

There's only one thing for it. If I don't run, she'll never let it go. 'More twigs, I'll get some now... back in a bit...'

38

Friday, 23rd December
In Alice's holiday cottage: Fluffy cardigans and reality checks

This morning all the concealer in the world wouldn't have hidden the dark circles under my eyes, so I decided not to bother. When I get back to the cottage, even though Alice's make-up is so perfect it could have been applied by a professional, her eyelids are like cream puffs and her eyes are even redder than Johnny's were. At a guess she's been crying buckets. On balance I decide it's not the moment to tell her Jess sorted the flower arrangements and is going to remake the buttonholes and bouquets for the morning, and that while she was busy I got all the chair covers and tablecloths on. Or that two catering lorries have arrived and that each one's bigger than the entire Brides by the Sea building. But whereas some things can be left for later, others need to be dealt with.

'I see you're wearing my slippers.' Sorry, but I can't let this go. What is it with Alice and my stuff? She has three different pairs of perfectly nice brocade slippers of her own. So why did she have to help herself to my scruffy old Ugg boots?

She takes a sip of what I assume is Winter Pimms, pushes a pack of crystallised ginger in my direction and tucks her feet further under her on the sofa. 'Sorry, but they're just so unbelievably warm and comfy. And comforting.'

'I know they are.' My voice is soaring. 'That's why I wear them.' There's nothing like sheepskin boots for a long day in the studio in winter. Or for when your sister is running out on her wedding.

At least she has the decency to look slightly ashamed. 'I'd never tried them before. They seemed to suit people who were more relaxed than me.' Only Alice could make Uggs look smart, and somehow with her grey tailored slacks meticulously tucked in to the tops, she does.

'Poor Alice. You need to be more chilled. Maybe let go a bit more.' Not that she's ever needed my advice, or that I've ever given it before, but it's slipped out before I realise.

'You could be right.' If she needs to think about that for a minute, it's probably because me telling her what to do is such a departure. For both of us. She draws in a breath, then goes on. 'Do you know, Dan actually called me bossy?' It's more of a statement than a question.

Somehow I'm relieved she's the one who's raised the 'B' word, not me. And of everything Dan said, that this is what she's seized on rather than the Bridezilla thing. What's more, it's taken twenty-four hours for her to react.

'You're planning a wedding – maybe you need to be bossy.'

I say, because it's a fair point. 'Ever since we were kids, you've been one who got things done. Telling people what to do is part of who you are. And mostly we love you for it.' I send her a grin to soften what's coming next. 'Not often, but *very* occasionally – it can get too much.'

She's rubbing her nails, and as she speaks she sounds wistful. 'When we were kids I was always trying to be perfect. To make things perfect. Mum was always so busy and I just wanted to bring order to all that chaos in the house. To make things okay for both of us.'

I smile. 'Whereas I sat in the middle of the chaos and it didn't bother me.' Very much as I do now, although even I concede my laundry is currently a little out of control. 'As the older one, you definitely had it hard, where I had it easy.' I can see that now, even if I was blind to it while it was happening. But maybe that's when she started being so exacting.

She sighs. 'You were the one everyone liked, the one who had fun. I always envied you for being so free. And so lovable.'

How weird is that? 'I had no idea.'

'And when you came down to live with Gran, I felt shut out. You were there for each other and didn't need me any more.'

Maybe that's why she was always too busy to come down. 'You always looked after me so well when we were young. But you were so perfect, I was always in your shadow. Back then all I wanted was to be clever and driven like you, so Mum and Dad would praise me. I'd have given anything to pass my maths,' I say. Not that I've thought of it before, but right now I'm actually happy to be me rather than her. Exactly as I am.

'How strange it's taken us until now to find out.' Alice is

pondering. 'Jess is bossy isn't she?' She's obviously been thinking about this one. 'But people still like her.'

I laugh, because this has to be the proverbial pot-and-kettle scenario. 'Good for me that she is bossy, or I wouldn't get anything done. Maybe she's the substitute organised older sister I can't live without.'

Alice smiles, then she narrows her eyes. 'For what it's worth, I'm sorry I didn't buy one of your dresses to start with.'

I shrug. Somehow I can't imagine Alice as she was when she ordered her dress, coming to Brides by the Sea. 'How could you, when you didn't even know I made them.' It seems strange now that I hid it from her for so long. 'Anyway, those slips have only been around this week. Given you hate lace, I doubt my other designs would have worked for you.' All the same, I'm happy she's said it.

She slides her phone out of the pocket of her cardigan. 'Jules sent some pictures through.'

Good old Jules. He takes the most fabulous photos. I lean in to see and as she flicks through the pictures, there's a lump in my throat. 'Babe…' There's something about seeing my own sister looking so beautiful in the half light of the studio that makes my eyes prick. The slender lines of her neck. The amazing way the silk flows around the angles of her body. But it's not the old hard-boiled Alice I'm looking at here. Somehow Jules has sliced through her brittle shell and completely captured her inner vulnerability. The Alice in the photos is the Alice who cries. The Alice who wishes she was someone else. The Alice who has to borrow my slippers because she needs to be comforted. And it's nothing to do with my dresses at all, but suddenly I'm sniffing and scraping away the tears from under my eyelashes.

'You okay?' As she gives me a nudge, there are tears in her eyes too.

'Fine.' I pass her a tissue and we both blow our noses very loudly. 'You just look... so... lovely. That's all.'

Alice sighs. 'You know, if things hadn't gone off the rails...' From her extra-loud sniff, she must mean between Dan and her. 'I'd have been really happy and very proud to wear one of these dresses of yours. They're truly wonderful.'

'Thanks.' I rub my nose again and give her a squeeze on the Ugg.

She pulls her cardi around her. 'Those big bridesmaids dresses wouldn't have worked with your dress, though, would they?'

'They wouldn't?' I'm not sure I can give an unbiased opinion on the glitter explosions in question.

'Definitely not. We'd have needed something much lower-key.'

I take it we're still talking hypothetically. 'Maybe something simpler. Cloud grey tulle over satin might have looked pretty.' I know this is my dream not hers, but whatever. We're only pretending here, after all. 'With white cropped cardigans. Maybe in angora.'

She's propping her chin on her fist and staring into the distance. 'I'd never thought of cardigans.'

Which is when I take my reality check. We're sitting here talking about notional bridesmaids' dresses for an imaginary wedding, when what we should be doing is getting the bride and groom together to settle their differences.

'Hey, maybe we should be thinking about packing up and getting over to the manor?'

Alice taps her palms on her knees. 'Yes, Immie's coming in to do the changeover any time now, ready for when the guests arrive.'

That thought sends me scooting into the bathroom. Leaving the pregnancy tests out in full view on the shelf was my silent thought-transfer way of reminding Alice she might like to try one. Given the packs are unopened, obviously she hasn't. But if Immie comes and finds them it'll launch us into a whole new set of difficult questions with impossible answers. I whisk them back into the living room and slide them into my satchel next to the wedding manual. Which is still being carted around. If anyone needs proof I'm an incorrigible optimist this is it.

Alice still hasn't got up. 'Funny, not many of our friends have started their families yet.' She's still sounding as dreamy as when she talked about angora cardigans.

Visible tests are having some impact, then, even if not the desired one. But at least she's thinking about kids. 'Most people have careers first and families in their thirties.' I smile, hoping that's a suitable family-neutral comment that puts Alice in the right demographic.

As she gets to her feet she yawns. 'Apart from Johnny, obviously.'

My stomach lurches so hard I almost follow it across the room. I take a moment to yank my voice down from the high-pitched squeak that's escaping from my throat. 'Sorry? Who?' Somehow I can't believe what she's just said.

'Dan's best man. Who else do you think I mean?'

Crap. If I'm about to bring my breakfast up on the rug, it's a complete over-reaction. Why shouldn't he have kids? If it never crossed my mind, I'm the idiot here.

It's the perfect chance to drip in some information here. 'We actually knew each other vaguely at uni. And?' I want to shake her because she's answering so slowly.

'Nothing really. I think he's got a son, that's all. So what I'm saying is, not everyone's waited to have kids.'

'Right.' I manage to keep my voice level, but I'm bracing myself. The guests will be here in a few hours. And most likely I'll be facing Johnny's partner and his family. How did I not think of this before? And why the hell does it bother me so much? 'Cool. Great. Shall we pack then?'

Just for now I'm wishing Jess would come and revive me. A tumblerful of her Christmas Crash would be nowhere near enough.

39

Friday, 23rd December
At Rose Hill Manor: Merde alors

This last week we've kind of got used to having the Manor House to ourselves. So it's a shock to arrive at the open front door to find a cluster of taxis and a whole load of strangers rushing around with holdalls and rucksacks.

'Amazing tree… it's so huge… so Christmassy.' In the flurry of shouting and air kissing in the entrance hall, I spot Hetty, the bridesmaid who's been on her way from New York for what seems like forever, and give a mental cheer. If this is the catering team, that's another tick on the to-do list.

The sax solo on 'I wish it could be Christmas every day' is wafting through from the door to the reception rooms, which probably means that Quinn's still playing with his disco. So at the very least there's a guarantee of yummy food and non-stop dancing for the next three days.

I catch Alice's eye between the colourful padded jackets in the hall. 'I'll leave you to it and take our bags up.' Then I make a dash for the stairs.

The plan was that Alice and I would share a room on the second floor for tonight, then Alice would move down to the first-floor Master Suite for the wedding night. Even though it's tucked up under the eaves, our room is spacious and the large window has views down to the lake. The two double beds are deliciously deep and chunky with more cushions and pillows than I can count. In the rush of the day I've somehow overlooked lunch, so when I see the stack of Turkish Delight waiting on the coffee table, I dip straight in. As the icing sugar sweetness of rosewater melts on my tongue, I screw up my courage to try out the white sofa. I'm used to white dresses. White sofas, not so much. But it's feather-bed soft and as I sink into it, part of me wants to stay curled up in this attic haven forever.

It takes quite a few trips up and down the wide staircases to get everything up to our room. Before I leave again I get the test kits out of my satchel and put them in the bathroom. Let's face it, the last thing I want is to go scattering those amongst the guests. Although, who'd have thought an unopened pack of Clearblue would turn around and bite me on the bum quite so hard. As for why I feel like a sofa that's had the stuffing removed, it's about so much more than just missing lunch.

Johnny has a son?

Given I've pretty much exhausted my first to-do list, my next task is to sprinkle cupid dust on Dan and Alice, which is inevitably going to involve Johnny too. But given Alice is busy in the kitchens, I'm going to take a moment. I reckon I've got half an hour to get my head around this kid thing. I'm itching to get to the beach, but given there's no time for that, I'll have to make do with a walk down to the jetty. As I slip out of the front door and out onto the drive, and wind my scarf around my face, the icy wind has dropped. I'm just about to branch off towards the water's edge, when I hear the sound of blowing and a thunder of hooves on the gravel. Even though my heart is already beating somewhere approximately around stomach level, what I see over my shoulder makes it sink a little bit further.

Just who I wanted to see. Not.

Johnny's legs are dangling by Snowball's flanks and his cheeks are flushed as he pulls to a halt beside me. 'Hello you. We've been out letting off steam before tomorrow. Just in case the carriage is getting an outing.' As he leans forward and pats Snowball's neck, the horse snorts and flicks his tail.

That's the funny thing. All that time at uni he never let on he could ride. I push thoughts about children right to the back of my head. Just to make sure, I visualise a pirate trunk, slam the lid hard and then sit on it. It seems to have worked.

'No saddle?' I say, wondering how Johnny is staying on the horse's bare back without stirrups. 'Why don't you fall off?'

That seems to amuse him. 'You sit deep; it's all about balance. A couple of minutes of bareback riding is the most fun there is.' He slides down and the next thing is he's standing beside me. 'Want a go?'

He has to be joking. 'Definitely not.' I'm not known for my good sense of balance.

'Here.' He takes hold of my hand and pushes it onto the horse's neck. 'Grasp his mane, bend your knee, I'll give you a leg up.'

'Waaaaaaaaaahhh…' Somehow, before I know what's happening, I've landed on top of Snowball and his body is warm and solid underneath me. His mane is curiously coarse and wiry as I clamp my fingers around it and hang on for dear life. 'A- Alice has got enough p-problems, without a brides-maid with… with a b-broken neck.'

'Okay up there?' Johnny doesn't look at all sorry. 'Are you going on your own, or shall I come too?'

As it happens I don't have to answer that, because a second later Johnny gets up behind me and next thing I know his arms slide past my sides.

'Just relax,' he says, which might just be one of the most stupid things anyone has ever said to me. 'Move with the horse. We'll take it slowly, he's got a very smooth pace.'

There's a lurch and then the horse's back is swaying in a gentle rhythm as he walks.

'Like it?' Johnny asks.

In a strange way, I already do. 'Maybe.'

'You can see over the hedges.' He laughs. 'Hold on tight, we'll go into the field, then we can go a bit faster.'

As we go through the open gate and speed up, it gets bumpier. But the horse's back is broad, Johnny's arms are clamped around me. And suddenly when I look down, the ground is whizzing past my feet and my breath is being knocked out of my body every time the horse hits the ground.

If I weren't panting so hard it would almost feel like flying. We go once around the field and come to a breathless halt back by the gate.

'So how much fun was that?' Johnny slides back onto the ground.

A second later I follow, slithering down Snowball's flank. I'm breathing in the sweet musky warmth of his coat as my feet thud onto the ground again.

'Johnny, have you got a child?' So much for slamming imaginary trunk lids. It's out before I know, although that raspy croak sounds nothing like me. My mouth is parched and my pulse is banging in my ears as I wait for the reply.

'A child?' Johnny has the reins in his hand and he screws up his face as if he doesn't understand. 'You know I have.'

I certainly do not. This is news to me. 'I do?' It comes out as a squeak. For a moment I feel like I'm going mad. However many times I'm supposed to have heard this, right now my legs don't feel strong enough to hold me up.

'I definitely told you. Jake, he's twelve.' He sounds as matter of fact as any guy talking about the kid they've had for – well, twelve years.

Let's face it, if this kid is twelve, Johnny's had long enough to get his head around it, even if I haven't. As if I'd forget something as major as a child. I lock my knees, try to shut out that my stomach has dematerialised and do the maths. So Johnny's had Jake the whole time I've known him. So much for what we were saying about not knowing people at uni. Seeing as there's no reason on earth why this should matter to me a jot, I shut out the howl in my head. Instead I go for the next normal question that pops into my mind. 'So is he coming to the wedding, then?' And then there's the deafening silent sub-text. *What about his mum?*

'No, he had a better offer.' Johnny's dismissive head shake could be about anything. 'Disneyland with his grandparents. They wanted to take him before he got too old to enjoy it.'

'Shit.' A child who's close to growing out of Disneyland? That's a big child. You hear about twelve-year-olds who are taller than their mothers. And we're back to her again. 'I mean brill. Who doesn't love Mickey Mouse? And the US of A?' I'm hearing myself jabber.

Johnny shrugs. 'I think it was maybe a Frozen Spectacular rather than Mickey. And it's actually Paris not Florida.'

He's talking as if it's all so familiar. Like he picked up a Disney Knowledge package from the labour ward, along with his child. And, of course, his partner.

Johnny slides his hand up the horse's neck and springs up. With one easy movement, he's astride the horse's back again. 'By the way, have you had chance to talk to Alice yet?' And we've moved on from kids as fast as we got onto them.

My nose is on a level with Johnny's knee and I'm flailing to find some meaningful information to pass on. 'She's miserable enough to be wearing my slippers. Eating crystallised ginger like there's no tomorrow. And I think she knows she hasn't been that easy to be with.'

'Excellent.' He's grinning down at me as he gathers the reins. 'Sounds like we may need the carriage after all.'

He gives an upwards nod. 'And if I didn't know better, I'd say that sky was full of snow.'

Now I've heard it all. 'No, everyone says it's too cold to snow.' Not that I know shit all about weather.

He laughs. 'That's what they said yesterday. It's way warmer now than it was last night, you can surely feel that, Fi?' As Johnny squeezes his legs against Snowball's sides, the horse tenses. 'Great, well, enjoy your walk, then. I'll find Dan and catch up with you soon.' And the next moment the horse is tearing off towards the house, his white tail streaming out behind him.

And I'm left, opening and closing my mouth, staring up at the clouds.

40

Getting Alice and Dan together to talk when a) the first guests are starting to arrive and b) they're going out of their way to avoid each other, is easier said than done. Eventually I half shoo, half tempt her up to the bedroom.

'Okay, here's the Winter Warmer I promised.' I push her onto the sofa and shove a tumbler into her hand. 'You'll feel way better when you've had five minutes away from the buzz.' Lucky for me, Quinn's disco is both migrane-inducing and non-stop, which was a great excuse to head up here.

Alice leans back against the cushions and takes a glug. 'It's great to get away from the noise and those scented candles smell very soothing.'

Which means they're doing exactly what it says on the tin.

I've lined them up along the mantelpiece and I'm thanking my lucky stars Alice's forward planning provided us with so much choice in the candle box. 'They're vanilla. Calming and warming. Just what you need.' I send her a reassuring smile. I chose them because the label claims vanilla's a natural aphrodisiac. But I'll keep that bit to myself. 'Here, why not put on my Uggs too?' Can you tell I'm pulling out all the stops here?

'Thanks.' She's looking at me quizzically as she pulls on my boots. 'You look nice tonight. What's different?' So much for the softer Alice. She's still dishing a good backhanded compliment.

I squirm under the scrutiny. 'Maybe it's the dress?' Poppy's playsuit to be exact, but I'm hoping it'll conform to Alice's smart clothes request, as demanded the day she arrived. Even if it's technically still shorts, most people would read it as a skirt, and it has to be better than ripped denims. 'I don't often wear bright pink, but I fell in love with the flamingo print on this one.' It goes with my flamingo pyjamas too, so no one can accuse me of an uncoordinated travel wardrobe.

She nods. 'It makes you look more grown up. Older, but in a good way.' There she goes again.

'Thanks.' Right now I feel about a hundred and ten. Take it from me, if you want a relaxing life, don't ever get involved in your sister's wedding. I glance at my phone for the sixth time in as many minutes. When Johnny promised to be along as soon as he could, I assumed he meant today not tomorrow.

She shifts on the sofa. 'Lovely as this is, I mustn't stay up here too long.'

Maybe a sleep-inducing candle would have been a better choice if I'm hoping to keep her until they come. 'Actually…' Given they still haven't arrived, it might be best to 'fess up here. 'Dan's on his way. I think he might want to talk.'

She shakes her head, closes her eyes and pinches up her mouth. 'I'm not sure I have anything to say to him.' Not very helpful.

From what Johnny implies, I suspect Dan may feel the same way, but I can't tell her that. 'I think he may want to apologise.' Nor can I let her know how much I'm relying on the alchemy of those vanilla candles. 'It might be nice if you could say sorry too? For upsetting him, if nothing else?'

She gives a sniff. 'I don't know about that.' Never giving in is what makes Alice strong, but at times – like now – it's maddening.

'You two are so great together, you just need to reconnect.' I'm pleading here, even though, right now I could happily shake her. 'Remember how much better you are together than apart. How miserable you'd be without each other. How much you…' I'm about to say 'love each other', but there's a tap on the door. 'Come in.' *And for goodness sake hurry up.*

'Hi…' Johnny's head comes first, then Dan follows. From the way he does a leap, then staggers forwards, I suspect he's been propelled by a mighty push from behind.

As for Alice falling in love with him all over again, he's looking more ill than hunky. Fingers crossed her candle-induced lust can see past the bags under his eyes. As for escape-room games, if there was a key for this door I'd lock these two in and bugger letting them out after an hour. I'd only let them out when they promised they wanted to marry each other.

I grab my bag and make a run for the landing. 'Great, we'll see you two later, then. Have fun.' It's only when I'm out I realise I left my car keys on the table.

41

Friday, 23rd December
At Rose Hill Manor: A frosty reception

How long should you wait outside a door when there's a potential reconciliation going on which you may have to help with?

After two minutes, I look at Johnny, who's leaning against the wall next to me under the sloping ceiling of the landing. 'I'm guessing if Dan was going to get thrown out, he'd be with us by now.' So I take it that's a good sign.

Johnny frowns. 'If it's any help at all, he's feeling very guilty for chickening out and not showing up sooner.'

If we're swapping confessions, I'll throw in my contribution too. 'And possibly, deep down, Alice does see she's been slightly exacting.'

He sighs and taps his fingers on the wall. 'So there should

be some common ground.' After five minutes, when the door is still closed, he looks back at me again. 'Maybe we've done all we can here. For now.'

'They might need some privacy too.' Thinking of the vanilla here and hearing their low voices on the other side of the door is encouraging. But the smallest sign of make-up sex noises, I'll be out of here like a shot.

Johnny shakes his head. 'Believe me, they're a country mile away from that.' Which sounds a lot less hopeful than I'd thought.

'If they do make up, I'll have to race across to Brides by the Sea to pick up some dresses for tomorrow.' Hopefully Johnny will miss that Alice's as yet un-chosen wedding dress is one of them.

'I could run you into St Aidan now,' he says. 'So long as you don't mind a van full of welding gear. I'd still be back in time to take Dan to the farm later.'

Given where my car keys are, it's an offer I can't refuse. I mean, it's possible Alice and Dan may not come out of there until morning. And I'm torn between thinking I can't stand a whole trip to St Aidan with Johnny, and thinking it might be the last chance I ever get to drive with him. Not that I'm wishing my life away, but three short days from now, whatever happens with the wedding, Christmas will be over. And we'll all be saying our goodbyes and heading off back to our lives again.

'How about we sing along to some Christmas tunes?' I say, as we climb into his van. Singing seems like a suitably safe way to fill the silence. 'If we don't grab our chance to be cheesy, it'll all be over for another year.'

He laughs. 'I offered you a ride, I didn't sign up for a singalong.' But despite his protests, he's soon happily hollering along to 'Frosty the Snowman' as we bump along the back roads into St Aidan. What's more, he seems to know all the words to The Pogues' 'Fairy Tale of New York'. And 'Christmas Wrapping by The Waitresses', too.

Just for a few miles I can pretend he's how I used to think of him, before the awkwardness between us, before I found out he had a family. What's weird is that for all those years, when I've thought about him, it's always been as a single guy. Alone. Just like me. Somehow in my head, even though time moved on, he always stayed how he used to be. It never dawned on me he'd have a wife or a partner, let alone kids. Which shows how much I was dealing with daydreams. How much it was just me and my wishful thinking. As we pull up into the mews, the sparkle of the shop windows against the darkness of the street brings me back to real life.

'I'll be as quick as I can,' I promise, flicking on the lights on the stairs up to the studio. 'If you don't mind coming up, I could use some extra hands for carrying.'

Just like everyone else, once we're upstairs, Johnny heads straight across to the windows. 'What a view.'

'Everyone says that,' I say, as I whisk along the slips and tops on the rail, pulling off the ones Alice liked and slipping them into dress covers.

He's craning his neck to get a better view of the beach between the rooftops below. 'The breakers look amazing in the moonlight. And you can see the lights of ships out at sea. I'm surprised you ever get any work done up here.'

I laugh as I pick out some sashes, ribbons and delicate

diamanté belts. 'I actually do my best work sitting on the beach.'

'Fi.' He's staring at me. Hard. 'Nice dress by the way. What happened to the shorts?'

I roll my eyes, but only because it's taken him so long to catch up. 'Alice sent them on a Christmas break, expect them back Monday.'

As his brief smile fades, he's still lingering by the window. 'Actually, I was thinking about what we were talking about before.'

Alice and Dan, Snowball, Christmas songs, Mickey Mouse…? 'Right.'

'About Jake.'

'Oh that.' I force out a smile. 'I'd almost forgotten.' No way am I going to say I've barely thought about anything else since this morning.

Johnny clears his throat. 'He was born when I was at uni doing my first degree. His mum and I aren't together. We went out briefly and she found out she was pregnant later. That was why I was doing the kind of post-grad degree where I got paid – so I could support them. And why it was vital I went straight on into a job once I finished.' The words mount up in the silence of the studio.

'You had a baby all the time I knew you at uni?' And somehow managed not to say? I'm not sure which part I'm most shocked about. Both facts eclipse the relief that he's not with Jake's mum. Although that's not to say he isn't with someone else.

'I didn't broadcast it at uni. It wasn't something twenty-year-old students related to. Some dads in my situation run a mile, but I wanted to be involved. Take full responsibility.'

I laugh. 'So you were right. All that talking and I didn't know you at all.' Not that I should have, given I was just another girl in the downstairs flat.

'I loved hearing about your dreams to see the world. It was like an escape. With a baby to support, I assumed I'd never get to go anywhere, ever.'

'Shows how little we knew, doesn't it? You were heading for an ace job that let you travel anyway.' If my laugh was light before, now it's got a bitter ring, which I really didn't intend.

'I know I didn't tell you about Jake at uni, but I definitely mentioned him later. Didn't you get in touch when you came back one time?' He screws up his face, as if it's a distant memory. Which, let's face it, it is.

'I'm not sure.' Except I am. Because I only got in touch the once. That time I crashed back home a few months into my disaster gap-year trip, to be with Gran, pinning all my hopes on Johnny wanting to be with me. I'd never be that pathetic now. When he didn't reply I threw my phone in the harbour. It's probably still there.

'Why I remember is Jake was in hospital with meningitis. I tried to ring later, but I couldn't get through. So I texted back and obviously I mentioned him, to explain why I hadn't replied sooner.'

I know zilch about kids, but I do know meningitis is every parent's nightmare. 'Shit, was he okay?'

Johnny shrugs. 'There were complications, it was tough, but he pulled through.'

'Phew, that's good.' It takes seconds to sink in. All those years ago, when I gave up on him because I thought he wasn't interested, he was in hospital with his son. And he actually texted back? And tried to ring. If a steamroller had run over my stomach, I couldn't feel any flatter. Or any more crushed. 'I changed my phone shortly after I got back, but back then they gave out new numbers with every handset. So that would have been a text and calls I didn't get.' My voice trails off.

'And I always assumed it was because of Jake that you didn't reply.' He rubs his head, then clamps his hands behind his head. 'Well, who'd have thought?'

So we both spent the best part of ten years resenting the other for not replying. I'm not sure there's any easy way back from that. It's not even as positive as a clash of coincidences. It's more like a complete mismatch of disconnections. You might think it would be whoop-di-do, what the hell, let's pick up from where we left off. But it's not like that. At all. I'm someone else now. I've moved on with my life. And so has he.

'Well, now we've cleared that up, then. Thanks for sharing… I guess I need to think about bridesmaids' dresses.' The way I'm clapping my hands isn't like me at all. But at least a real problem might blank out the frustration. The screaming futility at the way I misread the situation back then. Banging my head against a wall wouldn't begin to put it right. It's so long ago, there's not even any point kicking myself for my mistake.

'Bridesmaids' dresses?' Johnny looks as bemused as I felt when he leapfrogged to talking about Jake.

'We need four.' I'm rattling now and it's helping. 'Don't ask why, it's just another crazy fuck-up, in this whole arse-up mess of a wedding. I'm going to raid the rails in the Bridesmaids' Beach Hut. Fingers crossed for variations on cloud grey tulle. If not, I've got a lot of sewing to do.'

42

Friday, 23rd December
At Rose Hill Manor: Sparks, secrets and wedding nights

'So how did it go with Dan?'

When I shove my way back into our bedroom, my hands are high in the air and I'm holding at least ten dresses. And Alice is on her own again, scrunched on the sofa. It's not that I'm being nosey with this question, either. But given we've been to hell and back for this wedding in the last week, I'd say I'm invested. Bloody invested.

What's more, I've checked on our parents on the way up and given them Alice's excuses. They're ensconced in the second-best suite, next to the Master. Alice's choice. It said in the Huffington Post that no one ever manages sex on their wedding night these days, so the parents having the room next door to the bride probably isn't that crucial. Not that I'd have put them there if this was my wedding. But it's not. And thank Christmas for that.

In Alice's words, our parents were the last people she could face when her wedding was on the skids. Well, that last part was me, but you get the idea. There are times when, much as you love them, you haven't got it in you to deal with them. Once I took away the scented candles, checked my dad's tie for tomorrow, tuned them in to Radio 4, found tumblers for their Gaviscon, and put new batteries in my mum's camera, they were all good.

So Alice owes me. Given she's my roomie for tonight, for payback I want her to talk non-stop, about anything at all. It's the only way to block out the white noise in my head. If I think any more about Johnny I might just go crazy.

'So…' I prompt.

'It was good at first with Dan… then not so good.' She screws up her face.

Not what I need to hear. 'Didn't you snog and make up?' I'm kicking myself that the crate of mistletoe is still untouched in the boot room. I seriously messed up by neglecting to hang a sprig from the bedroom beam in time for their reunion. Throwing open the wardrobe doors, I begin to hang up the dresses. Although at this rate they won't even be coming out of their covers.

'Snog?' Alice's eye roll is disparaging. 'We're not teenagers, Sera. Dan apologised very nicely. Then I said sorry too, although I'm not sure what for exactly.' As she stares at the frosted swag draped across the fireplace, her look is wistful. 'Actually it was lovely. I can't remember the last time we curled up and talked. And for a while, even though the bags under his eyes were shocking, he actually looked at me as if he truly loved me.'

Exactly why we opted for vanilla not lavender. It occurs to me I should offer Dan's excuses. 'Those bags are probably because he's been too upset to sleep.' On balance that sounds better than saying he got rat-arsed on his way to find a post box. 'So what the hell went so wrong?'

'I'm not sure.' She drags in a long breath. If she carries on twisting her bob around her fingers like that, hair and make-up aren't going to have anything left to work with when they get here in the morning. 'Everything was fine up until I mentioned the night with George.'

'Oh my.' My groan's out before I can stop it. I don't mean to be judgemental, but sometimes I despair of Alice. 'How was spilling the beans about spending the night with your ex, who also happens to be your first love, supposed to help?' Talk about hurling herself off a proverbial cliff.

Her sniff is starchy. 'I couldn't go forward to my wedding vows with a secret like that between us.' She looks horrified that I thought she might. Then she sticks out her chin like she used to when she was taking on the world, when she was little. 'If bloody Dan had turned up when he was supposed to, I wouldn't even have gone to see George. It's not as if there was a spark. Seeing George made me certain I wanted Dan.'

'And did you get the zero spark bit across to Dan?'

She gives a snort. 'Obviously not. He was too busy being sarcastic to listen to anything. One minute the lines of communication were blissfully open, the next he totally pulled up the drawbridge on me. And then he left.'

Be careful what you wish for. When I wanted to block out the white noise, I didn't mean like this.

As I flop down next to her on the sofa and the downy cushions close around me, I make a mental note to buy one like this for myself, next time around. 'Dan's only upset because he cares about you,' I say. Not for the first time, and probably not for the last. 'When he takes time to think about George, he'll see it for what it is. I'll get Johnny to explain to him in the morning.' I smile at her. 'It's Christmas Eve tomorrow, you know.'

She doesn't need me to tell her it's the day she's supposed to be getting married. That's the trouble with weddings. When there are wobbles, the timeframe makes the pressure huge. Especially for the bridesmaids. I can already see I'm going to be rushing around like a fly with a blue bum from first light. Again.

As Alice prods at my Uggs her voice has gone all wobbly. 'If there's even the tiniest bit of frost, I'll be *so* happy.' The slippers are still on her feet rather than mine, obviously.

Hopefully there'll be so much excitement tomorrow, she'll forget the white Christmas part of her dream. Because there's no way I can tell her it's got warmer and she's going to be disappointed. Instead I go to look out at the moonlight, to see if it's as spectacular on the lake as it was on the sea earlier. The way the light splashes across the water, it almost is, even without the breakers. The moon is washing across the gardens too, but as I stare down at the ghostly blue grass, a small random fleck drifts across the view.

'Alice.'

Then there's another.

And another.

When Johnny said it was going to snow I really didn't believe him.

Alice sits up. 'That print really suits you, Sera. Is it flamingos? You should wear dresses more often.'

'Thanks.' Someone's definitely been out with the fairy dust. I mean, when did Alice ever give a full-on compliment like that? If I wasn't so shocked at what I'm looking at through the window, I might have fainted on the spot. As it is, there's no time to be dramatic. 'Alice, please, just you get yourself over here. Like, now, would be good. For fuck's sake, just hurry up.'

'What?'

I fling the window open and thrust out my hand, because I can hardly believe what I'm seeing here. Sure enough, when I wave my hand around, a flake lands on my palm. Who'd have thought one tiny fragment of ice crystals could make my heart whirl so fast. But I don't want to spoil it. So I wait. As Alice pushes herself up off the sofa at approximately the speed of a snail, or, come to think of it, the speed of Jess on her way out of a bar, I'm asking myself exactly how much Pimms Alice has necked. It feels like a whole winter later when she arrives at my elbow and I nudge her. 'Look.'

Even though the flecks are bigger now, it takes a few seconds for her to focus. 'Snow?' She sticks her hand into the cold night air, snatches a flake in her fist. Then rubs it on her face. And that's all it takes to wake her up.

'It's a sign Sera. I *am* getting married. Of course I'm getting married. How could I ever think I might not be?' She's jumping up and down, flinging out her arms and hugging me in a way that's very unlike her.

So at least we have a bride now. Or possibly a Snow Queen. Or with any luck, both. Whether we also have a bridegroom is another question entirely.

43

Saturday, December 24th, Christmas Eve
At Rose Hill Manor: Snow drifts and style icons

When the warble of Alice's phone alarm wakes me at seven on Christmas Eve morning, two things hit me.

First – how the hell am I waking up? Because despite hitting the Winter Warmers last thing with Alice, after our mammoth session trying on dresses, with the mayhem in my head about Johnny, I didn't ever expect to fall asleep.

And second – the silence outside. Rose Hill Manor is in the country, but even at dawn there's always the noise of a distant tractor or a passing car. As I open one eye, although the light from the dawn sky is already seeping across the ceiling, apart from Alice's gentle breathing from under her quilt, it's as if there's a blanket of quiet over the world.

Only one thing makes that happen.

I slide down off the bed, pulling a cardi over my pyjamas, as I head for the window. 'Alice, there might be…' When I look outside the lights on the terrace below are washing across the garden. 'Oh my… did you wish for snow, Alice?' There's so much of it, someone must have. When I made my wish for snow, I distinctly remember specifying a dusting. An inch at most. Not a bloody avalanche. And this isn't any ordinary amount. Where there were trees and bushes and lawns before, now there's only whiteness. The kind of deep drifty whiteness that brings life to a total halt.

If I saw that view on any other day, regardless of my Johnny stress, I'd give a little whoop of excitement at the novelty, then dive straight back under the covers to grab a few more zeds. As it is, the kick of adrenalin in my chest has me running for my boots.

'Snow?' Alice is doing one of those slow-motion wake-ups you see in fifties' movies. She rolls over, wrist above her head, dark hair spread out over the pillow, a beatific grin on her face. 'Really? That's wonderful.'

It could be wonderful. It would be. If a hundred-plus guests weren't trying to reach her wedding in rural Cornwall. And despite Alice's three-year insistence that her wedding was going to be a whiteout, there isn't a single contingency plan in the wedding manual for snowy roads. How come Alice, empress of the risk assessment, has managed to overlook this? Whatever happened to snow chains for the registrars and a hundred and fifty pairs of wellies for the revellers? And someone needs to sort this. Leaving her cooing, I wrench my way out to the landing and hurtle down the stairs. Then, as I burst out of the front door, I run straight into a knee-high snow drift.

'Arghhhhhhh' I gasp as the snow spills over the tops of my boots and collects in clumps around my bare ankles. Talk about brain freeze, this is so cold it burns. Except, as I stand, legs in two holes, marooned in my snow pile, I realise this isn't a drift. This is it. The snow is the same even depth for as far as I can see. It's plastered against tree trunks. Clumped along branches. It's not even like something off a Christmas card, because it's pretty much obliterated everything.

'Talk about Scott of the Antarctic... what do we do now?' I'm still muttering to myself, when a distant rumble makes me stiffen. It gets louder as I listen. A tractor? As its lights speed into view, it's threading its way between the trees on the lane, lumps of snow flying off its huge wheels. Somehow it's forging a way down the drive, thrusting the snow to one side as it travels. As it blasts around the front of the house with a deafening roar, I let out a scream as I'm pelted with snow spray. Then a second later, the engine cuts out and the sound of Freddie Mercury singing 'Don't Stop Me Now' bounces off the trees. The music stops, the tractor door opens, and Rafe jumps down, followed by Poppy.

'Woohoo, amazing or what?' Poppy's cheeks are pink where they're peeping out over the top of her scarf. 'We've come to tell you not to worry.' It's alright for her to say that. She's wearing red-spotted wellies, not short biker boots. And her sister isn't trying to get married and have a Christmas house party to boot.

Rafe raises his eyebrows and grins. 'That was quite a snow dump, but there's definitely no need to panic. We've got this covered.'

Panic? They read my mind, then. 'How come you're out so early?'

'Farmers are always up at the crack of dawn because they never go to bed.' Poppy laughs. 'Anyway, first things first, we can't do anything until you admire my new Barbour jacket. It's a present from Rafe that was supposed to be for tomorrow, but Santa delivered it today due to the weather.' As she comes towards me she holds out her arm for me to sniff. 'Doesn't it smell fab?'

'Very smart,' I say, as I have a quiet swoon over the delicious scent of wax oil. If that had been the kind of early Christmas present Quinn had in mind, we might have been doing business. 'Does this mean you're a proper country girl now?'

Rafe laughs. 'She's practically an honorary farmer.'

Poppy gives him nudge. 'I'm not sure I'd go that far.'

'And in return I got a London T-shirt with a picture of The Shard.' As Rafe opens his own Barbour, and lifts up his jumper for a T-shirt inspection, his ear-to-ear grin gives away how pleased he is. These are his own ears too, not fake elf ones like Quinn's.

'Top marks for style, both of you.' I'm truly hoping they aren't judging my cardi, jimjam shorts and biker boots in return. Although realistically, as a bridesmaid, until I put my dress on, this is pretty much me for the morning.

Poppy gives Rafe a teasing nudge. 'Anyway Mr Fashion Icon, get over yourself and tell Sera where we're up to with the wedding.'

'Okay.' Rafe gives a cough. 'So the council are clearing the main road to St Aidan, the local farmers are out doing the smaller lanes, we'll sort out the drive here, clear a parking area and make a turning circle for the carriage.' He rubs his hands together. 'And the guys from the farm are meeting the sleeper train from London with our fleet of four-by-fours and Land Rovers. They'll bring guests from the station to the cottages. And then they'll bring them on here.'

I'm amazed that the problems I'd envisaged are melting away, even if the snow isn't. 'Brilliant. Thanks so much for all this.'

Poppy grins. 'Given you've filled the cottages to bursting over Christmas, it's the least we can do. Then we'll bring the cake over here too. And Rafe will pick up the registrars.' She's making it seem easy. 'The only bad news is that the hair and make-up team from London rang the farm to say they've only made it as far as Sussex. I let Jess know and she's rounding up her crew. They'll be here as soon as they can be.'

'That's awesome.' I'm so relieved. With yesterday's complications I never got around to making a list for today, but it seems like they covered most things there.

'Anyway, we'd better get off. Snow at a wedding is a first for us.' Rafe laughs. 'We'll think of it as practice for when we do weddings all year round.'

'We certainly won't need the snow machines,' I say. Which reminds me of one last thing to check. 'Any signs of life from the guys' cottage yet?'

Poppy smiles as she clambers up into the tractor. 'They were out early. Quinn was heading off for a swim in the sea, but decided to build a snowman instead.'

I can't help rolling my eyes at that. 'No surprise there, then.'

'And Dan was out pacing,' Rafe adds as he swings up into the cab after her. 'I'd take that as a good sign. Pacing is what grooms do before breakfast on their wedding day.'

At least he hasn't run away. Yet.

I hold up my arm to stop them as I have a last thought. 'A very important message for Johnny. Tell him, if there are any problems at all, to come and find me. I'll mostly be in the top-floor bedroom.' For once I don't give a damn about the bedroom innuendo and 'fingers crossed' the next time I see Johnny is when we help Alice into the carriage.

44

Saturday, December 24th, Christmas Eve
In the bridesmaid's bedroom at Rose Hill Manor:
Tangles and envelopes

After the early start, there's plenty of time for the bridesmaids to make the final touches to the ballroom and the winter-garden ceremony area while we wait for the beautifying ladies to arrive. While Alice gets to laze in her bath, the four of us bridesmaids zoom in all directions downstairs. We soon have the place cards, candles, jars of flowers and favours spread around the tables. As we put the buttonholes out for guests to collect on their way in, next to the replacement post box, I cringe at the trouble it caused. As for the flowers, Jess has done wonders with the bouquets. Alice has the simple bundle of white rose buds she'd set her heart on. And the bridesmaids' gypsophila posies are like mini snowstorms as they sit waiting in their Mason jars, when we take them upstairs with us to get ready.

However good Alice's own hair and make-up team are, let's face it, they're stuck in a snow drift. Which frankly is as much use to us as a waterproof teabag. Jess's hair and make-up team are legendary and, luckily for us, they're *here*.

At long last we're perched on the beds and the sofa, sipping prosecco, and nibbling on tiny smoked-salmon blinis, and pancetta and cherry tomato tartlets that fellow bridesmaid and caterer Hetty has brought up. After a couple of glasses of wine on an empty stomach, everyone suddenly cares a lot less than they did.

'Right, I'll go first for make-up.' Proving to the London ladies they aren't about to get their faces scraped off by some country bumpkins is the least I can do. As I get up and make my way to the waiting chair, I'm already the teensiest bit dizzy, although I'm not sure if it's down to the fizz or sheer terror about the day to come.

I'm not quite sure what Jess's make-up girls do. It involves getting sprayed like a car, which I admit might look pretty alarming if you come from Hampstead, even if that is the world centre of colonic irrigation. Enough to say that afterwards all those awful dark circles have disappeared from under my eyes and my skin looks radiant. But in a good way. What's more, I'm transformed. Instead of being a bridesmaid about to have a breakdown, I'm me again. Only me on the best day ever. Woohoo to that.

'You're looking completely rejuvenated and beautiful, babes.' Hetty says, as she stifles a yawn. 'Bagsy I'm next. And please tell me that spray obliterates jet lag too.' She's generous, and everybody loves her. How else would she get an entire team to follow her to Cornwall and agree to work flat out over Christmas? If I wasn't already pinned down by a harpy with a hairbrush, I'd hug her for that.

Mandy, the hairdresser, stands behind me, pulls on a lock of my hair and eyes me in the pop-up mirror. 'So, straight and glossy, or wavy?'

I knew this was coming. Alice is hell-bent on making me into her rather than me. 'Straight hair will look neat, but you might as well get married with a stranger as your bridesmaid.' My wail is heartfelt and the imploring look I send her is directed at my slippers too. Given she's swiped them again, I reckon she owes me this one.

'Beachy waves, but tamed?' Mandy gives another tug on my scalp.

Alice takes another large gulp of fizz. 'Go on, then. Be beachy.'

I'm guessing I have the bubbly to thank for that. Half an hour later the results are awesome. If I could hide one of these women in my bedroom to do this to me before I left home every day, I damn well would. Although, thinking about it, I might not get anything done afterwards, because I'd be too busy swishing my hair around. And knowing how much trouble I have even keeping track of my shorts in the morning, hoping to fit in a hair-tonging session too is pretty unrealistic. My current low-maintenance hair routine is to run my fingers through it. End of. But I suspect even the new, chilled, Ugg-boot-wearing version of Alice would still have a fit at the idea of me leaving the house without brushing my hair.

'Okay.' As I give my head another experimental shake, the waves bounce, then flick back into perfect place. I could so get used to this. 'I'm ready except for the dress, so I'll nip down and see how things are going.' Catching a glimpse of myself in the mirror as I whoosh down the stairs, I can't help but think if my instant transformation was a boob job I'd have gone from an A cup to a whopping FF.

As I slip past the Christmas tree in the hall I catch sight of Poppy through the door to the dining room, next to a stack of cake boxes, so I glide on through.

'Anything I can do to help?'

She gently sets down the top tier of the cake on her stack, stepping back to check it's centralised. Then she turns around. 'Wow, are you gorgeous or what?'

The little twirl I give her ends with a peck on her cheek. 'Mwah! And still in my cardi and pjs too.'

Poppy gives a frown. 'Have you sorted out the dresses for the wedding yet?'

'As soon as it started snowing Alice got all enthusiastic about dresses. We were still trying them on at two this morning, but in the end we're going with grey tulle for the bridesmaids.' I give a cheering sign because there's no expressing how pretty they are, even if they are from my own range.

'Tab, so wishes do come true.' She smiles and hands me a spatula of buttercream, then moves back to work on the cake. As I lick, I watch in awe as she shakes a sieve, scattering icing sugar over the impressive four-tier cake, then begins to arrange frosted fruit and white rose buds around the ledges.

'Your nude cakes are usually colourful, but this one is stunning all in white.'

She pops a tiny white posy on the top and we both stand back.

'Completely amazing. Alice is going to love it.' I squeeze Poppy into a huge hug. 'I can't begin to thank you for making it.'

'You're welcome.' As she squeezes me back I get another waft of delicious new wax jacket from her sweater.

'One last thing.' I might as well try my luck before I dash off, because after the spatula taster of vanilla, the towers of glistening cupcakes further along the table are making my mouth water. 'Any chance of a cupcake? Canapes are completely delish, but they're built for London-sized stomachs, not Cornish ones.'

She laughs. 'I brought you an emergency supply, in case you needed a sugar rescue. In the blue box over there. With your name on.'

Now you can see why I've missed her so much. 'I'm sooooo pleased you're back.' She gets another even bigger hug for that, then I grab my box and make a run for the stairs before I get all emotional.

When I get back upstairs the room's the same as when I left, but there's not a hangover or a tired eye in sight. What's more, Alice, Hetty, Jo and Sophie have gone, and there are four supermodels in their places, wearing their dressing gowns, their hair almost done. I'm standing marvelling at the transformations, when there's a knock on the door behind me.

For a second I swear my heart stops. Then my stomach plummets. I told Johnny he could find me up here. And if this is Johnny, what the hell has gone wrong at the farm? Even before I put my hand on the knob, I'm ready to cry. I'm hesitating, but it's only to prolong the time before everything crashes around our ears. To give us a few more happy moments.

'Hello…' There's another knock.

Alice turns impatiently. 'Open the door, Sera, don't keep Jules waiting on the landing.'

'Jules?' My knees feel like they're about to give way.

'Obviously. He's here for our getting-ready shots.'

'Right.' I do as I'm told.

A second later Jules swings straight past me, making a bee line for Alice. Next minute she's engulfed in one of those spectacular air kiss embraces he does. He showers her with photographer love, while leaving every molecule of her foundation and bob perfectly intact. All whilst holding his camera bags and tripods, and unwinding his stripy scarf at the same time.

'What a day.' He slides his holdalls on to the floor. 'I've been wishing *so* hard for snow. This is my first full-on white-out wedding. At Christmas too. The pictures are going to be phenomenal. Sensational. Awesome. Fabulous. All of the above, even.'

I take it he's excited. And at least we know whose fault the avalanche is now. I lean my back against the wall, hook my left foot around my right ankle. Watching Jules whisking around snapping photos will give my blood pressure a chance to drop.

I'm just starting to breathe again, a long time later, when there's another knock on the door. This time round it's less of a shock. Talk about déjà vu. By the time my hand is on the handle, my heart is racing, but I've convinced myself it's probably our mum. So when I open the door and my eyes lock on Johnny's face, my stomach goes into spasm so fast, I'm practically sick on his feet. If I squeeze out onto the landing, maybe I can keep this away from Alice.

'What's happened?' My mouth's so dry, all that comes out is a whisper.

He stares at me. 'Nothing, why?' He gives my shorts a little tug. 'More flamingos then?'

How can he talk about fabric prints when the wedding's going down the pan? As I double over and hug my clenching gut, I notice the creases in Johnny's trousers. 'But you're wearing your suit?' As I let my gaze run up his body a little bit of me manages a silent 'phwoar'. What is it about guys in nice suits? Focus, Sera. 'Where the hell's Dan?'

Johnny's talking slowly, using his patient voice. 'Dan's safe at the farm with Quinn. As planned.' From his passing frown he's suddenly doubting putting 'Quinn' and 'safe' in the same sentence. 'And I'm in a suit because there's a wedding.' He gives me a teasing nudge with his elbow. 'Alice and Dan? Getting married? Why there's a houseful of people downstairs? Please tell me you haven't forgotten?'

When your body goes into flight mode, it's hard to back-pedal. 'But you were coming to find me… if there was a problem.'

Johnny scratches his head, as if he hasn't got a clue about that. 'Sorry, I'm actually here with something from Dan. For Alice.'

'Right.'

'To make up for yesterday. It's all in the letter.' He pulls an envelope out of his pocket and passes it to me. It says *Alice* on the front, in Dan's strong, honest hand-writing. Then Johnny puts a small box wrapped in silver paper into my hand too. 'This was meant for Christmas, but it's probably more important she gets it now.' The wrinkles in Johnny's brow tell me how anxious he is.

'Lovely.' My head's still trying to catch up with the U-turn. 'I'll give them to her straight away.'

'Great. I'll see you soon, then. With the carriage.' Johnny's backing down the landing. Just before he disappears down the stairs he stops. 'By the way, Fi, you look beautiful.' The smile he flashes is one I haven't seen lately. Possibly for years. 'Just saying.' And then he's gone.

45

Saturday, December 24th, Christmas Eve
In the bridesmaid's bedroom at Rose Hill Manor:
This is to say…

Amore, Alice,
This is to say that however wonderful the wedding manual
is – and ours is brilliant – weddings are about so
much more than disco floors, and post boxes, and white
dresses.

Weddings are about two people, moving on to a future
together, simply because they can't bear to think of living
their life any other way. And I truly hope that's us, Alice.
I love you and I want to marry you, simply because I want
to be with you forever. And I hope I haven't wrecked my
chances by stuffing up so spectacularly. If/when we move
on with our life, please let's make that a life where we work

less, where we make time for talking, and holidays, and
doing what we do best – being us.
   Please make my day and marry me.
   I love you, Dan xxx

Okay, it's meant for Alice. But we're bridesmaids. We're
invested. Bloody invested. Even before she's opened the envelope, we're looking over her shoulder. And we're sighing with
her, and smiling with her, and sniffling with her, as she
murmurs her way through it. And we're all dipping into our
pockets for hankies by the end.

'Holy shit, you have to marry him after that, whatever he's
done,' Hetty says, as she blows her nose on a man-size tissue
with all the decorum of an elephant.

'Don't forget the pressie.' I push the box at her. If we're
going by the rule of presents, 'the smaller the box, the bigger
the value', this is going to be a stonker. And my money's on
some gorgeous earrings.

We wait, as she takes forever to pull off the paper.

Hetty's right behind her. 'Another note… on the outside of
the box. Come on, hurry up and unfold it…'

Alice rubs her nose. 'It's folded very tight… and it's a
PS…'

P.S.
I know eternity rings are supposed to be some way down
the line, but given how long we waited to get married, I
couldn't wait any longer to get you yours. This ring was
meant as a gift for tomorrow, our first Christmas together,
to tell you how much I want our love to last forever. But

just in case you were thinking of changing your mind today,
I'm hoping it might remind you what a catch I am – wink
;) As it's meant for infinity, hopefully getting it a day early
won't make much difference in the long run.
  Love you always, D x
  P.P.S. I wished for snow x

'Oh my, it's *another* ring.' As I lean in to read, I'm smiling at Dan's jokes and welling up at the love. Two majorly significant rings in one day. And snow too. How lucky is Alice?

'Open the box, open the box, open the box…' For someone whose work demands they're cool in a crisis, Hetty's very hyped.

As Alice does as she's told, we let out a collective brides-maids' gasp. 'Oh wow… beautiful… amazing…'

The ring is simple platinum, a single beautiful half-band of diamonds. And maybe just for once, we're all thinking it would have been worth every minute of going to hell and back for three years making this wedding happen, if this is what we got at the end of it. And as early Christmas presents go, this one's definitely a bride-clincher.

Alice scrapes her finger under her lashes. 'Good thing we're waterproof here. I'll put it on my right hand for now.' She gives me a watery smile. 'Remind me to swap my engagement ring too, nearer the time.'

Jules, who's been hanging back at a respectful distance, snapping away silently with a zoom lens, looks at his watch. 'The registrars usually arrive well in advance to talk you through the ceremony. So "nearer the time" isn't so very far away. Sophie, how about you bring Alice's mum along for a few quick pictures with Alice. And then you might like to hurry along with those last hair and make-up details, and get into your dresses, ladies.'

When Jess talks about the photographers running the weddings, she's not joking is she?

As if I ever imagined I'd be okay with my sister, the bride, in one of my dress designs, and all the bridesmaids wearing them too, including me. Let's face it, when I first said I'd do anything not to wear the glitter explosion of a dress, I'd have drawn the line at swapping to a Seraphina East.

But right now it feels like the most natural thing in the world.

46

Saturday, December 24th, Christmas Eve
In the Winter Garden at Rose Hill Manor:
Bells and pointy toes

'Who'd have thought Alice's dream of arriving at her wedding like a Snow Queen would actually come true?' I say to Rafe as we stamp our feet. 'Although not thinking it through as far as the white wellies was an oversight. Good thing Poppy's red-spotty wellies fitted.' Even though the guys have cleared a path through the snow, Alice can't risk ruining her dainty shoes, so I'm waiting here with her white satin pumps so she can swap before she goes inside.

'If you didn't know there were a hundred and fifty wedding guests on the other side of those doors, you could believe we were in an Arctic wasteland.' Rafe laughs.

When Johnny drew up around the front of the house earlier,

we bundled Alice and her wonderful white fur cape into the carriage, along with my dad in his scarf and overcoat, to be driven the short distance around to the garden. We took the short cut through the house, and we're now outside the double doors that lead from the garden into the ceremony room. Rafe's waiting with me because he's going to take over with Snowball and the carriage, so Johnny can come inside.

As another icy gust of wind whistles across the garden, I pull my little fur jacket closer around my neck. 'They're taking ages to get here, given it's approximately a hundred yards.'

Rafe shrugs deeper into his Barbour. 'You don't actually get much more photogenic than a bride in a horse-drawn carriage, in snow, at Christmas. It's like the top trumps of wedding conditions. And given this is Jules, he'll be stopping the carriage for a shot of every vista.'

'Let's hope he hasn't been run over on the way round,' I say, although I'm only half joking here. If anything happens to Jules, I'm not sure Jess has any more photographers up her sleeve.

I'm stamping my feet, because my toes in my white leather kitten-heeled ankle boots – pause for you to vom at the thought of those – are already freezing. On the upside, if my feet are numb with cold, at least I can't feel the pain where the pointy toes nip. And yes, it might surprise you, but I *am* wearing them. I didn't rebel and put on my biker boots, because seeing as I got my way, and I'm wafting around on my own cloud of happiness in my lovely grey tulle and taffeta skirt, the least I could do for Alice was to wear her choice of boots. Even if they're the last thing in the world I'd ever put on my feet myself, but whatever. Just this once I'm happy to suffer.

The other bridesmaids are waiting on their own clouds of happiness, just inside the doors. Somehow I thought once Hetty arrived, she'd automatically pick up the head bridesmaid reins from me, but she hasn't. So I'm first in line to support Alice here, clutching her pumps, a hankie, a spare copy of her vows, not that she's going to lose her own bag between getting into the carriage and getting out of it, I hope. And a bag for the wellies. As well as my posy.

Rafe thrusts his hands deeper into his pockets. 'Don't worry, Jules knows how to look after himself.' As we hear the jingle of bells we both stiffen. Then as the carriage comes into view through the trees, Rafe smiles at me. 'See, I told you whatever happened, it would all work out. Doesn't she look beautiful?' There's a catch in his voice as he speaks.

Despite Alice being snuggled inside her huge white hood, her face is terrified and pale rather than regal. I swallow hard. 'You must get used to this, seeing it so often,' I say, because if I keep talking I'm less likely to start blubbing.

Rafe gives my arm a squeeze. 'It's always great when the bride arrives. After that everyone can relax. Ten minutes from now you'll be knocking back the bubbly.'

I laugh. 'We've already downed a startling amount of prosecco considering it's not even lunchtime yet.' And I'm determined to pace myself. Between us, I'm definitely not going to be the proverbial pissed bridesmaid here. Although it's funny, with all the adrenalin rushing through my body, I'm barely feeling the effects of the alcohol at all.

We watch as the carriage slows to a halt. 'Snowball's stamping his feet too, look, and his breath's all steamy.'

Rafe sighs as Jules directs Alice down the carriage steps.

'More pictures. This part always takes an age.' He pats me on the shoulder as he sees Johnny jumping down from the carriage. 'I'd better go, have a wonderful day.'

And then suddenly Alice and my dad are here. One minute I'm on the floor, pulling off Alice's wellies, the next her cloak lands on top of me like a dead weight.

And just when I think I'm going to suffocate, there's a familiar voice. 'Great job, Fi. I'll take this and the wellies, give me your jacket too.' Johnny's here, scooping the cloak into his arms, pulling me up, sliding off my jacket.

Then it's just Alice and me, looking at each other. We're so close, I can't even see her dress properly. She's biting her lip, and as she pulls me into a hug, mostly she's just squeaking and snuffling. 'Thank you, Sera… and don't forget, you're going to be my witness.'

Jules takes a moment to capture our sisterly squish, then he dashes inside.

'All set?' I ask, as I push her away again.

Alice does a teary nod, and takes my dad's arm. This is possibly the first time in my life I've seen him without his papers and his reading glasses.

As someone throws open the doors, I can already hear the first tinkling bars of their music playing, and see the rows of backs and the muslin bows on the chairs. It's Christmas, it's snowy, it had to be 'Somewhere Only We Know'. It's only a surprise because I just didn't have Alice down as such a softie. Somehow I never actually thought quite this far. As I get ready to follow Alice down the aisle I'm just so happy, because we've actually made it to the end of the wedding manual.

I'm grinning at her, because that's the only way I can keep

back my tears. 'Come on, what we are waiting for. Let's go and get you married.'

***

'Candles and white roses, and clouds of fairy lights, it's amazing.' Hetty's beside me, smiling, whispering as I step back to my seat with Alice's bouquet. 'And that dress… it's so beautiful.'

Beside Dan's broad back in his tweed suit, Alice is slender, her simple silk shift hanging in gentle folds, the tiny spangles on the chiffon top glistening as they catch the light.

'I've never seen anyone actually get married in one of my dresses before,' I whisper back. It's quite a funny feeling. It makes my chest all tight. I'm kind of bursting because I'm so proud of Alice, and yet I'm all scrunched up inside, because I'm trying so hard not to howl. Because I'm so happy. I'm still all wobbly from the moment when Alice arrived next to Dan and he saw her for the first time. If she ever doubted he loved her, the look on his face then was enough to chase every bit of doubt away. Loved-up didn't begin to cover it.

As for the repeating bits, Dan is gruff, but decided. And Alice is sniffing so much, her voice has practically disappeared. And when it comes to the mission statement part, she swallows her words, so no one can hear what she's saying. The only bit we get is at the end, where she says 'I love you, Dan', but that's all good. And Dan's promises are pretty much what he said in the letter last night.

Hetty smiles at me as Dan comes to the end of his speech. 'So heartfelt…' The tears gushing down her cheeks have to be testing her make-up to the limit.

I blow my nose and stuff my hanky back up the sleeve of my fluffy cardigan. 'She's so lucky, isn't she?' Not that I've ever imagined wanting a husband, or a wedding. Nor that I ever will. But for this one moment only, I'm kind of converted. The rose tints on my wedding goggles are turned full on.

And then bish bash bosh, who'd have thought it could be so fast, but they're man and wife, they've had their wedding snog – despite not being teenagers – and they're on their way over to the signing table, and someone's pushing me over there too. As Alice sits down and leans forward with the pen, the row of pearl buttons down the back of her jacket shine, all the way from the nape of her neck to her waist.

As Johnny arrives at my side the waft of delicious aftershave is pretty surprising. Somehow, I'd have thought he'd smell of Snowball, but he doesn't. If he's signing, I guess it means he *is* best man number one after all. And I really am chief brides-maid, however much of a ditz I am.

His voice is low as he leans towards my ear. 'Great job on the dresses, Fi. And not a flamingo in sight.'

'A flamingo-free zone.' I whisper back. There's no way I'm letting on I'm still wearing my flamingo shorts under my dress. A bridesmaid has to keep some secrets. 'You scrub up pretty well yourself.'

He gives me a nudge. 'Catch you later, I made sure we're sitting together.'

Then Johnny and I sign our names on the register too, and everyone laughs at the bit where the registrar pretends to give the certificate to Alice, because it's the woman who's going to be boss. Even though they have no idea what thin ice they're skating on there.

Rafe, wise man, was right about everything working out, and he was completely right a second time too. Ten minutes later, we're all filing into the ballroom, heading for the bubbly.

And I'm left wondering how the hell something so small and simple and beautiful as Alice and Dan getting married could ever have seemed so difficult.

47

Saturday, December 24th, Christmas Eve
In the ballroom at Rose Hill Manor: More bubbly?

'So you do know, I'm claiming the first dance with you.' Quinn's leaning over, topping up my bubbly again, as he's done every time I've taken a sip, pretty much ever since we sat down. Which seems like hours ago. 'Given the other best man signed the register, it's only fair.' His lower lip is sticking out so far, he's almost pouting. As for how I've ended up sitting next to Alice and Quinn rather than Alice and Johnny? Swapping place cards – whoever did it – is pretty childish for guys of their age.

We're relaxing after the most delicious four-course wedding breakfast ever. After three courses of deliciousness I was pretty certain I was so full, I couldn't eat another thing. Then a medley of puddings arrived and proved me wrong. Chocolate profiteroles to die for, dreamy lemony Eton Mess, mouth-melting mini meringues and delectable heart-shaped hot-chocolate brownies. As our plates.are finally whisked away, a waiter follows filling up our toasting glasses.

'What, more bubbly?' I'm gawping at the two full glasses in front of me. As if I haven't got through enough already, courtesy of Quinn. Although Johnny might have been right when he said I was getting a taste for champers, because it's going down faster and faster as the afternoon goes on. So fast, I'm starting to feel like I could almost be turning into Jess. I lean back in my seat and nod at Quinn. 'Now I see why we needed so much crystalware.'

'I knew Alice would love those jars in the end too.' Quinn's sounding very smug as he twiddles with a rose. 'Personally I'd have skipped the speeches and the toasts and cut straight to the dancing. But Alice is insisting.'

'Aren't you doing the best man's speech then, Quinn?' I can see Johnny setting up his laptop and a screen, at the end of the top table. Given Quinn's done his best to physically wedge himself between me and Johnny at every opportunity, it's the most I've seen of him since the ceremony.

Quinn gives a grimace. 'I'll say a few words, obviously, but Johnny muscled in on that one too. By the time I came on board, he'd already finished a mash-up of video clips and pictures, and the speech. I didn't get a look in.'

Which, roughly translated, probably means when there was work to be done, Quinn made himself scarce. But no doubt he will be around to take the credit. No change there, then.

Alice slides back into her seat next to me. 'Dan, Dad and you best men will have to wait. I'm doing my speech first.'

Quinn rolls his eyes up to the twigs and fairy lights overhead. 'Since when did you decide to do a speech?'

'Keep up.' Alice gives him the kind of less-significant-than-a-slug look she used to reserve for me. Come to think of it, it's days since I saw that look. 'If you aren't up to speed, Quinn, that's hardly my fault.' As Dan pulls up his chair and takes her hand, she gives Jules a nod. 'Are you all ready?'

As Dan sits down next to Alice, Jules dashes over. No idea what he's done with his cameras, but given he's waving both thumbs in the air, we're about to roll into the speeches. I'm just hoping they're funny enough to keep me awake, because after all those puddings, I'm pretty much ready to fall asleep.

'So,' Alice clears her throat. 'Traditionally, the bride doesn't make a speech, but today I'm making an exception, because there's something very special I need to say.'

That jolts me out of my slumber. Holy crap, is she about to announce that she's pregnant? Although I seriously doubt it, given she still doesn't have the first clue about that. I let my eyelids droop again.

'What you might not know is that a week ago I arrived in Cornwall for a wedding I'd planned so meticulously, I assumed it would happen on its own. But I couldn't have been more wrong.' She takes a deep breath and smiles around the room. 'I also came to Cornwall expecting to find my baby sister sitting on a beach...'

Okay. The word 'sister' jerks me back to life. Like when the teacher suddenly points at you in a lesson. My heart is hammering against my chest wall as I fold my arms and shift uncomfortably in my seat. Where is she going with this?

Wherever it is, she's got that determined look on her face. And she's not swallowing her words now.

'That was my biggest surprise. Because while I'd been looking the other way my baby sister, Sera, had grown up. Okay, she was still wearing her ripped denim shorts. But instead of the teenager I remembered her as, I found the most amazing, successful dress designer. A woman, who, with her incredible friends, has put our whole wedding back together piece by piece as it fell apart – and made it more beautiful than I could ever have imagined.'

Oh my. Who'd have thought? And whereas once if this happened, I'd have been crawling under the table with embarrassment, somehow this time I'm not. Because I didn't do this on my own. I'm here, taking this one for the team. Who I really hope she's going to mention.

Alice swallows hard before she goes on. 'Without my wonderful sister, we wouldn't actually be here now. Sera is the one whose strength and single-mindedness, whose wisdom and talent, actually made this wedding happen. I've always been the one to look after her, but this time she's looked after me, and you have no idea how loved that makes me feel. Her friends, Poppy, Rafe and Immie from Daisy Hill Farm, and Jess from Brides by the Sea, Jules the photographer, and the whole of the Blue Watch from the fire brigade threw themselves into the job. With every successive problem, they came up with a solution. Whatever I say, there aren't enough words in the world to thank them all. So I'd like to raise a toast to all those lovely people. But most of all, please raise your glasses and toast my wonderful, amazing sister.'

As she holds her glass up, everyone follows and I'm not

even bothering to bite back my tears. They're sliding down my cheeks like heavy rain cascading down a window. At the end of the table Johnny leans forward and gives me a nod and the proudest smile of all time.

'Sera, I love you so much – and thank you. Especially for your slippers.'

There's a general chinking of glasses. For a moment I don't know if I should be drinking or not, but in the end I take the hugest glug that has me laughing and choking all at the same time.

Alice is still standing. 'Right, that's me done. Over to you boys. I'm going to hug my sister.'

And next minute she's dragging me into the biggest hug of my life.

48

Saturday, December 24th, Christmas Eve
In the ballroom at Rose Hill Manor: Tart but not sour

'This floor totally is awesome, Quinn.' As he twirls me around, I put my mouth close to his ear and yell to be heard over the pulsing beat. Multi-coloured lights are flashing under our feet as we dance. I'm the first to admit I was sniffy about the whole idea, but in the end it's phenomenal. Dancing on a floor that changes colour with the music is awesome, even if it does make my head spin. As for Quinn's choice of track, great as it is to dance to, 'I knew the bride when she used to rock and roll' seems like another of Quinn's digs at Alice. But knowing Alice she'll get him back for it.

Despite what Quinn said about first dances, it's now way past midnight. Before that we were too busy. Johnny and I volunteered for cake slicing and distribution – a good move, given how yummy Poppy's cake is. That's the thing about having a hundred and fifty people around for the weekend. There's always a job to do or someone needing help. We had endless chairs to shift around, my mum lost her glasses, then her camera. I lost count of how many group hugs I took pictures of.

As for Quinn, the way he's spinning me around now, we could be on *Strictly Come Dancing*. And our first dance has sprawled into more. So long as I relax and move with him, it's like he's doing the dancing for both of us. By the end of the track, I'm throwing off my cardi, wiping the sweat off my forehead and wishing I hadn't kept my shorts on under my dress after all.

'There's nothing like a light show under your feet.' Quinn grins.

One more question before I disentangle myself from his hand and head off to get my breath back. I'm back shouting in his ear again for this. 'How come you dance so well?'

He grins and dips to my ear. 'It's a great way to stay fit – when I'm away from the beach that is.'

And I'm sure it doesn't do him any harm with the women either. Anyone who can dance like that will never be short of partners.

'Thanks anyway,' I yell, and begin to back off the floor.

'No, you can't leave now, Sera. The fun's hardly started.' There's the hint of a whine as he tugs at my wrist. As he pulls me towards him, the floor throbs from purple to red, then progresses to flashing black-and-white zig zags. 'Whatever happened to dancing the night away? Then tomorrow we'll hit the beach first thing, for a Christmas-morning swim.'

'Excuse me?' Much as I love the beach, I'd planned to spend the morning catching up on sleep, maybe having an Alice-type soak, in time to emerge for a huge Christmas lunch at three. Breaking the ice on the sea doesn't exactly fit in with my plans. Nor does sliding seamlessly from night to morning. What's more, he's definitely skipped over the bit where I go back to my room. On my own.

'If you insist on sitting down, I'll come with you.' The way his arm slides over my shoulder and guides me off the dance floor and across the ballroom towards the drinks, it could be just another slinky salsa move. Except it stays there. 'We'll grab some cocktails and find a sofa to sink into.'

Downing cocktails is not exactly top of my wish list for tonight. Especially not with Quinn. As for us sinking into a sofa together, that's pretty much top of my 'not to do' list.

Not that I'm going chasing after Johnny, but I scan every last corner for him, just in case he's arrived, so I can make my escape from Quinn. I spot Sophie in the kind of clinch I wouldn't be interrupting, and Hetty chasing after a waiter. 'Or maybe we should dance again?' Given Quinn's become as clingy as a limpet, it's my safest bet.

'Great plan, but let's get those cocktails first.'

The colourful mix of glasses, fruit, bottles, ice buckets and cocktail shakers on the table he steers me towards could have come from a magazine picture. Despite it being midnight, the guy behind the table is still pristine in his white shirt and bow tie. He smiles. 'What can I get you?'

I'm eyeing the array of drinks on offer, working out if a Diet Pepsi and ice is even possible, but Quinn gets there before me.

'Two large mojitos, please.' He sends me a grin as the waiter begins to pour. 'Handmade, these are something else.'

A few minutes later a frosted tumbler arrives in my hand. Pushing the mint sprig to one side, I pop the straw in my mouth and take a sip. 'Fab.' I send Quinn a nod of appreciation for getting this so right. 'It's tart but not sour, deliciously limey and minty.' Once I begin to suck, I'm so parched from the dancing, it practically goes down in one.

'That's my girl.' He raises his eyebrows as he puts his empty glass back on the table. 'Not so much like Alice after all, then.'

In seconds we're back on the dance floor again. And that's how it goes. Cocktails, dancing, cocktails, dancing. At some point I must have lost the kitten-heeled boots, although I can't remember where, or when. But a whole lot later, when I accidentally step on Quinn's foot, my feet are bare. I'm vaguely wobbly, but I don't actually give a damn about randomly bumping into people, because somehow I've arrived at a happy place, where I actually want to hug the whole world. Even Quinn. Although I'm still not quite drunk enough to think that's a good idea.

I lean in to Quinn as yet another Christmas song ends. 'There's not so many dancing people now – I mean people dancing.' It may be a good thing it's less crowded if I'm trampling people.

'Leaving a party at two?' As he tilts his forehead to touch mine, mine is so sweaty we stick. 'They must be lightweights.' He takes hold of my hand again. 'Let's have another drink.' Which has to be Quinn's most-used phrase of the day.

We leave the flashing floor, but I'm barely noticing the colours any more. As the piano notes of the next track come through the speaker stacks, there's a sudden rush towards the dance floor, as everyone recognises the song. Then there's a tap on my shoulder and I look around. 'Johnny, where have you been? I was looking for you.' Somehow I've missed him before, but he's here now. And letting him know how hard I've been looking for him is probably down to the cocktails. But right now I'm not sure I care who knows.

He's eyeing Quinn levelly. 'I think this one's mine, Quinn.'

For a second Quinn looks like he's going to nut him. Then he backs away. 'Okay, I'll get our drinks, see you back here in four, Sera.'

The next moment Johnny's taken my hand and we're winding our way back into the crush of bodies, as the electric guitar slices into the introduction. And then the drums crash in, and when the lyrics come, deep down I just know... Oasis. 'Don't Look Back in Anger'.

'Yay, this is one of my favourite feel-good drunken dancing songs...' I'm yelling at Johnny as I fall towards him. 'In the world, ever...' And suddenly I'm twenty all over again, if not fifteen.

He grabs me around the waist as he catches me. 'Oasis?' He's propping me up with his shoulder, helping me get my balance back. 'It's a great song for a last dance.'

I don't quite get what he means by that, but I don't care, because the music is making me smile, hugely, just because it always does. Beside us, everyone's pretty much in the same euphoric cloud as me. As mixes go, you don't get more heady than pure nostalgia and a free bar. By the time the chorus comes, I've got my balance back. I'm waving my hands in the air and shouting at the top of my voice, going totally bonkers, along with everyone else. When we get to the *don't look back in anger* line, Johnny and I are shouting it at each other. And the way it means so much to us both is sending shivers shooting all over my scalp.

When it finally goes all quiet and the music fades, I fall against Johnny again and this time my hands land on his shoulders. 'I'm guessing this is our song.' I'm filled with this deep-down sadness, which is nothing to do with Johnny and me, and how angry we've been with each other for all these years. I've momentarily forgotten that. For me it's the sadness I always get when that song ends, simply because I want it to go on forever. If I was on my own in the studio, I'd flick it straight back to the start and listen to it all over again.

Johnny pulls the corners of his mouth down. 'I guess you're right, Fi.'

I shout in his ear. 'That's the bloody annoying thing about discos – not being able to get instant replay.' 'Merry Christmas Everybody' is blasting out now. But the feel-good moment is over and my feet are throbbing as hard as the floor.

He gives a shrug, then dips towards me. 'Alice says it's your bedtime. Sorry, but she asked me to take you up. Undo your zip, check you're okay.' He puts his arm around me to guide me. 'Or maybe I shouldn't have told you that?'

'So that explains the last dance bit?' I'm furious with Alice for wrecking my fun. 'Why exactly?' I'm sticking my chin out.

He gives a shrug. 'Probably because she saw you falling over and she's looking out for you.'

I let out a snort of disgust. 'Thanks for that. I'm not that drunk.' Considering what I've consumed, that is. What's more, if Alice hasn't been drinking, everyone will look drunk to her.

And if Alice sent the most tactful best man here, I hate to think how the other one would have put it.

'Fine.' Now he's taking my hand and being all conciliatory. 'If you're all good we can stay longer? Dance some more?'

But as I sink against the warmth of Johnny's body, I'm suddenly not minding so much. As for undoing my zip… Whereas Quinn definitely couldn't be trusted with that job, we both already know Johnny proved he can do that and walk away. He's one hundred per cent up to the job of seeing me to bed and complying with Alice's 'no sex' rules. Because we both know that's what he did last time he undid my zip after a party. Despite all my efforts to persuade him otherwise.

I smile up at him. 'No, I'm ready to go.'

And somehow I can't wait to see how he's going to play it this time around.

49

Saturday, December 24th, Christmas Eve
In my bedroom: Uggs and a disaster area

'I can't actually believe it's over.'

We've made it up two flights of stairs 'without incident' and we're pushing our way through the door into my room. In other words, I didn't fall over and we didn't snog.

Johnny laughs. 'It's a long way from over. In six hours' time, we'll be starting again. Come here...'

Almost before the door has closed, he's whipped down the zip of my dress and jumped back to a safe distance. And I'm guessing he's all done here.

'Thanks.' As I run my hands through my hair, despite a few tangles, it's still silky enough to feel like it belongs to someone else. 'Can you see my Uggs anywhere?' If I slip my feet into them, I know I'll feel better.

Johnny laughs. 'Good luck with that one.'

Even though the hair and make-up ladies have done their best to tidy before leaving, the room is still like a disaster area. There are bottles and half-drunk glasses of prosecco scattered across the coffee tables along with the remnants of canapes, and towels strewn across the floor.

'I know it's messy in here, but my Uggs should be easy enough to find.' It's no worse than my bedroom at home on a bad day, but I'm skimming over that.

He laughs again. 'No, what I mean is, Alice said she'd taken them. She had them on under her wedding dress when I last saw her.'

Lucky I can see the funny side. And that I got my own toast. But there are times when all a girl wants are her Uggs. 'Borrowing from the bridesmaid is a bride's prerogative. For one day only.' I seize a piece of flamingo fabric from the floor. 'Yay, here we go, at least she left me my pyjama top. Give me a minute.' I dive into the bathroom. And if I clean my teeth while I'm there, it's for no reason other than because I'm on my way to bed.

As I come out and slip my dress onto a hanger, Johnny's still over by the door, his jacket slung over one shoulder. There's a pang of disappointment in my chest that he's about to follow Alice's instructions to the letter. I'm scouring the room, for some reason, to delay him leaving, although I seriously doubt flat prosecco and wizened tomato tarts will help me any. Then I spot gold – there's an open packet of crisps on the bedside table.

'Fancy a crisp while you're here? They're hand-cooked, smoky bacon, totally delish. At least they were this morning.

Or maybe a drink?' So long as he likes tap water we're all good.

He blinks and shifts his back, where he's leaning against the wall. 'Sorry. I was miles away. I should go.'

Dammit. Wrong answer. But just to be certain he's completely decided, I cross the room. When I come to a halt, my toes are practically brushing his brogues and my nose is level with the open neck of his shirt. I'm so close I'm checking out the tan on the skin of his neck. Very slowly I lift my hand upwards. As I slide it to rest on his jaw, I sense the catch in his breathing. As his stubble pricks my fingers, there's the bang of a heart, but I'm not sure if it's mine or his.

He locks his fingers around my wrist. 'Don't make this hard, Sera.'

Talk about a déjà vu action replay of our last time together. Except I'm possibly less drunk this time. More tired. And if he says anything about bad timing, I'll hit the roof, given it's taken bloody years to get back here.

Gently he turns his face into my palm. I'm feeling the shiver of his lips on my wrist, when there's a scuffle outside the door. We freeze and watch. As the handle turns and the door slides open, slowly I pull back my hand. By the time Quinn tiptoes in, I've taken a step back and my arms are folded across my cami top.

'Holy shit, what the hell are *you* doing here?' Quinn leaps backwards as he spits the words at Johnny.

'The same as you, I hope.' Johnny's voice is level. 'Checking Sera's okay. Which she is.' He grabs the door and hauls it open. 'In which case, I'll see you out.'

'Not so fast.' Quinn puts his hand on his hip, stands his ground and waggles a rum bottle. 'Maybe *you* should be the one to leave, Johnny, given Sera and I agreed we'd have a night cap. You know the old saying, three's a crowd.' He's recovered enough to give a low laugh.

Johnny leaves the door and wanders behind me shaking his head. 'Grab what you need from the bathroom, Sera. We'll go to mine.'

'What?' I'm not following.

Johnny's voice is low. 'Don't argue, just get your stuff and come with me. Like now would be good, please.' The look he flashes me tells me he's not joking.

'Okay.' I'm not exactly clear what he means by stuff, but I go to the bathroom and get my wash bag. As I see my cardigan hanging on the sofa edge as I pass, I grab that too. And a moment later, he's propelling me down the landing towards his room.

50

Saturday, December 24th, Christmas Eve
In Johnny's bedroom: Broom handles and lucky women.

'You jump into bed, I'll take the sofa.'

Johnny's turning back the quilt for me as I take in sloping ceilings very like the ones in my own room. Although because this room's smaller the double bed he's shooing me towards is the only one.

'We could top and tail?' Even as I say it I'm remembering the urban legend of the girl at school who lost her virginity doing just that. Lucky woman.

'Don't argue. Just get in.' He's wearing his non-negotiable face.

'I take it that's a no then?'

He ignores that and shakes out a couple of the cashmere throws Alice provided. 'We'll talk in the morning.'

When I'm less drunk. That's the subtext. And between us, with my alcohol-inflamed lust, it's not a talk I'm aching for.

As I ease my bottom onto the bed, I sniff. 'If this is about Alice's rule, it's damned hypocritical.' I'm sounding like a petulant kid because I feel like one. 'She's probably bonking my Uggs off in the wedding suite as we speak.'

Johnny's trying not to smile as he disappears into the bathroom. When he comes back a few moments later, he's in low-slung cotton lounge pants and a T-shirt. 'She is the bride.' At least he's laughing off my grumbling. 'Anyway, she's probably going straight to sleep too. It said in *The Huffington Post* no one has sex on their wedding night any more.'

'Whatever.' That's exactly where I read the same thing, but I'm not going to admit we have that in common right now.

He tugs at his hair. 'Anyway Alice isn't singlehandedly trying to ruin your wedding enjoyment with her rule. That's her way of subtly suggesting you steer clear of a certain groomsman.'

'Sorry?' There's only one person she could mean. 'Quinn?' If my voice is a shriek it's because I'm gobsmacked.

'He does have a hideous track record of hitting on bridesmaids. That was Alice's attempt to keep him in check. And to flag up a warning to everyone else.'

And saving me from falling flat on my face, which I so nearly did, even though I missed the point completely. And I thought she was being a control freak. 'And that's why I'm in here with you now?'

'Yes… and no.' He sighs. 'I'm sorry for exploiting the situation, but I kind of liked the idea of talking to you as we went to sleep. And you being here when I wake up. I'm happy to take the sofa to get that.'

The night of the ball, when I hurled myself at him, I still ended up in my own bed that night. In my own room, in the suite he'd booked. And when I didn't hear from him when I threw my phone into the harbour, I took it that he'd hated how that weekend panned out. Although the fact he did try to get in touch means that wasn't the ultimate humiliation I've taken it as. And now we're here, I have to ask.

'Why did you ask me to that uni ball before I went off travelling?' Not that I want to rake over the past, but I've always been curious to know.

The way he's sitting on the arm of the sofa, he's not intending to go straight to sleep. 'Once you left uni, I missed you. A lot. But you had your life mapped out and I was determined not to get in the way.' He gives a sheepish shrug. 'The ball was the perfect one-off excuse to see you before you left for your first world trip. I'm sorry if it was selfish.'

My lips are twitching. 'I had a lovely time. Once you finally decided to give in, that is.' Or do I mean put out? Those two days we spent in bed go down as the best of my entire life.

He looks at me steadily. 'I didn't mean for that to happen. All the same, I'm pleased it did.' He's smiling at me now. 'It kept me going for years.'

Whereas with me, it stopped me dead. My love life never quite moved on from the awesomeness of that weekend. 'Considering you were such a babe magnet back in the day, you play very hard to get with me.' And as a grumble, it's entirely justified. I mean, I'm in bed on my own, aren't I? Again.

He frowns. 'I was hardly that.'

'Excuse me, you took a different girl home every night.' But never me. If I was less polite, I'd have called him a man-whore.

'You surely don't think I…' He lets out a long sigh. 'For the record, if there were queues of women, it was only because I had a car and they wanted a lift. Believe me, I love Jake, and it's awesome having him in my life, but ending up with an unplanned baby puts casual sex in a whole new light. I didn't go there. Apart from that weekend of the ball, obviously. You were never the one I took home at uni, but only because I knew it would have been too hard to take you home and not end up in bed with you.

Now he tells me. 'You're managing to walk away tonight.' It's a fair point.

'You've got me there.' His smile splits into a grin. 'At least this way you won't wake up tomorrow and regret what you did.'

'I'm a lot less drunk than you think.' Well someone's got to tell him. Now I'm snuggled under the duvet, I'm barely wobbly.

'See how you feel when you've got a clear head in the morning.' He sends me a wink. 'Without the mojito goggles.' He rubs his hand on his chin. 'In any case, not everyone travels with multi packs of condoms.'

'Right. Good point. I know I don't.' My shrug goes with my admission. He's talking about Quinn's bulk supply there. And partly explaining too. It's obvious he hasn't brought any either. 'Alice fell down badly on that one. She could have had mince-pie-flavoured ones too.'

Johnny laughs. 'Fancy remembering champagne truffles and a nut cracker and forgetting the most essential essentials.'

As I look at the pink and gold truffle box on the bedside table, something beyond it catches my eye. 'Hey, you've still got the knitted bears from the shop. Weren't they meant to be a wedding present?' As I look at them nestling against the lamp, I feel all squishy inside because I've found my old friends again.

Johnny wrinkles his nose. 'I'm not sure they're Alice's thing.'

'But you bought them specially.'

A guilty flicker flashes across his face. 'No, I actually bought them because I saw your name on the window and wanted an excuse to go into the shop.' He shrugs in response to my horrified stare. 'What? I could hardly go in and say I wanted a wedding dress, could I?'

I'm wailing now. 'I loved those bears. They'd been in the shop for years, Jess should never have sold them to you.'

'Remember that time you were knitting at uni?' If he's trying for diversion tactics it's working.

I shudder at the thought. 'As if I could forget anything that traumatic.' We were supposed to knit a small item of clothing and I insisted on knitting a wedding dress with a train and practically had a nervous breakdown. 'I had to use broom handles to get the holey effect and I was knitting day and night for weeks.'

He laughs. 'Can you see why it was dull and boring when you left?'

And I quietly take us back to what's way more important. 'Promise you'll keep the bears... or at least let me buy them back.' Although given the figure he paid was monstrous and equivalent to several arms and a leg, I might need to pay in instalments.

'I promise...' He laughs. 'Or, you could always have a quiet word with Santa.'

'Of course. Why didn't I think of that?' Somehow, in all the excitement, I'd almost forgotten. 'When we wake up, it'll be Christmas morning.' It's funny how some years the magic isn't there and others there's so much it makes your head woozy. And it's nothing at all to do with the ten Gin Slings you just had. But whatever it is, you're so happy you feel like your chest could burst. And it's as if there's star dust twinkling on the ceiling, entirely without the help of Blue Watch, or Celestial Skies. 'Hasn't it just been the most perfect day?'

He nods. 'It has.' There's mischief in his eyes as he stands, turns and reaches upwards. 'You know Alice hasn't failed entirely…'

As I lean back, the pillow pile is so big I'm practically sitting up. 'How come?'

He's striding across the room towards the bed, his cheeks slicing into those delicious creases as he tries to hold back his smile. And there's a green sprig dangling from his hand.

'She gave us mistletoe…'

'So she did…' And a second later, as his lips brush against mine and I taste a mix of minty toothpaste and hot velvet guy, I'm damned glad I stayed the distance and hung mistletoe in *every* room.

51

Sunday, 25th December, Christmas Day
In Johnny's bedroom: Serviettes and dazzling smiles

'So, I'll see you again very soon, bed-head.'

It's seven-thirty, Johnny's grinning at me from the bed as he speaks, and if it seems like no time at all since we finally fell asleep curled around each other, that's probably because it is. But my idea is to make a fast getaway before everyone gets up, so no one sees me doing my bridesmaid's walk of shame, along the landing in my pyjamas. And so far I'm failing. Spectacularly. Both with the speed and the leaving.

'Johnny... how about you go and jump in the harbour?' I'm laughing as I reply to his cheeking. But when I rake my fingers through my party hair, I know he's got a point. The sleek bouncing curls I went to sleep with have tangled into a disaster area. Try as I might, it's hard to make a slinky departure, when

I'm in bare feet, tugging my cardi down far enough to cover my shorts and my hair's like a bird's nest that's been hit by a force-ten gale. 'Right, this time I'm definitely going.'

No more last-minute lingering snogs. I've rubbed my cheek on the stubble of his chin enough times. And yes, it is so blissful, it almost feels like I'm dreaming. The memory imprint should be strong enough to last while I grab a shower and get downstairs for coffee. Where we'll be 'accidentally' meeting up, in approximately forty-five minutes. Ignoring that he's looking entirely edible lounging on top of the bed wearing only his boxers, I give a cringingly coy little wave and haul the door open. A second later I'm hurtling along the landing back to my own room.

***

Despite my exceptionally 'waaaaaaahhhh' hair situation, I manage my turn-around really fast. Aiming to hit Alice's pre-wedding standards, I slip on a dark-brown silk shift dress of Poppy's. Once it's toned down with my favourite black rose-print tights and my second-biggest biker boots I don't feel a million miles away from myself. As I wander into the ballroom the log fire is already crackling in the fireplace and Hetty's team are busy behind a serving table. Although the hushed voices and serious lack of breakfast-takers underline that this is very much a 'morning after' scenario.

I blink at the amazing array of food on offer as I nod at the waiter. 'Isn't this where I got my drinks last night?'

'Yes, we served the last cocktail and went straight on into breakfasts. It kind of wrong-foots the jet lag and the culture shock.' The groan he gives before he smiles is entirely under-standable. 'What can I get you?'

Now I'm here, my earlier determination to bolster myself with a full English to last until Christmas Dinner at three is waning. Despite the bacon rashers sizzling under my nose, my hunger pangs have all but disappeared. What's worse, where there should be a huge hole demanding breakfast, there's now an anxious fluttering telling me I couldn't eat a thing. 'Maybe a mango smoothie. And a coffee, please.' Hopefully the vitamin and caffeine combo will sort me out. Although, considering the cocktail mix I got stuck into late last night, my head is remarkably clear.

I carry my drinks to a table by the window. From here there's a view across the snowy garden, but more importantly I can keep an eye on everyone coming in without being obvious. There's no way I'd have made any progress with a fry-up. Fifteen minutes later, I've still only sipped half an inch off the top of my smoothie. What's more, I'm watching the doorway like – well, like a girl who's expecting a guy at any moment.

Although I'm also getting twitchy. Not that I'm the kind of girl who makes a habit of getting over-excited about seeing a guy. Apart from that one weekend years ago, but I don't exactly get a lot of practice at second dates. Or even first ones, come to that. I know our arrangement was fluid. But right now I'm asking myself where the hell Johnny's got to, because he's way later than we said. For all I know, he could be one of those guys with a full body maintenance and grooming routine that takes three hours every morning. Let's face it, when it comes to his personal habits, I'm in the dark.

Ten minutes later when I'm still on my own, in my head I've got him sitting with cucumber slices on his eyes, exfoliating and buffing as we speak. So when I see movement by the doorway my heart lurches. But it's not Johnny, it's Alice. And the way she's waving at me, she could be doing semaphore signals on a hillside a mile away, trying to attract my attention across a room when I'm already looking straight at her. As soon as she's picked up a drink, she comes over.

'Hello, sweetie.' Her beam is disgustingly dazzling for this time on this particular morning as she clunks down her tea. 'You're up early.' Coming from someone who's often up at six, even if it's only to go and find her colouring book, that's rich. 'I couldn't find my hairbrush in our room, so I popped in to see if I'd left it in yours. I saw your flamingo shorts on the floor, so I knew you'd come down for breakfast.'

If I'm having silent heart attacks, it's because she so nearly found me out. She's the kind of ace detective who reads your mind and tracks you down from your abandoned shorts. If she'd turned up earlier to look for that brush, it would have been obvious my bed hadn't been slept in and she'd be down on me like a ton of bricks. At the very least. As it is, I crumpled the duvet when I came back and the bathroom was full of steam from my shower.

'So did you find your brush?'

As she shakes her head, her hair does that moving-and-falling-back thing mine was doing yesterday. 'No, so I went back to ours, looked again, and found it under Dan's boxers.' She gives a guilty sigh. 'It's a bit of a mess in there.'

'You're allowed to leave your clothes on the floor on your wedding night.' I grin because one pair of boxers hanging loose is enough to cause a diplomatic incident for Alice. Then I hurry on to explain why I'm up, when on previous form I probably shouldn't be. 'I came down to grab an orange juice. I needed a vitamin boost after the long day yesterday.' Note, I'm blaming the long day not the long night.

She's suddenly staring at me like I'm some kind of exhibit. 'You've got a hangover?'

'Surprisingly, no.'

Her nod is smug. 'You've got me to thank for that. The cocktails were quarter-strength, so people who drank all day didn't collapse.'

I'm having a silent OMG moment here. 'What kind of control-freak waters down the drinks?'

Her expression is inscrutable. 'A sensible one.' She squeezes lemon into her tea and takes a sip. 'Anyway, moving on, you're looking lovely. Again. Dresses three days running – you'll be waving good bye to your shorts forever.'

Between us, no one's looking that great this morning. We both look like we're in desperate need of a visit from the make-up team. I suppose it's too much to hope that Alice asked them to come back again today.

'Somehow I don't think I'll be giving up on my shorts.' Although getting compliments from Alice is something I am getting used to. Wearing dresses hasn't been half as bad as I expected. Apart from the wind whooshing up my skirts, that is. 'Still got some on, just not showing them.' As I flick up my skirt she gets a flash of the kids' lycra games shorts I grabbed in the mini-market. 'Imagine the drafts without.'

'And Johnny saw you up to bed okay?'

Crap. That question sends my stomach into free-fall and

re-boots the fluttering. I fix my gaze on a point beyond the ballroom, out in the next room. And although I'm aching for Johnny to appear, if he's anywhere near, I'm willing him to hang on outside. Just until I get past this part with Alice. I clear my throat. 'Err – yes. I was one tired bridesmaid. I went out like a proverbial candle blowing in the wind.' Okay, it's a catastrophic mix of song lyrics. And it comes out as a squeak. But Alice seems oblivious.

'Johnny's great, I really like him.' Her beam is out of proportion to what she's discussing. Especially given she doesn't know I just climbed out of his bed. But maybe 'ecstatic' is the new 'normal' for a just-married woman wearing a fuchsia Mr and Mrs T-shirt over her white capri pants. I mean, when did Alice ever embrace pink?

I wrack my brain for a suitable reply. 'Mmmm, he seems cool.'

Alice is playing with her spoon now. 'I just met him in the hall on my way in.'

I'm about to sip from my glass, but somehow I end up coughing so hard my smoothie lands in a splat across the table. At least there's so much mess to mop up, Alice entirely fails to pick up my anxiety about Johnny. She thinks this is me being my usual clumsy self.

Predictable as ever, she shoots off for extra serviettes, then comes back and starts dabbing at the bits I've missed. 'Actually he asked me to tell you he was going for a walk on the beach.'

I look up much too sharply, so I have to wait a while to speak. When I eventually get around to one tiny word, it comes out as a croak. 'Right.' I can't think what the hell else to say, because I have no idea what he said to her. Or what's going on. What's he doing going to the beach when he was supposed to be coming for breakfast with me? And finally, I get to the right answer. 'Actually, I really don't know why he told you to tell me that.'

Her forehead crinkles into a frown. 'Did he seem alright last night? It's just when I saw him just now he looked a bit upset.'

'He was fine when I left him.' As an answer that's true, even if it is less than the whole story. 'Really…' Damn that I've said that because she's narrowing her eyes and getting all suspicious.

'What's wrong, Sera? What aren't you telling me?' Talk about penetrating stares. She'll be getting out the thumb screws any minute.

'Nothing…' One more glimpse of her dogged expression tells me I'm losing here. There's no point fighting. When Alice is like this, I may as well give in. 'Okay, you've got me. Johnny and I weren't just at uni at the same time, we were actually pretty close. Or I thought we were. Like we drank tea and ate cake. A lot of it.'

'I see.' She's tapping her fingernails on the table in that really annoying way.

Actually she doesn't see, at all, but she soon will. 'And we spent last night together…'

'Oh shit.'

Even though it's been my lifetime's ambition to hear Alice say the word 'shit', I still wish she hadn't said it about me. And this. And somehow I need to explain it away. 'It was a schoolgirl crush that lasted years, that's all. It was never going to come to anything.' Most probably never will, given he's getting

355

the hell out of here as we speak. 'And I completely messed up our chance of reconnecting again when I threw my phone into the harbour. But that was years ago.' I watch as she rubs her rings. It's okay for her. She's wearing her guarantee of eternal happiness.

'How did I not see this…' As she purses her lips her radiance has turned to a perplexed frown and her hand lands on top of mine. 'You're still in love with him aren't you?'

That question has me opening and closing my mouth like a guppy. 'I don't know, I'm not sure…' Except I am. I just never put it into words like that before. But what's weirder still is there's no way I could have ever have imagined having this conversation with Alice a week ago.

'Bloody hell, Sera, it's obvious you're in love. And of everyone I know, Johnny could really do with someone amazing to love him. Whatever's upset him, you can't just sit here.'

'I can't?' She's right. I should be heading for the nearest duvet to hide under, and only coming out when it's New Year and they've all gone home. Although where would that get me? If I'd done that every time I felt like it the last few days, this wedding would never have happened. 'Actually, you're right. I can't.' I spent all those years thinking he hated our weekend, when he didn't. Whatever's gone wrong now, I owe it to myself to find out what it is. To see if there's anything in my power I can do to make things right. Because somehow, possibly for the first time in my life, I suddenly feel like I deserve something good. A piece of happy of my own. It's as if I put everything on hold for years, and now I've got a second chance, I can't throw it away. I have to fight.

Alice's fingers close around mine. 'If it wasn't for you, we'd never have got married. None of this wonderful Christmas would be happening.' She glances around the room. Not that there's anyone here right now, given most people have paced themselves better than us and haven't got up at stupid o' clock. But we both know what she's meaning. 'I'm completely aware of how much we owe you. Think of this as payback. Come on, get your coat. I'm taking you to the beach to find him. I'm not taking no for an answer.'

52

Sunday, December 25th, Christmas Day
On the beach at St Aidan:
Pantomime horses and billowing hems

'What the hell are you doing on the beach? We're supposed to be drinking coffee and eating fucking cornflakes.'

Okay, I know. When I planned what I was going to say to Johnny in my head, it was much quieter. Way more polite. Without the swearing. Although my shriek is pretty much wiped out by a wind gust that blasts through at thirty miles an hour. That's how fast it blows when the white horses scud right across the inky blue of the bay, like they are today. The sand grains get carried on the breeze and blast into your eyes, making them sting like crazy.

I'm a little bit hoarse anyway, because Alice and I sang all the way here, yelling out the Christmas songs like we were in a pantomime-singing competition, where one side of the theatre has to sing louder than the other. Then as she drove along the seafront and we finally spotted Johnny, hunched against the wind, the last thing she said to me before I slammed the car door was, 'Be calm and be kind.' So I blew that right away too.

'This is so screwed up.' As Johnny yells back at me his hair is standing on end and his cheeks are pale and drawn. A million miles away from the laughing guy I left on the bed less than a couple of hours ago.

'What's screwed up?' I'm just not getting this.

His hands are in his pockets and he's walking backwards into the wind, facing me. 'I'm the stupid one, for not bothering to ask.' As he shakes his head, he stoops, picks up a stone and hurls it down the beach. 'I just assumed you'd be on your own, like me. More fool me for not finding out first. It's my mistake. Now I stop to think about it, it's obvious someone like you would be with someone. I can't think why I didn't…'

'Sorry? What did you say?' I'm scrunching up my face, because I haven't got the foggiest idea what he's talking about. What's more, I've seriously found the limitation of dresses. Battling to keep this mini shift from blowing over my head or taking off like a kite is major hard work. 'With someone? Why would you think I'm with someone?' Wherever has he got that idea from?

Johnny stops. 'The pregnancy test in your bathroom. You forgot your wash bag, I saw it when I dropped it back. I completely understand why you weren't going to tell me.'

'Oh fuck…' Somehow that doesn't begin to cover it. As I catch up, I take a deep breath. 'There was a test open in my bathroom?'

He squints at me. 'You know there was. On the basin. I hated myself for looking, but once I saw it, I couldn't help it.'

Crap, crap, crap. So much for Alice hunting for a hairbrush. 'Johnny. Johnny. It wasn't mine. It isn't my test.'

'But it was positive.'

I put my hands over my ears. 'Waaaaaaaaaaaahhhhhhhh don't tell me that…' Too late. Oh my God, Alice. If I'm honest, it's only what I knew in my heart already. And thank Christmas Alice came round to the idea herself. Even if she has accidentally created mayhem, it's a bride's prerogative. And she's unknowingly gone some way to putting it right. I just hope she realises that after tomorrow, special privileges are over. She's back to being a normal person. End of.

His face crumples in disbelief. 'Who else would come into your bathroom to use your pregnancy test?'

If ever there's a time to roll my eyes, it's now. 'It's a very long story.' I can't begin to go into it here. 'I bought the tests, but I promise I didn't pee on the stick. I'm definitely not pregnant. Or with anyone else. Okay?' That should cover most points without blowing Alice's secret.

'Really?' He's visibly deflating in front of me. It's as if he daren't believe what I'm telling him. 'I'm sorry for rushing off, it was such a shock when I saw it.'

'I can imagine. It's a shock for me, just hearing about it. And I'm sure whoever it is will share their news. When they're ready.'

He's tugging at his hair. 'I don't give a damn who it is. Knowing you aren't with anyone else is enough for me.'

'So does that mean breakfast's back on again, then?' Because if it does, regardless of the fluttering, right now I feel like I could eat a metaphorical horse. Not one related to Snowball. Obviously.

'Breakfast?' He's blinking, looking like he's battling shell shock. 'Now you're talking. Who'd have thought we'd be needing that?'

53

Sunday, December 25th, Christmas Day
At Brides by the Sea: Coffee and little bit more to say

'Here we go. Two Christmas morning breakfasts of mince pies and coffee…'

Johnny and I raiding the kitchen at Brides by the Sea was always going to be a better bet than hitting the fridge at my gran's cottage. Carried up to the studio on a tray, so we don't have to clear up the crumbs downstairs afterwards. As I set it down on the table by the window, Johnny swings two high stools into place.

'Festive and warming, what's not to like? It's homely up here too. With all the lace snippets and half-made dresses, it reminds me of your room at uni.' The colour is ebbing back into his cheeks, although he still looks like he was the one who drank his own volume in cocktails rather than me.

I made the coffee strong enough to stand your spoon up in, so my first sip is so bitter it makes me shiver. But it gives me the instantaneous caffeine kick I was hoping for. 'Except you could fit ten of those bedrooms in here.'

Johnny demolishes his first mince pie in two gulps, then takes another. 'Coming here gives us space to have that talk I wanted too.'

If my stomach has just perked up, that news deflates it immediately. 'Given the last chat we had up here, I might do a runner down the beach instead.'

When Johnny rubs his face, it's so drawn he almost loses his thumb in the hollow under his cheekbone. 'It's nothing scary.' He gives a half-laugh. 'Thinking I'd lost you yet again, I owe it to you to explain a few things.'

I take a nibble of mince pie and force myself to stay on my stool. 'Okay...'

He drags in a breath. 'When you were at uni I'd have given anything to have got together, but you were so set on living abroad and I had Jake. To be a part of his life I had to stay nearby. Which was a million miles away from the globetrotting life you wanted.' He props his hand on his forehead and looks at me sideways. 'Back then I was completely crushed by the weight of my responsibilities. However desperate I was to have you in my life, you deserved so much more than I had to offer. In the end I decided I loved you too much to ask you to give up on your dreams.'

'Oh my poor Johnny.' I put my hand on top of his and squeeze, because what he's saying is literally wringing my heart out too. If only he'd said, I'd have stayed with him in a heartbeat. But there's no point labouring that now. 'I actually loved you so much, I wouldn't have minded.' I just wish I'd believed in myself enough back then to tell him.

He squeezes my fingers in return. 'Thank you for saying that. Actually there were some very hard times. Having a child wasn't what I planned, the shock took a few years to adjust to. But I wouldn't change it now. If there's anything good about being years late getting together, it's that you've missed the difficult parts.'

The way he's talking about getting together as if we are is warming me up as much as the steaming coffee.

He wrinkles up his nose. 'I was pretty tied up with Jake. A couple of times when I did meet people, there was always something missing. It wasn't right, because they weren't you.'

I'm beaming and it's from sheer relief. 'Same here. No one else compared, so I could never be bothered.' As we're being totally honest here, I'm going to have to tell him. 'Actually I didn't lose my phone all those years ago. When I came back to be with Gran, the one thing I'd pinned my hopes on was us meeting up again. I was so disappointed when you didn't text back, after two weeks of waiting I flung my phone in the harbour. How stupid is that?'

His sigh is deep. 'No more stupid than me not being open about how I felt in the first place.' He pulls down the corners of his mouth. 'We're older now; Jake's older too. We're at a better place in our lives. We're both old enough to know what we want – at least I know I do.'

Awesome doesn't begin to cover it. 'Me too. And we're both established in our careers. I thought I was grown up, but it's strange how much this last week has changed me. I always felt like the family failure, but I don't any more. Helping make the wedding happen let me find my super-powers.'

Johnny laughs. 'I always knew about those, though. They're why no one else ever came close.'

If I was on a cloud of happiness yesterday, today it's like I've landed on the moon. I half-close my eyes and lean towards him. I can almost taste the spicy warmth of the kiss even before it arrives. A few seconds later, when he still hasn't met my lips, I open my eyes to see where he is. He's a mile away. Not even close.

As he pulls his gaze back from where he's been staring down to the beach, his brow furrows into a frown. 'There's still a little bit more to say…' His hand lands on my knee. 'About Jake.'

'Have you got any pictures?' I don't want to push, but at the same time I'm longing to know what he looks like.

Johnny's eyebrows go up. 'Only about five thousand. Would you like to see a couple? I sorted some specially.' As he pulls out his phone the lines on his face soften. 'I'm bit of a prouddad bore, so cut me off before I send you to sleep.'

My pulse is pounding with anticipation. As I lean in for the first close-up, for a second my voice whooshes away, because the resemblance is huge. The boy looking back at me is like a junior Johnny. 'Oh my, he's got exactly the same grin as you. And your floppy brown hair.' I reach out and push back the same piece that's trailing down over Johnny's forehead.

'We are both ridiculously good-looking, obviously.' Johnny's cheeks crease as he smiles and he flicks through the next few photos.

As I snuggle against the warmth of Johnny's elbow, I'm

watching Jake on a pony, Jake sitting in the sea, Jake lying back on his pillows, laughing like a mini-version of his dad. 'Hey, nice pyjamas…'

'Superman ones. They're ironic, obviously.'

As he flicks onto wider views, I catch a glimpse of Jake on arm crutches and my heart gives a jump. Then we're back to ponies, one with a birthday cake and candles, the next one Jake's in a wheelchair. And in the next too. And my stomach is contracting and my heart is aching, and somehow I'm putting my arm around Johnny. 'So are you going to tell me about it, then?'

As he turns towards me his voice is low. 'The wheelchair's because he has a lot of problems with his joints. There were complications with the meningitis. There was brain damage, he has epilepsy too.'

'Oh no…' I'm so shocked I can barely manage a whisper.

Johnny rubs his jaw. 'We were so close to losing him. But when it happens, believe me, you'd settle for anything to get to keep them with you.'

'I'm so sorry.'

'He was only four, but he was so damned brave. I'd have given the world for it to have been me not him.'

'Four?' However hard I swallow, my face is crumpling. As I stand up, he turns and I fit into the gap between his knees. 'That must have been so awful.'

He drags me towards him. 'It's that cliché – every parent's worst nightmare. At the time it felt like it was happening to someone else. You contacted me a few days in, but eventually I got it together to ring, then sent a text explaining what had been going on. Hoping to meet up. I thought you didn't get back to me because you couldn't cope and didn't want to get involved. It's why I didn't try to find you.'

Worse and worse. 'I'd never think like that.' As I press my cheek against his there are tears streaming down both our faces.

'I know that now.' As he crushes me against him, his chest is shuddering.

My tears are soaking his sweatshirt, but I don't care.

Johnny is rubbing his nose and sniffing, 'It's actually way more okay than you think. Jake's amazing. Life is about what we can do, not what we can't. You'll find out when you meet him.'

'I'd really like that.'

Our foreheads are touching as his dark-brown eyes meet mine, I see his lashes are clumped.

I nod. No wonder Alice told me Johnny needed someone to love him. 'I might be years late, but I'm getting back to you now. I would like to see you again. Very much. And I can't think of anything better than spending time together. And getting to know Jake too.'

His lips twitch into a smile. 'That's exactly the answer I was hoping for. We've got so long to make up for. And there's so much to find out about each other. I can't wait.'

He's so right about that. 'That's true. I still don't even know where you actually live, because I've been trying not to ask questions. Or what on earth we're going to do once the wedding's over and you go away again... Or how we'll ever mesh our lives...' I'm sounding panicky because I am. That's how it is with huge events. You're so busy working up to them, you don't get to see beyond them. Regardless of Johnny, my life plans never got beyond the day after Boxing Day, when the wedding ends. And the clearing up, obviously.

Johnny laughs. 'For starters, I'm in Bristol, which isn't so far away. In a flat that's way too big for me, and desperately in need of someone to leave their leopard print leggings on the floor and make it feel like home.'

I want to hug him more than ever. 'I could maybe help you out with that one.'

He pulls me towards him and rests his chin on my head. 'Don't worry. We've got a lot of catching up to do, but I promise, I'll do whatever it takes to make this work. Think of it as an adventure, we'll go one step at a time. So long as we're together, there's no rush.'

'Together sounds good.'

'So what do you say to Christmas dinner for our first date? Once we've had our next Christmas Morning kiss, obviously.'

'That would be…' Perfect. Except I never get to the last bit, because his lips land on mine. And a second later I dive into the deepest mocha-and-mince-pie snog of my life.

54

Sunday, December 25th, Christmas Day
In the ballroom at Rose Hill Manor: Lashings of sauce

Christmas dinner for a hundred and fifty the afternoon after a huge wedding could be chaotic. Hog roast, with all the trimmings. Apple sauce, sage and onion stuffing, the crispiest roast potatoes in the world ever, Yorkshire puddings, mash, roast parsnips, sausages, pigs-in-blankets, a zillion different vegetables and ladlefuls of gravy. With stuffed courgettes and filo parcels for the vegetarians. And in the event, it's mayhem. Every one of Alice's glasses are in use again. But somehow it works. And it's beyond delicious.

Rafe and Poppy were supposed to be having lunch with his family, but they come over afterwards and still arrive in time to eat a second lunch with us. It turns out Rafe and Johnny could talk for England about horses and machinery, and we let them get on with it. Immie and Chas are there too, with Immie's son Morgan. Jules has come along, complete with his mum, and her hollow legs. And between us, she's looking so stunning, I suspect she had the entire make-up team to work on her before she left. Jules is ecstatic to expand the wedding album into his first coverage of a house party. And Jess is here too. She's sweet-talked her latest conquest slash pick-up into driving her over, so she doesn't have to hold back on the macaroons. As for the cocktails, it's like Jaggers' White Christmas Night revisited.

It's lovely to have all my friends around me.

Somewhere in between clearing the plates and the arrival of the flaming Christmas puddings Alice comes over to our Brides by the Sea cluster. All it takes is one small nod from her. Next thing, she's herding me off to the deserted winter garden with all the expertise of a sheepdog splitting a single sheep from the flock. Which just goes to show, I've still got a lot to learn in the people-handling area, but whatever. At least I've made a start.

She waits until we're an inch through the door and then she swoops. 'So how did it go at the beach with Johnny? Did you find out what the problem was?'

If she'd stuck to the first question, it would have been easier. There are times when the only way forward is to come straight out with it. And fast. Like now. 'There was a pregnancy test in my bathroom, Johnny thought it was mine and assumed I was with someone else.' On balance I decide to leave out the word 'pregnant'.

Alice's mouth is open. 'Bloody hell, Sera, I'm so sorry, that was my fault. I never thought.' At least that's got the admission over. 'On the upside, I forgot to say earlier, but while I was there peeing on sticks in your bathroom, I did bring your slippers back.'

'Thanks for that.' I'm shaking my head and laughing at the same time. 'So should I be saying congratulations?' It's a very tentative enquiry. Whatever the evidence, if you're going round asking people if they're up the duff, you have to be a bit careful. I raise my eye brows, hold my breath and wait.

But it's fine, because Alice's eyes are popping and her face lights up. 'Yeeeess. It's sooooo exciting.' It comes out as a strangled squeal and she's flapping her hands wildly. As she pulls me into a huge hug she drops her voice. 'We're keeping it to ourselves for now. But Dan's totally over the moon.'

Better and better. 'Finding out you're having a baby on Christmas morning – as presents go, they don't come much better, do they?'

Alice's wild smile turns smugger. 'Dan giving me my eternity ring on our first Christmas was a lot to compete with but I reckon my baby news has topped it.'

'I'm so happy for you. When did you actually realise?' Sorry, but I have to ask.

She laughs. 'I've been feeling sick for a while, but I thought it was nerves. You can imagine the stack of crystallised ginger I've got through. But the penny dropped that day at the shop. There's no other reason you'd grow out of your wedding dress in a month. Not when you're running around like a Bridezilla in a mist.' She's on the nail with that description, but I'm glad she said it, not me.

I try to forget that I was the one who went haring around buying multi-packs of Clearblue, and look as if it just hit me now. 'It's obvious when you think about it.' There's no need to tell her Jess was onto her too.

'Well, thanks for getting the tests. I didn't take one before, because I didn't want it to cloud my pre-wedding judgement. If the baby's a girl, we'll definitely be calling it Seraphina, though. Which shows you how hugely grateful I am.'

'That's so cool.' I'm torn between being so touched, I've got a lump in my throat, and wanting to spare the poor baby the hell I went through as a child. 'Although maybe don't do that. It's got so many letters, I was the last person in the class to be able to write my name.'

'Maybe we could have it as a middle name, then.' She gives a shrug and another guilty smile. 'Actually, at the moment I'm calling it Ugg.'

Heaven help us. Now I've heard it all. 'Brilliant.' If I'd wondered what project she was going to go on to after the wedding, I've found my answer. A baby. Perfect. Hours on from a positive test, she's already organising names. Between us, it wouldn't surprise me if she'd already started her baby-planner spread sheet.

'No more Winter Warmers either.' I take it this will come as the biggest shock of all to Alice, but her anticipated shriek of horror doesn't come.

'Hell no,' she says. 'Have you seen what's in that stuff? It's practically neat brandy.'

Which reminds me of another piece of shocking news. 'You might need to wave your "no sex" flag at Quinn and Hetty. He practically ate her under the mistletoe earlier.'

Alice rolls her eyes. 'That flag was for you, silly. You probably noticed, Quinn can be *very* persuasive, but he never sticks around. I refused to let him charm his way into your... well wherever... then break my baby sister's heart. Whereas Hetty knows exactly what she's doing and, what's more, she'll have a fabulous time. He's got a reputation for being great in bed.'

'Sorry?'

'Don't worry, Hetty will have him for breakfast, then spit him out.'

Alice carries on. 'So I take it from the snogging that you and Johnny sorted yourselves out?'

Excuse me? I thought we were being pretty 'hands off' in public, although our thighs have practically been welded together since we came into the ballroom. Somehow, now he's almost mine, I don't want to let him go.

'We did.' Those two little words don't quite express how much we've gone through. How much we mean to each other. 'Thank you for the mercy-dash anyway. I couldn't have done it without you.'

As her hand lands on my arm, her frown is anxious. 'And you know about...?'

I nod. 'His boy, Jake.'

'I was asking Dan earlier, and he says Johnny's a wonderful dad. Just think, we'll all be able to go to the park together, how lovely will that be?'

It's great she's embracing parenthood so enthusiastically for both of us, although I'm not sure she's factored in the age gap there. I'm saved from explaining because Dan comes in and calls us back to the ballroom for Christmas pudding and rum sauce with lashings of cream. Then we work our way past a cheese course, through to coffee and chocolate logs, and home-made rum truffles. And just when we think we can't eat or drink any more, Quinn sends the champagne round again. He does a toast and suggests we all come back and do the same again next year. As if.

Then we move seamlessly on to opening the presents. Quinn gives the bridesmaids' sweatshirts with our names on the back, and the message on the front 'I will kiss guys for mince pies'. Looks like he's covering all bases there. Dream on, Quinn. And Alice has bought us all silk pillow cases so we can sleep without getting folds in our faces and bed hair. Yay to that.

And as Johnny and I are totally unprepared for presents, we make promises instead. He promises to teach me to ride and I promise to let him. I promise to knit him a jumper, but we both know that's more to make him laugh than because it's going to happen. And he promises me something really special for later and I say 'back at you' because I think I know where he's going with that one.

As for my own gifts, I give everyone key rings with stars made from driftwood and washed-up glass, and Christmas-tree ornaments made from shells from the beach, so they'll always be reminded of the Christmas they came to St Aidan, when Alice and Dan got married. Although, between us, I doubt they'll forget a wedding quite this mega in a hurry.

55

Sunday, December 25th, Christmas Day
At Rose Hill Manor

'So are you ready for your very special, once in a lifetime, present, Fi?'

It's a lot later when Johnny comes up to me in the ballroom, takes my hand and leads me out into the hallway. It's ages since he left to prepare this special present, which I suspect is bedroom or bathroom-related. Maybe with a few gorgeous scented candles thrown in too. If we're talking rose petals on the bed here, he's been gone so long he's pretty much had time to grow the roses, not just sprinkle them. I'm expecting to head for the stairs, so it's a big surprise when we veer towards the front door.

'Okay, put this on. Alice says it's okay to borrow it.' He's holding up Alice's huge white fur cape.

I hesitate. 'I know I've come a long way this last week, but I'm not sure I'm up to being a snow queen.' Even if it is payback time for her borrowing my Uggs.

Johnny laughs. 'I get where you're coming from. Here, take my parka instead.'

So I do. I can't believe it's taken me so long to discover how amazing it is to wrap myself in my boyfriend's coat. I'm guessing it's okay to call him that. It's as if I'm wearing his scent like an animal's pelt. And, believe me, now I've finally found him again, I'll be hanging on very tightly.

Then as we open the door and head outside into the snow there's a familiar snort, a stamping of hooves and a jingle of bells.

'Snowball? And the carriage…' I let out a gasp, because it's so much more than just that. It's waiting for us a few yards from the door, as if it's landed from a film set. Both the carriage and Snowball's harness are twinkling with fairy-light strands, and there are candles flickering in the carriage lights. 'Oh, Johnny, it's beautiful.' He must have been working like the wind to get all this done so fast.

Johnny jumps up into the high driver's seat and pulls me up to sit beside him. 'With snow at Christmas and a carriage, we had to go for a moonlight drive.' One shake of the reins and Snowball sets off up the drive at a trot.

As the freezing air rushes past my face, I hook my arm around Johnny's back and snuggle my head into the crook of his neck. 'This is magical, I feel like a fairy princess. And even though it's dark the snow is so bright.' With the light splashing down from the moon, the folds of the white-covered landscape are luminous and the snow crust sparkles.

'As first dates go, today has been pretty awesome.' Johnny's breath is coming out in clouds as he shouts over the rumble of the wheels and the clip clop of Snowball's shoes. 'Finding you has made this my best Christmas yet.' He turns and grins at me. 'In case I didn't say before, Fi, I love you.'

I think he may have mentioned it earlier, but hearing it again, my chest feels like it might just burst. 'I love you too, Johnny.' Shouting at the top of my voice as we rush down the lane towards the village is the most perfect way to tell him. 'I love you, I love you, I love you.'

'Whoa, Snowball.' As we circle and turn around at the crossroads, we pull to a halt, and a second later Johnny dips and pulls me into a long, delicious snowy kiss that only stops much later, when Snowball begins to stamp impatiently. Johnny laughs as he breaks away. 'Someone's anxious to get back to his hay net. And we've got another two days of hard partying ahead of us.'

Whereas some guests are just warming up, my stamina is running out fast. 'I'm looking forward to curling up in front of the fire with a mulled wine.'

Johnny gives a low laugh as he slides his mouth over mine again. 'Once we go to bed tonight, I seriously doubt we'll get up again before New Year.'

Which sounds perfect to me. 'Talking of New Year, do you suppose with my new super powers I'll get my laundry under control too?' Telling people what I think is an awesome step forward but clean undies and shorts in neat piles would be something else. Especially if Johnny and I are going to be weekend roomies from now on.

'Shall I be honest?' He's twiddling with the tangles in my

hair. 'Expressing yourself and being assertive are great life skills, but it's way better to be yourself. Thongs under your sofa cushions are part of the fun of coming to yours. I love you as you are, I don't want you to change.'

I appreciate the pressure's off. Not that I'm intending to turn into Alice, but given how well those lists worked, folded clothes might be a logical next step.

'One more thing too.' He dips into his pocket and pushes something soft and small into my hands.

I know what they are is straight away. 'The knitted bride and groom bears.' I thought he'd forgotten them. 'Thank you so much, you've no idea how happy I am to see them again.'

The twinkle in his eye is as bright as the string of fairy lights twisted around the reins. 'They definitely belong in the shop. But I would like to borrow them back… if ever I need them, that is… which I'm hoping we will.'

'I'm sure we can arrange that, Sir.' I say, in my best shop-assistant voice. And even though I know Jess was purring when she sold them to him less than ten days ago, that is nothing compared to my beam now.

'You know the old saying, "a best man's for life, not just for Christmas"?' As he tilts his head, he's biting back his smile. 'It means I'm here to stay. Just saying.'

'Whereas I'd heard it was a bridesmaid for life,' I laugh.

'So now we've got that sorted out, we can get on with our first date, and the rest of our lives.' As Johnny shakes the reins the carriage creaks and Snowball begins to trot back down the lane.

'Sounds like a plan,' I say, then squeal because I sound so unlike myself. 'Dammit, I'm talking like a wedding manual.'

'So you are.' Luckily Johnny sounds amused rather than horrified. 'That's what happens when you've just pulled off the wedding of the year.' As he winks, he's shouting over the jingle of the bells on Snowball's harness. 'On the upside, we'll know exactly how to do it when it comes to our turn.'

He grins at me and as his words sink in, our eyes lock. We're both reliving the last ten days. And as we stare at each other, we break into a spontaneous 'Waaaaaaaaaaaaaaahhhhhhhhh.'

Waaaaaaaahhh because we could never face going through that all over again. Waaaaaaaahhh because it all turned out so wonderfully. And waaaaaaaaahhh because the thought of it ever being our turn is way beyond exciting. Even if it isn't going to be right away.

And we're still laughing as we turn back down the drive and thread our way back between the trees to where the windows of the house are glowing orange against the snow.

Acknowledgements

A big thank you…

To my wonderful editor Charlotte Ledger, who is talented, brilliant, supportive and lovely – all at the same time. This series belongs to both of us. To Kimberley Young and the team at HarperCollins for three wonderful covers and all-round expertise and support.

To Debbie Johnson and Zara Stoneley, and my writing friends across the world, for sharing and caring. To my friends, the fabulous bloggers, who spread the word.

To High Street Bride guru, Samantha Birch, for all her help. A special shout-out for the fabulous Emily Bridal of Sheffield, whose shop and dresses are so beautiful. And thanks to amazing cake baker, Caroline Tranter, for bringing the cakes in the book to life and for letting us use her fab pictures.

Big hugs and Happy Anniversary to India and Richard for their amazing wedding, which is where this series began. And more hugs and good luck to Anna and Jamie for their very own Sequins and Snowflakes wedding in February. To my whole family for cheering me on all the way. To Max for being a techy wizard, for making me tea and bringing me cake. And big love to my own hero, Phil… for being there every day and never letting me give up.

Favourite Christmas Cocktails
from Brides by the Sea

In case you'd like to try a taste of Brides by the Sea at home, here's how to make some of the fab cocktails and drinks featured in this book. Don't stress too much about the quantities. At Brides by the Sea it's much more about sloshing it in and having a good time. As Jess would say, LET THE FUN BEGIN...

WONDERFUL WHITE CHRISTMAS COCKTAIL

This is the perfect Christmas drink... Cream, shaken with ice, vodka, peppermint schnapps and white crème de cacao, served with a candy cane. Yum.

Ingredients:

2 tablespoons double cream
2 tablespoons vodka
2 tablespoons peppermint schnapps
2 tablespoons white crème de cacao
I cupful ice cubes
Candy cane to garnish

Pour the ingredients into a cocktail shaker and shake until chilled. Strain into chilled glasses, then add the candy cane.

SNOWBALLS

Simple to make and delish to drink long or short. I love the cherries and the name.

Ingredients:

1 part Advocat
3 parts chilled lemonade
Squeeze of lime to taste
Cocktail cherries

Pour Advocat into a glass, top up with lemonade and add a squeeze of lime to taste, and decorate with cherries.

For an extra luxury, add a dash of vodka or cream.

For a special Christmassy touch, dip the glass rims in melted white chocolate and dessicated coconut.

This can be drunk long in tall glasses, or in shorter ones, with less lemonade.

ICE QUEEN COCKTAILS

As delectable as their name…

Ingredients:

One and a half ounces white rum
Three quarters of an ounce fresh lime juice
1 teaspoon crème de menthe
One ounce prosecco or cava
Lime twists to garnish

Pop the rum, lime juice and crème de menthe in a cocktail shaker with ice and shake until chilled. Strain into glasses, top up with sparkling wine and garnish with a lime twist.

WHITE RUSSIAN COCKTAILS

Simple to make, but if you save the cream to add at the end, you get snow caps on the ice mountains.

Ingredients:

30 ml Tia Maria or coffee-flavoured liqueur
30 ml vodka
125 ml fresh cream
Ice cubes

Combine the ingredients in a mixing glass, then pour over ice cubes in the serving glass.

Or, for a dramatic snowy-topped drink, put ice in the serving glass, pour the coffee liqueur and vodka over, and then float the cream on the top.

Strain into glasses, top up with sparkling wine and garnish with a lime twist.

And last but not least...

Jane Linfoot

ALICE'S WINTER WARMER

Alice loved her Winter Warmers because they were warming and relaxing.

These are made with Pimms No 3 Winter Cup, the winter version of the summer drink, which is fortified with brandy and spices.

150 ml Pimms No 3 Winter Cup
450 ml apple juice
(One part Pimms No 3 to three parts apple juice)
Apple slices
Orange slices

For large quantities, warm the Pimms and apple juice in a saucepan, then transfer to a serving jug and add fruit slices.

Alice warmed hers in a pan and drank it from a glass mug, usually without the fruit slices.

Cheers!

Happy Christmas,

Love Jane x

Favourite Recipes from Brides by the Sea

Tempted by the mouth-watering treats Poppy bakes in the book? Now you can try them for yourself!

COFFEE CUPCAKES TOPPED WITH TOASTED ALMONDS

Sera often turns to Poppy's cupcakes to rescue her at stressful times. She particularly loves coffee cupcakes with toasted almonds on top. Here's Poppy's recipe.

Ingredients:
For the cupcakes:
150g sugar
150g butter

150g self-raising flour, sieved
3 eggs
Two heaped teaspoons instant coffee
A little warm water to dissolve the coffee

For the icing:
100g butter (softened)
200g icing sugar, sieved
Two heaped teaspoons instant coffee
A little warm water to dissolve the coffee

For the topping:
100g flaked almonds

Method for the sponge cakes:
1. Preheat the oven, 170C Fan/ Gas Mark 5/ 190C Electric. Prepare a 12 sectioned cupcake tin with your chosen cupcake cases.
2. Cream the butter and sugar together in a large bowl until light and fluffy, using an electric whisk.
3. Add the eggs, and mix again.
4. Add the sieved flour, and fold into the mixture until it's all combined.
5. Put the coffee granules into a cup, and add a tiny amount of water. Mix until the coffee has dissolved, then add to the cake mixture. Stir gently until it's all mixed in and the mixture is a uniform colour. You can vary the amount of coffee, to give a darker or lighter cake.
6. Spoon the mixture into the cases, filling to about 2/3 up the side, to allow for the cakes to rise.

7. Bake in the oven for 15-20 minutes until golden brown and cooked all the way through. (Check by sticking a sharp knife in. If it comes out clean then that means they're done.)
8. Place on a cooling tray, and ice when cool.

Method for the buttercream icing:

You can make the buttercream icing while the cupcakes are in the oven.

1. Sieve the icing sugar into a bowl. Add the softened butter and cream together.
2. Put the coffee granules into a cup, and add a tiny amount of water. Mix until the coffee has dissolved, then add to the icing. Mix until the icing is a uniform colour. Use more or less coffee depending on how dark you'd like your icing.
3. Spoon the icing into a piping bag, with the pipe of your choice. When the cupcakes are cool, pipe the icing in swirls on top of the cupcakes.

For the nut topping:

1. Heat a knob of butter in a frying pan, add the nuts, and stir over a gentle heat until the almond flakes are toasted and golden brown.
2. Leave the toasted almonds to cool, then and sprinkle on top of the cupcakes as soon as they are iced.

As an alternative to almonds, walnut halves also work well with the coffee icing. You can pop these on top of the icing without toasting them

These are totally delish!!

EASY PEASY CHOCOLATE BROWNIES

The day of Alice's wedding dress disaster the girls end up in Poppy's kitchen eating chocolate brownies. The beauty of this recipe is that it uses Nutella chocolate spread which contains lots of the ingredients for brownies, already combined. So all you have to do is to add flour and eggs to Nutella, mix it together, and bake. Easy peasy, the brownies really are mouth-wateringly delish – and there's plenty of opportunity for brownie mix tasting too.

Ingredients:
300g Nutella
2 eggs (free range ones if you're going to taste the mixture!)
60g self-raising flour

Directions:
Put ingredients in a bowl. Mix it together until smooth. Spoon into greased baking tin (20cm square), or muffin/bun cases.

For extra pizazz sprinkle on a few chopped hazelnuts.

Bake in oven at 350F (180C), for 30 mins if baking as a cake. If cooking muffin/bun case brownies cook for 10-15 mins, or until centres are baked through, depending on the size. (Check by sticking a sharp knife in, it comes out clean when they're done, although they are also nice slightly sticky in the middle.)

Eat when hot, or leave to cool. If you're making the cake version, cut into squares.

Yummy.

Hope you enjoy these tastes of Brides by Sea,

love Jane x